Praise for

MAGGIE
STIEFVATER

Best Book to Curl Up With
Glamour

"If you are a fan of *Twilight*, then you will love *Shiver*"
Waterstone's Books Quarterly

"A magnificent and haunting love story"
Youngscot.org

"Literary methadone . . . all-consuming"
Sunday Telegraph

"This bittersweet tale had the
publishing world buzzing"
Glamour

"Full of deliciously illicit, star-crossed love"
Financial Times

ABOUT THE AUTHOR

Maggie Stiefvater's life decisions have revolved around her inability to be gainfully

employed. Talking to yourself, staring into space, and coming to work in your pyjamas are frowned upon when you're a waitress, calligraphy instructor, or technical editor (all of which she's tried), but are highly prized traits in novelists and artists (she's made her living as one or the other since she was twenty-two). Maggie now lives a surprisingly eccentric life in the middle of nowhere, Virginia, with her charmingly straight-laced husband, two kids, and multiple neurotic dogs.

L♥ve Maggie

www.maggiestiefvater.com

@mstiefvater

MAGGIE STIEFVATER

THE RAVEN BOYS

SCHOLASTIC

for Brenna, who is good at looking for things

Scholastic Children's Books
An imprint of Scholastic Ltd
Euston House, 24 Eversholt Street
London, NW1 1DB, UK
Registered office: Westfield Road, Southam, Warwickshire, CV47 0RA
SCHOLASTIC and associated logos are trademarks and/or
registered trademarks of Scholastic Inc.

First published in the US by Scholastic Inc, 2012
This edition published in the UK by Scholastic Ltd, 2012

Text copyright © Maggie Stiefvater, 2012
Cover Raven artwork by Adam S. Doyle 2012

The right of Maggie Stiefvater to be identified as the author
of this work has been asserted by her.

ISBN 978 1407 13461 1

Printed and bound by CPI Group (UK) Ltd, Croydon, CR0 4YY
Papers used by Scholastic Children's Books are made
from wood grown in sustainable forests.

18

This is a work of fiction. Names, characters, places,
incidents and dialogues are products of the author's imagination
or are used fictitiously. Any resemblance to actual people, living or dead,
events or locales is entirely coincidental.

www.scholastic.co.uk/zone
www.maggiestiefvater.com

*Deep into that darkness peering, long I stood
there, wondering, fearing,
Doubting, dreaming dreams no mortal ever
dared to dream before. . .*

—Edgar Allan Poe

*A dreamer is one who can only find his way by
moonlight, and his punishment is that he sees the
dawn before the rest of the world.*

—Oscar Wilde

PROLOGUE

Blue Sargent had forgotten how many times she'd been told that she would kill her true love.

Her family traded in predictions. These predictions tended, however, to run towards the nonspecific. Things like: *Something terrible will happen to you today. It might involve the number six.* Or: *Money is coming. Open your hand for it.* Or: *You have a big decision and it will not make itself.*

The people who came to the little, bright blue house at 300 Fox Way didn't mind the imprecise nature of their fortunes. It became a game, a challenge, to realize the exact moment that the predictions came true. When a van carrying six people wheeled into a client's car two hours after his psychic reading, he could nod with a sense of accomplishment and release. When a neighbour offered to buy another client's old lawnmower if she was looking for a bit of extra cash, she could recall the promise of money coming and sell it with the sense that the transaction had been foretold. Or when a third client heard his wife say, *This is a decision that has to be made,* he could remember the same words being said by Maura Sargent over a spread of tarot cards and then leap decisively to action.

But the imprecise nature of the fortunes stole some

of their power. The predictions could be dismissed as coincidences, hunches. They were a chuckle in the Walmart car park when you ran into an old friend as promised. A shiver when the number seventeen appeared on an electric bill. A realization that even if you had discovered the future, it really didn't change how you lived in the present. They were truth, but they weren't all of the truth.

"I should tell you," Maura always advised her new clients, "that this reading will be accurate, but not specific."

It was easier that way.

But this was not what Blue was told. Again and again, she had her fingers spread wide, her palm examined, her cards plucked from velvet-edged decks and spread across the fuzz of a family friend's living room carpet. Thumbs were pressed to the mystical, invisible third eye that was said to lie between everyone's eyebrows. Runes were cast and dreams interpreted, tea leaves scrutinized and séances conducted.

All the women came to the same conclusion, blunt and inexplicably specific. What they all agreed on, in many different clairvoyant languages, was this:

If Blue was to kiss her true love, he would die.

For a long time, this bothered Blue. The warning was specific, certainly, but in the way of a fairy tale. It didn't say how her true love would die. It didn't say how long after the kiss he would survive. Did it have to be a kiss on the lips? Would a chaste peck on the back of his palm prove as deadly?

Until she was eleven, Blue was convinced she would silently contract an infectious disease. One press of her lips to her hypothetical soulmate and he, too, would die in a consumptive battle untreatable by modern medicine. When she was thirteen, Blue decided that jealousy would kill him instead – an old boyfriend emerging at the moment of that first kiss, bearing a handgun and a heart full of hurt.

When she turned fifteen, Blue concluded that her mother's tarot cards were just a pack of playing cards and that the dreams of her mother and the other clairvoyant women were fuelled by mixed drinks rather than otherworldly insight, and so the prediction didn't matter.

She knew better, though. The predictions that came out of 300 Fox Way were unspecific, but undeniably true. Her mother had dreamt Blue's broken wrist on the first day of school. Her aunt Jimi predicted Maura's tax return to within ten dollars. Her older cousin Orla always began to hum her favourite song a few minutes before it came on the radio.

No one in the house ever really doubted that Blue was destined to kill her true love with a kiss. It was a threat, however, that had been around for so long that it had lost its force. Picturing six-year-old Blue in love was such a far-off thing as to be imaginary.

And by sixteen, Blue had decided she would never fall in love, so it didn't matter.

But that belief changed when her mother's half sister Neeve came to their little town of Henrietta. Neeve had got famous for doing loudly what Blue's mother did quietly. Maura's readings were done in her front room, mostly for residents of Henrietta and the valley around it. Neeve, on the other hand, did her readings on television at five o'clock in the morning. She had a website featuring old soft-focus photographs of her staring unerringly at the viewer. Four books on the supernatural bore her name on the cover.

Blue had never met Neeve, so she knew more about

her half aunt from a cursory web search than from personal experience.

Blue wasn't sure why Neeve was coming to visit, but she knew her imminent arrival spurred a legion of whispered conversations between Maura and her two best friends, Persephone and Calla – the sort of conversations that trailed off into sipping coffee and tapping pens on the table when Blue entered the room. But Blue wasn't particularly concerned about Neeve's arrival; what was one more woman in a house filled to the brim with them?

Neeve finally appeared on a spring evening when the already long shadows of the mountains to the west seemed even longer than usual. When Blue opened the door for her, she thought, for a moment, that Neeve was an unfamiliar old woman, but then her eyes grew used to the stretched crimson light coming through the trees, and she saw that Neeve was barely older than her mother, which was not very old at all.

Outside, in the distance, hounds were crying. Blue was familiar enough with their voices; each fall, the Aglionby Hunt Club rode out with horses and foxhounds nearly every weekend. Blue knew what their frantic howls meant at that moment: they were on the chase.

"You're Maura's daughter," Neeve said, and before Blue could answer, she added, "this is the year you'll fall in love."

ONE

It was freezing in the churchyard, even before the dead arrived.

Every year, Blue and her mother, Maura, had come to the same place, and every year it was chilly. But this year, without Maura here with her, it felt colder.

It was April 24, St Mark's Eve. For most people, St Mark's Day came and went without note. It wasn't a school holiday. No presents were exchanged. There were no costumes or festivals. There were no St Mark's Day sales, no St Mark's Day cards in the shops, no special television programmes that aired only once a year. No one marked April 25 on their calendar. In fact, most of the living were unaware that St Mark even had a day named in his honour.

But the dead remembered.

As Blue sat shivering on the stone wall, she reasoned that at least, at the *very* least, it wasn't raining this year.

Every St Mark's Eve, this was where Maura and Blue came: an isolated church so old that its name had been forgotten. The ruin was cupped in the densely wooded hills outside of Henrietta, still several miles from the mountains proper. Only the exterior walls remained; the roof and floors had long ago collapsed inside. What hadn't rotted away was hidden under hungry vines and rancid-smelling saplings. The church was surrounded by a stone wall, broken only by a lychgate just large enough for a coffin and its bearers. A stubborn path that seemed impervious to weeds led through to the old church door.

"Ah," hissed Neeve, plump but strangely elegant as she sat beside Blue on the wall. Blue was struck again, as she had been struck the first time she'd met Neeve, by her oddly lovely hands. Chubby wrists led to soft, child-like palms and slender fingers with oval nails.

"Ah," Neeve murmured again. "Tonight is a night."

She said it like this: "Tonight is a *night*" and when she did, Blue felt her skin creep a little. Blue had sat watch with her mother for the past ten St Mark's Eves, but tonight felt different.

Tonight was a *night*.

This year, for the first time, and for reasons Blue didn't understand, Maura had sent Neeve to do the church watch in her place. Her mother had asked Blue if she would go along as usual, but it wasn't really a question. Blue had always gone; she would go this time. It was not as if she had made plans for St Mark's Eve. But she had to be asked. Maura had decided sometime before Blue's birth that it was barbaric to order children about, and so Blue had grown up surrounded by imperative question marks.

Blue opened and closed her chilly fists. The top edges of her fingerless gloves were fraying; she'd done a bad job knitting them last year, but they had a certain trashy chic to them. If she hadn't been so vain, Blue could've worn the boring but functional gloves she'd been given for Christmas. But she *was* vain, so instead she had her fraying fingerless gloves, infinitely cooler though also colder, and no one to see them but Neeve and the dead.

April days in Henrietta were quite often fair, tender things, coaxing sleeping trees to bud and love-mad ladybirds to beat against windowpanes. But not tonight. It felt like winter.

Blue glanced at her watch. A few minutes until eleven. The old legends recommended the church watch be kept at midnight, but the dead kept poor time, especially when there wasn't a moon.

Unlike Blue, who didn't tend towards patience, Neeve was a regal statue on the old church wall: hands folded, ankles crossed beneath a long wool skirt. Blue, huddled, shorter and thinner, was a restless, sightless gargoyle. It wasn't a night for her ordinary eyes. It was a night for seers and psychics, witches and mediums.

In other words, the rest of her family.

Out of the silence, Neeve asked, "Do you hear anything?" Her eyes glittered in the black.

"No," Blue answered, because she didn't. Then she wondered if Neeve had asked because Neeve *did*.

Neeve was looking at her with the same gaze that she wore in all of her photos on the website – the deliberately unnerving, otherworldly stare that lasted several more seconds than was comfortable. A few days after Neeve had arrived, Blue had been distressed enough to mention it to Maura. They had both been crammed into the single bathroom, Blue getting ready for school, Maura for work.

Blue, trying to clip all of the various bits of her dark hair back into a vestigial ponytail, had asked, "Does she have to stare like that?"

In the shower, her mother drew patterns in the steamed glass door. She had paused to laugh, a flash of her skin visible through the long intersecting lines she had drawn. "Oh, that's just Neeve's trademark."

Blue thought there were probably better things to be known for.

In the churchyard, Neeve said enigmatically, "There is a lot to hear."

The thing was, there wasn't. In the summer, the foothills were alive with insects buzzing, mockingbirds whistling back and forth, ravens yelling at cars. But it was too cool, tonight, for anything to be awake yet.

"I don't hear things like that," Blue said, a little surprised Neeve wasn't already aware. In Blue's intensely clairvoyant family, she was a fluke, an outsider to the vibrant conversation her mother and aunts and cousins held with a world hidden to most people. The only thing that was special about her was something that she herself couldn't experience. "I hear as much of the conversation as the telephone. I just make things louder for everyone else."

Neeve still hadn't looked away. "So that's why Maura was so eager for you to come along. Does she have you at all her readings as well?"

Blue shuddered at the thought. A fair number of the clients who entered 300 Fox Way were miserable women hoping Maura would see love and money in their future. The idea of being trapped in the house with that all day was excruciating. Blue knew it had to be very tempting for her mother to have Blue present, making her psychic powers stronger. When she was younger, she'd never appreciated how little Maura called on her to join in a reading, but now that Blue understood how well she honed other people's talents, she was impressed at Maura's restraint.

"Not unless it's a very important one," she replied.

Neeve's gaze had edged over the subtle line between discomfiting and creepy. She said, "It's something to be proud of, you know. To make someone else's psychic gift stronger is a rare and valuable thing."

"Oh, *pshaw*," Blue said, but not cruelly. She meant to be funny. She'd had sixteen years to get used to the idea that she wasn't privy to the supernatural. She didn't want Neeve to think she was experiencing an identity crisis over it. She tugged a string on her glove.

"And you have plenty of time to grow into your own intuitive talents," Neeve added. Her gaze seemed hungry.

Blue didn't reply. She wasn't interested in telling other people's futures. She was interested in going out and finding her own.

Neeve finally dropped her eyes. Tracing an idle finger through the dirt on the stones between them, she said, "I passed by a school on the way into town. Aglionby Academy. Is that where you go?"

Blue's eyes widened with humour. But of course Neeve, an outsider, couldn't know. Still, surely she could have guessed from the massive stone great hall and the car park full of cars that spoke German that it wasn't the sort of school that they could afford.

"It's an all-boys school. For politicians' sons and oil barons' sons and for" – Blue struggled to think of who else might be rich enough to send their kids to Aglionby – "the sons of mistresses living off hush money."

Neeve raised an eyebrow without looking up.

"No, really, they're awful," Blue said. April was a bad time for the Aglionby boys; as it warmed up, the convertibles appeared, bearing boys in shorts so tacky that only the rich would dare to wear them. During the school week, they all wore the Aglionby uniform: khaki trousers and a V-neck jumper with a raven emblem. It was an easy way to identify the advancing army. Raven boys.

Blue continued. "They think they're better than us and that we're all falling all over ourselves for them, and they drink themselves senseless every weekend and spray-paint the Henrietta exit sign."

Aglionby Academy was the number one reason Blue had developed her two rules: one, stay away from boys, because they were trouble. And two, stay away from Aglionby boys, because they were bastards.

"You seem like a very sensible teen," Neeve said, which annoyed Blue, because she already knew she was a very sensible teen. When you had as little money as the Sargents did, sensibility in all matters was ingrained young.

In the ambient light from the nearly full moon, Blue caught sight of what Neeve had drawn in the dirt. She asked, "What is that? Mom drew that."

"Did she?" Neeve asked. They studied the pattern. It was three curving, intersecting lines, making a long sort of triangle. "Did she say what it was?"

"She was drawing it on the shower door. I didn't ask."

"I dreamt it," Neeve said, in a flat voice that sent an unpleasant shudder along the back of Blue's neck. "I wanted to see what it looked like drawn out." She rubbed her palm through the pattern, then abruptly held up a beautiful hand.

She said, "I think they're coming."

This was why Blue and Neeve were here. Every year, Maura sat on the wall, knees pulled up to her chin, staring at nothing, and recited names to Blue. To Blue, the churchyard remained empty, but to Maura, it was full of the dead. Not the currently dead, but the spirits of those who would die in the next twelve months. For Blue, it had always been like hearing one half of a conversation. Sometimes her mother would recognize the spirits, but often she would have to lean forward to ask them their names. Maura had once explained that if Blue wasn't there, she couldn't convince them to answer her – the dead couldn't see Maura without Blue's presence.

Blue never grew tired of feeling particularly needed, but sometimes she wished *needed* felt less like a synonym for *useful*.

The church watch was critical for one of Maura's most unusual services. So long as clients lived in the area, she guaranteed to let them know if they or a local loved one was bound to die in the next twelve months. Who wouldn't pay for that? Well, the true answer was: most of the world, as most people didn't believe in psychics.

"Can you see anything?" Blue asked. She gave her numb hands a bracing rub before snatching up a notebook and pen from the wall.

Neeve was very still. "Something just touched my hair."

Again, a shiver thrilled up Blue's arms. "One of them?"

In a husky voice, Neeve said, "The future dead have to follow the corpse road through the gate. This is probably another . . . spirit called by your energy. I didn't realize what an effect you would have."

Maura had never mentioned *other* dead people being attracted by Blue. Perhaps she hadn't wanted to scare her. Or maybe Maura just hadn't seen them – maybe she was as blind to these other spirits as Blue was.

Blue became uncomfortably aware of the slightest breeze touching her face, lifting Neeve's curly hair. Invisible, orderly spirits of not yet truly dead people were one thing. Ghosts that weren't compelled to stay on the path were another.

"Are they—" Blue started.

"Who are you? Robert Neuhmann," Neeve interrupted. "What's your name? Ruth Vert. What's your name? Frances Powell."

Scratching quickly to catch up, Blue printed the names phonetically as Neeve solicited them. Every so often, she lifted her eyes to the path, trying to glimpse – *something*. But as always, there was only the overgrown crabgrass, the barely visible oak trees. The black mouth of the church, accepting invisible spirits.

Nothing to hear, nothing to see. No evidence of the dead except for their names written in the notebook in her hand.

Maybe Neeve was right. Maybe Blue was having a bit of an identity crisis. Some days it did seem a little unfair that all of the wonder and power that surrounded her family was passed to Blue in the form of paperwork.

At least I can still be a part of it, Blue thought grimly, although she felt about as included as a seeing eye dog. She held the notebook up to her face, close, close, close, so she could read it in the darkness. It was like a roster of names popular seventy and eighty years before: Dorothy, Ralph, Clarence, Esther, Herbert, Melvin.

A lot of the same last names, too. The valley was dominated

by several old families that were large if not powerful.

Somewhere outside of Blue's thoughts, Neeve's tone became more emphatic.

"What's your name?" she asked. "*Excuse* me. What is your name?" Her consternated expression looked wrong on her face. Out of habit, Blue followed Neeve's gaze to the centre of the courtyard.

And she saw someone.

Blue's heart hammered like a fist to her breastbone. On the other side of the heartbeat, he was still there. Where there should have been nothing, there was a person.

"I see him," Blue said. "Neeve, *I see him*."

Blue had always imagined the procession of spirits to be an orderly thing, but this spirit wandered, hesitant. It was a young man in trousers and a jumper, hair rumpled. He was not quite transparent, but he wasn't quite there, either. His figure was as murky as dirty water, his face indistinct. There was no identifying feature to him apart from his youth.

He was so young – that was the hardest part to get used to.

As Blue watched, he paused and put his fingers to the side of his nose and his temple. It was such a strangely *living* gesture that Blue felt a little sick. Then he stumbled forward, as if jostled from behind.

"Get his name," Neeve hissed. "He won't answer me and I need to get the others!"

"Me?" Blue replied, but she slid off the wall. Her heart was still ramming inside her ribcage. She asked, feeling a little foolish, "What's your name?"

He didn't seem to hear her. Without a twitch of

acknowledgement, he began to move again, slow and bewildered, towards the church door.

Is this how we make our way to death? Blue wondered. *A stumbling fade-out instead of a self-aware finale?*

As Neeve began again to call out questions to the others, Blue made her way towards the wanderer.

"Who are you?" she called from a safe distance, as he dropped his forehead into his hands. His form had no outline at all, she saw now, and his face was truly featureless. There was nothing about him, really, that made him human shaped, but still, she saw a boy. There was something telling her mind what he was, even if it wasn't telling her eyes.

There was no thrill in seeing him, as she had thought there would be. All she could think was, *He will be dead within a year.* How did Maura bear it?

Blue stole closer. She was close enough to touch him as he began to walk again, but still he made no sign of seeing her.

This near to him, her hands were freezing. Her heart was freezing. Invisible spirits with no warmth of their own sucked at her energy, pulling goosebumps up her arms.

The young man stood on the threshold of the church and Blue knew, just *knew*, that if he stepped into the church, she would lose the chance to get his name.

"Please," Blue said, softer than before. She reached out a hand and touched the very edge of his not-there jumper. Cold flooded through her like dread. She tried to steady herself with what she'd always been told: spirits drew all their energy from their surroundings. All she was feeling was him using her to stay visible.

But it still felt a lot like dread.

She asked, "Will you tell me your name?"

He faced her and she realized with shock that he wore an Aglionby jumper.

"Gansey," he said. Though his voice was quiet, it wasn't a whisper. It was a real voice spoken from some place almost too far away to hear.

Blue couldn't stop staring at his mussed hair, the suggestion of staring eyes, the raven on his jumper. His shoulders were soaked, she saw, and the rest of his clothing rain spattered, from a storm that hadn't happened yet. This close, she could smell something minty that she wasn't sure was unique to him or unique to spirits.

He was so real. When it finally happened, when she finally saw him, it didn't feel like magic at all. It felt like looking into the grave and seeing it look back at her.

"Is that all?" she whispered.

Gansey closed his eyes. "That's all there is."

He fell to his knees – a soundless gesture for a boy with no real body. One hand splayed in the dirt, fingers pressed to the ground. Blue saw the blackness of the church more clearly than the curved shape of his shoulder.

"Neeve," Blue said. "Neeve, he's – dying."

Neeve had come to stand just behind her. She replied, "Not yet."

Gansey was nearly gone now, fading into the church, or the church fading into him.

Blue's voice was breathier than she would have liked. "Why – why can I see him?"

Neeve glanced over her shoulder, either because there were more spirits coming or because there weren't – Blue couldn't tell. By the time she looked back, Gansey had vanished entirely. Already Blue felt warmth returning to her skin, but something behind her lungs felt icy. A dangerous, sucking sadness seemed to be opening up inside her: grief or regret.

"There are only two reasons a non-seer would see a spirit on St Mark's Eve, Blue. Either you're his true love," Neeve said, "or you killed him."

TWO

"It's me," said Gansey.

He turned around so that he was facing his car. The Camaro's bright orange hood was up, more as a symbol of defeat than for any practical use. Adam, friend of cars everywhere, might have been able to determine what was wrong with it this time, but Gansey certainly couldn't. He'd managed to roll to a stop about a metre off the interstate and now the car's fat tyres sat off-kilter on top of lumpy tufts of valley grass. A lorry roared by without pause; the Camaro rocked in its wake.

On the other end of the phone, his room-mate Ronan Lynch replied, "You missed World Hist. I thought you were dead in a ditch."

Gansey flipped his wrist around to examine his watch. He had missed a lot more than World History. It was eleven o'clock, and already the chilliness of last night seemed improbable. A gnat was stuck in the perspiration on his skin next to the watchband; he flicked it off. Gansey had camped, once, when he was younger. It had involved tents. Sleeping bags. An idling Range Rover parked nearby for when he and his father lost interest. As an experience, it had not been anything like last night.

He asked, "Did you get notes for me?"

"No," Ronan replied. "I thought you were dead in a ditch."

Gansey blew grit off his lips and readjusted the phone against his cheek. *He* would've got notes for Ronan. "The Pig stopped. Come get me."

A sedan slowed as it passed, the occupants staring out of the window. Gansey was not an unpleasant-looking boy and the Camaro was not too hard on the eyes, either, but this attention had less to do with comeliness and more to do with the novelty of an Aglionby boy broken down by the side of the road in an impudently orange car. Gansey was well aware that there was nothing little Henrietta, Virginia, preferred over seeing humiliating things happen to Aglionby boys, unless it was seeing humiliating things happen to their families.

Ronan said, "Come on, man."

"It's not like you're going to class. You know what, it'll be lunch break anyway." Then he added, perfunctory, "Please."

Ronan was silent for a long moment. He was good at silence; he knew it made people uncomfortable. But Gansey was immune from long exposure. He leaned into the car to see if he had any food in the glovebox while he waited for Ronan to speak. Next to an EpiPen, there was a stick of beef jerky, but the jerky had expired two years ago. Possibly it had been there when he'd bought the car.

"Where are you?" Ronan asked, finally.

"Next to the Henrietta sign on 64. Bring me a burger. And a few gallons of petrol." The car had not run out of petrol, but it couldn't hurt.

Ronan's voice was acidic. "Gansey."

"Bring Adam, too."

Ronan hung up. Gansey stripped off his jumper and threw it in the back of the Camaro. The tiny back of the car was a cluttered marriage of everyday things — a chemistry textbook, a Frappuccino-stained notebook, a half-zipped CD binder with naked discs slithering out across the seat — and the supplies he'd acquired during his eighteen months in Henrietta. Rumpled maps, computer printouts, ever-present journal, torch, willow stick. When Gansey plucked a digital recorder out of the mess, a pizza receipt (one large deep-dish, half sausage, half avocado) fluttered to the seat, joining a half-dozen receipts identical except for the date.

All night he'd sat outside the monstrously modern Church of the Holy Redeemer, recorder running, ears straining, waiting for — something. The atmosphere had been less than magical. Possibly not the best place to try to make contact with the future dead, but Gansey had maintained high hopes for the power of St Mark's Eve. It wasn't that he'd expected to see the dead. All of the sources said that church watchers had to possess "the second sight" and Gansey barely possessed first sight before he put his contacts in. He'd just hoped for—

Something. And that was what he had got. He just wasn't quite sure what that *something* was yet.

The digital recorder in hand, Gansey settled himself against the rear tyre to wait, letting the car shield him from the buffeting of passing vehicles. On the other side of the guard rail, a greening field stretched out and down to the trees. Beyond it all rose the mysterious blue crest of the mountains.

On the dusty toe of his shoe, Gansey drew the arcing

shape of the promised supernatural energy line that had led him here.

As the mountain breeze rushed over his ears, it sounded like a hushed shout – not a whisper, but a loud cry from almost too far away to hear.

The thing was, Henrietta looked like a place where magic could happen. The valley seemed to whisper secrets. It was easier to believe that they wouldn't give themselves up to Gansey rather than that they didn't exist at all.

Please just tell me where you are.

His heart hurt with the wanting of it, the hurt no less painful for being difficult to explain.

Ronan Lynch's shark-nosed BMW pulled in behind the Camaro, its normally glossy charcoal paint dusted green with pollen. Gansey felt the bass of the stereo in his feet a moment before he made out the tune. When he stood up, Ronan was just opening his door. In the passenger seat was Adam Parrish, the third member of the foursome that made up Gansey's closest friends. The knot of Adam's tie was neat above the collar of his jumper. One slender hand pressed Ronan's thin mobile phone tightly to his ear.

Through the open car door, Adam and Gansey exchanged the briefest of looks. Adam's knitted eyebrows asked, *Did you find anything?* and Gansey's widened eyes replied, *You tell me.*

Adam, frowning now, spun the volume knob down on the stereo and said something into the phone.

Ronan slammed the car door – he slammed everything – before heading to the boot. He said, "My dick brother wants us to meet him at Nino's tonight. With *Ashley*."

"Is that who's on the phone?" Gansey asked. "What's *Ashley*?"

Ronan hefted a container of petrol from the boot, making little effort to keep the greasy container from contacting his clothing. Like Gansey, he wore the Aglionby uniform, but, as always, he managed to make it look as disreputable as possible. His tie was knotted with a method best described as *contempt* and his shirttails were ragged beneath the bottom of his jumper. His smile was thin and sharp. If his BMW was shark-like, it had learned how from him. "Declan's latest. We're meant to look pretty for her."

Gansey resented having to play nicely with Ronan's older brother, a senior at Aglionby, but he understood why they had to. Freedom in the Lynch family was a complicated thing, and at the moment, Declan held the keys to it.

Ronan traded the fuel can for the digital recorder. "He wants to do it tonight because he knows I have class."

The fuel-tank lid for the Camaro was located behind the spring-loaded licence plate, and Ronan watched silently as Gansey simultaneously wrestled with the lid, the container of petrol and the licence plate.

"You could have done this," Gansey told him. "Since you don't care about crapping up your shirt."

Unsympathetic, Ronan scratched at an old, brown scab beneath the five knotted leather bands he wore around his wrist. Last week, he and Adam had taken turns dragging each other on a moving dolly behind the BMW, and they both still had the marks to show it.

"Ask me if I found something," Gansey said.

Sighing, Ronan twitched the recorder towards Gansey. "Did you find anything?"

Ronan didn't sound very interested, but that was part of the Ronan Lynch brand. It was impossible to tell how deep his uninterest truly was.

Fuel was leeching slowly into Gansey's expensive chinos, the second pair he'd ruined in a month. It wasn't that he meant to be careless – as Adam told him again and again, "Things cost *money*, Gansey" – it was just that he never seemed to realize the consequences of his actions until too late. "Something. I recorded about four hours of audio and there's – something. But I don't know what it means." He gestured to the recorder. "Give it a whirl."

Turning to stare out over the interstate, Ronan pressed PLAY. For a moment there was merely silence, broken only by icy-sounding shrills of crickets. Then, Gansey's voice:

"Gansey," it said.

There was a long pause. Gansey rubbed a finger slowly along the pocked chrome of the Camaro's bumper. It was still strange to hear himself on the recording, with no memory of saying the words.

Then, as if from very far away, a female voice, the words hard to make out: "Is that all?"

Ronan's eyes darted to Gansey, wary.

Gansey lifted his finger: *Wait*. Murmured voices, quieter than before, hissed from the recorder, nothing clear about them except the cadence: questions and answers. And then his disembodied voice spoke out of the recorder again:

"That's all there is."

Ronan cast a glance back over to Gansey beside the car, doing what Gansey thought of as his smoker breath: long inhale through flared nostrils, slow exhale through parted lips.

Ronan did not smoke. He preferred his habits with hangovers.

He stopped the recorder and said, "You're dripping petrol on your trousers, geezer."

"Aren't you going to ask me what was happening when I recorded that?"

Ronan didn't ask. He just kept looking at Gansey, which was the same thing.

"Nothing was happening. That's what. I was staring at a car park full of bugs that shouldn't be alive when it's this cold overnight, and there was nothing."

Gansey hadn't really been sure if he'd pick up anything in the car park, even if he was in the right place. According to the ley hunters he'd spoken to, the ley line sometimes transmitted voices across its length, throwing sounds hundreds of miles and dozens of years from when they'd first been heard. A sort of audio haunting, an unpredictable radio transmission where nearly anything on the ley line could be a receiver: a recorder, a stereo, a pair of well-tuned human ears. Lacking any psychic ability, Gansey had brought the recorder, as the noises were often only audible when played back. The strange thing in all this was not the other voices on the player. The strange thing was *Gansey's* voice: Gansey was quite certain he was not a spirit.

"I didn't *say* anything, Ronan. All night long, I didn't say anything. So what's my voice doing on the recorder?"

"How did you know it was there?"

"I was listening to what I'd recorded while I was driving back. Nothing, nothing, nothing, and then: my voice. Then the Pig stopped."

"Coincidence?" Ronan asked. "I think not."

It was meant to be sarcastic. Gansey had said *I don't believe in coincidences* so often that he no longer needed to.

Gansey asked, "Well, what do you think?"

"Holy grail, finally," Ronan replied, too sarcastic to be any use at all.

But the fact was this: Gansey had spent the last four years working with the thinnest scraps of evidence possible and the barely heard voice was all the encouragement he needed. His eighteen months in Henrietta had used some of the sketchiest scraps of all as he searched for a ley line – a perfectly straight, supernatural energy path that connected spiritual places – and the elusive tomb he hoped lay along its path. This was just an occupational hazard of looking for an invisible energy line. It was . . . well, *invisible*.

And possibly hypothetical, but Gansey refused to consider that notion. In seventeen years of life, he'd already found dozens of things people hadn't known could be found, and he fully intended to add the ley line, the tomb, and the tomb's royal occupant to that list of items.

A museum curator in New Mexico had once told Gansey, *Son, you have an uncanny knack for discovering oddities.* An astonished Roman historian commented, *You look under rocks no one else thinks to pick up, slick.* And a very old British professor had said, *The world turns out its pockets for you, boy.* The key, Gansey found, was that you had to believe that they existed; you had to realize they were part of something bigger. Some secrets only gave themselves up to those who'd proven themselves worthy.

The way Gansey saw it was this: if you had a special knack for finding things, it meant you owed the world to look.

"Hey, is that Whelk?" Ronan asked.

A car had slowed considerably as it passed them, affording them a glimpse of its overly curious driver. Gansey had to agree that the driver did look a lot like their resentful Latin teacher, an Aglionby alumnus by the unfortunate name of Barrington Whelk. Gansey, owing to his official title of Richard "Dick" Campbell Gansey III, was fairly immune to posh names, but even he had to admit there wasn't much forgivable about Barrington Whelk.

"Hey, don't stop and help or anything," Ronan snapped after the car. "Hey, runt. What went down with Declan?"

This last part was directed at Adam as he climbed out of the BMW with Ronan's phone still in hand. He offered it to Ronan, who shook his head disdainfully. Ronan despised all phones, including his own.

Adam said, "He's coming by at five tonight."

Unlike Ronan, Adam's Aglionby jumper was second-hand, but he'd taken great care to be certain it was impeccable. He was slim and tall, with dusty hair unevenly cropped above a fine-boned, tanned face. He was a sepia photograph.

"Joy," Gansey replied. "You'll be there, right?"

"Am I invited?" Adam could be peculiarly polite. When he was uncertain about something, his Southern accent always made an appearance, and it was in evidence now.

Adam never needed an invitation. He and Ronan must've fought. Unsurprising. If it had a social security number, Ronan had fought with it.

"Don't be stupid," Gansey replied, and graciously accepted the grease-splotched fast-food bag that Adam offered. "Thanks."

"Ronan got it," Adam said. In matters of money, he was quick to assign credit or blame.

Gansey looked to Ronan, who lounged against the Camaro, absently biting one of the leather straps on his wrist. Gansey said, "Tell me there's no sauce on this burger."

Dropping the strap from his teeth, Ronan scoffed. "Please."

"No pickle, either," Adam said, crouching behind the car. He'd not only brought two small containers of fuel additive, but also a rag to place between the container of petrol and his khakis; he made the entire process look commonplace. Adam tried so hard to hide his roots, but they came out in the smallest of gestures.

Now Gansey grinned, the warmth of discovery starting to course through him. "So, pop quiz, Mr Parrish. Three things that appear in the vicinity of ley lines?"

"Black dogs," Adam said indulgently. "Demonic presences."

"Camaros," Ronan inserted.

Gansey continued as if he hadn't spoken. "And ghosts. Ronan, queue up the evidence if you would."

The three of them stood there in the late morning sun as Adam screwed the fuel-tank lid back on and Ronan rewound the player. A long way away, over the mountains, a red-tailed hawk screamed thinly. Ronan pressed PLAY again and they listened to Gansey say his name into thin air. Adam frowned distantly, listening, the warm day reddening his cheeks.

It could have been any one of the mornings in the last year and a half. Ronan and Adam would make up by the end of the day, Gansey's teachers would forgive him for missing class, then he and Adam and Ronan and Noah would go out for pizza, four against Declan.

Adam said, "Try the car."

Leaving the door hanging open, Gansey crashed on to the driver's seat. In the background, Ronan played the recording again. For some reason, from this distance, the sound of the voices made the hair on his arms stand slowly. Something inside him said that this unconscious speech meant the start of something different, although he didn't know what yet.

"Come on, Pig!" snarled Ronan. Someone laid on their horn as they blew by on the highway.

Gansey turned the key. The engine turned over once, paused for the briefest of moments – and then roared to deafening life. The Camaro lived to fight another day. The radio was even working, playing the Stevie Nicks song that always sounded to Gansey like it was about a one-winged dove. He tried one of the French fries they'd brought him. They were cold.

Adam leaned into the car. "We'll follow you back to the school. It'll get you back, but it's not done yet," he said. "There's still something wrong with it."

"Great," Gansey replied, loudly, to be heard over the engine. In the background, the BMW pumped out a nearly inaudible bass line as Ronan dissolved what was left of his heart in electronic loops. "So, suggestions?"

Reaching into his pocket, Adam retrieved a piece of paper and offered it to him.

"What's this?" Gansey studied Adam's erratic handwriting. His letters always looked like they were running from something. "A number for a psychic?"

"If you didn't find anything last night, this was going to be next. Now you have something to ask them about."

Gansey considered. Psychics tended to tell him he had money coming his way and that he was destined for great things. The first one he knew was always true and the second one he was afraid might be. But maybe with this new clue, with a new psychic, they'd have something else to say.

"OK," he agreed. "So what am I asking them?"

Adam handed him the digital recorder. He knocked the top of the Camaro once, twice, pensive.

"That seems obvious," he answered. "We find out who you were talking to."

THREE

Mornings at 300 Fox Way were fearful, jumbled things. Elbows in sides and lines for the bathroom and people snapping over tea bags placed into cups that already had tea bags in them. There was school for Blue and work for some of the more productive (or less intuitive) aunts. Toast got burned, cereal went soggy, the refrigerator door hung open and expectant for minutes at a time. Keys jingled as car pools were hastily decided.

Partway through breakfast, the phone would begin to ring and Maura would say, "That's the universe calling for you on line two, Orla" or something like that, and Jimi or Orla or one of the other aunts or half aunts or friends would fight over who had to pick it up on the upstairs phone. Two years ago, Blue's cousin Orla had decided that a call-in psychic line would be a lucrative addition and, after some brief skirmishes with Maura about public image, Orla won. "Winning" involved Orla waiting until Maura was at a conference over a weekend to secretively set up the line, and it was not so much a sore spot as the memory of a sore spot. Calls started coming in around seven a.m., and some days a dollar a minute felt more worth it than others.

Mornings were a sport. One that Blue liked to think she was getting better at.

But the day after the church watch, Blue didn't have to worry about battling for the bathroom or trying to make a packed lunch while Orla dropped toast butter-side down. When she woke up, her normally morning-bright room had the breath-held dimness of afternoon. In the next room over, Orla was talking to either her boyfriend or to one of the psychic hotline callers. With Orla, it was difficult to tell the difference between the two sorts of calls. Both of them left Blue thinking she ought to shower afterwards.

Blue took over the bathroom uncontested, where she gave most of her attention to her hair. Her dark hair was cut in a bob, long enough to plausibly pull back but short enough that it required an assembly of clips to do so successfully. The end result was a spiky, uneven ponytail populated by escaped chunks and mismatched clips; it looked eccentric and unkempt. Blue had worked hard to get it that way.

"*Mom*," she said as she jumped down the crooked stairs. Maura was at the kitchen counter making a mess of some kind of loose tea. It smelled appalling.

Her mother didn't turn around. On the counter on either side of her were green, oceanic drifts of loose herbs. "You don't have to run everywhere."

"*You* do," Blue retorted. "Why didn't you wake me up for school?"

"I did," Maura said. "Twice." Then, to herself, "Dammit."

From the table, Neeve's mild voice said, "Do you need my help with that, Maura?" She sat at the table with a cup of tea, looking plump and angelic as always, no sign of having lost any sleep the night before. Neeve stared at Blue, who tried to avoid eye contact.

"I'm perfectly capable of making a damn meditation tea, thank you," Maura said. To Blue, she added, "I told the school you had the flu. I emphasized that you were vomiting. Remember to look peaked tomorrow."

Blue pressed the heels of her hands to her eyes. She'd never missed class the day after the church watch. Been sleepy, perhaps, but never wasted like last night.

"Was it because I saw him?" she asked Neeve, lowering her hands. She wished that she couldn't remember the boy so clearly. Or rather, the *idea* of him, his hand sprawled on the ground. She wished she could un-see it. "Is that why I slept so long?"

"It's because you let fifteen spirits walk through your body while you chatted with a dead boy," Maura replied tersely, before Neeve could speak. "From what I've heard, anyway. Christ, is this what these leaves are supposed to smell like?"

Blue turned to Neeve, who continued to sip her tea with a sanguine air. "Is that true? Is it because spirits walked through me?"

"You *did* let them draw energy from you," Neeve replied. "You have quite a lot, but not that much."

Blue had two immediate thoughts about this. One was *I have quite a lot of energy?* and the other was *I think I am annoyed.* It was not as if she had intentionally allowed the spirits to draw power from her.

"You should teach her to protect herself," Neeve told Maura.

"I *have* taught her some things. I'm not an entirely wretched mother," Maura said, handing Blue a cup of tea.

Blue said, "I'm not trying this. It smells awful." She retrieved a cup of yoghurt from the fridge. Then, in solidarity with her mother, she told Neeve, "I've never had to protect myself at the church watch before."

Neeve mused, "That's surprising. You amplify energy fields so much, I'm surprised they don't find you, even here."

"Oh, stop," Maura said, sounding irritable. "There is nothing frightening about dead people."

Blue was still seeing Gansey's ghostly posture, defeated and bewildered. She said, "Mom, the church-watch spirits – can you ever prevent their deaths? By warning them?"

The phone rang then. It shrilled twice and kept going, which meant Orla was still on the line with the other caller.

"Damn Orla!" Maura said, though Orla wasn't around to hear it.

"I'll get it," Neeve said.

"Oh, but—" Maura didn't finish what she was going to say. Blue wondered if she was thinking that Neeve normally worked for a lot more than a dollar a minute.

"I know what you're thinking," her mother said, after Neeve had left the kitchen. "Most of them die from heart attacks and cancer and other things that just can't be helped. That boy is going to die."

Blue was beginning to feel a phantom of the sensation she'd felt before, that strange grief. "I don't think an Aglionby boy will die from a heart attack. Why do you bother telling your clients?"

"So they can get their things in order and do everything they want to do before they die." Her mother turned then, fixing Blue with a very knowing gaze. She looked as impressive as someone could look when standing barefoot in jeans, holding a mug of tea reeking of rotting soil.

"I'm not going to stop you from trying to warn him, Blue. But you need to know he's not going to believe you, even if you find him, and it's probably not going to save him, even if he knows. You might keep him from doing something stupid. Or you might just ruin the last few months of his life."

"You're a Pollyanna," Blue snapped. But she knew Maura was right – at least about the first part. Most everyone who met her thought her mother did parlour tricks for a living. What did Blue think she would do – track down an Aglionby student, tap on the window of his Land Rover or Lexus, and warn him to have his brakes checked and life-insurance policy updated?

"I probably can't stop you from meeting him anyway," Maura said. "I mean, if Neeve is right about why you saw him. You're fated to meet him."

"Fate," Blue replied, glowering at her mother, "is a very weighty word to throw around before breakfast."

"Everyone else," said Maura, "had breakfast a very long time ago."

The stairs creaked as Neeve returned. "Wrong number," she said in her affectless way. "Do you get many?"

"We're one number off from a gentlemen escort company," Maura replied.

"Ah," Neeve said. "That explains it. Blue," she added, as she settled back down at the table again, "if you'd like, I can try to see what killed him."

This got both Maura's and Blue's attention in a hurry.

"*Yes*," Blue said.

Maura started to reply, then merely pressed her lips back together.

Neeve asked, "Do we have any grape juice?"

Puzzled, Blue went to the fridge and held up a jug questioningly. "Cran-grape?"

"That will work fine."

Maura, her face still complicated, reached into the cupboard and drew out a dark blue salad bowl. She set it in front of Neeve, not gently.

"I won't be responsible for anything that you see," Maura said.

Blue asked, "What? What is that supposed to mean?"

Neither of them answered.

With a soft smile on her soft face, Neeve poured the juice into the bowl until it reached the edge. Maura turned off the light switch. The outside suddenly seemed vivid in comparison to the dim kitchen. The April-bright trees pressed against the windows of the breakfast area, green leaf upon green leaf upon glass, and Blue was suddenly very aware of being surrounded by trees, of having a sense of being in the middle of a still wood.

"If you are going to watch, please be quiet," Neeve remarked, looking at no one in particular. Blue jerked out a chair and sat. Maura leaned on the counter and crossed her arms. It was rare to see Maura upset but not doing something about it.

Neeve asked, "What was his name again?"

"He only said *Gansey*." She felt self-conscious saying his name. Somehow the idea that she would have a hand in his life or his death made his nominal existence in this kitchen her responsibility.

"That's enough."

Neeve leaned over the bowl, her lips moving, her dark reflection moving slowly in the bowl. Blue kept thinking of what her mother had said:

I won't be responsible for anything that you see.

It made this thing they did seem bigger than it usually felt. Further away from a trick of nature and closer to a religion.

Finally, Neeve murmured. Though Blue couldn't hear any particular meaning in the wordless sound, Maura looked abruptly triumphant.

"Well," Neeve said. "This is a thing."

She said it like, "This is a *thing*," and Blue already knew how that turned out.

"What did you see?" Blue asked. "How did he die?"

Neeve didn't take her eyes off Maura. She was asking a question, somehow, at the same time that she answered. "I saw him. And then he disappeared. Into absolutely nothing."

Maura flipped her hands. Blue knew the gesture well. Her mother had used it to end many an argument after she'd delivered a winning line. Only this time the winning line had been delivered by a bowl of cran-grape juice, and Blue had no idea what it meant.

Neeve said, "One moment he was there, and the next, he didn't exist."

"It happens," Maura said. "Here in Henrietta. There is some place – or places – that I can't see. Other times, I see" – and here she *didn't* look at Blue in such a way that Blue noticed that her mother was trying hard not to look at her – "things I wouldn't expect."

Now Blue was recalling the countless times her mother had insisted that they stay in Henrietta, even as it became more expensive to live here, even when opportunities to go to other towns opened up. Blue had once intercepted a set of emails on her mother's computer; one of Maura's male clients had ardently begged Maura to bring Blue "and whatever else you cannot live without" to his row house in Baltimore. In the reply, Maura had sternly informed him that this was not a possibility, for many reasons, chief of which that she would not leave Henrietta and least of which that she didn't know if he was an axe murderer. He had emailed back only a sad-face smiley. Blue always wondered what became of him.

"I would like to know what you saw," Blue said. "What is 'nothing'?"

Neeve said, "I was following the boy we saw last night to his death. I felt it was close, chronologically, but then he disappeared into some place I couldn't see. I don't know how to explain it. I thought it was me."

"It's not," Maura said. When she saw that Blue was still curious, she explained, "It's like when there's no picture on the television but you can tell it's still on. That's what it looks like. I've never seen someone go into it before, though."

"Well, he went into it." Neeve pushed the bowl away from her. "You said that's not all. What else will that show me?"

Maura said, "Channels that don't show up on basic cable."

Neeve tapped her beautiful fingers on the table, just once, and then she said, "You didn't tell me about this before."

"It didn't seem relevant," Maura replied.

"A place where young men can disappear seems quite relevant. Your daughter's skill also seems quite relevant." Neeve levelled her eternal gaze on Maura, who pushed off the counter and turned away.

"I have work this afternoon," Blue said finally, when she realized that the conversation had perished. The reflection of the leaves outside rippled slowly in the bowl, a forest still, but darkly.

"Are you really going to work in that?" Maura asked.

Blue looked at her clothing. It involved a few thin layering shirts, including one she had altered using a method called *shredding*. "What's wrong with it?"

Maura shrugged. "Nothing. I always wanted an eccentric daughter. I just never realized how well my evil plans were working. How late do you work?"

"Seven. Well, probably later. Cialina is supposed to work until seven-thirty but she's been saying all week that her brother got her tickets for *Evening* and if only someone would take over the last half hour. . ."

"You could say no. What's *Evening*? Is that the one where all the girls die with hatchets?"

"That's the one." As Blue slurped down her yoghurt, she spared a quick glance at Neeve, who was still frowning at the bowl of juice, pushed just out of her reach. "OK, I'm out."

She pushed back her chair. Maura was quiet in that heavy way that was louder than talking. Blue took her time tossing her yoghurt into the rubbish bin and dropping her spoon into the sink beside her mother, then she turned to go upstairs for her shoes.

"Blue," Maura said finally. "I don't have to tell you not to kiss anyone, right?"

FOUR

Adam Parrish had been Gansey's friend for eighteen months, and he knew that certain things came along with their friendship. Namely, believing in the super-natural, tolerating Gansey's troubled relationship with money and coexisting with Gansey's other friends. The former two were problematic only when they took time away from Aglionby, and the latter was only problematic when it was Ronan Lynch.

Gansey had once told Adam that he was afraid most people didn't know how to handle Ronan. What he meant by this was that he was worried that one day someone would fall on Ronan and cut themselves.

Sometimes Adam wondered if Ronan had been like *Ronan* before the Lynch brothers' father had died, but only Gansey had known him then. Well, Gansey and Declan, but Declan seemed incapable of handling his brother now – which was why he'd been careful to schedule his visit while Ronan was in class.

Outside of 1136 Monmouth, Adam waited on the first-storey landing with Declan and his girlfriend. Girlfriend, in fluttering white silk, looked a lot like Brianna, or Kayleigh, or whoever Declan's last girlfriend had been. They all had blonde, shoulder-length hair and eyebrows that matched

Declan's dark leather shoes. Declan, wearing the suit that his senior-year political internship required, looked thirty. Adam wondered if he would look that official in a suit, or if his childhood would betray him and render him ridiculous.

"Thanks for meeting us," Declan said.

Adam replied, "No problem."

Really, the reason he had agreed to walk with Declan and Girlfriend from Aglionby had nothing to do with kindness and everything to do with a nagging hunch. Lately, Adam had felt as if someone had been . . . *looking in* on their search for the ley line. He wasn't quite sure how to put this feeling into concrete terms. It was a stare caught out of the corner of his eye, a set of scuffed footprints in the stairwell that didn't seem to belong to any of the boys, a library clerk telling him an arcane text had been checked out by someone else right after he had returned it. He didn't want to trouble Gansey with it until he was certain, though. Things seemed to weigh heavily enough on Gansey as it was.

It wasn't that Adam wondered if Declan was spying on them. Adam knew he was, but he believed that had everything to do with Ronan and nothing to do with the ley line. Still, it wouldn't hurt to do a bit of observation.

Currently, Girlfriend was glancing around in the furtive way that was more noticeable for its furtiveness. 1136 Monmouth was a hungry-looking brick factory, gutted and black-eyed, growing out of an overgrown lot that took up nearly all of the street. A clue to the building's original identity was painted on the eastern side of the building: MONMOUTH MANUFACTURING. But for all their research, neither Gansey nor Adam had been able to figure out precisely what Monmouth had manufactured. Something that had required eight-metre ceilings and wide open spaces; something that had left moisture stains on the floor and gouges in the brick walls. Something that the world no longer needed.

At the top of the first-floor staircase, Declan whispered all this knowledge into Girlfriend's ear, and she giggled nervously, as if it were a secret. Adam watched the way Declan's lip barely brushed the bottom of Girlfriend's earlobe as he spoke to her; he looked away just as Declan glanced up.

Adam was very good at watching without being watched. Only Gansey ever seemed to catch him at it.

Girlfriend pointed out of the cracked window towards the car park below; Declan followed her gaze to the black, angry curves Gansey and Ronan had left doing doughnuts. Declan's expression hardened; even if they were all Gansey's doing, he'd assume it was Ronan.

Adam had knocked already, but he knocked again – one long, two short, his signal. "It will be messy," he apologized.

This was more for the benefit of Declan's girlfriend than it was for Declan, who knew full well what state the apartment would be in. Adam suspected Declan somehow found the mess charming to outsiders; Declan was calculating, if anything. His goal was Ashley's virtue, and every step of tonight would have been planned with that in mind, even this brief stop at Monmouth Manufacturing.

There was still no answer.

"Should I call?" Declan asked.

Adam tried the knob, which was locked, and then jimmied it with his knee, lifting the door on its hinges a bit. It swung open. Girlfriend made a noise of approval, but the success of the break-in had more to do with the door's failings than Adam's strengths.

They stepped into the apartment and Girlfriend tipped her head back, back, back. The high ceiling soared above them, exposed iron beams holding up the roof. Gansey's invented apartment was a dreamer's laboratory. The entire first floor, thousands of square feet, spread out before them. Two of the walls were made up of old windows – dozens of tiny, warped panes, except for a few clear ones Gansey had replaced – and the other two walls were covered with maps: the mountains of Virginia, of Wales, of Europe. Marker-pen lines arced across each of them. Across the floor, a telescope peered at the western sky; at its feet lay piles of arcane electronics meant to measure magnetic activity.

And everywhere, everywhere, there were books. Not the tidy stacks of an intellectual attempting to impress, but the slumping piles of a scholar obsessed. Some of the books weren't in English. Some of the books were dictionaries for the languages that some of the other books were in. Some of the books were actually *Sports Illustrated* Swimsuit Editions.

Adam felt the familiar pang. Not jealousy, just *wanting*. One day, he'd have enough money to have a place like this. A place that looked on the outside like Adam looked on the inside.

A small voice within Adam asked whether he would ever look this grand on the inside, or if it was something you had to be born into. Gansey was the way he was because he had lived with money when he was small, like a virtuoso placed at a piano bench as soon as he could sit. Adam, a latecomer, a usurper, still stumbled over his clumsy Henrietta accent and kept his change in a cereal box under his bed.

Beside Declan, Girlfriend held her hands to her chest in an unconscious reaction to masculine nakedness. In this case, the naked party was not a person, but a thing: Gansey's bed, nothing but two mattresses on a bare metal frame, sitting baldly in the middle of the room, barely made. It was somehow intimate in its complete lack of privacy.

Gansey himself sat at an old desk with his back to them, gazing out of an east-facing window and tapping a pen. His fat journal lay open near him, the pages fluttering with glued-in book passages and dark with notes. Adam was struck, as he occasionally was, by Gansey's agelessness: an old man in a young body, or a young man in an old man's life.

"It's us," Adam said.

When Gansey didn't reply, Adam led the way to his oblivious friend. Girlfriend made a variety of noises that all began with the letter O. With a variety of cereal boxes, packing containers, and house paint, Gansey had built a knee-high replica of the town of Henrietta in the centre of the room, and so the three visitors were forced to walk down Main Street in order to reach the desk. Adam knew the truth: these buildings were a symptom of Gansey's insomnia. A new wall for every night awake.

Adam stopped just beside Gansey. The area around him smelled strongly of mint from the leaf he chewed absently.

Adam tapped the earbud in Gansey's right ear and his friend startled.

Gansey jumped to his feet. "Why, hello."

As always, there was an all-American war hero look to him, coded in his tousled brown hair, his summer-narrowed hazel eyes, the straight nose that ancient Anglo-Saxons had graciously passed on to him. Everything about him suggested valour and power and a firm handshake.

Girlfriend stared.

Adam remembered finding him intimidating when he first met him. There were two Ganseys: the one who lived inside his skin, and the one Gansey put on in the morning when he slid his wallet into the back pocket of his chinos. The former was troubled and passionate, with no discernible accent to Adam's ears, and the latter bristled with latent power as he greeted people with the slippery, handsome accent of old Virginia money. It was a mystery to Adam how he could not seem to see both versions of Gansey at the same time.

"I didn't hear you knock," Gansey said unnecessarily. He knocked fists with Adam. Coming from Gansey, the gesture was at once charming and self-conscious, a borrowed phrase of a another language.

"Ashley, this is Gansey," Declan said, in his pleasant, neutral voice. It was a voice that reported tornado damage and cold fronts. Narrated side effects of small blue pills. Explained the safety procedures of this 747 we're flying in today. He added, "Dick Gansey."

If Gansey was thinking Declan's girlfriend was expendable, a renewable resource, he didn't show it. He merely said, voice just a little chilly as he corrected, "As Declan knows, it's my father who's Dick. For me, it's just Gansey."

Ashley looked more shocked than amused. "*Dick?*"

"Family name," Gansey said, with the weary air of someone trotting out a tired joke. "I try my best to ignore it."

"You're Aglionby, right? This place is crazy. Why don't you live on the school grounds?" Ashley asked.

"Because I own this building," Gansey said. "It's a better investment than paying for dorm housing. You can't sell your dorm after you're done with school. And where did that money go? Nowhere."

Dick Gansey III hated to be told that he sounded like Dick Gansey II, but right then, he did. Both of them could trot out logic on a nice little leash, wearing a smart plaid jacket, when they wanted to.

"God," Ashley remarked. She glanced at Adam. Her eyes didn't linger, but still, he remembered the fray on the shoulder of his jumper.

Don't pick at it. She's not looking at it. No one else notices it.

With effort, Adam squared his shoulders and tried to inhabit the uniform as easily as Gansey or Ronan.

"Ash, you won't believe why Gansey came here, of all places," Declan said. "Tell her, Gansey."

Gansey couldn't resist talking about Glendower. He never could. He asked, "How much do you know about Welsh kings?"

Ashley pursed her lips, her fingers pinching the skin at the base of her throat. "Mmmm. Llewellyn? Glendower? English Marcher lords?"

The smile on Gansey's face could have lit coal mines. Adam hadn't known about Llewellyn or Glendower when he'd first met Gansey. Gansey had needed to describe how Owain Glyndŵr – Owen Glendower to non-Welsh speakers – a medieval Welsh noble, had fought against the English for Welsh freedom and then, when capture seemed inevitable, disappeared from the island and from history altogether.

But Gansey never minded retelling the story. He'd related the events like they'd just happened, thrilled again by the magical signs that had accompanied Glendower's birth, the rumours of his power of invisibility, the impossible victories against larger armies and, finally, his mysterious escape.

When Gansey spoke, Adam saw the green swell of the Welsh foothills, the wide glistening surface of the River Dee, the unforgiving northern mountains that Glendower vanished into. In Gansey's stories, Owain Glyndŵr could never die.

Listening to him tell the story now, it was clear to Adam that Glendower was more than a historical figure to Gansey. He was everything Gansey wished he could be: wise and brave, sure of his path, touched by the supernatural, respected by all, survived by his legacy.

Gansey, now fully warmed to his tale, enchanted again by the mystery of it, asked Ashley, "Have you heard of the legends of sleeping kings? The legends that heroes like Llewellyn and Glendower and Arthur aren't really dead, but are instead sleeping in tombs, waiting to be woken up?"

Ashley blinked vapidly, then said, "Sounds like a metaphor."

Perhaps she wasn't as dumb as they'd thought.

"Maybe so," Gansey said. He made a grandiose gesture to the maps on the wall, covered with the ley lines he believed Glendower had travelled along. Sweeping up the journal behind him, he paged through maps and notes as examples. "I think Glendower's body was brought over to the New World. Specifically, here. Virginia. I want to find where he's buried."

To Adam's relief, Gansey left out the part about how he believed the legends that said Glendower was still alive, centuries later. He left out the part about how he believed the eternally sleeping Glendower would grant a favour to whoever woke him. He left out the part about how it haunted him, this need to find this long-lost king. He left out the midnight phone calls to Adam when he couldn't sleep for obsessing about his search. He left out the microfiche and the museums, the newspaper features and the metal detectors, the frequent flier miles and the battered foreign language phrase books.

And he left out all the parts about magic and the ley line.

"That's crazy," Ashley said. Her eyes were locked on the journal. "Why do you think he's here?"

There were two possible versions of this answer. One was grounded merely in history and was infinitely suitable for general consumption. The other added divining rods and magic to the equation. Some days, some rotten days, Adam believed the former, and only barely. But being Gansey's friend meant that more often he hoped for the latter. This was where Ronan, much to Adam's dissatisfaction, excelled: his belief in the supernatural explanation was unwavering. Adam's faith was imperfect.

Ashley, either because she was transient or because she'd been deemed sceptical, got the historical version. In his best professor voice, Gansey explained a bit about Welsh place names in the area, fifteenth-century artefacts found buried in Virginia soil, and historical support for an early, pre-Columbus Welsh landing in America.

Midway through the lecture, Noah – Monmouth Manufacturing's reclusive third resident – emerged from the meticulous room directly next to the office Ronan had claimed as his bedroom. Noah's bed shared the tiny space with a piece of mysterious equipment Adam guessed was some sort of printing press.

Noah, stepping further into the room, didn't so much smile at Ashley as goggle at her. He wasn't the best with new people.

"That's Noah," Declan said. He said it in a way that

confirmed Adam's assumption: Monmouth Manufacturing and the boys who lived in it were a tourist stop for Declan and Ashley, a conversation piece for a later dinner.

Noah extended his hand.

"Oh! Your hand is *cold.*" Ashley cupped her fingers against her shirt to warm them.

"I've been dead for seven years," Noah said. "That's as warm as they get."

Noah, unlike his pristine room, always seemed a little grubby. There was something out of place about his clothing, his mostly combed-back fair hair. His unkempt uniform always made Adam feel a little less like he stuck out. It was hard to feel like part of the Aglionby crowd when standing next to Gansey, whose crisp-as-George-Washington white collared shirt alone cost more than Adam's bicycle (anyone who said you couldn't tell the difference between a shirt from the mall and a shirt made by a clever Italian man had never seen the latter), or even Ronan, who had spent nine hundred dollars on a tattoo merely to piss off his brother.

Ashley's obliging giggle was cut off as Ronan's bedroom door opened. A cloud like there would never be sun again crossed Declan's face.

Ronan and Declan Lynch were undeniably brothers, with the same dark brown hair and sharp nose, but Declan was solid where Ronan was brittle. Declan's wide jaw and smile said, *Vote for me* while Ronan's buzzed head and thin mouth warned that this species was poisonous.

"Ronan," Declan said. On the phone with Adam earlier, he had asked, *When will Ronan* not *be available?* "I thought you had tennis."

"I did," Ronan replied.

There was a moment of silence, where Declan considered what he wanted to say in front of Ashley, and Ronan enjoyed the effect that awkward silence had on his brother. The two elder Lynch brothers – there were three total at Aglionby – had been at odds for as long as Adam had known them. Unlike most of the world, Gansey preferred Ronan to his elder brother Declan, and so the lines had been drawn. Adam suspected Gansey's preference was because Ronan was earnest even if he was horrible, and with Gansey, honesty was golden.

Declan waited a second too long to speak, and Ronan crossed his arms over his chest. "You've got quite the guy here, Ashley. You'll have a great night with him and then some other girl can have a great night with him tomorrow."

A fly buzzed against a windowpane far above their heads. Behind Ronan, his door, covered with photocopies of his speeding tickets, drifted closed.

Ashley's mouth didn't make an O so much as a sideways D. A second too late, Gansey punched Ronan in the arm.

"He's sorry," Gansey said.

Ashley's mouth was slowly closing. She blinked at the map of Wales and back to Ronan. He'd chosen his weapon well: only the truth, untempered by kindness.

"My brother is—" said Declan. But he didn't finish. There wasn't anything he could say that Ronan hadn't already proven. He said, "We're going now. Ronan, I think you need to reconsider your—" But again, he had no words to end the sentence. His brother had taken all the catchy ones.

Declan snagged Ashley's hand, jerking her attention away and towards the apartment door.

"Declan," Gansey started.

"Don't try to make this better," Declan warned. As he pulled Ashley out into the tiny stairwell and down the stairs, Adam heard the beginnings of damage control: *He has problems, I told you, I tried to make sure he wouldn't be here, he's the one who found Dad, it messed him up, let's go get seafood instead, don't you think we look like lobster tonight? We do.*

The moment the apartment door was closed, Gansey said, "Come on, Ronan."

Ronan's expression was still incendiary. His code of honour left no room for infidelity, for casual relationships. It wasn't that he didn't condone them; he couldn't understand them.

"So he's a man-whore. It's not your problem," Gansey said. Ronan was not really Gansey's problem, either, in Adam's opinion, but they'd had this argument before.

One of Ronan's eyebrows was raised, sharp as a razor.

Gansey strapped his journal closed. "That doesn't work on me. *She* had nothing to do with you and Declan." He said *you and Declan* like it was a physical object, something you could pick up and look underneath. "You treated her badly. You made the rest of us look bad."

Ronan looked chastened, but Adam knew better. Ronan wasn't sorry for his behaviour; he was only sorry that Gansey had been there to see him. What lived between the Lynch brothers was dark enough to hide anyone else's feelings.

But surely Gansey knew that as well as Adam. He ran his thumb back and forth across his bottom lip, a habit he never seemed to notice and Adam never bothered to point out. Catching Adam's gaze, he said, "Christ, now I feel dirty. Come on. Let's go to Nino's. We'll get pizza and I'll call that psychic and the whole goddamn world will sort itself out."

This was why Adam could forgive that shallow, glossy version of Gansey he'd first met. Because of his money and his good family name, because of his handsome smile and his easy laugh, because he liked people and (despite his fears to the contrary) they liked him back, Gansey could've had any and all of the friends that he wanted. Instead he had chosen the three of them, three guys who should've, for three different reasons, been friendless.

"I'm not coming," Noah said.

"Need some more alone time?" Ronan asked.

"Ronan," Gansey interjected. "Set your weapons to stun, will you? Noah, we won't make you eat. Adam?"

Adam glanced up, distracted. His mind had wandered from Ronan's bad behaviour to Ashley's interest in the journal, and he was wondering if it was more than the ordinary curiosity people possessed when faced with Gansey and his obsessive accessories. He knew Gansey would find him overly suspicious, unnecessarily proprietary of a search Gansey was more than willing to share with most people.

But Gansey and Adam sought Glendower for different reasons. Gansey longed for him like Arthur longed for the grail, drawn by a desperate but nebulous need to be useful to the world, to make sure his life meant something beyond champagne parties and white collars, by some complicated longing to settle an argument that waged deep inside himself.

Adam, on the other hand, needed that royal favour.

And that meant they needed to be the ones to wake Glendower. They needed to be the ones to find him first.

"Parrish," Gansey repeated. "Come on."

Adam made a face. He felt it would take more than pizza to improve Ronan's character.

But Gansey was already grabbing the car keys to the Pig and stepping around his miniature Henrietta. Even though Ronan was snarling and Noah was sighing and Adam was hesitating, he didn't turn to verify that they were coming. He knew they were. In three different ways, he'd earned them all days or weeks or months before, and when it came to it, they'd all follow him anywhere.

"*Excelsior,*" said Gansey, and shut the door behind them.

FIVE

Barrington Whelk was feeling less than sprightly as he slouched down the hall of Whitman House, the Aglionby admin building. It was five p.m., the school day well over, and he'd only left his town house in order to pick up homework that had to be graded before the next day. Afternoon light spilled in the tall, many-paned windows to his left; on the right was a hum of voices from the staff offices. These old buildings looked like museums at this time of day.

"Barrington, I thought you were out today. You look terrible. You sick?"

Whelk didn't immediately formulate an answer. For all intents and purposes, he *was* still out. The question asker was Jonah Milo, the well-scrubbed eleventh- and twelfth-grade English teacher. Despite an affinity for plaid and thin-legged corduroy trousers, Milo wasn't unbearable, but Whelk didn't care to discuss his absence from class this morning with him. St Mark's Eve was beginning to have a sheen of tradition for him, one that involved spending most of the night getting smashed before falling asleep on his kitchenette floor just before dawn. This year he'd had the forethought to request St Mark's Day off. Teaching Latin to Aglionby boys was punishment enough. Teaching it with a hangover was excruciating.

Finally, Whelk merely held up the grubby stack of handwritten homework assignments as answer. Milo's widened his eyes at the sight of the name written on the topmost paper.

"Ronan Lynch! Is that his homework?"

Flipping the stack around to read the name on the front, Whelk agreed that it was. As he did, a few boys on their way to crew team practice crashed past, pushing him into Milo. The students probably didn't even realize they were being disrespectful; Whelk was barely older than they were, and his dramatically large features made him look younger. It was still easy to mistake him for one of the students.

Milo disentangled himself from Whelk. "How do you get him to come to class?"

The mere mention of Ronan Lynch's name had scraped something raw inside Whelk. Because it was never Ronan by himself, it was Ronan as part of the inseparable threesome: Ronan Lynch, Richard Gansey and Adam Parrish. All of the boys in his class were affluent, confident, arrogant, but the three of them, more than anyone else, reminded him of what he'd lost.

Whelk struggled to remember if Ronan had ever missed a class with him. The days of the school year blurred together, one long and unending day that began with Whelk parking his crappy car next to the beautiful Aglionby cars, shouldering his way past laughing, thoughtless boys, standing in front of a room of students who were glassy-eyed at best and derisive at worst. And at the end of the day

Whelk, alone and haunted, never, ever able to forget that he was once one of them.

When did this become my life?

Whelk shrugged. "I don't remember him skipping."

"You have him with Gansey, though, don't you?" Milo asked. "That explains it. Those two are tight as ticks."

It was a strange, old expression, one that Whelk hadn't heard since his own days at Aglionby, when he, too, had been tight as ticks with his room-mate Czerny. He felt a hollowness inside him, like he was hungry, like he should've stayed home and drunk more to commemorate this miserable day.

He swam back to the present, looking at the attendance sheet the supply teacher had left. "Ronan was in class today, but Gansey wasn't. Not in mine, anyway."

"Oh, that's probably because of that St Mark's Day hoopla he was talking about," Milo said.

This got Whelk's attention. No one knew that today was St Mark's Day. No one celebrated St Mark's Day, not even St Mark's mother. Only Whelk and Czerny, treasure hunters and troublemakers, cared about its existence.

Whelk said, "Beg pardon?"

"I don't know what all's going on," Milo replied. One of the other teachers said hi to him on the way out of the staffroom, and Milo looked over his shoulder to reply. Whelk imagined grabbing Milo's arm, forcing his attention back his way. It took all of his effort to wait instead. Turning back around, Milo seemed to sense Whelk's interest, because he added, "He hasn't talked to you about it? He wouldn't shut up about it yesterday. It's that ley line stuff he's always on about."

Ley line.

If no one knew about St Mark's Day, *truly* no one knew about ley lines. Certainly no one in Henrietta, Virginia. Certainly not one of Aglionby's richest pupils. Definitely not in conjunction with St Mark's Day. This was Whelk's quest, Whelk's treasure, Whelk's teen years. Why was Richard Gansey III talking about it?

With the words *ley line* spoken aloud, a memory was conjured: Whelk in a dense wood, sweat collected on his upper lip. He was seventeen and shivering. Every time his heart beat, red lines streaked in the corners of his vision, the trees darkening with his pulse. It made the leaves seem like they were all moving, though there was no wind. Czerny was on the ground. Not dead, but *dying.* His legs still pedalled on the uneven surface beside his red car, making drifts of fallen leaves behind him. His face was just . . . done. In Whelk's head, unearthly voices hissed and whispered, words blurred and stretched together.

"Some sort of energy source or something," Milo said.

Whelk was suddenly afraid that Milo could see the memory on him, could hear the inexplicable voices in his head, incomprehensible but nonetheless present ever since that failed day.

Whelk schooled his features, though what he was really thinking was: *If someone else is looking here, I must have been right. It must be here.*

"What did he say he was doing with the ley line?" he asked with studied calm.

"I don't know. Ask him about it. I'm sure he'd love to talk your ear off about it." Milo looked over his shoulder as the secretary joined them in the hall, her bag on her arm, her jacket in her hand. Her eyeliner was smudged after a long day in the office.

"We talking about Gansey the third and his New Age obsession?" the secretary asked. She had a pencil stuck in her hair to keep it up and Whelk stared at the stray strands that wound up around the lead. It was clear to him from the way she stood that she secretly found Milo attractive, despite the plaid and the corduroy and the beard. She asked, "Do you know how much Gansey senior is worth? I wonder if he knows what his kid spends all his time on. Man, sometimes these entitled little bastards make me want to slit my wrists. Jonah, are you coming with me for a smoke break or not?"

"I quit," said Milo. He cast a quick, uneasy glance from the secretary to Whelk, and Whelk knew he was thinking about how much Whelk's father had been worth, once upon a time, and how little he was worth now, long after the trials had left the front pages of the newspapers. All the junior faculty and the admin staff hated the Aglionby boys, hated them for what they had and what they stood for, and Whelk knew they were all secretly pleased that he had fallen down among their ranks.

"How about you, Barry?" the secretary asked. Then she answered her own question: "No, you don't smoke, you're too pretty for that. Oh well, I'll go myself."

Milo turned to go as well.

"Feel better," he said kindly, although Whelk had never said he was sick.

The voices in Whelk's head were a roar, but for once, his own thoughts had drowned them out.

"I think I do already," said Whelk.

It was possible that Czerny's death wasn't for nothing after all.

SIX

Blue wouldn't really describe herself as a waitress. After all, she also taught penmanship to third graders, made wreaths for the Society for Ladies of Perpetual Health, walked dogs that belonged to inhabitants of Henrietta's poshest condo complex and replaced bedding plants for the elderly ladies of their neighbourhood. Really, being a waitress at Nino's was the least of things she did. But the hours were flexible, it was the most legitimate-looking entry on her already bizarre résumé, and it certainly paid the best.

There was really only one problem with Nino's, and it was that for all practical purposes, it belonged to Aglionby. The restaurant was six streets over from the iron-gated Aglionby campus at the very edge of the historic downtown. It wasn't the nicest place in Henrietta. There were others with bigger televisions and louder music, but none of them had managed to grip the school's imagination like Nino's. Just to know that Nino's was the place to be was a rite of passage; if you could be seduced by Morton's Sports Bar on Third, you didn't deserve to be in the inner circle.

So the Aglionby boys at Nino's were not just Aglionby students, but they were the most Aglionby that the school had to offer. Loud, pushy, entitled.

Blue had seen enough of the raven boys to last a lifetime.

Tonight, the music was already loud enough to paralyse the finer parts of her personality. She tied on her apron, tuned out the Beastie Boys as best she could, and put her tip-earning smile on.

Close to the beginning of her shift, four boys came through the front door, letting a cold hiss of fresh air into the room that smelled of oregano and beer. In the window beside the boys, a neon light that said *Since 1976* lit their faces a Limesicle green. The boy in front was talking on his mobile phone even as he showed Cialina four fingers to indicate party size. Raven boys were good at multitasking, so long as all tasks were exclusively to benefit themselves.

As Cialina hurried by, her apron pocket stuffed with tickets to deliver, Blue handed her four greasy menus. Cialina's hair floated above her head with static electricity and abject stress.

Blue asked, very unwilling, "Do you want me to take that table?"

"Are you kidding?" Cialina replied, eyeing the four boys. Having finally ended his call, the first one slid into one of the orange vinyl booths. The tallest of them knocked his head on the green cut-glass light hanging over the table; the others laughed generously at him. He said, *Bitch*. A tattoo snaked out above his collar as he swivelled to sit down. There was something hungry about all of the boys.

Blue didn't want them anyway.

What she wanted was a job that wouldn't suck all the thoughts out of her head and replace them with the leering call of a synthesizer. Sometimes, Blue would creep outside for an infinitesimal break, and as she lay her head back against the brick wall of the alley behind the restaurant, she'd dream idly about careers studying tree rings. Swimming with manta rays. Scouring Costa Rica to find out more about the scale-crested pygmy tyrant.

Really, she didn't know if she'd truly like to find out more about the pygmy tyrant. She just liked the name, because, for a five-foot-tall girl, *pygmy tyrant* sounded like a career.

All of those imagined lives seemed pretty far away from Nino's.

Just a few minutes after Blue's shift began, the manager signalled to Blue from the kitchen. Tonight it was Donny. Nino's had about fifteen managers, all of them related to the owner and none of them high-school graduates.

Donny managed to both lounge and offer the phone at once. "Your parent. Uh, mother."

But there was no need to clarify, because Blue didn't really know who her other parent was. Actually, she'd tried to pester Maura about her father before, but her mother had neatly slithered out of that line of questioning.

Plucking the phone from Donny's hand, Blue tucked herself back into the corner of the kitchen, next to a terminally greasy fridge and a large-basined sink. Despite her care, she still got jostled every few moments.

"Mom, I'm working."

"Don't panic. Are you sitting? You probably don't need to sit. Well, possibly. At least lean on something. He called. To schedule a reading."

"Who, Mom? Speak louder. It's loud here."

"*Gansey.*"

For a moment, Blue didn't understand. Then realization

tumbled down, weighting her feet. Her voice was a bit faint. "When . . . did you schedule it for?"

"Tomorrow afternoon. It was the fastest I could get him in. I *tried* to get him in sooner, but he said he had school. Do you have a shift tomorrow?"

"I'm changing it," Blue replied immediately. It was someone else saying the words, though. The real Blue was back in the churchyard, hearing his voice say *Gansey*.

"Yes, you are. Go work."

As she hung up, she could feel her pulse fluttering. It was real. He was real.

It was all true and terribly, terribly specific.

It seemed foolish to be here, now, busing tables and filling drinks and smiling at strangers. She wanted to be home, leaning back against the cool bark of the spreading beech tree behind the house, trying to decide what this changed about her life. Neeve had said this was the year she'd fall in love. Maura had said that she'd kill her true love if she kissed him. Gansey was supposed to die this year. What were the odds? Gansey had to be her true love. He had to be. Because there was no way she was going to kill someone.

Is this the way life is supposed to be? Maybe it would be better not to know.

Something touched her shoulder.

Touching was strictly against Blue's policy. No one was to touch her person while she was at Nino's, and especially no one was to touch her now, when she was having a crisis. She whirled.

"Can. I. Help. You?"

Before her stood the multitasking mobile phone Aglionby

boy, looking tidy and presidential. His watch looked as if it cost more than her mother's car and every area of exposed skin was a flattering shade of tan. Blue had never figured out how Aglionby boys managed to tan earlier than locals. It probably had something to do with things like spring break and places like Costa Rica and the Spanish coast. President Mobile Phone had probably been closer to a pygmy tyrant than she would ever be.

"I certainly hope so," he said, in a way that indicated less hope and more certainty. He had to speak loudly to be heard and he had to incline his head to meet her eyes. There was something annoyingly impressive about him, an impression that he was very tall, although he was no taller than most boys. "My socially inhibited friend Adam thinks you're cute, but he's unwilling to make a move. Over there. Not the smudgy one. Not the sulky one."

Blue, largely against her will, glanced to the booth he pointed to. Three boys sat at it: one was smudgy, just as he said, with a rumpled, faded look about his person, like his body had been laundered too many times. The one who'd hit the light was handsome and his head was shaved; a soldier in a war where the enemy was everyone else. And the third was – elegant. It was not the right word for him, but it was close. He was fine boned and a little fragile looking, with blue eyes pretty enough for a girl.

Despite her better instincts, Blue felt a flutter of interest. "So?" she asked.

"So would you do me a favour and come over and talk to him?"

Blue used one millisecond of her time to imagine what that might be like, throwing herself at a booth of raven boys and wading through awkward, vaguely sexist conversation. Despite the comeliness of the boy in the booth, it was not a pleasant millisecond.

"What exactly is it you think I'm going to talk to him about?

President Mobile Phone looked unconcerned. "We'll think of something. We're interesting people."

Blue doubted it. But the elegant boy was rather elegant. And he looked genuinely horrified that his friend was talking to her, which was slightly endearing. For one brief, brief moment that she was later ashamed of and bemused by, Blue considered telling President Mobile Phone when her shift ended. But then Donny called her name from the kitchen and she remembered rules number one and two.

She said, "Do you see how I'm wearing this apron? It means I'm working. For a living."

The unconcerned expression didn't flag. He said, "I'll take care of it."

She echoed, "Take care of it?"

"Yeah. How much do you make in an hour? I'll take care of it. And I'll talk to your manager."

For a moment, Blue was actually lost for words. She had never believed people who claimed to be speechless, but she was. She opened her mouth, and at first, all that came out was air. Then something like the beginning of a laugh. Then, finally, she managed to sputter, "I am not a *prostitute*."

The Aglionby boy appeared puzzled for a long moment, and then realization dawned. "Oh, that was not how I meant it. That is not what I said."

"That *is* what you said! You think you can just *pay* me to talk to your friend? Clearly you pay most of your female companions by the hour and don't know how it works with the real world, but . . . but. . ." Blue remembered that she was working to a point, but not what that point was. Indignation had eliminated all higher functions and all that remained was the desire to slap him. The boy opened his mouth to protest and her thought came back to her all in a rush. "Most girls, when they're interested in a guy, will sit with them *for free*."

To his credit, the Aglionby boy didn't speak right away. Instead, he thought for a moment and then he said, without heat, "You said you were working for living. I thought it'd be rude to not take that into account. I'm sorry you're insulted. I see where you're coming from, but I feel it's a little unfair that you're not doing the same for me."

"I *feel* you're being condescending," Blue said.

In the background, she caught a glimpse of Soldier Boy making a plane of his hand. It was crashing and weaving towards the table surface while Smudgy Boy gulped laughter down. The elegant boy held his palm over his face in exaggerated horror, fingers spread just enough that she could see his wince.

"Dear God," remarked President Mobile Phone. "I don't know what else to say."

"'Sorry'," she recommended.

"I said that already."

Blue considered. "Then, 'bye'."

He made a little gesture at his chest that she thought was supposed to mean he was curtsying or bowing or something sarcastically gentleman-like. Calla would've flipped him off, but Blue just stuffed her hands in her apron pockets.

As President Mobile Phone headed back to his table and

picked up a fat leather journal that seemed incongruous with the rest of him, the soldier boy let out a derisive laugh and she heard him mimic, ". . . 'not a prostitute'" Beside him, the elegant boy ducked his head. His ears were bright pink.

Not for a hundred dollars, Blue thought. *Not for two hundred dollars.*

But she had to confess she was a little undone by the blushing ears. It didn't seem very . . . Aglionby. Did raven boys get embarrassed?

She'd stared a moment too long. The elegant boy looked up and caught her gaze. His eyebrows were drawn together, remorseful rather than cruel, making her doubt herself.

But then she flushed, hearing again President Mobile Phone's voice saying *I'll take care of it*. She shot him a foul look, a real Calla number, and whirled back towards the kitchen.

Neeve had to be wrong. She'd never fall in love with one of them.

SEVEN

"Tell me again," Gansey asked Adam, "why you think a psychic is a good idea?"

The pizzas had been demolished (no help from Noah), which made Gansey feel better and Ronan feel worse. By the end the meal, Ronan had picked off all his moving-dolly scabs and he would've picked off Adam's as well if he'd let him. Gansey sent him outside to blow off steam and Noah to babysit him.

Now Gansey and Adam stood in line while a woman argued about mushroom topping with the cashier.

"They deal in energy work," said Adam, just loud enough to be heard over the blaring music. He studied his arm where he'd worried his own scab off. The skin beneath looked a little angry. Looking up, he peered over his shoulder, probably looking for the evil, *not-a-prostitute* waitress. Part of Gansey felt guilty for botching Adam's chances with her. The other part felt he'd possibly saved Adam from having his spinal cord ripped out and devoured.

It was possible, Gansey thought, that he'd once again been oblivious about money. He hadn't *meant* to be offensive but, in retrospect, it was possible he had been. This was going to eat at him all evening. He vowed, as he had a hundred times before, to consider his words better.

Adam continued, "The ley lines are energy. Energy and energy."

"Matchy matchy," Gansey replied. "If the psychic is for real."

Adam said, "Beggars can't be choosers."

Gansey looked at the handwritten ticket for the pizza in his hand. According to the bubbly writing, their waitress's name had been Cialina. She'd included her telephone number, but it was hard to say which boy she'd been hoping to attract. Some of the parties at the table were less dangerous to consort with than others. *She* clearly hadn't found him condescending.

Which was probably because she hadn't heard him speak.

All night. This was going to bother him *all night*. He said, "I wish we had a sense of how wide the lines were. I don't know if we're looking for a thread or a highway, even after all this time. We could've been feet away from it and never known."

Adam's neck might have broken from all the looking around he was doing. There was still no sign of the waitress. He looked tired, up too late too many nights in a row working and studying. Gansey hated seeing him like this, but nothing he thought of in his head sounded like something he could actually say to him. Adam wouldn't tolerate pity.

"We know they can be dowsed, so they can't be that narrow," Adam said. He rubbed the back of his hand against his temple.

That was what had brought Gansey to Henrietta in the first place: months of dowsing and research. Later, he'd tried to dowse the line more precisely with Adam. They'd circled the town with a willow divining rod and an electromagnetic-frequency reader, swapping the instruments between the two of them. The machine had spiked strangely a few times, and Gansey had thought he'd felt the divining rod twitch in his hands in time with it, but it might have been wishful thinking by that point.

I could tell him his grades are going to go to hell if he doesn't cut back on his hours, Gansey thought, looking at the dark skin beneath Adam's eyes. If he made it about him, Adam wouldn't interpret it as charity. He considered how to frame it so that it sounded selfish: *You're no good to me if you get mono or something.* Adam would see through that in a second.

Instead, Gansey said, "We need a solid point A before we even start thinking about point B."

But they had point A. They even had point B. The problem was just that the points were too large. Gansey had a map torn from a book depicting Virginia with the ley line marked darkly across it. Like the ley-line enthusiasts in the UK, American ley-line seekers determined key spiritual places and drew lines between them until the arc of the ley line became obvious. It seemed like all the work had been done for them already.

But the creators of those maps had never meant for them to be used as *road* maps; they were too approximate. One of the maps listed merely New York City, Washington, D.C., and Pilot Mountain, North Carolina, as possible reference points. Each of those points was kilometres wide, and even the finest of pencil lines drawn on a map was no narrower than ten metres – even eliminating the possibilities left them with thousands of acres where the ley line could be. Thousands of acres where Glendower could be, if he was along the ley line at all.

"I wonder," Adam mused aloud, "if we could electrify either the rods or the line. Hook up a car battery to them or something."

If you got a loan, you could stop working until after college. No, that would immediately birth an argument. Gansey shook his head a little, more at his own thoughts than at Adam's comment. He said, "That sounds like either the beginning of a torture session or a music video."

Adam's searching-for-devil-waitress face had given way to his brilliant-idea face. The fatigue melted away. "Well, amplification. That's all I was thinking. Something to make it louder and easier to follow."

It wasn't an awful idea. Last year in Montana, Gansey had interviewed a lightning-strike victim. The boy had been sitting on his quad bike in the doorway of a cattle barn when he was struck, and the incident had left him with an inexplicable fear of being indoors and an uncanny ability to follow one of the western ley lines using only a bent bit of radio antenna. For two days, they'd trailed together across fields carved by glaciers and marked by round hay bales higher than their heads, finding hidden water sources and tiny caves and lightning-burned stumps and strangely marked stones. Gansey had tried to convince the boy to come back to the East Coast to perform his same miracle on the ley line there, but the boy's newly pathological fear of the indoors ruled out all plane and car travel. And it was a long walk.

Still, it wasn't an entirely useless exercise. It was further proof of the amorphous theory Adam had just described: ley lines and electricity could be linked. Energy and energy.

Matchy matchy.

As he moved up to the counter, Gansey became aware that Noah was lurking at his elbow, looking strained and urgent. Both were typical for Noah, so Gansey was not immediately troubled. He passed a folded-over packet of notes to the cashier. Noah continued to hover.

"Noah, what?" demanded Gansey.

Noah seemed about to put his hands in his pockets and then didn't. Noah's hands seemed to belong fewer places than other people's. He eventually just let them hang as he looked at Gansey. He said, "Declan's here."

An immediate scan of the restaurant offered nothing. Gansey demanded, "Where?"

"Car park," Noah said. "He and Ronan—"

Not bothering to wait for the rest of the sentence, Gansey burst out into the black evening. Scrambling around the side of the building, he skidded on to the car park just in time to see Ronan throw a punch.

The swing was infinite.

From the looks of it, it was the opening act. In the sickly green light of a buzzing streetlamp, Ronan had an unbreakable stance and an expression hard as granite. There was no wavering in the line of the blow; he had accepted the consequences of wherever his fist landed long before he began the punch.

From his father, Gansey had got a head for logic, an affection for research and a trust fund the size of most state lotteries.

From their father, the Lynch brothers had got indefatigable egos, a decade of obscure Irish music instrument lessons and the ability to box like they meant it. Niall Lynch had not been around very much, but when he had been, he had been an excellent teacher.

"*Ronan!*" Gansey shouted, too late.

Declan went down, but before Gansey even had time to form a plan of action, he was back up again, fist smacking into his brother. Ronan released a string of profanity so varied and pointed that Gansey was amazed that the words alone didn't slay Declan. Arms windmilled. Knees met chests. Elbows rammed into faces. Then Ronan grabbed Declan's suit coat and used it to throw him on to the mirrorlike hood of Declan's Volvo.

"Not the fucking car!" snarled Declan, his lip bloody.

The story of the Lynch family was this: once upon a time, a man named Niall Lynch had three sons, one of whom loved his father more than the others. Niall Lynch was handsome and charismatic and rich and mysterious, and one day, he was dragged from his charcoal-grey BMW and beaten to death with a tyre iron. It was a Wednesday. On Thursday, his son Ronan found his body in the driveway. On Friday, their mother stopped speaking and never spoke again.

On Saturday, the Lynch brothers found that their father's death left them rich and homeless. The will forbade them to touch anything in the house – their clothing, the furniture. Their silent mother. The will demanded they immediately move into Aglionby housing. Declan, the eldest, was meant to control the funds and their lives until his brothers reached eighteen.

On Sunday, Ronan stole his deceased father's car.

On Monday, the Lynch brothers stopped being friends.

Ripping Ronan from the Volvo, Declan hit his brother hard enough that even Gansey felt it. Ashley, her light hair more visible than the rest of her, blinked at him from inside the Volvo.

Gansey took several strides across the car park. "Ronan!"

Ronan didn't even turn his head. A grim smile, more skeleton than boy, was etched on to his mouth as the brothers whirled around. This was a real fight, not for show, and it played in fast-forward. Someone would be unconscious before Gansey had time to cry havoc, and he just didn't have time to take someone to the ER tonight.

Gansey sprang, seizing Ronan's arm in mid-swing. Ronan still had fingers hooked inside Declan's mouth, though, and Declan already had a fist flying from behind, like a violent embrace. So it was Gansey who got Declan's blow. Something wet misted his arm. He was fairly certain it was spit, but it was possible it was blood. He shouted a word he'd learned from his sister, Helen.

Ronan had Declan by the knot of his burgundy tie, and Declan gripped the back of his brother's skull with one white-knuckled hand. Gansey might as well have not been there. With a neat flick of his wrist, Ronan smacked Declan's head off the driver's side door of the Volvo. It made a sick, wet sound. Declan's hand fell away.

Gansey seized the opportunity to propel Ronan about two metres away. Jerking in his grip, Ronan jackrabbited his legs on the tarmac. He was unbelievably strong.

"Quit it," Gansey panted. "You're ruining your face."

Ronan twisted, all muscle and adrenaline. Declan, his suit looking more bedraggled than any suit ought to look, started back towards them. He had a hell of a bruise rising on his temple, but he looked ready to go again. There was no way of telling what had set them off – a new home nurse for their mother, a poor grade at school, an unexplained credit card bill. Maybe just Ashley.

Across the car park, the manager of Nino's emerged from the front entrance. It wouldn't be long before the cops were called. *Where was Adam?*

"Declan," Gansey said, voice full of warning, "if you come back over here, I swear. . ."

With a jerk of his chin, Declan spit blood at the tarmac. His lip was bleeding, but his teeth were still good. "Fine. He's your dog, Gansey. You leash him. Keep him from getting kicked out of Aglionby. I wash my hands of him."

"I wish," snarled Ronan. His entire body was rigid underneath Gansey's hand. He wore his hatred like a cruel second skin.

Declan said, "You're such a piece of shit, Ronan. If Dad saw—" and this made Ronan burst forward again. Gansey clamped arms around Ronan's chest and dragged him back.

"Why are you even *here*?" Gansey asked Declan.

"Ashley had to use the bathroom," Declan replied crisply. "I should be able to stop where I like, don't you think?"

The last time Gansey had been in the Nino's co-ed bathroom, it had smelled like vomit and beer. On one of the walls, a red Sharpie had scrawled the word *BEEZLEBUB* and Ronan's number below. It was hard to imagine Declan *choosing* to inflict Nino's facilities on his girlfriend. Gansey's voice was short. "*I* think you should just go. This isn't getting solved tonight."

Declan laughed, just once. A big, careless laugh, full of round vowels. He clearly found nothing about Ronan funny.

"Ask him if he's going to get by with a B this year," he told Gansey. "Do you *ever* go to class, Ronan?"

Behind Declan, Ashley peered out of the driver's side window. She'd rolled down the window to listen; she didn't look nearly as much like an idiot when she thought no one was paying any attention to her. It seemed like justice that perhaps this time, Declan was the one getting played.

"I'm not saying you're wrong, Declan," Gansey said. His ear throbbed where it had been boxed. He could feel Ronan's pulse crashing in his arm where he restrained him. His vow to consider his words more carefully came back to him, and so he framed the rest of the statement in his head before saying it out loud. "But you are not Niall Lynch, and you won't ever be. And you'd get ahead a lot faster if you stopped trying."

Gansey released Ronan.

Ronan didn't move, though, and neither did Declan, as if by saying their father's name, Gansey had cast a spell. They wore matching raw expressions. Different wounds inflicted by the same weapon.

"I'm only trying to help," Declan said finally, but he sounded defeated. There was a time, a few months ago, when Gansey would've believed him.

Next to Gansey, Ronan's hands hung open at his sides. Sometimes, after Adam had been hit, there was something remote and absent in his eyes, like his body belonged to someone else. When Ronan was hit, it was the opposite; he became so urgently present that it was as if he'd been sleeping before.

Ronan told his brother, "I'll never forgive you."

The Volvo's window hissed closed, as if Ashley had just realized that this had become a conversation she wasn't meant to hear.

Sucking on his bloody lip, Declan looked at the ground for a bare moment. Then he straightened and adjusted his tie.

"Wouldn't mean much from you any more," he said, and tugged open the Volvo's door.

As he slid into the driver's seat, Declan said, "I don't want to talk about it" to Ashley and slammed the door shut. The Volvo's tyres squealed as they bit into the tarmac, and then Gansey and Ronan were left standing next to each other in the strange dim light of the car park. A street away, a dog barked balefully, three times. Ronan touched his pinkie finger to his eyebrow to check for blood, but there was none, just a raised, angry bump.

"Fix it," Gansey said. He wasn't entirely sure that whatever Ronan had done, or failed to do, was easily corrected, but he was sure that it must be corrected. The only reason Ronan was allowed to stay at Monmouth Manufacturing was because his grades were acceptable. "Whatever it is. Don't let him be right."

Ronan said, low, just for Gansey, "I want to quit."

"One more year."

"I don't want to do this for another year." He kicked a piece of gravel under the Camaro. Now his voice did rise, but only in ferocity, not in volume. "Another year, and then I get strangled with a necktie like Declan? I'm not a damn politician, Gansey. I'm not a banker."

Gansey wasn't, either, but it didn't mean he wanted to leave school. The pain in Ronan's voice meant he couldn't have any in his when he said, "Just graduate, and do whatever you want."

The trust funds from their fathers had ensured that neither of them had to work for a living, ever, if they didn't choose to. They were extraneous parts in the machine that was society, a fact that sat differently on Ronan's shoulders than Gansey's.

Ronan looked angry, but he was in the mood where he was going to look angry no matter what. "I don't know what I want. I don't know what the hell I am."

He got into the Camaro.

"You promised me," Gansey said through the open car door.

Ronan didn't look up. "I know what I did, Gansey."

"Don't forget."

When Ronan slammed the door, it echoed across the car park in the too-loud way of sounds after dark. Gansey joined Adam at his safely distant vantage point. In comparison to Ronan, Adam looked clean, self-contained, utterly in control. From somewhere, he had got a rubber ball printed with a SpongeBob logo, and he bounced it with a pensive expression.

"I convinced them not to call the cops," Adam said. He was good at making things quiet.

Gansey let out his breath. Tonight, he didn't have it in him to talk to the police on Ronan's behalf.

Tell me I'm doing the right thing with Ronan. Tell me this is how to find the old Ronan. Tell me I'm not ruining him by keeping him away from Declan.

But Adam had already told Gansey he thought Ronan needed to learn to clean up his own messes. It was only Gansey who seemed afraid that Ronan would learn to live in the dirt.

So he merely asked, "Where's Noah?"

"He's coming. I think he was leaving a tip." Adam dropped the ball and caught it again. He had an almost mechanical way of snapping his fingers around the ball as it bounced back towards him; one moment his hand was open and empty, and the next, tight shut around it.

Bounce. Snap.

Gansey said, "So, Ashley."

"*Yes,*" Adam replied, as if he'd been waiting for him to bring her up.

"Quite some eyes on her." It was an expression his dad used all the time, a family catchphrase for someone nosy.

Adam asked, "Do you think she's really here for Declan?"

"Why else would she be here?"

"Glendower," Adam replied immediately.

Gansey laughed, but Adam didn't. "Really, why else?"

Instead of answering, Adam twisted his hand and released the rubber ball. He'd chosen his trajectory carefully: the ball bounced off the greasy asphalt once, struck one of the Camaro's tyres, and arced high in the air, disappearing in the black. He stepped forward in time for it to slap in his palm. Gansey made an approving noise.

Adam said, "I don't think you should talk to people about it any more."

"It's not a secret."

"Maybe it should be."

Adam's uneasiness was contagious, but logically, there was nothing to support suspicion. For four years, Gansey had been searching for Glendower, freely admitting this fact to all and any who showed interest, and he'd never seen the slightest evidence of anyone else sharing his precise quest. He had to admit, however, that the suggestion of that possibility gave him a peculiarly unpleasant feeling.

He said, "It's all out there, Adam. Pretty much everything I've done is public record. It's too late for it to be a secret. It was too late years ago."

"Come on, Gansey," Adam said with some heat. "Don't you feel it? Don't you feel. . .?"

"Feel what?" Gansey despised fighting with Adam, and somehow this felt like a fight.

Unsuccessfully, Adam struggled to put his thoughts into words. Finally, he replied: "*Observed.*"

Across the car park, Noah had finally emerged from Nino's and he slouched towards them. In the Camaro, Ronan's silhouetted form lay back in the seat, head tilted as if he slept. Close by, Gansey could smell roses and grass mowed for the first time that year, and farther away, he smelled damp earth coming to life beneath last year's fallen leaves, and water running over rocks in mountain crooks where humans never walked. Perhaps Adam was right. There was something pregnant about the night, he thought, something out of sight opening its eyes.

This time, when Adam dropped the ball, it was Gansey's hand that reached out to snap it up.

"Do you think there would be any point to someone spying on us," Gansey said, "if we weren't on the right track?"

EIGHT

By the time Blue made her slow way outside, weariness had extinguished her anxiety. She sucked in a huge breath of the cool night air. It didn't even seem like it could be the same substance that filtered through Nino's air-conditioning vents.

She tilted her head back to look at the stars. Here, on the edge of downtown, there weren't enough streetlights to obliterate the stars completely. Ursa Major, Leo, Cepheus. Her breaths came easier and slower with each familiar constellation she found.

The chain was cold as Blue unlocked her bike. Across the car park, muffled conversations faded in and out. Footsteps scuffed across the tarmac somewhere close behind her. Even when they were quiet, people really were the noisiest animals.

One day, she would live some place where she could stand outside her house and see only stars, no streetlights, where she could feel as close as she ever got to sharing her mother's gift. When she looked at the stars, something tugged at her, something that urged her to see more than stars, to make sense of the chaotic firmament, to pull an image from it. But it never made sense. She only ever saw Leo and Cepheus, Scorpio and Draco. Maybe she just needed more horizon and less city. The only thing was, she didn't really want to see the future. What she wanted was to see something no one else could see or would see, and maybe that was asking for more magic than was in the world.

"Excuse me, um, miss – hi."

The voice was careful, masculine and local; the vowels had all the edges sanded off. Blue turned with a lukewarm expression.

To her surprise, it was Elegant Boy, face gaunter and older in the distant streetlight. He was alone. No sign of President Mobile Phone, the smudgy one, or their hostile friend. One hand steadied his bike. The other was tucked neatly in his pocket. His uncertain posture didn't quite track with the raven-breasted jumper and she caught a glimpse of a worn bit of seam on the shoulder before he shrugged it under his ear as if he was cold.

"Hi," Blue said, softer than she would've if she hadn't noticed the fray. She didn't know what sort of Aglionby boy wore hand-me-down jumpers. "Adam, is it?"

He gave a jerky, abashed nod. Blue looked at his bike. She didn't know what sort of Aglionby boy rode a bicycle instead of driving a car, either.

"I was on my way home," Adam said, "And I thought I recognized you over here. I wanted to say sorry. About what happened earlier. I didn't tell him to do that and I wanted you to know."

It didn't escape Blue that his slightly accented voice was as nice as his looks. It was all Henrietta sunset: hot front-porch swings and cold iced-tea glasses, cicadas louder than your thoughts. He glanced over his shoulder, then, at the sound of a car on a side street. When he looked back to her, he still wore a wary expression, and Blue saw that this expression – a wrinkle pinched between his eyebrows, mouth tense – was his normal one. It fitted his features perfectly, matched up with every line around his mouth and eyes. *This Aglionby boy isn't often happy*, she thought.

"Well, that's nice of you," she said. "But it's not you that needed to apologize."

Adam said, "I can't let him take all the blame. I mean, he *was* right. I did want to talk to you. But I didn't want to just – try to pick you up."

This was where she ought to brush him off. But she was stymied by his blush at the table; his honest expression; his newly minted, uncertain smile. His face was just strange enough that she wanted to keep looking at it.

The fact was that she'd never been flirted with by someone who she wanted to succeed at it.

Don't do it! warned the voice inside Blue.

But she asked, "And what is it you *wanted* to do?"

"Talk," he said. In his local accent, it was a long word and it seemed less of a synonym for *speak* than it was for *confess*. She couldn't help but look at the thin, pleasant line of his mouth. He added, "I guess I could have just saved a lot of trouble by coming up to talk to you in the first place. Other people's ideas always seem to get me into more trouble."

Blue was about to tell him how Orla's ideas got everyone into trouble at her house, too, but then she realized he would say something else and then she would reply and it could go on all night. Something about Adam told her that this was a boy she could have a *conversation* with. Out of nowhere, Maura's voice was in Blue's head. *I don't have to tell you not to kiss anyone, right?*

And just like that, Blue was done. She was, as Neeve

pointed out, a sensible girl. Even the very best outcome here could only end in torment. She blew out a breath.

"It wasn't about what he was saying about you, anyway. It was that he offered me money," she said, putting her foot on the bike pedal. The thing was not to imagine what it would've been like to stay and talk. When Blue didn't have enough money for something, the worst thing in the world was to imagine what it would've been like to have whatever the something was.

Adam sighed, as if he recognized her retreat. "He doesn't know. He's stupid about money."

"And you aren't?"

He just levelled her with a very steady look. It wasn't an expression that left room for folly.

Blue tipped her head back, staring up at the stars. It was strange to imagine how quickly they wheeled across the sky: a vast movement too far away for her to detect. *Leo, Leo Minor, Orion's Belt.* If she had been her mother or her aunts or her cousins, scrying up through the heavens, would she see what she ought to say to Adam?

She asked, "Are you coming back to Nino's?"

"Am I invited?"

She smiled in reply. It felt like a very dangerous thing, that smile, like something Maura wouldn't be pleased with.

Blue had two rules: stay away from boys, because they're trouble, and stay away from raven boys, because they were bastards.

But those rules didn't seem to apply to Adam. Fumbling in her pocket, she pulled out a tissue and wrote her name and the phone number for 300 Fox Way on it. Heart thumping, she folded it up and handed it to him.

Adam said only, "I'm glad I came back." Turning his long self around, he began to push his dolefully squeaking bike back the way he'd come.

Blue pressed her fingers to her face.

I gave a boy my number.

I gave a raven *boy* my number.

Hugging her arms around herself, she imagined a future argument with her mother. *Giving someone your number doesn't mean you're going to kiss him.*

Blue jumped when the rear door of the restaurant cracked open. But it was only Donny, his expression clearing when he saw her. In his hand was a tantalizingly fat leather-bound book that Blue knew instantly. She'd seen it in President Mobile Phone's hands.

Donny asked, "Do you know who left this behind? Is it yours?"

Meeting him halfway across the lot, Blue accepted the journal and flipped it open. The journal didn't immediately choose a page to open to; it was so well-worn and well-stuffed that every page claimed seniority. It finally split down the middle, obeying gravity instead of use.

The page it opened to was a mishmash of yellowed clippings from books and newspapers. Red pen underlined a few phrases, added commentary in the margins (*Luray Caverns count as spiritual place? crows = ravens?*), and jotted a neatly boxed list titled "Welsh-Influenced Place Names Near Henrietta". Blue recognized most of the towns listed. Welsh Hills, Glen Bower, Harlech, Machinleth.

"I didn't really read it," Donny said. "I just wanted to see if there was a name in there to return it. But then I saw that it was — well, it's your stuff."

By this, he meant it was what he expected of a psychic's daughter.

"I think I know who it belongs to," Blue said. She had no immediate thought other than wanting to spend more time flipping through its pages. "I'll take it."

After Donny had returned inside the restaurant, she flipped the journal back open. Now she had time to marvel at the sheer density of it. Even if the content hadn't immediately caught her, the feel of the thing would have. There were so many of the clippings she'd noticed before that the journal wouldn't stay book-shaped unless tied shut with leather wrappings. Pages and pages were devoted to these ripped and scissored excerpts, and there was an undeniable tactile pleasure to browsing. Blue ran her fingers over the varied surfaces. Creamy, thick artist paper with a slender, elegant font. Thin, browning paper with spidery serif. Slick, utilitarian white stock with an artless modern type. Ragged-edged newspaper in a brittle shade of yellow.

Then there were the notes, made with a half-dozen different pens and markers, but all in the same business-like hand. They circled and pointed and underlined *very urgently*. They made bulleted lists and eager exclamation points in the margins. They contradicted one another and referred to one another in third person. Lines became cross-hatching became doodles of mountains became squirrelly tyre tracks behind fast-looking cars.

It took her a while to make sense of what the journal was really about. It was organized into rough sections, but it was clear that whoever had created it had run out of space in some and begun anew later in the journal. There was a section on ley lines, invisible energy lines that connected spiritual places.

There was a section on Owain Glyndŵr,, the Raven King. There was a section about legends of sleeping knights who waited beneath mountains for discovery and new life. There was a section of strange stories about sacrificed kings and ancient water goddesses and all of the old things that ravens represented.

More than anything, the journal *wanted*. It wanted more than it could hold, more than words could describe, more than diagrams could illustrate. Longing burst from the pages, in every frantic line and every hectic sketch and every dark-printed definition. There was something pained and melancholy about it.

A familiar shape stood out from the rest of the doodles. Three intersecting lines: a long, beaked triangle. It was the same shape Neeve had drawn in the churchyard dust. The same shape her mother had drawn on the steamed shower door.

Blue flattened the page to get a better look. This section was on ley lines: "mystical energy roads that connect spiritual places". Throughout the journal, the writer had doodled the three lines again and again, along with a sickly-looking Stonehenge, strangely elongated horses, and a labelled sketch of a burial mound. There was no explanation of the symbol.

It couldn't be a coincidence.

There was no way this journal could possibly belong to that presidential raven boy. Someone must've given it to him.

Maybe, she thought, *it's Adam's.*

He gave her the same sensation as the journal did: the sense of magic, of possibility, of anxious danger. That same feeling as when Neeve had said that a spirit touched her hair.

Blue thought, *I wish you had been Gansey*. But as soon as she thought it, she knew it wasn't true. Because whoever Gansey was, he didn't have long to live.

NINE

Gansey woke in the night to find the moon full on his face and his phone ringing.

He fumbled for where it was nestled in the blankets beside him. Blind without his glasses or contacts, he had to hold the screen a few centimetres from his eyes to read the caller ID: MALORY, R. Now Gansey understood the bizarre timing of the call. Dr Roger Malory lived in Sussex, a five-hour time difference from Henrietta. Midnight in Virginia was five in the morning for Malory-the-early-riser. Malory was one of the prime authorities on British ley lines. He was either eighty or one hundred or two hundred years old and had written three books on the subject, all classics in the (very limited) field. They'd met the summer Gansey was splitting his time between Wales and London. Malory had been the first one to take fifteen-year-old Gansey seriously, a favour for which Gansey would not soon stop being grateful for.

"Gansey," Malory said warmly, knowing better than to call him by his Christian name. Without further preamble, Malory launched into a one-sided conversation about the weather, the historical society's past four meetings and how frustrating his neighbour with the collie was. Gansey understood about three quarters of the monologue. After living in the UK for nearly a year, Gansey was good with accents, but Malory's was often difficult, due to a combination of slurring, chewing, extreme age, bad breeding and a poor phone connection.

Getting out of bed to crouch beside his model of Henrietta, Gansey half-listened for a polite twelve minutes before breaking in, gently. "It's nice of you to call."

"I found a very interesting textual source," Malory said. There was a sound like he was either chewing or wrapping something in cellophane. Gansey had seen his flat and it was quite possible he was doing both. "Who suggested that the ley lines are dormant. Sleeping. Sound familiar?"

"Like Glendower! So what does that mean?"

"Might explain why they're so hard to dowse. If they're still present but not active, the energy would be very faint and irregular. In Surrey, I was following a line with this fellow – twenty kilometres, rotten weather, raindrops like turnips – and then it just disappeared."

Retrieving a tube of glue and some cardboard shingles, Gansey used the strong moonlight to work on a roof while Malory went on about rain. He asked, "Did your source say anything about waking the ley lines up? If Glendower can be woken, the ley lines could be, too, right?"

"That's the thought."

"But all it takes to wake Glendower is discovery. People have been *walking* all over the ley lines."

"Oh no, Mr Gansey, that's where you're mistaken. The spirit roads are underground. Even if they weren't always, they're now covered by metres of dirt accumulated over the centuries," Malory said. "No one's really touched them for hundreds of years. You and I, we don't walk the lines. We just follow the echoes."

Gansey recalled how the trail had seemed to come and go for no reason while he and Adam dowsed the lines. Malory's theory had a ring of plausibility, and, really, that was all he needed. He wanted nothing more than to start scouring his books for further support for this new idea, school day be damned. He felt a rare stab of resentment at being a teen, being tied to Aglionby; maybe this was how Ronan felt all the time.

"OK. So we go to them underground. Caves, maybe?"

"Oh, caves are dreadful things," Malory replied. "Do you know how many people die in caves every year?"

Gansey replied that he was sure he didn't.

"Thousands," Malory assured him. "They are like elephant graveyards. Much better to stay aboveground. Spelunking is more dangerous than motorcycle racing. No, this source was all about a ritual way to wake the spirit roads from the surface, letting the ley line know of your presence. You'd do a symbolic laying of hands on the energy there in Marianna."

"Henrietta."

"Texas?"

Whenever Gansey talked to British people about America, they always seemed to think he meant Texas. He said, "Virginia."

"Right," agreed Malory warmly. "Think how easy it would be to follow that spirit road to Glendower if it's shouting loud instead of whispering. You find it, perform the ritual, follow it to your king."

When Malory said it, it sounded inevitable.

Follow it to your king.

Gansey closed his eyes to calm his pulse. He saw a dimly

grey image of a king in repose, hands folded on his chest, a sword by his right side, a cup by his left. This slumbering figure was dizzyingly important to Gansey in a way that he couldn't begin to understand or shape. It was something more, something bigger, something that mattered. Something without a price tag. Something earned.

"Now, the text was not quite clear on how to perform the ritual," Malory admitted. He rambled about the vagaries of historical documents, and Gansey only paid a little attention until he finished with, "I'm going to try it on the Lockyer road. I'll let you know how it goes."

"Brilliant," Gansey said. "I can't say thanks enough."

"Give my regards to your mother."

"I wi—"

"You're lucky you still have your mother at your age. When I was about your age, my mother was murdered by the British health-care system. She was perfectly fine until she was admitted after a little cough..."

Gansey half-listened to Malory's oft-repeated story of the government's failure to cure his mother's throat cancer. Malory sounded quite cheerful by the time the phone had gone silent.

Now Gansey felt infected by the chase; he needed to talk to someone before the unfinished feeling of the quest ate him from the inside out. Adam would be the best, but the odds were good that Ronan, who swung wildly between insomnia and hypersomnia, would be awake.

He'd only made it halfway to Ronan's room before the thought struck him that it was empty. Standing in the dark doorway, Gansey whispered Ronan's name, and then, when that got no response, spoke it aloud.

Ronan's room was not to be broached, but Gansey did it anyway. Putting his hand on the bed, he found it unmade and cool, the blankets thrown aside with the speed of Ronan's going. Gansey hammered Noah's closed door with a fist while fumbling to dial Ronan's number with his other hand. It rang twice before Ronan's voicemail said merely, "Ronan Lynch."

Gansey cut off the recorded voice mid-word, his pulse tripping. For a long moment he debated, and then he dialled another number. This time, it was Adam's voice that answered, low with sleep and caution. "Gansey?"

"Ronan's gone."

Adam was quiet. It was not just that Ronan had vanished, it was that he had vanished after a fight with Declan. But it wasn't an easy thing to leave the Parrish household in the middle of the night. The consequences of getting caught could leave physical evidence, and it was getting too warm for long sleeves. Gansey felt wretched for asking this of him.

Outside, a midnight bird cried, high and piercing. The little replica of Henrietta was eerie in the half-light, the die-cast cars parked on the streets appearing as though they had just paused. Gansey always thought that, after dark, it felt like anything could happen. At night, Henrietta felt like magic, and at night, magic felt like it might be a terrible thing.

"I'll check the park," Adam whispered finally. "And, uh, the bridge, I guess."

Adam hung up so softly that it took Gansey a moment to realize the connection had ended. He pressed his fingertips to his eyes, which was how Noah found him.

"You're going to look for him?" Noah asked. He looked pale and insubstantial in the yellow, late-night light of the room behind him; the skin beneath his eyes was darker than anything. He looked less like Noah than the suggestion of Noah. "Check the church."

Noah didn't say he would go along, and Gansey didn't ask him to. Six months ago, the only time it had ever mattered, Noah had found Ronan in an introspective pool of his own blood, and so he was exempt from ever having to look again. Noah hadn't gone with Gansey to the hospital afterwards, and Adam had been caught trying to sneak out, so it was only Gansey who'd been with Ronan when they stitched his skin whole again. It had been a long time ago, but also, it was no time at all.

Sometimes, Gansey felt like his life was made up of a dozen hours that he could never forget.

Pulling on his jacket, he headed out into the greenish light of the chilly car park. The hood of Ronan's BMW was cold, so it hadn't been driven recently. Wherever he'd gone, he'd gone on foot. The church, its spire illuminated by dusky yellow light, was within walking distance. So was Nino's. So was the old bridge with the fast current rushing away beneath it.

He started to walk. His mind was logical, but his traitorous heart stuttered from beat to beat. He wasn't naive; he carried no illusions that he'd ever recover the Ronan Lynch he'd known before Niall died. But he didn't want to lose the Ronan Lynch he had now.

Despite the strong moonlight, the entrance to St Agnes lay in total darkness. Shivering a bit, Gansey put his hand on the great iron ring that pulled open the church door, unsure if it would be unlocked. He'd only been to St Agnes once, on Easter, because Ronan's younger brother,

Matthew, had asked them all to come. He wouldn't have thought of it as a place someone like Ronan would go in the middle of the night, but then again, he wouldn't have pegged Ronan as a churchgoer at all. And yet all of the Lynch brothers went to St Agnes every Sunday. For an hour, they managed to sit next to one another in a pew even when they couldn't meet one another's eyes over a restaurant table.

Stepping through the black arch of the entrance, Gansey thought, *Noah is good at finding things.* He hoped that Noah was right about Ronan.

The church enveloped Gansey in an incense-scented pocket of air, a rare enough smell that it instantly evoked half a dozen memories of family weddings, funerals and baptisms, every one of them summer. How strange that a season should be held captive in one breath of trapped air.

"Ronan?" The word was sucked into the empty space. It echoed off the unseeable ceiling far overhead so it was only his own voice, in the end, that answered him.

The subdued aisle light made peaked shadows of arches. The darkness and uncertainty crushed Gansey's ribs as small as a fist, his breathless lungs reminding him of yet another long-ago summer day, the afternoon he first realized there was such a thing as magic in the world.

And there Ronan was, stretched out on one of the shadowed pews, an arm hanging off the edge, the other skewed above his head, his body a darker bit of black in an already black world. He wasn't moving.

Gansey thought, *Not tonight. Please don't let it be tonight.*

Edging into the pew behind Ronan, he put his hand on the other boy's shoulder, as if he could merely wake him, praying that by assuming it so, it would be true. The shoulder was warm below his hand; he smelled alcohol.

"Wake up, dude," he said. The words didn't sound light, though he meant them to.

Ronan's shoulder shifted and his face turned. For a brief, unchained moment, Gansey had a sudden thought that he was too late and Ronan was dead after all, and that his corpse woke now only because Gansey had commanded it to. But then Ronan's brilliant blue eyes opened, and the moment dissipated.

Gansey let out a sigh. "You bastard."

Ronan said plainly, "I couldn't dream." Then, taking in Gansey's stricken expression, he added, "I promised you it wouldn't happen again."

Gansey tried again to keep his voice light, but failed. "But you're a liar."

"I think," Ronan replied, "that you're mistaking me for my brother."

The church was quiet and full around them; it seemed brighter now that Ronan's eyes were open, as if the building had been asleep as well.

"When I told you I didn't want you getting drunk at Monmouth, I didn't mean I wanted you drunk somewhere else."

Ronan, with only a little slurring, replied, "Pot calling the kettle black."

With dignity, Gansey said, "I drink. I do not get drunk."

Ronan's eyes dropped to something he held near his chest.

"What is that?" Gansey asked.

Next to his chest, Ronan's fingers curled around a dark

object. When Gansey reached down to uncurl his grip, he felt something warm and living, a rapid pulse against his fingertips. He snatched his hand away.

"Christ," said Gansey, trying to make sense of what he'd felt. "Is that a bird?"

Ronan slowly sat up, still holding his cargo close. Another whuff of alcohol-laced breath drifted towards Gansey.

"Raven." There was a long pause as Ronan regarded his hand. "Maybe a crow. But I doubt it. I . . . yeah, seriously doubt it. *Corvus corax*."

Even drunk, Ronan knew the Latin name for the common raven.

And it was not just a raven, Gansey saw. It was a tiny foundling, featherless mouth still a baby's smile, wings still days and nights and days away from flight. He wasn't sure he would want to touch something that looked so easily destroyable.

The raven was Glendower's bird. The Raven King, he was called, from a long line of kings associated with the bird. Legend had it that Glendower could speak to ravens, and vice versa. It was only one of the reasons why Gansey was here in Henrietta, a town known for its ravens. His skin prickled.

"Where did it come from?"

Ronan's fingers were a compassionate cage around the raven's breast. It didn't look real in his hands. "I found it."

"People find pennies," Gansey replied. "Or car keys. Or four-leaf clovers."

"And ravens," Ronan said. "You're just jealous 'cause" – at this point, he had to stop to regroup his beer-sluggish thoughts – "you didn't find one, too."

The bird had just crapped between Ronan's fingers on to the pew beside him. Holding the fledgling in one hand, Ronan used a church bulletin to scrape the majority of the mess off the wood. He offered the soiled paper to Gansey. The weekly prayer requests were spattered with white.

Gansey only took the paper because he didn't trust Ronan to bother finding a place to throw it out. With some distaste, he asked, "What if I implement a no-pets policy at the apartment?"

"Well, hell, man," Ronan replied, with a savage smile, "you can't just throw out Noah like that."

It took Gansey a moment to realize that Ronan had made a joke, and by then, it was too late to laugh. In any case, he knew he was going to let the bird return with them to Monmouth Manufacturing, because he saw the possessive way Ronan held it. Already the raven looked up at him, beak cracked hopefully, dependent.

Gansey relented. "Come on. We're going back. Get up."

As Ronan unsteadily climbed to his feet, the raven hunched down in his hands, becoming all beak and body, no neck. He said, "Get used to some turbulence, you little bastard."

"You can't name it that."

"Her name's Chainsaw," replied Ronan, without looking up. Then: "Noah. You're creepy as hell back there."

In the deep, shadowed entrance of the church, Noah stood silently. For a second, all that seemed to be visible was his pale face; his dark clothing invisible and his eyes chasms into someplace unknowable. Then he stepped into the light and he was rumpled and familiar as always.

"I thought you weren't coming," Gansey said.

Noah's gaze travelled past them to the altar, then up to the dark, unseeable ceiling. He said, with typical bravery, "The apartment was creepy."

"Freak," Ronan remarked, but Noah seemed unconcerned.

Gansey pulled open the door to the pavement. No sign of Adam. Guilt for calling him out for a false alarm was beginning to settle in. Though . . . he wasn't entirely certain it was a false alarm. *Something* had happened, even if he wasn't yet sure what. "Where did you say you found that bird again?"

"In my head." Ronan's laugh was a sharp jackal cry.

"Dangerous place," commented Noah.

Ronan stumbled, all his edges blunted by alcohol, and the raven in his hands let out a feeble sound more percussive than vocal. He replied, "Not for a chainsaw."

Back out in the hard spring night, Gansey tipped his head back. Now that he knew that Ronan was all right, he could see that Henrietta after dark was a beautiful place, a patchwork town embroidered with black tree branches.

A *raven*, of all the birds for Ronan to turn up with.

Gansey didn't believe in coincidences.

TEN

Whelk was not sleeping.

Back when he was an Aglionby boy, sleep had come easy – and why shouldn't it have? Like Czerny and the rest of his classmates, he slept two or four or six hours on weekdays, up late, up early, and then performed marathon sleeping sessions on the weekend. And when he did sleep, it was hours of easy, dreamless sleep. No – he knew that was false. Everyone dreamed, only some forgot.

Now, however, he rarely closed his eyes for longer than a few hours at a stretch. He rolled in his bedsheets. He sat bolt upright, woken by whispers. He nodded off on his leather sofa, the only piece of furniture the government hadn't seized. His sleep patterns and energy seemed dictated by something larger and more powerful than himself, ebbing and flowing like an uneven tide. Attempts to chart it left him frustrated: he seemed more wakeful at the full moon and after thunderstorms, but beyond that, it was difficult to predict. In his mind, he imagined that it was the magnetic pulse of the ley line itself, somehow invited into his body through Czerny's death.

Sleep deprivation made his life an imaginary thing, his days a ribbon floating aimlessly in water.

It was nearly a full moon and it had not been long since it rained, so Whelk was awake.

He sat in a T-shirt and boxers in front of the computer screen, operating the mouse with the unprincipled and dubious productivity of the fatigued. All in a rush, the countless voices invaded his head, whispering and hissing. They sounded like the static that buzzed over phone lines in the vicinity of the ley line. Like the wind before a storm front. Like the trees themselves conspiring. As always, Whelk couldn't pick out any words, and he couldn't understand the conversation. But he did understand one thing: something strange had just happened in Henrietta, and the voices couldn't stop talking about it.

For the first time in years, Whelk retrieved his old county maps from his tiny hall wardrobe. He had no table and the counter-top was cluttered with opened packages of microwave lasagne and plates with stale bread crusts on them, so he spread the maps out in the bathroom instead. A spider in the bathtub skidded out of his way when he flattened a map against the surface.

Czerny, you're in a better place than me, I think.

But he didn't really believe that. He had no idea what had become of Czerny's soul or spirit or whatever you wanted to call what had been Czerny, but if Whelk had been cursed with whispering voices merely by his part in the ritual, Czerny's fate must've been worse.

Whelk stood back and crossed his arms, studying the dozens of marks and notations he'd made on the maps over the course of his search. Czerny's impossible handwriting, always in red, noted energy levels along the possible path of the ley line. Back then, it had been a game, a treasure hunt. A play for glory. Was it true? It didn't matter. It was an expensive exercise in strategy with the East Coast as the playing field. Looking for patterns, Whelk had painstakingly drawn circles around areas of interest on one of the topographical maps. A circle around an old copse of ash trees where the energy levels were always high. A circle around a ruined church that wildlife seemed to avoid. A circle around the place Czerny had died.

Of course, he had drawn the circle *before* Czerny had died. The place, a sinister group of oak trees, had been notable because of old words carved into one of the trunks. Latin. It seemed incomplete, difficult to translate, and Whelk's best guess was "the second road". The energy levels were promising there, though, if inconsistent. Surely this, then, was on the ley line.

Czerny and Whelk had returned a half-dozen times, taking readings (next to the circle, there were six different numbers in Czerny's handwriting), digging in the dirt for possible artefacts, watching overnight for signs of supernatural activity. Whelk had constructed his most complicated and sensitive dowsing rod yet, two metal wires bent at a ninety-degree angle and inserted into a metal tube handle so that they could swing freely. They'd dowsed the area around it, trying to establish for certain the path of the line.

But it remained spotty, coming in and out of focus like a distant radio station. The lines needed to be woken, to have their frequencies honed, the volume turned up.

Czerny and Whelk made plans to attempt the ritual in the oak grove. They weren't quite sure of the process, though. All Whelk could find out was that the line loved reciprocity and sacrifice, but that was frustratingly vague. No other information presented itself, so they kept pushing it back. Over winter break. Spring break. End of the school year.

Then Whelk's mother had called and told Whelk that his father had been arrested for unethical business practices and income tax evasion. It turned out the company had been trading with war criminals, a fact his mother knew and Whelk had guessed, and the FBI had been watching for years. Overnight, the Whelks lost everything.

It was in the papers the next day, the catastrophic crash of the Whelk family fortune. Both of Whelk's girlfriends left him. Well, the second one was technically Czerny's, so perhaps that didn't count. The whole thing was all very public. The Virginia playboy, heir to the Whelk fortune, suddenly evicted from his Aglionby dorm, relieved of his social life, freed from any hope of his Ivy League future, watching his car being loaded on to a truck and his room emptied of speakers and furniture.

The last time Whelk had looked at this map had been as he stood in his dorm room, realizing that the only thing he had left was the ten-dollar note in his pocket. None of his credit cards meant anything any more.

Czerny had pulled up in his red Mustang. He hadn't got out of the car.

"Does this make you white trash now?" he'd asked. Czerny didn't really have a sense of humour. He just sometimes said things that happened to be funny. Whelk, standing in the wreckage of his life, didn't laugh this time.

The ley line wasn't a game any more.

"Unlock your door," Whelk had told him. "We're doing the ritual."

ELEVEN

One hour and twenty-three minutes before Blue's alarm was supposed to go off for school, she was woken by the front door closing. Grey dawn light filtered in her bedroom window, making diffuse shadows of the leaves pressed against the glass. She tried not to resent her lost one hour and twenty-three minutes of sleep.

Footsteps started up the staircase. Blue caught the sound of her mother's voice.

"...was up waiting for you."

"Some things are better done at night." This was Neeve. Though her voice was smaller than Maura's, it was crisper, somehow, and carried well. "Henrietta is quite a place, isn't it?"

"I didn't ask you to look at Henrietta," Maura replied, in a stage whisper. She sounded – protective.

"It is difficult not to. It shouts," Neeve said. Her next words were lost in the sound of a creaking stair.

Maura's reply was obscured as she, too, started to climb the stairs, but it sounded like, "I would prefer if you left Blue out of this."

Blue went very still.

Neeve said, "I'm only telling you what I'm finding. If

he vanished at the same time that . . . possible they're linked. Do you not want her to know who he is?"

Another stair groaned. Blue thought, *Why can't they talk without creaking up the stairs at the same time!*

Maura snapped, "I don't see how that would be easier for anyone."

Neeve murmured a reply.

"This is already getting out of hand," her mother said. "It was barely more than typing his name into a search engine, and now. . ."

Blue strained her ears. It felt like she hadn't heard her mother use a masculine pronoun for quite a long time, with the exception of Gansey.

It was possible, Blue thought after a long moment, that Maura meant Blue's father. None of the awkward conversations Blue had attempted with her mother had ever got her any information about him, just nonsensical humourous replies (*He is Santa Claus. He was a bank robber. He's currently in orbit*) that changed every time she asked. In Blue's head, he was a dashing heroic figure who'd had to vanish because of a tragic past. Possibly to a witness protection programme. She liked to imagine him stealing a glimpse of her over the back-garden fence, proudly watching his strange daughter daydream under the beech tree.

Blue was awfully fond of her father, considering she'd never met him.

Somewhere in the depths of the house, a door closed, and then there was once more the sort of night-silence that is hard to disturb. After a long moment, Blue reached over to the plastic bin that served as her bedside table and retrieved the journal. She rested a hand on the cool leather cover. The surface of it felt like the cool, smooth bark of the beech tree behind the house. As when she touched the beech tree, she felt at once comforted and anxious: reassured and driven to action.

Henrietta is quite a place, Neeve had said. The journal seemed to agree. A place for what, she wasn't sure.

Blue didn't mean to fall asleep, but she did, for another hour and twelve minutes. It wasn't her alarm that woke her this time, either. It was a single thought shouted in her brain:

Today is the day Gansey comes for his reading.

Embroiled in the daily routine of getting ready for school, the conversation between Maura and Neeve seemed more commonplace than it had before. But the journal was still as magical. Sitting on the edge of her bed, Blue touched one of the quotes.

The king sleeps still, under a mountain, and around him is assembled his warriors and his herds and his riches. By his right hand is his cup, filled with possibility. On his breast nestles his sword, waiting, too, to wake. Fortunate is the soul who finds the king and is brave enough to call him to wakefulness, for the king will grant him a favour, as wondrous as can be imagined by a mortal man.

She closed the pages. It felt as if there were a larger, terribly curious Blue inside her that was about to bust out of the smaller, more sensible Blue that held her. For a long moment she let the journal rest on her legs, the cover cool against her palms.

A favour.

If she had a favour, what would she ask? To not have to worry about money? To know who her father had been? To travel the world? To see what her mother saw?

The thought rang through her brain again:

Today is the day Gansey comes for his reading.

What will he be like?

Maybe, if she was standing before that sleeping king, she'd ask the king to save Gansey's life.

"Blue, I hope you're awake!" Orla screamed from downstairs. Blue needed to leave soon if she was to make the bike trip to school on time. In a few weeks, it would be an uncomfortably hot ride.

Possibly, she would ask a sleeping king for a car.

I wish I could just cut class today.

It wasn't that Blue dreaded high school; it just felt like ... a holding pattern. And it wasn't as if she was bullied; it hadn't taken her very long to discover that the weirder she looked on the outside — the more she let other kids realize that she wasn't like them, from the very beginning — the less likely she was to be picked on or ignored. The fact was, by the time she got to high school, being weird and proud of it was an asset. Suddenly cool, Blue could've happily had any number of friends. And she *had* tried. But the problem with being weird was that everyone else was *normal*.

So her family remained her closest friends, school remained a chore and Blue remained secretly hopeful that, somewhere out there in the world, there were other odd people like her. Even if they didn't seem to be in Henrietta.

It was possible, she thought, that Adam was also odd.

"*BLUE!*" Orla bellowed again. "*SCHOOL.*"

With the journal held fast to her chest, Blue headed towards the red-painted door at the end of the hall. On her way, she had to pass the frenzy of activity in the Phone/Sewing/Cat Room and the furious battle for the bathroom. The room behind the red door belonged to Persephone, one of Maura's two best friends. The door was ajar, but still, Blue knocked softly. Persephone was a poor but energetic sleeper; her midnight shouting and nocturnal leg paddling ensured that she never had to share a room. It also meant that she grabbed sleep when she could; Blue didn't want to wake her.

Persephone's tiny, breathy voice said, "It's available. I mean, open."

Pushing open the door, Blue found Persephone sitting at the card table beside the window. When pressed, people often remembered Persephone's hair: a long, wavy white-blonde mane that fell to the back of her thighs. If they got past her hair, they sometimes recalled her dresses – elaborate, frothy creations or quizzical smocks. And if they made it past that, they were unsettled by her eyes, true mirror black, the pupils hidden in the darkness.

Currently, Persephone held a pencil with a strangely childlike grip. When she saw Blue, she frowned in a pointy sort of way.

"Good morning," Blue said.

"Good morning," Persephone echoed. "It's too early. My words aren't working, so I'll just use as many of the ones that work for you as possible."

She twirled a hand around in a vague sort of way.

Blue took this as a sign to find a place to sit. Most of the bed was covered by strange, embroidered leggings and checked tights running in place, but she found a place to lean her butt on the edge. The whole room smelled familiar, like oranges, or baby powder, or maybe like a new textbook.

"Sleep badly?" Blue asked.

"Badly," Persephone echoed again. Then, "Oh, well, that's not quite true. I'll have to use my own words after all."

"What are you working on?"

Often, Persephone was working on her eternal PhD thesis, but because it was a process that seemed to require vexed music and frequent snacks, she rarely did it during the morning rush.

"Just a little something," Persephone said sadly. Or perhaps thoughtfully. It was hard to tell the difference, and Blue didn't like to ask. Persephone had a lover or a husband who was dead or overseas – it was always difficult to know details when it came to Persephone – and she seemed to miss him, or at least to notice that he was gone, which was notable for Persephone. Again, Blue didn't like to ask. From Maura, Blue had inherited a dislike of watching people cry, so she never liked to steer the conversation in a way that might result in tears.

Persephone tilted her paper up so Blue could see it. She'd just written the word *three* three times, in three different handwritings, and a few centimetres beneath it, she'd copied a recipe for banana cream pie.

"Important things come in threes?" Blue suggested. It was one of Maura's favourite sayings.

Persephone underlined *tablespoon* next to the word *vanilla* in the recipe. Her voice was faraway and vague. "Or sevens. That is a lot of vanilla. One wonders if that is a typo."

"One wonders," repeated Blue.

"*Blue!*" Maura shouted up. "Are you gone yet?"

Blue didn't reply, because Persephone disliked high-pitched sounds and shouting back seemed to qualify as one. Instead, she said, "I found something. If I show it to you, will you not tell anybody else about it?"

But this was a silly question. Persephone barely told anybody anything even when it wasn't a secret.

When Blue handed over the journal, Persephone asked, "Should I open it?"

Blue flapped a hand. *Yes, and quickly.* She fidgeted back and forth on the bed while Persephone paged through, her face betraying nothing.

Finally, Blue asked, "Well?"

"It's very nice," Persephone said politely.

"It's not mine."

"Well, I can see *that*."

"It was left behind at Ni – wait, why do you say that?"

Persephone paged back and forth. Her dainty, child's voice was soft enough that Blue had to hold her breath to hear it. "This is clearly a boy's journal. Also, it's taking him for ever to find this thing. You'd have already found it."

"*BLUE!*" roared Maura. "*I'M NOT SHOUTING AGAIN!*"

"What do you think I should do about it?" Blue asked.

As Blue had, Persephone ran her fingers over the varying grains of the papers. She realized Persephone was right; if the journal had been hers, she would've just copied down the information she needed, rather than all this cutting and pasting. The fragments were intriguing but unnecessary; whoever put that journal together must love the hunt itself, the process of research. The aesthetic properties of the journal couldn't be accidental; it was an academic piece of art.

"Well," Persephone said. "First, you might find out whose journal it is."

Blue's shoulders sagged. It was a relentlessly proper answer, and one that she might have expected from Maura or Calla. Of course she knew she had to return it to its rightful owner. But then where would the fun of it go?

Persephone added, "Then I think you'd better find out if it's true, don't you?"

TWELVE

Adam wasn't waiting by the bank of postboxes in the morning.

The first time that Gansey had come to pick up Adam, he'd driven past the entrance to Adam's neighbourhood. Actually, more properly, he'd used it as a place to turn around and head back the way he'd come. The road was two ruts through a field — even *driveway* was too lofty a word for it — and it was impossible to believe, at first look, that it led to a single house, much less a collection of them. Once Gansey had found the house, things had gone even more poorly. At the sight of Gansey's Aglionby jumper, Adam's father had charged out, firing on all cylinders. For weeks after that, Ronan had called Gansey "the S.R.F.", where the *S* stood for *Soft*, the *R* stood for *Rich*, and the *F* for something else.

Now Adam just met Gansey where the tarmac ended.

But there was no one waiting by the clustered herd of postboxes now. It was just empty space, and a lot of it. This part of the valley was endlessly flat in comparison to the other side of Henrietta, and somehow this field was always several degrees drier and more colourless than the rest of the valley, like both the major roads and the rain avoided it. Even at eight in the morning, there were no shadows anywhere in the world.

Peering down the desiccated drive, Gansey tried the house phone, but it merely rang. His watch said he had eighteen minutes to make the fifteen-minute drive to school.

He waited. The engine threw the car to and fro as the Pig idled. He watched the gearshift knob rattle. His feet were roasting from proximity to the V-8. The entire cabin was beginning to stink of petrol.

He called Monmouth Manufacturing. Noah answered, sounding like he'd been woken.

"Noah," Gansey said loudly, to be heard over the engine. Noah had let him leave his journal behind at Nino's after all, and its absence was surprisingly unsettling. "Do you remember Adam saying he had work after school today?"

On the days that Adam had work, he often rode his bike in so that he'd have it to get to places later.

Noah grunted to the negative.

Sixteen minutes until class.

"Call me if he calls," Gansey said.

"I won't be here," Noah replied. "I'm almost gone anyway."

Gansey hung up and unsuccessfully tried the house again. Adam's mother might be there but not answering, but he didn't really have time to go back into the neighbourhood and investigate.

He could cut class.

Gansey tossed the phone on to the passenger seat. "Come on, Adam."

Of all of the places Gansey had attended boarding school – and he'd attended many in his four years of underage wandering – Aglionby Academy was his father's favourite, which meant it was the most likely to land its student body in the Ivy League.

Or the Senate. It also meant, however, that it was the most difficult school Gansey had ever been to. Before Henrietta, he'd made his search for Glendower his primary activity, and school had been a distant second. Gansey was clever enough and he was good at studying if nothing else, so it hadn't been a problem to skip classes or push homework to the bottom of the list. But at Aglionby, there were no failing grades. If you dropped below a B average, you were out on your ass. And Dick Gansey II had let his son know that if he couldn't hack it in a private school, Gansey was cut out of the will.

He'd said it nicely, though, over a plate of fettuccine.

Gansey couldn't cut class. Not after missing school the day before. That was what it came down to. Fourteen minutes to make a fifteen-minute drive to school, and Adam not waiting.

He felt the old fear creeping slowly out of his lungs.

Don't panic. You were wrong about Ronan last night. You have to stop this. Death isn't as close as you think.

Dispirited, Gansey tried the home phone one more time. Nothing. He had to go. Adam must've taken his bike, he must've had work, he must've had errands to run and forgotten to tell him. The rutted drive down to the neighbourhood was still empty.

Come on, Adam.

Wiping his palms on his trousers, he put his hands back on the steering wheel and headed for the school.

Gansey didn't get a chance to see if Adam had made it to

Aglionby until third period, when they both had Latin. This was, inexplicably, the only class Ronan never missed. Ronan was head of class in Latin. He studied joylessly but relentlessly, as if his life depended on it. Directly behind him was Adam, Aglionby's star pupil, otherwise at the top of every class that he took. Like Ronan, Adam studied relentlessly, because his future life *did* depend on it.

For his part, Gansey preferred French. He told Helen there was very little purpose to a language that couldn't be used to translate a menu, but really, French was just easier for him to learn; his mother spoke a little. He'd originally resigned himself to taking Latin in order to translate historical texts for Glendower research, but Ronan's proficiency at the language robbed Gansey's study of any urgency.

Latin was held in Borden House, a small frame house on the other side of the Aglionby campus from Welch Hall, the main academic building. As Gansey strode hurriedly across the centre green, Ronan appeared, knocking Gansey's arm. His eyes looked like he hadn't slept in days.

Ronan hissed, "Where's Parrish?"

"He didn't come in with me today," Gansey said, mood sinking. Ronan and Adam shared second period. "You haven't seen him yet?"

"Wasn't in class."

Behind Gansey, someone punched his shoulder blade and said, *Gansey boy!* as they trotted by. Gansey half-heartedly lifted three fingers, the signal of the rowing team.

"I tried calling him at the house," he said.

Ronan replied, "Well, Poor Boy needs a mobile."

A few months earlier, Gansey had offered to buy Adam a mobile phone, and by so doing had launched the longest fight they'd ever had, a week of silence that had resolved itself only when Ronan did something more offensive than either of them could accomplish.

"Lynch!"

Gansey looked in the direction of the voice; Ronan didn't. The owner of the voice was halfway across the green, difficult to identify in the homogenous Aglionby uniform.

"Lynch!" the call came again. "I'm going to fuck you up."

Ronan still didn't look up. He adjusted the strap on his shoulder and continued stalking across the grass.

"What's that about?" Gansey demanded.

"Some people don't take losing very well," Ronan replied.

"Was that Kavinsky? Don't tell me you've been racing again."

"Don't ask me, then."

Gansey contemplated if he could give Ronan a curfew. Or if he should quit rowing to spend more time with him on Fridays – he *knew* that was when Ronan got into trouble with the BMW. Maybe he could convince Ronan to. . .

Ronan adjusted the strap on his shoulder again, and this time, Gansey took a closer look at it. The bag it belonged to was distinctly larger than his usual, and he handled it gingerly, as if it might spill.

Gansey asked, "Why are you carrying that bag? Oh my God, you have that bird in there, don't you."

"She has to be fed every two hours."

"How do you know?"

"Jesus, the internet, Gansey." Ronan pulled open the door to Borden House; as soon as they breached the threshold, everything within sight was covered with navy blue carpet.

"If you got caught with that thing—" But Gansey couldn't think of a suitable threat. What was the punishment for smuggling a live bird into classes? He wasn't certain there was precedent. He finished, instead, "If it dies in your bag, I forbid you to throw it out in a classroom."

"*She*," Ronan corrected. "It's a she."

"I'd buy that if it had any defining sexual characteristics. It had better not have bird flu or something." But he wasn't thinking about Ronan's raven. He was thinking about Adam not being in class.

Ronan and Gansey took their usual seats in the back of the navy-carpeted classroom. At the front of the room, Whelk was writing verbs on the board.

When Gansey and Ronan had come in, Whelk had stopped writing mid-word: *internec*— Though there was no reason to think Whelk cared about their conversation, Gansey had the strange idea that the lifted piece of chalk in Whelk's hand was because of them, that the Latin teacher had stopped writing merely to listen in. Adam's suspicion really was beginning to rub off on him.

Ronan caught Whelk's eye and held it in an unfriendly sort of way. Despite his interest in Latin, Ronan had declared their Latin teacher a socially awkward shitbird earlier in the year and further clarified that he didn't like him. Because he despised everyone, Ronan wasn't a good judge of character, but Gansey had to agree that there was something discomfiting about Whelk. A few times, Gansey had tried to hold a conversation with him about Roman history, knowing full well the effect an enthusiastic academic conversation could have on an otherwise listless grade. But Whelk was too young to be a mentor and too old to be a peer, and Gansey couldn't find an angle.

Ronan kept staring at Whelk. He was good at staring. There was something about his stare that took something from the other person.

The Latin teacher flicked his glance awkwardly away from them. Having dealt with Whelk's curiosity, Ronan asked, "What are you going to do about Parrish?"

"I guess I'm going to go by there after class. Right?"

"He's probably sick."

They looked at each other. *We're already making excuses for him*, Gansey thought.

Ronan peered inside his bag again. In the darkness, Gansey just caught a glimpse of the raven's beak. Usually, Gansey would've basked once more in the odds of Ronan of finding a raven, but at the moment, with Adam missing, his quest didn't feel like magic; it felt like years spent piecing together coincidences, and all he had made from it was a strange cloth – too heavy to carry, too light to do any good at all.

"Mr Gansey, Mr Lynch?"

Whelk had managed to suddenly manifest beside their desks. Both boys looked up at him. Gansey, polite. Ronan, hostile.

"You seem to have an extremely large bag today, Mr Lynch," Whelk said.

"You know what they say about men with large bags," Ronan replied. "*Ostendes tuum et ostendam meus?*"

Gansey had no idea what Ronan had just said, but he was certain from Ronan's smirk that it wasn't entirely polite.

Whelk's expression confirmed Gansey's suspicion, but he merely rapped on Ronan's desk with his knuckles and moved off. "Being a shit in Latin isn't the way to an A," Gansey said. Ronan's smile was golden. "It was last year." At the front of the room, Whelk began class. Adam never showed.

THIRTEEN

"Mom, why is Neeve here?" Blue asked.

Like her mother, she was standing on the kitchen table. The moment she'd come back from school, Maura had enlisted her help for changing the bulbs in the badly designed stained-glass creation that hung over the table. The complicated process required at least three hands and tended to be left until most of the bulbs had burned out. Blue hadn't minded helping. She needed something to keep her mind off Gansey's looming appointment. And off Adam's failure to call. When she thought about giving him her number the night before, she felt weightless and uncertain.

"She's family," Maura replied grimly. She savagely gripped the fixture's chain as she wrestled with a stubborn bulb.

"Family that comes home in the middle of the night?"

Maura shot Blue a dark look. "You were born with larger ears than I remember. She's just helping me look for something while she's here."

The front door opened. Neither of them thought anything of it, as both Calla and Persephone were about the house somewhere. Calla was less likely, as she was an irascible, sedentary creature of habit, but Persephone tended to get caught in odd draughts and blow around.

Adjusting her grip on the stained glass, Blue asked, "What sort of something?"

"Blue."

"What sort of something?"

"A some*one*," Maura said, finally.

"What sort of *someone*?"

But before her mother had time to reply, they heard a man's voice:

"That is a strange way to run a business."

They both turned slowly. Blue's arms had been lifted for so long they felt rubbery when she lowered them. The owner of the voice stood in the doorway to the front hall, his hands in his pockets. He was not old, maybe mid-twenties, with a shock of black hair. He was handsome in a way that required a bit of work from the viewer. All of his facial features seemed just a little too large for his face.

Maura glanced at Blue, an eyebrow lifted. Blue lifted one shoulder in response. He didn't seem like he was here to murder them or steal any portable electronics.

"And that," her mother said, releasing the beleaguered light fixture, "is a very strange way to enter someone's home."

"I'm sorry," the young man said. "There is a sign out front saying this is a place of business."

There was indeed a sign out front, hand-painted – though Blue didn't know by whose hand – that read PSYCHIC. And, beneath that:

"By appointment only," Maura told the man. She grimaced into the kitchen. Blue had left a basket of clean laundry by the kitchen counter and one of her mother's mauve lacy bras sat on top in full view. Blue refused to feel guilty. It wasn't as if she had expected men to be wandering through the kitchen.

The man said, "Well then, I'd like to make an appointment."

A voice from the doorway to the stairs made all three of them turn.

"We could do a triple reading for you," Persephone said.

She stood at the base of the stairs, small and pale and made largely of hair. The man stared at her, though Blue wasn't certain if this was because he was considering Persephone's proposal or because Persephone was quite a lot to take in at first glance.

"What," the man asked finally, "is that?"

It took Blue a moment to realize that he meant "triple reading" rather than Persephone. Maura jumped off the table, landing with enough force that the glasses in the cabinet rattled. Blue climbed down more respectfully. She was, after all, holding a box of light bulbs.

Maura explained, "It's when three of us – Persephone, Calla, and I – read your cards at the same time and compare our interpretations. She doesn't offer that to just anyone, you know."

"Is it more expensive?"

"Not if you change that one stubborn bulb," Maura said, wiping her hands off on her jeans.

"Fine," said the man, but he sounded vexed about it.

Maura gestured for Blue to give a light bulb to the man, and then she said, "Persephone, would you get Calla?"

"Oh dear," Persephone said in a small voice – and Persephone's voice was already quite small, so her small voice was indeed tiny – but she turned and went up the stairs. Her bare feet were soundless as she did.

Maura eyed Blue, asking a question with her expression. Blue shrugged an agreement.

"My daughter, Blue, will be in the room, if you don't mind. She makes the reading more clear."

With an uninterested glance at Blue, the man climbed on to the table, which creaked a bit under the weight. He grunted as he tried to twist the stubborn bulb.

"Now you see the problem," Maura said. "What is your name?"

"Ah," he said, giving the bulb a jerk. "Can we leave this anonymous?"

Maura said, "We're psychics, not strippers."

Blue laughed, but the man didn't. She thought this was rather unfair of him; maybe it was in slightly poor taste, but it was funny.

The kitchen abruptly lightened as the new bulb screwed into place. Without comment, he stepped on to a chair and then to the floor.

"We'll be discreet," Maura promised. She gestured for him to follow her.

In the reading room, the man looked around with clinical interest. His gaze passed over the candles, the pot plants, the incense burners, the elaborate dining room chandelier, the rustic table that dominated the room, the lace curtains, and finally landed on a framed photograph of Steve Martin.

"Signed," Maura said with some pride, noticing his attention. Then: "Ah, Calla."

Calla blew into the room, her eyebrows quite angry at

being disturbed. She was wearing lipstick in a dangerous shade of plum, which made her mouth a small, pursed diamond under her pointy nose. Calla gave the man a lacerating look that plumbed the depths of his soul and found it wanting. Then she plucked her deck of cards from a shelf by Maura's head and flopped into a chair at the end of the table. Behind her, Persephone stood in the doorway, her hands clasping and unclasping each other. Blue slid hastily into a chair at the end of the table. The room seemed a lot smaller than it had a few minutes before. This was mostly Calla's fault.

Persephone said, in a kind voice, "Have a seat," and Calla said, in an unkind one, "What is it you want to know?"

The man dropped into a seat. Maura took the chair opposite from him at the table, with Calla and Persephone (and Persephone's hair) on either side of her. Blue was, as always, just a little apart.

"I would rather not say," the man said. "Maybe you'll tell me."

Calla's plum smile was positively fiendish. "Maybe."

Maura slid her deck of cards across the table to the man and told him to shuffle them. He did so with proficiency and little self-consciousness. When he was done, Persephone and Calla did the same.

"You've been to a reading before," Maura noted.

He made only a vaguely grumbling noise of assent. Blue could see he thought that any information would let them fake the reading. Still, she didn't think he was a sceptic. He was merely sceptical of *them*.

Maura slid her deck back from the man. She'd had her deck for as long as Blue had been paying attention, and the edges were fuzzy with handling. They were a standard tarot deck, only as impressive as she made them. She selected ten cards and laid them out. Calla did the same with her slightly crisper deck – she'd replaced them a few years ago after an unfortunate incident had made her lose her taste for her previous deck. The room was quiet enough to hear the rustle of their cards against the uneven, pocked surface of the reading table.

Persephone held her cards in her long, long hands, eyeing the man for a pregnant moment. Finally, she contributed only two cards, one at the beginning of the spread and one at the end. Blue loved watching Persephone lay down her cards; the limpid turn of her wrist and the *swick* of the card always made it seem like a sleight of hand or a ballet movement. Even the cards themselves seemed more otherworldly. Persephone's cards were slightly larger than Maura's and Calla's, and the art on them was curious. Spidery lines and smudgy backgrounds suggested the figures on each card; Blue had never seen another deck like it. Maura had told Blue once that it was hard to ask Persephone questions that you didn't absolutely need the answer to, so Blue had never found out where the deck had come from.

Now that the cards were laid out, Maura, Calla and Persephone studied the shape of them. Blue struggled to see over their huddled heads. She tried to ignore that, this close to the man, he had the overpowering chemical scent of a manly shower gel. The sort that normally came in a black bottle and was called something like SHOCK or EXCITE or BLUNT TRAUMA.

Calla was the first to speak. She flipped the three of swords around for the man to look at. On her card, the three swords stabbed into a dark, bleeding heart the colour of her lips. "You've lost someone close to you."

The man looked at his hands. "I have lost. . ." he started, then considered before finishing, ". . .many things."

Maura pursed her lips. One of Calla's eyebrows edged towards her hair. They darted glances at each other. Blue knew them both well enough to interpret the looks. Maura's asked, *What do you think?* Calla's said, *This is off.* Persephone's said nothing.

Maura touched the edge of the five of pentacles. "Money's a concern," she noted. On her card, a man with a crutch limped through snow under a stained–glass window while a woman held a shawl beneath her chin.

She added, "Because of a woman."

The man's gaze was unflinching. "My parents had considerable resources. My father was implicated in a business scandal. Now they're divorced and there is no money. Not for me."

It was a strangely unpleasant way to put it. Relentlessly factual.

Maura wiped her palms on her slacks. She gestured to another card. "And now you're in a tedious job. It's something you're good at but tired of."

His lips were thin with the truth of it.

Persephone touched the first card she had drawn. The knight of pentacles. An armoured man with cold eyes surveyed a field from the back of a horse, a coin in his hand. Blue thought if she looked closely at the coin, she could see a shape in it. Three curving lines, a long, beaked triangle. The shape from the churchyard, from Maura's unmindful drawing, from the journal.

But no, when she looked harder, it was just a faintly drawn, five-pointed star. The pentacle for which the card was named.

Persephone finally spoke. In her small, precise voice, she told the man, "You're looking for something."

The man's head jerked towards her.

Calla's card, beside Persephone's, was also the knight of pentacles. It was unusual for two decks to agree exactly. Even stranger was to see that Maura's card was also the knight of pentacles. Three cold-eyed knights surveyed the land before them.

Three again.

Calla said bitterly, "You're willing to do whatever it takes to find it. You've been working at it for years."

"*Yes*," the man snapped, surprising them all with the ferocity of his response. "But how much longer? Will I find it?"

The three women scanned the cards again, looking for an answer to his question. Blue looked, too. She might not have had the sight, but she knew what the cards were supposed to mean. Her attention moved from the Tower, which meant his life was about to change dramatically, to the last card in the reading, the page of cups. Blue glanced at her frowning mother. It wasn't that the page of cups was a negative card; in fact, it was the card Maura always said she thought represented Blue when she was doing a reading for herself.

You're the page of cups, Maura had told her once. *Look at all that potential she holds in that cup. Look, she even looks like you.*

And there was not just one page of cups in this reading.

Like the knight of pentacles, it was tripled. Three young people holding a cup of full of potential, all wearing Blue's face. Maura's expression was dark, dark, dark.

Blue's skin prickled. Suddenly, she felt as if there was no end to the fates she was tied to. Gansey, Adam, that unseeable place in Neeve's scrying bowl, this strange man sitting beside her. Her pulse was racing.

Maura stood up so quickly that her chair keeled back against the wall.

"The reading's done," she snapped.

Persephone's gaze wandered up to Maura's face, bewildered, and Calla looked confused but delighted at the appearance of conflict. Blue didn't recognize her mother's face.

"Excuse me?" the man asked. "The other cards—"

"You heard her," Calla said, all acid. Blue didn't know if Calla was also uneasy, or if she was merely backing Maura up. "The reading's over."

"Get out of my house," Maura said. Then, with an obvious attempt at solicitude, "Now. Thank you. Goodbye."

Calla moved aside for Maura to whirl past her to the front door. Maura pointed over the threshold.

Rising to his feet, the man said, "I'm incredibly insulted."

Maura didn't reply. As soon as he was clear of the doorway, she slammed the door shut behind him. The dishes in the cupboards rattled once again.

Calla had moved to the window. She drew the curtains aside and leaned her forehead against the glass to watch him leave.

Maura paced back and forth beside the table. Blue thought of asking a question, then stopped, then started again. Then stopped. It seemed wrong to ask a question if no one else was.

Persephone said, "What an unpleasant young man."

Calla let the curtains drift shut. She remarked, "I got his licence plate number."

"I hope he *never* finds what he's looking for," Maura said.

Retrieving her two cards from the table, Persephone said, a little regretfully, "He's trying awfully hard. I rather think he'll find *something*."

Maura whirled towards Blue. "Blue, if you ever see that man again, you just walk the other way."

"No," Calla corrected. "Kick him in the nuts. Then *run* the other way."

FOURTEEN

Helen, Gansey's older sister, called right as Gansey got to the Parrishes' dirt road. Accepting phone calls in the Pig was always tricky. The Camaro was a stick shift, to start with, and as loud as a lorry, to end with, and in between those two things were a host of steering problems, electrical interferences and grimy gearshift knobs. The upshot was that Helen was barely audible and Gansey nearly drove into the ditch.

"When is Mom's birthday?" Helen asked. Gansey was simultaneously pleased to hear her voice and annoyed to be bothered by something so trivial. For the most part, he and his sister got along well; Gansey siblings were a rare and complicated species, and they didn't have to pretend to be something they weren't around each other.

"You're the wedding planner," Gansey said as a dog ripped out of nowhere. It barked furiously, trying to bite the Camaro's tyres. "Shouldn't dates be your realm of expertise?"

"That means you don't remember," Helen replied. "And I'm not a wedding planner any more. Well. Part-time. Well. Full-time, but not every day."

Helen did not *need* to be anything. She didn't have careers, she had hobbies that involved other people's lives.

"I do remember," he said tensely. "It's May tenth." A lab mix tied in front of the first house bayed dolorously as he passed.

The other dog continued to worry at his tyres, a snarl ascending with the engine note. Three kids in sleeveless shirts stood in one of the yards shooting milk jugs with BB guns; they shouted *Hey, Hollywood!* and affably aimed guns at the Pig's tyres. They pretended to hold phones by their ears. Gansey felt a peculiar stab at the three of them, their camaraderie, their belonging, products of their surroundings. He wasn't sure if it was pity or envy. Everywhere was dust.

Helen asked, "Where are you? You sound like you're on the set of a Guy Ritchie movie."

"I'm going to see a friend."

"The mean one, or the white trash one?"

"Helen."

She replied, "Sorry. I meant Captain Frigid or Trailer-Park Boy."

"*Helen*."

Adam didn't live in a trailer park, technically, since every house was a double-wide. Adam had told him that the last of the single-wide trailers had been taken out a few years ago, but he had said it ironically, like even he knew that doubling the size of the trailers didn't change much.

"Dad calls them worse things," Helen said. "Mom said one of your weird New Age books was delivered to the house yesterday. Are you coming home anytime soon?"

"Maybe," Gansey said. Somehow seeing his parents always reminded him of how little he'd accomplished, how similar he and Helen were, how many red ties he owned, how he was slowly growing up to be everything Ronan was afraid of becoming. He pulled in front of the light blue double-wide where the Parrishes lived. "Maybe for Mom's birthday. I have to go. Things might get ugly."

The phone speaker made Helen's laugh a hissing, pitch-less thing. "Listen to you, sounding all badass. I bet you're just listening to a CD called 'The Sounds of Crime' while you cruise for chicks outside the Old Navy in your Camaro."

"Bye, Helen," said Gansey. He clicked END and climbed out.

Fat, shiny carpenter bees swooped at his head, distracted from their work of destroying the stairs. After he knocked, he looked out across the flat, ugly field of dead grass. The idea that you had to pay for the beauty in Henrietta should have occurred to him before then, but it hadn't. No matter how many times Adam told him he was foolish about money, he couldn't seem to get any wiser about it.

There is no spring here, Gansey realized, and the thought was unexpectedly grim.

Adam's mother answered his knock. She was a shadow of Adam – the same elongated features, the same wide-set eyes. In comparison to Gansey's mother, she seemed old and hard-edged.

"Adam's out back," she said, before he could ask her anything. She glanced to him and away, not holding his gaze. Gansey never failed to be amazed at how Adam's parents reacted to the Aglionby jumper. They knew everything they needed to about him before he even opened his mouth.

"Thanks," Gansey said, but the word felt like sawdust in his mouth, and in any case, she was already closing the door.

Under the old carport behind the house, he found Adam lying beneath an old Bonneville pulled up on to ramps, initially invisible in the cool blue shadows. An empty oil pan protruded from under the car. There was no sound coming from beneath the car, and Gansey suspected that Adam wasn't working so much as avoiding being in the house.

"Hey, tiger," Gansey said.

Adam's knees bent as if he were going to scoot himself out from under the car, but then he didn't.

"What's up?" he said flatly.

Gansey knew what this meant, this failure to immediately come out from beneath the car, and anger and guilt drew his chest tight. The most frustrating thing about the Adam situation was that Gansey couldn't control it. Not a single piece of it. He dropped a notebook on the worktable. "Those are notes from today. I couldn't tell them you were sick. You missed too much last month."

Adam's voice was even. "What did you tell them, then?"

One of the tools under the car made a half-hearted scraping sound.

"Come on, Parrish. Come out," Gansey said. "Get it over with."

Gansey jumped as a cold dog nose shoved into his dangling palm – the mutt that had so savagely attacked his tyres earlier. He reluctantly fondled one of her stumpy ears and then jerked his hand back as she leapt at the car, barking at Adam's feet when they started to move. The ripped knees of Adam's camo combat trousers appeared first, then his faded Coca-Cola T-shirt, then, finally, his face.

A bruise spread over his cheekbone, red and swelling as a galaxy. A darker one snaked over the bridge of his nose.

Gansey said immediately, "You're leaving with me."

"It will only make it worse when I come back," Adam told him.

"I mean for good. Move into Monmouth. Enough's enough."

Adam stood up. The dog pranced delightedly around his feet as if he'd been gone to another planet instead of merely underneath a car. Wearily, he asked, "And what about when Glendower takes you away from Henrietta?"

Gansey couldn't say it wouldn't happen. "You come with."

"I come with? Tell me how that would work. I lose all the work I put in at Aglionby. I have to play the game again at another school."

Adam had once told Gansey, *Rags to riches isn't a story anyone wants to hear until after it's done.* But it was a story that was hard to finish when Adam had missed school yet again. There was no happy ending without passing grades.

Gansey said, "You wouldn't have to go to a school like Aglionby. It doesn't have to be an Ivy League. There are different ways to be successful."

At once, Adam said, "I don't judge you for what you do, Gansey."

And this was an uneasy place to be, because Gansey knew it took a lot for Adam to accept his reasons for chasing Glendower. Adam had plenty of reasons to be indifferent about Gansey's nebulous anxiety, his questioning of why the universe had chosen him to be born to affluent parents, wondering if there was some greater purpose that he was alive. Gansey *knew* he had to make a difference, had to make a bigger mark on the world because of the head start he'd been given, or he was the worst sort of person out there.

The poor are sad they're poor, Adam had once mused, *and turns out the rich are sad they're rich.*

And Ronan had said, *Hey, I'm rich, and it doesn't bother me.*

Out loud, Gansey said, "Fine, then. We'd find another good school. We play the game. We make up a new life for you."

Adam reached past him to find a rag and began to wipe between each greasy finger. "I would have to find jobs, too. This didn't happen overnight. Do you know how long it took me to find these?"

He didn't mean working in the carport outside his father's double-wide. That was merely a chore. Adam held down three jobs, the most important of which was at the trailer factory just outside Henrietta.

"I could cover you until you found something."

There was a very long silence as Adam continued scrubbing his fingers. He didn't look up at Gansey. This was a conversation they'd had before, and entire days of arguments were replayed in the few moments of quiet. The words had been said often enough that they didn't need to be said again.

Success meant nothing to Adam if he hadn't done it for himself.

Gansey tried his best to keep his voice even, but a bit of heat crept in. "So you won't leave because of your pride? He'll kill you."

"You've watched too many cop shows."

"I've watched the evening news, Adam," Gansey snapped.

"Why don't you let Ronan teach you to fight? He's offered twice now. He means it."

With great care, Adam folded the greasy rag and draped it back over a toolbox. There was a lot of stuff in the carport. New tool racks and calendars of topless women and heavy-duty air compressors and other things Mr Parrish had decided were more valuable than Adam's school uniform. "Because then he *will* kill me."

"I don't follow."

Adam said, "He has a gun."

Gansey said, "Christ."

Laying a hand on the mutt's head – it drove her insane with happiness – Adam leaned out of the carport to look down the dirt road. He didn't have to tell Gansey what he was watching for.

"Come on, Adam," said Gansey. *Please.* "We'll make it work."

A wrinkle formed between Adam's eyebrows as he looked away. Not at the double-wides in the foreground, but past them, to the flat, endless field with its tufts of dry grass. So many things survived here without really living. He said, "It means I never get to be my own person. If I let you cover for me, then I'm yours. I'm his now, and then I'll be yours."

It struck Gansey harder than he thought it would. Some days, all that grounded him was the knowledge that his and Adam's friendship existed in a place that money couldn't influence. Anything that spoke to the contrary hurt Gansey more than he would have admitted out loud. With precision, he asked, "Is that what you think of me?"

"You don't know, Gansey," Adam said. "You don't know anything about money, even though you've got all of it. You don't know how it makes people look at me and at you. It's all they need to know about us. They'll think I'm your monkey."

I am only my money. It is all anyone sees, even Adam.

Gansey shot back, "You think your plans are going to keep working when you miss school and work because you let your dad pound the shit out of you? You're as bad as her. You think you deserve it."

Without warning, Adam slammed a small box of nails off the ledge beside him. The sound it made on the concrete startled both of them.

Adam turned his back to Gansey, his arms crossed.

"Don't pretend you know," he said. "Don't come here and pretend you know anything."

Gansey told himself to walk away. To say nothing else. Then he said, "Don't pretend you have anything to be proud of, then."

As soon as he said it, he knew that it wasn't fair, or even if it had been fair, it wasn't right. But he wasn't sorry he'd said it.

He went back to the Camaro and took his phone out to call Ronan, but the signal had completely disappeared, like it often did in Henrietta. Usually, Gansey took that as a sign that something supernatural was affecting the energy around the town, knocking down the signal and sometimes even the electricity.

Now, he thought it probably just meant he wasn't getting through to anyone.

Closing his eyes, he thought about the bruise on Adam's

face, with its spreading, soft edges, and the hard red mark over his nose. He imagined coming here one day and finding that Adam wasn't here, but in the hospital, or worse, that Adam was here, but that something important had been beaten out of him.

Even imagining it made him feel sick.

The car jerked then, and Gansey's eyes came open as the passenger door groaned.

"Wait, Gansey," Adam said, out of breath. He was all folded over to be able to see inside the car. His bruise looked ghastly. It made his skin seem transparent. "Don't leave like—"

Sliding his hands off the wheel and into his lap, Gansey peered up at him. This was the part where Adam was going to tell him not to take what he'd said personally. But it felt personal.

"I'm only trying to help."

"I know," Adam told him. "I know. But I can't do it that way. I can't live with myself that way."

Gansey didn't understand, but he nodded. He wanted it to be over; he wanted it to be yesterday, when he and Ronan and Adam were listening to the recorder and Adam's face was still unmarked. Behind Adam, he saw the figure of Mrs Parrish watching from the porch.

Adam closed his eyes for a minute. Gansey could see his irises moving underneath the thin skin of his eyelids, a dreamer awake.

And then, in one easy movement, he'd slid into the passenger seat. Gansey's mouth opened to form a question he didn't ask.

"Let's go," Adam said. He didn't look at Gansey. His

mother stared at them from the porch, but he didn't look at her, either. "The psychic was the plan, right? We're doing the plan."

"Yes. But—"

"I need to be back by ten."

Now Adam looked at Gansey. There was something fierce and chilling in his eyes, an unnamable something that Gansey was always afraid would eventually take over completely. This, he knew, was a compromise, a risky gift that he could choose to reject.

After a moment of hesitation, Gansey bumped knuckles with him over the gearshift. Adam rolled down the window and gripped the roof as if he needed to hold on.

As the Camaro headed slowly out of the single-track road, their path was blocked by a blue Toyota pickup truck, approaching from the other way. Adam's breath stopped audibly. Through the windscreen, Gansey met the eyes of Adam's father. Robert Parrish was a big thing, colourless as August, grown from the dust that surrounded the trailers. His eyes were dark and small and Gansey could see nothing of Adam in them.

Robert Parrish spat out of the window. He didn't pull over for them to pass. Adam's face was turned out to the cornfield, but Gansey didn't look away.

"You don't have to come," said Gansey, because he had to say it.

Adam's voice came from far away. "I'm coming."

Jerking the wheel of the car, Gansey revved the engine up high. The Pig stormed off the road, clouds of dirt exploding from the tyres, and slammed through the shallow ditch. His heart thudded with anticipation and danger and the desire to shout everything he thought about Adam's father *to* Adam's father.

As they charged back on to the driveway on the other side of the Toyota, Gansey could feel Robert Parrish's stare follow them.

The weight of that gaze seemed like a more substantial promise of the future than anything a psychic might tell him.

FIFTEEN

Of course, Gansey was not on time for his reading. The appointment time came and went. No Gansey. And, perhaps more disappointingly, no phone call from Adam. Blue pulled aside the curtains to glance up and down the street, but there was nothing but normal after-work traffic. Maura made excuses.

"Maybe he wrote down the wrong time," she said.

Blue didn't think he'd written down the wrong time.

Ten more minutes slouched by. Maura said, "Maybe he had car trouble."

Blue didn't think he had car trouble.

Calla retrieved the novel she'd been reading and started upstairs. Her voice carried down towards them. "That reminds me. You need to get that belt looked at on the Ford. I see a breakdown in your future. Next to that sketchy furniture store. A very ugly man with a mobile phone will stop and be overly helpful."

It was possible she really *did* see a breakdown in Maura's future, but it was also possible she was being hyperbolic. In any case, Maura made a note on the calendar.

"Maybe I accidentally told him tomorrow afternoon instead of today," Maura said.

Persephone murmured, *"That is always possible,"* and said, "Perhaps I will make a pie." Blue looked anxiously to Persephone. Pie making was a lengthy and loving process, and Persephone did not like to be interrupted during it. She wouldn't begin a pie if she really thought Gansey's arrival would interrupt her.

Maura eyed Persephone as well before retrieving a bag of yellow squash and a stick of butter from the fridge. Now Blue knew precisely how the rest of the day was going to go. Persephone would make something sweet. Maura would make something with butter. Eventually, Calla would reappear and make something involving sausage or bacon. It was how every evening went if a meal hadn't been planned in advance.

Blue didn't think that Maura had told Gansey tomorrow afternoon instead of today. What she thought was that Gansey had looked at the clock on his Mercedes-Benz's dashboard or Aston Martin's radio and had decided that the reading interfered with his rock climbing or racquetball. And then he'd blown it off, just like Adam had blown off calling her. She couldn't really be surprised. They'd done exactly what she expected from raven boys.

Just as Blue was getting ready to sulk upstairs with her knitting needles and her homework, Orla howled from the Phone Room, her wordless wail eventually resolving itself into words:

"There is a 1973 Camaro in front of the house! *It matches my nails!*"

The last time Blue had seen Orla's nails, they'd been a complicated paisley pattern. She wasn't exactly sure what a

1973 Camaro looked like, but she was sure that if it was paisley, it must be impressive. She was also certain that Orla must be on the phone, or she would've been down here ogling.

"Well, here we go," Maura said, abandoning her squash in the sink. Calla reappeared in the kitchen, exchanging a sharp look with Persephone.

Blue's stomach dropped to her feet.

Gansey. That's all there is.

The doorbell rang.

"Are you ready?" Calla asked Blue.

Gansey was the boy she either killed or fell in love with. Or both. There was no *being ready*. There just was this: Maura opening the door.

There were three boys in the doorway, backlit by the evening sun as Neeve had been so many weeks ago. Three sets of shoulders: one square, one built, one wiry.

"Sorry that I'm late," said the boy in front, with the square shoulders. The scent of mint rolled in with him, just as it had in the churchyard. "Will it be a problem?"

Blue knew that voice.

She reached for the railing of the stairs to keep her balance as President Mobile Phone stepped into the hallway.

Oh no. Not him. All this time she'd been wondering how Gansey might dic and it turned out she was going to strangle him. At Nino's, the blare of the music had drowned out the finer points of his voice and the odour of garlic had overwhelmed the scent of mint.

But now that she put two and two together, it seemed obvious.

In their hallway, he looked slightly less presidential,

but only because the heat had made him messily roll up the sleeves of his button-down shirt and remove his tie. His dusty brown hair was mussed, too, in that way that Virginia warmth always managed. But the watch was still there, large enough to knock out bank robbers, and he still had that handsome glow. The glow that meant that not only had he never been poor, but his father hadn't, nor his father's father, nor his father's father's father. She couldn't tell if he was actually tremendously good-looking or merely tremendously wealthy. Perhaps they were the same thing.

Gansey. This was Gansey.

And that meant that the journal belonged to him.

That meant that *Adam* belonged to him.

"Well," Maura said. It was clear her curiosity overruled all rules of scheduling. "It's not too late. Come into the reading room. Can I get some names?"

Because of course President Mobile Phone had brought most of his posse from Nino's, everyone but the smudgy boy. They filled the hallway to overflowing, somehow, the three of them, loud and male and so comfortable with one another that they allowed no one else to be comfortable with them. They were a pack of sleek animals armoured with their watches and their Top-Siders and the expensive cut of their uniforms. Even the sharp boy's tattoo, cutting up the knobs of his spine above his collar, was a weapon, somehow slicing at Blue.

"Gansey," President Mobile Phone said again, pointing to himself. "Adam. Ronan. Where do you want us? There?"

He pointed a hand towards the reading room, palm flat, like he was directing traffic.

"In there," Maura agreed. "This is my daughter, by the way. She'll be present for the reading, if you don't mind."

Gansey's eyes found Blue. He'd been smiling politely, but now his face froze in the middle of the smile.

"Hi, again," he said. "This is awkward."

"You've *met*?" Maura shot a poisonous look at Blue. Blue felt unfairly persecuted.

"Yes," Gansey replied, with dignity. "We had a discussion about alternative professions for women. I didn't realize she was your daughter. *Adam?*"

He shot a nearly as poisonous look at Adam, whose eyes were large. Adam was the only one not in uniform, and his palm was spread across his chest as if his fingers would cover his faded Coca-Cola T-shirt.

"I didn't know, either!" Adam said. If Blue had known *he* was coming, she might not have worn her baby blue top with the feathers sewn into the collar. He was staring at it. To Blue, he said, again, "I didn't know, I swear."

"What happened to your face?" Blue asked.

Adam shrugged ruefully. Either he or Ronan smelled like a parking garage. His voice was self-deprecating. "Do you think it makes me look tougher?"

What it did was make him look was more fragile and dirty, somehow, like a teacup unearthed from the soil, but Blue didn't say that.

Ronan said, "It makes you look like a loser."

"Ronan," said Gansey.

"*I need everyone to sit down!*" shouted Maura.

It was such an alarming thing to hear Maura shout that nearly everyone did, sinking or throwing themselves into the mismatched furniture in the reading room. Adam rubbed a hand over his cheekbone as if he could remove the bruise from it. Gansey sat in an armchair at the head of the table, his hands stretched over either arm like chairman of the board, one eyebrow raised as he looked at Steve Martin's framed face.

Only Calla and Ronan remained standing, and they regarded each other warily.

It still felt like there had never been this many people in the house, which was utterly untrue. It was possibly true that there had never been this many men in the house before. Certainly never this many raven boys.

Blue felt as if their very presence robbed something from her. They'd made her family dingy just by coming here.

"It is," Maura said, "too damn loud in here." The way she said it, though, holding one finger to her pulse, just under her jawbone, told Blue that it was not their voices that were too loud. It was something she was hearing inside her head. Persephone, too, was wincing.

"Do I need to leave?" Blue asked, though that was the last thing she wanted.

Gansey, misunderstanding, immediately asked her, "Why would you have to leave?"

"She makes things louder for us," Maura said. She was frowning over all of them as if she was trying to make sense of it. "And you three are . . . *very* loud already."

Blue's skin was hot. She could imagine herself heating like an electrical conduit, sparks from all parties travelling through her. What could these raven boys have going on under their skins that could deafen her mother? Was it all of them in conjunction, or was it merely Gansey, his energy screaming out the countdown to his death?

"What do you mean, very loud?" Gansey asked. He was, Blue thought, very clearly the ringleader of this little pack. They all kept looking to him for their cues of how to interpret the situation.

"I mean that there is something about your energies that is very. . ." Maura trailed off, losing interest in her own explanation. She turned to Persephone. Blue recognized the look exchanged between them. It was, *What is going on?* "How do we even do this?"

The way she asked it, distracted and vague, made Blue's stomach clench with nerves. Her mother was *undone.* For the second time, a reading seemed to be pushing her to a place she wasn't comfortable with.

"One at a time?" Persephone suggested, her voice nearly inaudible.

Calla said, "One-offs. You'll have to, or some of them will have to leave. They're just too noisy."

Adam and Gansey glanced at each other. Ronan picked at the leather straps around his wrist.

"What is a one-off?" Gansey asked. "How is it different from a regular reading?"

Calla spoke to Maura as if he hadn't said anything at all. "It doesn't matter what they want. It is what it is. Take it or leave it."

Maura's finger was still pressed under her jaw. She told Gansey, "A one-off is where you each draw just one card from a deck of tarot cards, and we interpret."

Gansey and Adam shared some sort of private conversation with their eyes. It was the sort of thing Blue was used to transpiring between her mother and Persephone or Calla, and she hadn't thought anyone else really capable of it.

It also made her feel strangely jealous; she wanted something like that, a bond strong enough to transcend words.

Adam's head jerked a nod in response to whatever Gansey's unspoken statement might have been, and Gansey said, "Whatever you're comfortable with."

Persephone and Maura momentarily debated, though it didn't seem like they'd be comfortable with anything at the moment.

"Wait," Persephone said as Maura produced her deck of cards. "Have Blue deal it."

It wasn't the first time Blue had been asked to deal the cards. Sometimes, at difficult or important readings, the women wanted Blue to touch the deck first, to hone whatever messages the cards might contain. This time, she was overly aware of the boys' attention as she took the cards from her mother. For the boys' benefit, she shuffled the deck in a slightly theatrical fashion, moving cards from one hand to another. She was very good at card tricks that didn't involve any psychic talent whatsoever. As the boys, impressed, watched the cards fly back and forth, Blue mused that she would make an excellent fake psychic.

No one volunteered immediately to go first, so she offered the deck to Adam. He met her gaze and held it for a moment. There was something forceful and intentional about the gesture, more aggressive than he'd been the night he approached her.

Selecting a card, Adam presented it to Maura.

"Two of swords," she said. Blue was over-aware of her mother's Henrietta accent, suddenly rural and uneducated sounding to her ear. Was that how *Blue* sounded?

Maura continued, "You're avoiding a hard choice. Acting

by not acting. You're ambitious, but you feel like someone's asking something of you you're not willing to give. Asking you to compromise your principles. Someone close to you, I think. Your father?"

"Brother, I think," Persephone said.

"I don't have a brother, ma'am," Adam replied. But Blue saw his eyes dart to Gansey.

"Do you want to ask a question?" Maura asked.

Adam considered. "What's the right choice?"

Maura and Persephone conferred. Maura replied, "There isn't a right one. Just one you can live with. There might be a third option that will suit you better, but right now, you're not seeing it because you're so involved with the other two. I'd guess from what I'm seeing that any other path would have to do with you going outside those other two options and making your own option. I'm also sensing you're a very analytical thinker. You've spent a lot of time learning to ignore your emotions, but I don't think this is a time for that."

"Thanks," Adam said. It wasn't quite the right thing to say, but it wasn't entirely wrong, either. Blue liked how polite he was. It seemed different than Gansey's politeness. When Gansey was polite, it made him powerful. When Adam was polite, he was giving power away.

It seemed right to leave Gansey for last, so Blue moved on to Ronan, though she was a little afraid of him. Something about him dripped venom, even though he hadn't spoken. Worst of all, in Blue's opinion, was that there was something about his antagonism that made her want to court his favour, to earn his approval. The approval of someone like him, who clearly cared for no one, seemed like it would be worth more.

To offer the deck to Ronan, Blue had to stand, because he still stood by the doorway near Calla. They looked ready to box.

When Blue fanned the cards, he scanned the women in the room and said, "I'm not taking one. Tell me something true first."

"Beg your pardon?" Calla said stiffly, answering for Maura.

Ronan's voice was glass, cold and brittle. "Everything you've told him could apply to anybody. Anybody with a pulse has doubts. Anybody alive has argued with their brother or their father. Tell me something no one else can tell me. Don't toss a playing card at me and spoon feed me some Jungian bullshit. Tell me something specific."

Blue's eyes narrowed. Persephone stuck out her tongue slightly, a habit born of uncertainty, not impudence. Maura shifted with annoyance. "We don't do specif—"

Calla interrupted. "A secret killed your father and you know what it was."

The room went deadly silent. Both Persephone and Maura were staring at Calla. Gansey and Adam were staring at Ronan. Blue was staring at Calla's hand.

Maura often called on Calla to do joint tarot readings, and Persephone sometimes called on her to interpret her dreams, but very rarely did anyone ask Calla to use one of her strangest gifts: psychometry. Calla had an uncanny ability to hold an object and sense its origin, feel its owner's thoughts, and see places the thing had been.

Now, Calla pulled her hand away; she'd reached to touch Ronan's tattoo right where it met his collar. His face was turned just slightly, looking to where her fingers had been.

There might have only been Ronan and Calla in the room. He was a head taller than her already, but he looked young beside her, like a lanky wildcat not yet up to weight. She was a lioness.

She hissed, "What are you?"

Ronan's smile chilled Blue. There was something empty in it.

"Ronan?" Gansey asked, concern in his voice.

"I'm waiting in the car." Without further comment, Ronan left, slamming the door hard enough that the dishes in the kitchen rattled.

Gansey turned an accusatory gaze on Calla. "His father's dead."

"I know," Calla said. Her eyes were slits.

Gansey's voice was cordial enough to pass straight through polite and on to rude. "I don't know how you found out, but that's a pretty lousy thing to throw at a kid."

"At a snake, you mean," Calla snarled back. "And what is it you came for, if you didn't believe we could do what we're charging you for? He asked for a specific. I gave him a specific. I'm sorry it wasn't puppies."

"Calla," Maura said, at the same time that Adam said, "Gansey."

Adam murmured something directly into Gansey's ear and then leaned back. A bone moved at Gansey's jawline. Blue saw him shift back into President Mobile Phone; she hadn't been aware, before, that he'd been anything else. Now she wished she'd been paying better attention, so she could've seen what was different about him.

Gansey said, "I'm sorry. Ronan is blunt, and he wasn't comfortable coming here in the first place. I wasn't trying to insinuate that you were less than genuine. Can we continue?"

He sounded so *old*, Blue thought. So formal in comparison to the other boys he'd brought. There was something intensely discomfiting about him, akin to how she felt compelled to impress Ronan. Something about Gansey made her feel so strongly *other* that it was as if she had to guard her emotions against him. She could not like him, or whatever it was about these boys that had drowned out her mother's psychic abilities and filled the room to overflowing would overwhelm her.

"You're fine," Maura said, though she looked at glowering Calla when she said it.

As Blue moved to where Gansey sat, she caught a glimpse of his car at the kerb: a flash of impossible orange, the sort of orange Orla would definitely paint her nails. It was not exactly what she'd have expected an Aglionby boy to drive — they liked new, shiny things, and this was an old, shiny thing — but it was clearly a raven boy's car nonetheless. And just then, Blue had a falling sensation, like things were happening too fast for her to properly absorb them. There *was* something odd and complicated about all of these boys, Blue thought — odd and complicated in the way that the journal was odd and complicated. Their lives were somehow a web, and she had somehow managed to do something to get herself stuck in the very edge of it. Whether that something had been done in the past or was going to be done in the future seemed irrelevant. In this room with Maura and Calla and Persephone, time felt circular.

She stopped in front of Gansey. This close, she again caught the scent of mint, and that made Blue's heart trip unsteadily.

Gansey looked down at the fanned deck of cards in her hands. When she saw him like that, she saw the bend of his shoulders and the back of his head, and she piercingly remembered his spirit, the boy she'd been afraid she'd fall in love with. That shade hadn't worn any of the effortless, breezy confidence of this raven boy in front of her.

What happens to you, Gansey? she wondered. *When do you become that person?*

Gansey looked up at her, and there was a crease between his eyebrows. "I don't know how to choose. Could you pick a card for me? Will that work?"

Out of the corner of her eye, Blue saw Adam shifting in his chair, frowning.

Persephone answered from behind Blue. "If you want it to."

"It's about intention," Maura added.

"I want you to," he said. "Please."

Blue fanned the cards across the table; they slithered loosely over the finish. She let her fingers float above them. Once, Maura had told her that the correct cards sometimes felt warm or tingly when her fingers were near them. For Blue, of course, each card felt identical. One, however, had slid further than the others, and that was the one she chose.

As she flipped it over, she let out a little helpless laugh.

The page of cups looked back at Blue with her own face. It felt like someone was laughing at her, but she had no one to blame for the selection of the card but herself.

When Maura saw it, her voice went still and remote. "Not that one. Make him choose another."

"Maura," said Persephone mildly, but Maura just waved her hand, dismissing her.

"Another one," she insisted.

"What's wrong with that one?" Gansey asked.

"It has Blue's energy on it," Maura said. "It wasn't meant to be yours. You'll have to pick it yourself."

Persephone moved her mouth back and forth, but she didn't say anything. Blue replaced the card and shuffled the deck with less drama than before.

When she offered the cards to him, Gansey turned his face away like he was pulling a raffle winner. His fingers grazed the edges of the cards, contemplative. He selected one, then flipped it over to show the room.

It was the page of cups.

He looked at the face on the card, and then at Blue's face, and Blue knew that he'd seen the similarity.

Maura leaned forward and snatched the card from his fingers. "Pick another one."

"*Now* why?" Gansey said. "What's wrong with that card? What does it mean?"

"Nothing's wrong with it," Maura replied. "It's just not yours."

Now, for the first time, Blue saw an edge of true aggravation to Gansey's expression, and it made her like him a little better.

So there was something below the raven boy exterior, maybe. Flippantly, Gansey snagged another card, clearly finished with this exercise. With flourish, he turned the card over and slapped it on the table.

Blue swallowed.

Maura said, "*That's* your card."

On the card on the table was a black knight astride a white horse. The knight's helmet was lifted so that it was obvious that his face was a bare skull dominated by eyeless sockets. The sun set beyond him and below his horse's hooves lay a corpse.

Outside the windows behind them, a breeze hissed audibly through the trees.

"Death." Gansey read the bottom of the card. He didn't sound surprised or alarmed. He just read the word like he would read *eggs* or *Cincinnati*.

"Great job, Maura," Calla said. Her arms were crossed firmly over her chest. "You going to interpret that for the kid?"

"Possibly we should just give him a refund," Persephone suggested, although Gansey had not paid yet.

"I thought that psychics didn't predict death," Adam said quietly. "I read that the Death card was only symbolic."

Maura and Calla and Persephone all made vague noises. Blue, utterly aware of the truth of Gansey's fate, felt ill. Aglionby boy or not, he was only her age, and he obviously had friends who cared for him and a life that involved a very orange car, and it was hideous to know he'd be dead in less than twelve months.

"Actually," Gansey said, "I don't care about that."

Every pair of eyes in the room was on him as he stood the card on its end to study it.

"I mean, the cards are very interesting," he said. He said *the cards are very interesting* like someone would say *this is very interesting* to a very strange sort of cake that they didn't quite want to finish. "And I don't want to discount what you do. But I didn't really come here to have my future told to me. I'm quite OK with finding that out for myself."

He cast a quick glance at Calla at this, obviously realizing that he was walking a fine line between "polite" and "Ronan".

"Really, I came because I was hoping to ask you a question about energy," Gansey continued. "I know you deal with energy work, and I've been trying to find a ley line I think is near Henrietta. Do you know anything about that?"

The journal!

"Ley line?" Maura repeated. "Maybe. I don't know if I know it by that name. What is it?"

Blue was a little stunned. She'd always thought her mother was the most truthful person around.

"They're straight energy lines that criss-cross the globe," Gansey explained. "They're supposed to connect major spiritual places. Adam thought you might know about them because you deal with energy."

It was obvious that he meant the corpse road, but Maura didn't offer any information. She just pressed her lips together and looked at Persephone and Calla. "Does that ring a bell to you two?"

Persephone pointed a finger straight in the air and then said, "I forgot about my pie crust."

She withdrew from the room. Calla said, "I'd have to think about it. I'm not good with specifics."

There was a faint, amused smile on Gansey's face that meant he knew they were lying. It was a strangely wise expression; once again Blue got the sense that he seemed older than the boys he'd brought with him.

"I'll look into it," Maura said. "If you leave your number, I can give you a call if I find out anything about it."

Gansey replied, coolly polite, "Oh, that's quite all right. How much for the reading?"

Standing, Maura said, "Oh, just twenty."

Blue thought this was criminal. Gansey clearly had spent more than twenty dollars on the laces for his Top-Siders.

He frowned at Maura over the top of his open wallet. There were a lot of notes in it. They could've been ones, but Blue doubted it. She could also see his driver's licence through a clear window; not closely enough to make out the details, but close enough to see that the name printed on it looked a lot longer than just *Gansey*. "Twenty?"

"Each," Blue added.

Calla coughed into her first.

Gansey's face cleared and he handed Maura sixty dollars. Quite obviously this was more what he'd been expecting to pay, and now the world was right again.

It was Adam, though, who Blue noticed then. He was looking at her, sharp-eyed, and she felt transparent and guilty. Not only about overcharging, but about Maura's lie. Blue had seen Gansey's spirit walk the corpse road and she had known his name before he walked in this door. Like her mother, she'd said nothing. So she was complicit.

"I'll show you out," Maura said. She was clearly eager to see them on the other side of the door. For a moment, it looked as if Gansey felt the same, but then he stopped. He paid an undue amount of attention to his wallet as he folded it and reinserted it into his pocket, and then he looked up to Maura and made a firm line of his mouth.

"Look, we're all adults here," he started.

Calla made a face as if she disagreed.

Gansey squared his shoulders and continued, "So I think we deserve the truth. Tell me you know something but you don't want to help me, if that's what's going on, but don't lie to me."

It was a brave thing to say, or an arrogant one, or maybe there was not enough of a difference between the two things to matter. Every head in the room swung to Maura.

She said, "I know something but I don't want to help you."

For the second time that day, Calla looked delighted. Blue's mouth was open. She closed it.

Gansey, however, just nodded, no more or less distressed than when Blue had retorted back to him at the restaurant. "All right, then. No, no, you can stay put. We'll let ourselves out."

And just like that, they did, Adam sending Blue a last look that she couldn't easily interpret. A second later, the Camaro revved high, and the tyres squealed out Gansey's true feelings. Then the house was quiet. It was a sucked-out silence, like the raven boys had taken all the sound in the neighbourhood with them.

Blue whirled on her mother. "*Mom.*" She was going to say something else, but all that she could manage was again, louder, "*Mom!*"

"Maura," Calla said, "that was very rude." Then she added, "I liked it."

Maura turned to Blue as if Calla hadn't spoken. "I don't want you to ever see him again."

Indignant, Blue cried, "Whatever happened to 'children should never be given orders'?"

"That was before Gansey." Maura flipped around the Death card, giving Blue a long time to stare at the skull inside the helmet. "This is the same as me telling you not to walk in front of a bus."

Several comebacks riffled through Blue's head before

she found one that she wanted. "Why? Neeve didn't see *me* on the corpse road. *I'm* not going to die in the next year."

"First of all, the corpse road is a promise, not a guarantee," Maura replied. "Second of all, there are other terrible fates besides death. Shall we talk about dismemberment? Paralysis? Endless psychological trauma? There is something really wrong with those boys. When your mother says don't walk in front of a bus, she has a good reason."

From the kitchen, Persephone's soft voice called, "If someone had stopped you from walking in front of a bus, Maura, Blue wouldn't be here."

Maura shot a frown in her direction, then swept her hand across the reading table as if she were clearing it of crumbs. "The best-case scenario here is that you make friends with a boy who's going to die."

"Ah," said Calla, in a very, very knowing way. "Now I see."

"Don't psychoanalyse me," her mother said.

"I already have. And I say again, 'ah'."

Maura sneered uncharacteristically, and then asked Calla, "What did you see when you touched that other boy? The raven boy?"

"They're all raven boys," Blue said.

Her mother shook her head. "No, he's more raven than the others."

Calla rubbed her fingertips together, as if she was wiping the memory of Ronan's tattoo from them. "It's like scrying into that weird space. There's so much coming out of him, it shouldn't be possible. Do you remember that woman who came in who was pregnant with quadruplets? It was like that, but worse."

"He's pregnant?" Blue asked.

"He's creating," Calla said. "That space is creating, too. I don't know how to say it any better than that."

Blue wondered what sort of creating they meant. *She* was always creating things – taking old things and cutting them up and making them better things. Taking things that already existed and transforming them into something else. This, she felt, was what most people meant when they called someone *creative*.

But she suspected that wasn't how Calla meant it. She suspected that what Calla meant was the true meaning of creative: to make a thing where before there was none.

Maura caught Blue's expression. She said, "I've never told you to do anything before, Blue. But I'm telling you now. Stay away from them."

SIXTEEN

The night following the reading, Gansey woke to a completely unfamiliar sound and fumbled for his glasses. It sounded a little like one of his room-mates was being killed by a possum, or possibly the final moments of a fatal cat fight. He wasn't certain of the specifics, but he was sure death was involved.

Noah stood in the doorway to his room, his face pathetic and long-suffering. "Make it stop," he said.

Ronan's room was sacred, and yet here Gansey was, twice in the same week, pushing the door open. He found the lamp on and Ronan hunched on the bed, wearing only boxers. Six months before, Ronan had got the intricate black tattoo that covered most of his back and snaked up his neck, and now the monochromatic lines of it were stark in the claustrophobic lamplight, more real than anything else in the room. It was a peculiar tattoo, both vicious and lovely, and every time Gansey saw it, he saw something different in the pattern. Tonight, nestled in an inked glen of wicked, beautiful flowers, was a beak where before he'd seen a scythe.

The ragged sound cut through the apartment again.

"What fresh hell is this?" Gansey asked pleasantly. Ronan

was wearing headphones as usual, so Gansey stretched forward far enough to tug them down around his neck. Music wailed faintly into the air.

Ronan lifted his head. As he did, the wicked flowers on his back shifted and hid behind his sharp shoulder blades. In his lap was the half-formed raven, its head tilted back, beak agape.

"I thought we were clear on what a closed door meant," Ronan said. He held a pair of tweezers in one hand.

"I thought we were clear that night was for sleeping."

Ronan shrugged. "Perhaps for you."

"Not tonight. Your pterodactyl woke me. Why is it making that sound?"

In response, Ronan dipped the tweezers into a plastic baggy on the blanket in front of him. Gansey wasn't certain he wanted to know what the grey substance was in the tweezers' grasp. As soon as the raven heard the rustle of the bag, it made the ghastly sound again – a rasping squeal that became a gurgle as it slurped down the offering. At once, it inspired both Gansey's compassion and his gag reflex.

"Well, this is not going to do," he said. "You're going to have to make it stop."

"She has to be fed," Ronan replied. The raven gargled down another bite. This time it sounded a lot like vacuuming potato salad. "It's only every two hours for the first six weeks."

"Can't you keep her downstairs?"

In reply, Ronan half-lifted the little bird towards him. "You tell me."

Gansey disliked having his kindness appealed to, especially when it had to war with his desire for sleep. There was, of course, no way that he would force the raven downstairs. It looked bite-sized and improbable. He wasn't certain if it was extremely cute or appallingly ugly and it bothered him that it managed to be both.

From behind him, Noah said, sounding pitiful, "I don't like that thing in here. It reminds me of. . ."

He trailed off, as he often did, and Ronan pointed the tweezers at him. "Hey, man. Stay out of my room."

"Shut up," Gansey told both of them. "That includes you, bird."

"Chainsaw."

Noah withdrew, but Gansey remained. For several minutes, he watched the raven slurp down grey slime while Ronan cooed at her. He was not the Ronan that Gansey had grown accustomed to, but neither was he the Ronan that Gansey had first met. It was clear now that the instrument wailing from the headphones was the Irish pipes. Gansey couldn't remember the last time Ronan had listened to Celtic music. Niall Lynch's music. All at once, he, too, missed Ronan's charismatic father. But more than that, he missed the Ronan that had existed when Niall Lynch had still been alive. This boy in front of him now, fragile bird in his hands, seemed like a compromise.

After a space, Gansey asked, "What did the psychic mean, Ronan? Earlier. About your father."

Ronan didn't lift his head, but Gansey watched the muscles in his back tighten, stretched as if they were suddenly carrying weight. "That's a very Declan question."

Gansey considered this. "No. No, I don't think it is."

"She was just full of shit."

Gansey considered this, too. "No, I don't think she was."

Ronan found his music player next to him on the bed

and paused it. When he replied, his voice was pitchless and naked. "She's one of those chicks who gets inside your head and fucks around with parts. She said it because she knew it would cause problems."

"Like what?"

"Like you asking me questions like Declan would," Ronan said. He offered the raven another grey mass, but she just stared up at him, transfixed. "Making me think about things I don't want to think about. Those sorts of problems. Among others. What's going on with your face, by the way?"

Gansey rubbed his chin, rueful. His skin felt reluctantly stubbled. He knew he was being diverted, but he allowed it. "Is it growing?"

"Dude, you aren't really going to do that beard thing, are you? I thought you were joking. You know that stopped being cool in the fourteenth century or whenever it was that Paul Bunyan lived." Ronan looked over his shoulder at him. He was sporting the five o'clock shadow that he was capable of growing at any time of the day. "Just stop. You look mangy."

"It's irrelevant. It's not growing. I'm doomed to be a man-child."

"If you keep saying things like 'man-child', we're done," Ronan said. "Hey, man. Don't let it get you down. Once your balls drop, that beard'll come in great. Like a fucking rug. You eat soup, it'll filter out the potatoes. Terrier style. Do you have hair on your legs? I've never noticed."

Gansey didn't dignify any of this with a response. With a sigh, he pushed off the wall and pointed at the raven. "I'm going back to bed. Keep that thing quiet. You so owe me, Lynch."

"Whatever," Ronan said.

Gansey retreated to his bed, though he didn't lie down. He reached for his journal, but it wasn't there; he'd left it at Nino's the night of the fight. He thought about calling Malory, but he didn't know what he wanted to ask. Something inside him felt like the night, hungry and wanting and black. He thought about the dark eyeholes of the skeletal knight on the Death card.

An insect was buzzing against the window, the sort of buzz-tap that came from an insect with some size to it. He thought about his EpiPen, far away in the glovebox of the car, too far away to be a useful antidote if it was needed. The insect was probably a fly or a stink bug or yet another crane fly, but the longer he lay there, the more he considered the idea that it could be a wasp or a bee.

It probably wasn't.

But he opened his eyes. Gansey climbed softly from the bed, bending to retrieve a shoe that lay on its side. Walking cautiously to the window, he searched for the sound of the insect. The shadow of the telescope was an elegant monster on the floor beside him.

Though the sound of buzzing had died away, it only took him a moment to find the insect on the window: a wasp, crawling up the narrow wooden frame of the window, swivelling back and forth. Gansey didn't move. He watched it climb and pause, climb and pause. The streetlights outside made a faint shadow of its legs, its curved body, the fine, insubstantial point of the stinger.

Two narratives coexisted in his head. One was the real image: the wasp climbing up the wood, oblivious to his presence. The other was a false image, a possibility: the wasp whirring into the air, finding Gansey's skin, dipping the stinger into him, Gansey's allergy making it a deadly weapon.

Long ago, his skin had crawled with hornets, their wings beating even when his heart hadn't.

His throat was tight and full.

"Gansey?"

Ronan's voice was just behind him, the timbre of it strange and initially unrecognizable. Gansey didn't turn around. The wasp had just twitched its wings, nearly lifting off.

"Shit, man!" Ronan said. There were three footsteps, very close together, the floor creaking like a shot, and then the shoe was snatched from Gansey's hand. Ronan shoved him aside and brought down the shoe on the window so hard that the glass should've broken. After the wasp's dry body had fallen to the floorboard, Ronan sought it out in the darkness and smashed it once more.

"Shit," Ronan said again. "Are you stupid?"

Gansey didn't know how to describe how it felt, to see death crawling centimetres from him, to know that in a few seconds, he could have gone from "a promising student" to "beyond saving". He turned to Ronan, who had painstakingly picked up the wasp by a broken wing, so that Gansey wouldn't step on it.

"What did you want?" he asked.

"What?" Ronan demanded.

"You came out for something."

Ronan chucked the wasp's small body into the waste basket by the desk. The bin was overflowing with crumpled papers, so the body bounced out and forced him to find a better crevice for it. "I can't even remember."

Gansey merely stood and waited for Ronan to say something else. Ronan fussed over the wasp for another few moments before he said anything, and when he finally did, he didn't look at Gansey. "What's this about you and Parrish leaving?"

It wasn't what Gansey had expected. He wasn't sure how to speak without hurting Ronan. He couldn't lie to him.

"You tell me what you heard and I'll tell you what's real."

"Noah told me," Ronan said, "that if you left, Parrish was going with you."

He had let jealousy sneak into his voice and that made Gansey's response cooler than it might have been. Gansey tried not to play favourites. "And what else did Noah have to say?"

With visible effort, Ronan pulled himself back, sorted himself out. None of the Lynch brothers liked to appear anything other than intentional, even if it was intentionally cruel. Instead of answering, he asked, "Do you not want me to come?"

Something stuck in Gansey's chest. "I would take all of you anywhere with me."

The moonlight made a strange sculpture of Ronan's face, a stark portrait incompletely moulded by a sculptor who had forgotten to work in compassion. He did his smoker's inhale, heavy on the intake through the nostrils, light on the exhale through his prison of teeth.

After a pause, he said, "The other night. There's something—"

But then he stopped without saying anything else. It was a full stop, the sort that Gansey associated with secrets and guilt. It was the stop that happened when you'd made up your mind to confess, but your mouth betrayed you in the end.

"There's what?"

Ronan muttered something. He shook the wastebasket.

"There's *what*, Ronan?"

He said, "This thing with Chainsaw and the psychic woman, and just, with Noah, and I just think there's something strange going on."

Gansey couldn't keep the exasperation from his voice. "'Strange' doesn't help me. I don't know what 'strange' means."

"I don't know, man, this sounds crazy to me. I don't know what to tell you. I mean strange like your voice on that recorder," Ronan replied. "Strange like the psychic's daughter. Things feel bigger. I don't know what I'm saying. I thought you would believe me, of all people."

"I don't even know what you're asking me to believe."

Ronan said, "It's starting, man."

Gansey crossed his arms. He could see the dark black wing of the dead wasp pressed against the mesh of the wastebasket. He waited for Ronan to elaborate, but all the other boy said was, "I catch you staring at a wasp again, though, I'm going to let it kill you. Screw that."

Without waiting for a reply, he turned away and retreated back to his room.

Slowly, Gansey picked up his shoe from where Ronan had left it. When he straightened, he realized Noah had drifted from his room to stand near Gansey. His anxious gaze flickered from Gansey to the wastebasket. The wasp's body had slipped down several centimetres, but it was still visible.

"What?" Gansey asked. Something about Noah's uneasy

face reminded him of the frightened faces surrounding him, hornets on his skin, the sky blue as death above him. A long, long time ago, he'd been given another chance, and lately, the weight of needing to make it matter felt heavier.

He looked away from Noah, out of the wall of windowpanes. Even now, it seemed to Gansey that he could feel the aching presence of the nearby mountains, like the space between him and the peaks was a tangible thing. It was as excruciating as the imagined sleeping countenance of Glendower.

Ronan was right. Things felt bigger. He may not have found the line, or the heart of the line, but something was happening, something was starting.

Noah said, "Don't throw it away."

SEVENTEEN

Several days later, Blue woke up sometime well before dawn.

Her room was cluttered with jagged shadows from the hall night-light. As they had every night since the reading, thoughts about Adam's elegant features and the memory of Gansey's bowed head crowded into her mind as soon as sleep relinquished its hold. Blue couldn't help replaying the chaotic episode over and over in her mind. Calla's volatile response to Ronan, Adam and Gansey's private language, the fact that Gansey was not just a spirit on the corpse road. But it wasn't just the boys that she was concerned with, though, sadly, it didn't seem likely that Adam would ever call now. No, the thing that seized her the most was the idea that her mother had forbidden her to do something. It pinched like a collar.

Blue pushed off the covers. She was getting up.

She bore a grudging fondness for the weird architecture of 300 Fox Way; it was a sort of half-hearted affection born of nostalgia more than any real feeling. But her feelings for the garden behind the house were anything but mixed. A great, spreading beech tree sheltered the entire back garden. Its beautiful, perfectly symmetrical canopy stretched from one fence line to the other, so dense that it tinted even the hottest summer day a lush green. Only the heaviest rain could penetrate the leaves. Blue had a satchelful of memories of standing by the massive, smooth trunk in the rain, hearing it hiss and tap and scatter across the canopy without ever reaching the ground. Standing under the beech tree, it felt like *she* was the beech, like the rain rolled off her leaves and off the bark, smooth as skin against her own.

With a little sigh, Blue made her way down to the kitchen. She pushed open the back door, using two hands to close it silently behind her. After dark, the garden was its own world, private and dim. The high wooden fence, covered with messy honeysuckle, blocked out the lights from neighbouring back porches, and the inscrutable canopy of the beech blocked the moonlight. Ordinarily, she would have had to wait several long minutes for her eyes to adjust to the relative dark, but not tonight.

Tonight, an eerie, uncertain light flickered on the trunk of the tree. Blue hesitated just outside the door, trying to make sense of the sputtering light as it shifted on the pale, grey bark. Laying a hand against the side of the house – it was still warm from the heat of the day – she leaned forward. From here, she saw a candle around the other side of the tree, nestled in the bare snake-roots of the beech. A tremulous flame vanished and lengthened and vanished again.

Blue took a step off the cracked brick patio, then another, glancing behind her again to see if anyone watched from the house. Whose project was this? A metre away from the candle was another tangle of smooth-skinned roots and a pool of black water had gathered in them. The water reflected the flickering light, like another candle beneath the black surface.

Blue held her breath tight inside her as she took another step.

In a loose jumper and broom skirt, Neeve knelt near the candle and the little root-pool. With her pretty hands folded in her lap, she was as motionless as the tree itself and as dark as the sky overhead.

Blue's breath came out in a rush when she first saw Neeve, and then, lifting her eyes to Neeve's barely visible face, her breath jerked out of her once more, as if the surprise were fresh again.

"Oh," Blue breathed. "I'm sorry. I didn't know you were here."

But Neeve didn't reply. When Blue looked closer, she saw that Neeve's eyes were unfocused. It was her eyebrows that really did it for Blue; they had no expression to them somehow. Even more vacuous than Neeve's eyes were those formless eyebrows, waiting for input, drawn in two straight, neutral lines.

Blue's first thought was something medical — weren't there seizures where the symptom was just sitting there? What were those called? — but then she thought of the bowl of cran-grape juice on the kitchen table. It was far more likely that she'd interrupted some sort of meditation.

But it didn't look like meditation. It looked like . . . a ritual. Her mother didn't do rituals. Maura had once told a client hotly, *I am not a witch.* And once she had said sadly to Persephone, *I am not a witch.* But perhaps Neeve was. Blue wasn't certain what the rules were in this situation.

"Who's there?" asked Neeve.

But it was not Neeve's voice. It was something deeper and farther away.

A nasty little shiver ran up Blue's arms. Somewhere in the tree above, a bird hissed. At least Blue thought it was a bird.

"Come into the light," said Neeve.

The water moved in the roots, or maybe it was merely the moving reflection of the solitary candle. As Blue cast her gaze wider, she saw a five-pointed star marked around the beech tree. One point was the candle, and another the pool of dark water. An unlit candle marked the third point and an empty bowl the fourth. For a moment, Blue thought that she was mistaken, that it was not a five-pointed star after all. But then she realized: Neeve was the final point.

"I know you are there," not-Neeve said, in the voice that sounded like dark places, far away from the sun. "I can smell you."

Something crawled very slowly up the back of Blue's neck, on the inside of her skin. It was such a hideously real creep that she was badly tempted to slap it or scratch it.

She wanted to go inside and pretend she had not come out, but she didn't want to leave Neeve behind if something—

Blue didn't want to think it, but she did.

She didn't want to leave Neeve behind if something *had* her.

"I am here," Blue said.

The candle flame stretched very, very long.

Not-Neeve asked, "What is your name?"

It occurred to Blue that she wasn't exactly certain that

Neeve's mouth moved when she spoke. It was hard to look at her face.

"Neeve," Blue lied.

"Come where I can see you."

There was definitely something moving in the little black pool. The water was reflecting colours that were not in the candle. They shifted and moved in a pattern completely unlike the movement of the flame.

Blue shivered. "I am invisible."

"Ahhhhhhh," sighed not-Neeve.

"Who are you?" Blue asked.

The candle flame reached tall, tall, thin to the point of breaking. It reached not for the sky but for Blue.

"Neeve," said not-Neeve.

There was something crafty now, to the dark voice. Something knowing and malicious, something that made Blue want to look over her shoulder. But she couldn't look away from that candle, because she was afraid the flame would touch her if she turned away.

"Where are you?" Blue asked.

"On the corpse road," not-Neeve growled.

Blue became aware that her breath clouded in front of her. Goosebumps pricked her arms, fast and painful. In the half-light of the candle, she saw that Neeve's breath was visible, too.

The cloud of Neeve's breath parted over the pool, like something physical was rising from the water to break the path of it.

Rushing forward, Blue kicked over the empty bowl, knocked over the unlit candle, scuffed dirt in the direction of the black pool.

The candle went out.

There was a minute of complete blackness. There was no sound, as if the tree and the garden around it were not in Henrietta any more. Despite the silence, Blue did not feel alone, and it was a terrible feeling.

I am inside a bubble, she thought furiously. *I am in a fortress. There is glass all around me. I can see out but nothing can get in. I am untouchable.* All of the visuals that Maura had given her to protect herself from psychic attack. It felt like nothing at all against the voice that had come out of Neeve.

But then there was nothing. Her goosebumps had disappeared as quickly as they'd come. Slowly, her eyes adjusted to the darkness – though it felt like light leeching back into the world – and she found Neeve, still kneeling by the pool of water.

"Neeve," whispered Blue.

For a moment, nothing happened, and then Neeve lifted her chin and her hands.

Please be Neeve. Please be Neeve.

Blue's entire body was poised to run.

Then she saw that Neeve's eyebrows were ordered and firm over her eyes, though her hands were quivering. Blue let out a relieved sigh.

"Blue?" Neeve asked. Her voice was quite normal. Then, with sudden understanding: "*Oh.* You won't tell your mother about this, will you?"

Blue stared at her. "I most certainly will! What was *that*? What were you doing?" Her heart was still going fast and she realized that she was terrified, now that she could think about it.

Neeve took in the broken pentagram, the knocked-over candle, the overturned bowl. "I was scrying."

Her mild voice only infuriated Blue.

"Scrying is what you did earlier. This was not the same thing!"

"I was scrying into that space I saw earlier. I was hoping to make contact with someone who was in it to find out what it was."

Blue's voice was not nearly as steady as she would've liked. "It *spoke*. It was *not you* when I came out here."

"Well," Neeve said, sounding a little cross, "that was your fault. You make everything stronger. I wasn't expecting you to be here, or I would've. . ."

She trailed off and looked at the stub of the candle, her head cocked. It wasn't a particularly human sort of gesture, and it made Blue remember the nasty chill she had got before.

"Would've what?" Blue demanded. She was a little cross, too, that she was somehow being blamed for whatever had just happened. "What *was* that? It said it was on the corpse road. Is that the same thing as a ley line?"

"Of course," Neeve said. "Henrietta's on a ley line."

That meant that Gansey was right. It also meant Blue knew exactly where the ley line ran, because she'd seen Gansey's spirit walk along it only a few days earlier.

"It's why it's easy to be a psychic here," Neeve said. "The energy is strong."

"Energy, like my energy?" Blue asked.

Neeve did a complicated hand gesture before picking up the candle. She held it upside down in front of her and pinched the wick to be certain it was entirely extinguished. "Energy like your energy. Feeds things. How did you put it? Makes the conversation louder. The light bulb brighter. Everything that needs energy to stay alive craves it, just like they crave your energy."

"What did you see?" Blue asked. "When you were—?"

"Scrying," Neeve finished for her, though Blue wasn't at all certain that was how she would've finished it. "There's someone who knows your name there. And there's someone else who is looking for this thing that you're looking for."

"That *I'm* looking for!" Blue echoed, dismayed. There was nothing *she* was looking for. Unless Neeve was talking about the mysterious Glendower. She recalled that feeling of connection, of feeling tied up in this web of raven boys and sleeping kings and ley lines. Of her mother saying to stay away from them.

"Yes, you know what it is," Neeve replied. "Ah. Everything seems so much clearer now."

Blue thought about that stretching, hungry candle flame, the shifting lights inside the pool of water. She felt cold somewhere very deep inside her. "You haven't said what that was yet. In the pool."

Neeve looked up then, all of her supplies gathered in her arms. Her gaze was the unbreakable one that could last an eternity.

"That's because I have no idea," she said.

EIGHTEEN

Whelk took the liberty of going through Gansey's locker before school the next day.

Gansey's locker, one of the few in use, was only a couple of doors down from Whelk's old one, and the feeling of opening it brought back a rush of memory and nostalgia. Once upon a time, this had been *him* – one of the wealthiest kids at Aglionby, with whichever friends he wanted, whichever Henrietta girls caught his eye, whichever classes he felt like going to. His father had no compunction about making an extra donation here or there to help Whelk pass a class he'd failed to attend for a few weeks. Whelk longed for his old car. The cops here had known his father well; they hadn't even bothered to pull Whelk over.

And now Gansey was a king here, and he didn't even know how to use it.

Thanks to Aglionby's honour code, there were no locks on any of the lockers, allowing Whelk to open Gansey's without any fuss. Inside, he found several dusty spiral-bound notebooks with only a few pages used in each. In case Gansey decided to come into school two hours early, Whelk left a note in the locker ("Belongings have been removed while we spray for roaches") and then retreated back to one of the unused staff bathrooms to examine his find.

Sitting cross-legged on the pristine but dusty tile beside the sink, what he found was that Richard Gansey III was more obsessed with the ley line than he had ever been. Something about the entire research process seemed . . . frantic.

What is wrong *with this kid?* Whelk wondered, and then immediately afterwards felt strange that he had grown old enough to think of Gansey as a kid.

Outside the bathroom, he heard heels clicking down the hallway. The scent of coffee drifted under the doorway; Aglionby was beginning to stir. Whelk flipped to the next notebook.

This one was not about the ley line. It was all historical stuff about the Welsh king Owen Glendower. Whelk was not interested. He skimmed, skimmed, skimmed, thinking it was unrelated, until he realized the case Gansey was making for tying the two elements together: Glendower and the ley line. Stooge or not, Gansey knew how to sell a story.

Whelk focused on one line.

Whoever wakes Glendower is granted a favour (limitless?) (supernatural?) (some sources say reciprocal/what does that mean?)

Czerny had never cared about the ultimate outcome of the ley line search. At first, Whelk hadn't, either. The appeal had merely been the riddle of it. Then one afternoon Czerny and Whelk, standing in the middle of what seemed to be a naturally formed circle of magnetically charged stones, had experimentally pushed one of the stones out of place. The resulting sizzle of energy had knocked them both off their feet and created a faint apparition of what looked like a woman.

The ley line was raw, uncontrollable, inexplicable energy. The stuff of legends.

Whoever controlled the ley line would be more than rich. Whoever controlled the ley line would be something that the other Aglionby boys could only hope to aspire to.

Czerny still hadn't cared, not really. He was the most mild, ambitionless creature Whelk had ever seen, which was probably why Whelk liked to hang out with him so much. Czerny didn't have a problem being no better than the other Aglionby students. He was content to trot along after Whelk. These days, when Whelk was trying to comfort himself, he told himself that Czerny was a sheep, but sometimes he slipped and remembered him as loyal instead.

They didn't have to be different things, did they?

"Glendower," Whelk said out loud, trying it out. The word echoed off the bathroom walls, hollow and metallic. He wondered what Gansey – strange, desperate Gansey – was thinking he'd ask for as a favour.

Climbing up off the bathroom floor, Whelk picked up all the notebooks. It would only take a few minutes to copy them in the staffroom, and if anyone asked, he'd tell them Gansey had asked him to.

Glendower.

If Whelk found him, he'd ask for what he'd wanted all along: to control the ley line.

NINETEEN

The following afternoon, Blue walked barefoot to the street in front of 300 Fox Way and sat on the kerb to wait for Calla beneath the blue-green trees. All afternoon Neeve had been locked up in her room and Maura had been doing angel-card readings for a group of out-of-towners on a writing retreat. So Blue had taken all afternoon to contemplate what to do about finding Neeve in the back garden. And what to do involved Calla.

She was just getting restless when Calla's carpool pulled up at the kerb.

"Are you putting yourself out with the trash?" Calla asked as she climbed out of the vehicle, which was blue-green like everything else in the day. She wore a strangely respectable dress with dubiously funky rhinestone sandals. Making a lackadaisical hand motion at the driver, she turned to Blue as the car drove away.

"I need to ask you a question," Blue said.

"And it's a question that sounds better next to a trash can? Hold this." Calla wrestled one of her bags off her arm and on to Blue's. She smelled of jasmine and chilli peppers, which meant she'd had a bad day at work. Blue wasn't entirely certain what Calla did for a living, but she knew it had something to do with Aglionby, paperwork and cursing at students, often on weekends. Whatever her job description was, it involved rewarding herself with burritos on bad days.

Calla began to stomp up the walk towards the front door.

Blue trailed helplessly after her, lugging the bag. It felt like it had books or bodies in it. "The house is full."

Only one of Calla's eyebrows was paying any attention. "It's always full."

They were nearly at the front door. Inside, every room was occupied with aunts and cousins and mothers. The sound of Persephone's angry PhD music was already audible. The only chance for privacy was outside.

Blue said, "I want to know why Neeve's here."

Calla stopped. She looked at Blue over her shoulder.

"Well, excuse you," she replied, not very pleasantly. "I'd like to know the cause of climate change, too, but no one's telling me that."

Clutching Calla's bag like a hostage, Blue insisted, "I'm not six any more. Maybe everyone else can see what they need to see in a pack of cards, but I'm tired of being left in the dark."

Now she had both of Calla's eyebrows' interest.

"Damn straight," Calla agreed. "I wondered when you were going to go all rebellious on us. Why aren't you asking your mother?"

"Because I'm angry at her for telling me what to do."

Calla shifted her weight. "Take another bag. What is it you propose?"

Blue accepted another bag; this one was dark brown, and managed to have corners. There seemed to be a box in it. "That you just tell me?"

Using one of her newly freed hands, Calla tapped a finger on her lip. Both her lips and the nail she used to tap were deeply indigo, the colour of octopus ink, the colour of the deepest shadows in the rocky front yard. "The only thing is, I'm not sure that what we've been told is the truth."

Blue felt a little lurch at that. The idea of lying to Calla or Maura or Persephone seemed ludicrous. Even if they didn't know the truth, they'd hear a lie. But there did seem to be something secretive about Neeve, about her scrying after hours, where she thought it likely no one would see her.

Calla said, "She was supposed to be here looking for someone."

"My father," Blue guessed.

Calla didn't say *yes* but she didn't say *no*, either. Instead, she replied, "But I think it's become something else for her, now that she's been here in Henrietta for a while."

They regarded each other for a moment, co-conspirators.

"My proposition is different, then," Blue said, finally. She tried to arch her eyebrow to match Calla's, but it felt a bit lacking. "We go through Neeve's stuff. You hold it and I'll stand next to you."

Calla's mouth became very small. Her psychometric reflections were often vague, but with Blue beside her, making her gift stronger? It had certainly been dramatic when she'd touched Ronan's tattoo. If she handled Neeve's things, they might get some concrete answers.

"Take this bag," Calla said, handing Blue the last of them. This one was the smallest of all, made of blood-red leather. It was impossibly heavy. While Blue worked out how to hold it with the others, Calla crossed her arms and tapped her indigo-nailed fingers on her upper arms.

"She'd have to be out of her room for at least an hour," Calla said. "And Maura would have to be otherwise occupied."

Calla had once observed that Maura had no pets because her principles took too much time to take care of. Maura was a big believer in many things, one of them personal privacy.

"But you will do it?"

"I'll find out more today," Calla said. "About their schedules. What's this?" Her attention had shifted to a car pulling up at the end of the walk. Both Calla and Blue tilted their heads to read the magnetic sign on the passenger door: FLOWERS BY ANDI! The driver rummaged in the back seat of her car for a full two minutes before heading up the walk with the world's smallest flower arrangement. Her fluffed bangs were larger than the flowers.

"It's hard to find this place!" the woman said.

Calla pursed her lips. She had a pure and fiery hatred for anything that could be classified as small talk.

"What's all this?" Calla asked. She made it sound as if the flowers were an unwanted kitten.

"This is for. . ." The woman fumbled for a card.

"Orla?" guessed Blue.

Orla was always getting sent flowers by various lovelorn men from Henrietta and beyond. It wasn't just flowers they sent. Some sent spa packages. Others sent fruit baskets. One, memorably, sent an oil portrait of Orla. He'd painted her in profile, so that the viewer could fully see Orla's long, elegant neck; her classic cheekbones; her romantic, heavy-lidded eyes; and her massive nose – her least favourite feature. Orla had broken up with him immediately.

"Blue?" the woman asked. "Blue Sargent?"

At first, Blue didn't understand that she meant that the flowers were for her. The woman had to thrust them towards her and then Calla had to take back one of her bags in order for Blue to be able to accept them. As the woman headed back to her car, Blue turned the arrangement in her hand. It was just a spray of baby's breath around a white carnation; they smelled prettier than they looked.

Calla commented, "The delivery must've cost more than the flowers."

Feeling around the wiry stems, Blue found a little card. Inside, a woman's scrawl had transcribed a message:

I hope you still want me to call. – Adam

Now the tiny bunch of flowers made sense. They matched Adam's frayed jumper.

"And you're blushing," Calla said disapprovingly. She held a hand out for them, which Blue smacked. With sarcasm, Calla added, "Whoever it is went all out, did they?"

Blue touched the edge of the white carnation to her chin. It was so light that it didn't feel like she was touching anything at all. It was no portrait or fruit basket, but she couldn't imagine Adam sending anything more dramatic. These little flowers were quiet and sparse, just like him. "I think they're pretty."

She had to bite her lip to keep a foolish smile inside. What she wanted to do was hug the flowers and then dance, but both seemed insensible.

"Who is he?" asked Calla.

"I'm being secretive. Take your bags back." Blue stretched out her arm so that Calla's brown bag and canvas bag slid down to Calla's open hands.

Calla shook her head, but she didn't look displeased. Deep down, Blue suspected she was a romantic.

"Calla?" Blue asked. "Do you think I should tell the boys where the corpse road is?"

Calla gazed at Blue for as long as a Neeve gaze. Then she said, "What makes you think I can answer that question?"

"Because you're an adult," Blue replied. "And you're supposed to have learned things on your way to old age."

"What I think," Calla said, "is that you've already made up your mind."

Blue dropped her eyes to the ground. It was true that she was kept awake at night by Gansey's journal and by the suggestion of something more to the world. It was also true that she was dogged by the idea that maybe, just maybe, there was a sleeping king and she would be able to lay her hand on his sleeping cheek and feel a centuries-old pulse beneath his skin.

But more important than either of those was her face on that page of cups card, a boy's rain-spattered shoulders in the churchyard and a voice saying, *Gansey. That's all there is.*

Once she'd seen his death laid out for him, and seen that he was real, and found out that she was meant to have a part in it, there had never been a chance she would just stand by and let it happen.

"Don't tell Mom," Blue said.

With a noncommittal grunt, Calla wrenched open the

door, leaving Blue and her flowers on the step. The blossoms weighed nothing at all, but to Blue, they felt like change.

Today, Blue thought, *is the day I stop listening to the future and start living it instead.*

"Blue, if you get to know him—" Calla started. She was standing half-in, half-out of the doorway. "You'd better guard your heart. Don't forget that he's going to die."

TWENTY

At the same time that his flowers were being delivered to 300 Fox Way, Adam arrived at Monmouth Manufacturing on his somewhat pathetic bicycle. Ronan and Noah were already out in the overgrown car park, building wooden ramps for some unholy purpose.

He tried twice to persuade his rusted kickstand to hold his bike up before laying it down on its side. Crabgrass poked up through the spokes. He asked, "When do you think Gansey will get here?"

Ronan didn't immediately answer him. He was lying as far beneath the BMW as he could, measuring the width of the tyres with a yellow hardware-shop ruler. "Ten inches, Noah."

Noah, standing next to a pile of plywood and four-by-fours, asked, "Is that all? That doesn't seem like very much."

"Would I lie to you? Ten. Inches." Ronan shoved himself from beneath the car and stared up at Adam. He'd let his five o'clock shadow become a multiday shadow, probably to spite Gansey's inability to grow facial hair. Now he looked like the sort of person women would hide their purses and babies from. "Who knows. When did he say?"

"Three."

Ronan climbed to his feet and they both turned to watch Noah working with the plywood for the ramps. *Working with* really meant *staring at*. Noah had his fingers held ten inches apart and he looked through the space between them to the wood below, perplexed. There were no tools in sight.

"What is your plan with these things anyway?" Adam asked.

Ronan smiled his lizard smile. "Ramp. BMW. The goddamn moon."

This was so like Ronan. His room inside Monmouth was filled with expensive toys, but, like a spoiled child, he ended up playing outside with sticks.

"The trajectory you're building doesn't suggest the moon," Adam replied. "It suggests the end of your suspension."

"I don't need your back talk, science guy."

He probably didn't. Ronan didn't need physics. He could intimidate even a piece of plywood into doing what he wanted. Crouching by his bike, Adam messed over the kickstand again, trying to see if he could pry it free without breaking it entirely.

"What's your malfunction, anyway?" Ronan asked.

"I'm trying to decide when I should call Blue." Saying it out loud was inviting ridicule from Ronan, but it was one of those facts that needed to be acknowledged.

Noah said, "He sent her flowers."

"How did you know?" Adam demanded, more mortified than curious.

Noah merely smiled in a far-off way. He kicked one of the wooden boards off the plywood, looking triumphant.

"To the psychic's? You know what that place was?" Ronan asked. "A castration palace. You date that girl, you should send her your nuts instead of flowers."

"You're a Neanderthal."

"Sometimes you sound just like Gansey," Ronan said.

"Sometimes you don't."

Noah laughed his breathy, nearly soundless laugh. Ronan spit on the ground beside the BMW.

"I didn't even realize that 'midget' was the Adam Parrish type," he said.

He wasn't being serious, but Adam was, all at once, fatigued with Ronan and his uselessness. Since the day of the fistfight at Nino's, Ronan had already got several notices in his student box at Aglionby, warning him of the dire things slated to befall him if he didn't begin to improve his grades. If he didn't begin attempting to *get* grades. Instead, Ronan was out here building ramps.

Some people envied Ronan's money. Adam envied his time. To be as rich as Ronan was to be able to go to school and do nothing else, to have luxurious swathes of time in which to study and write papers and sleep. Adam wouldn't admit it to anyone, least of all Gansey, but he was *tired*. He was tired of squeezing homework in between his part-time jobs, of squeezing in sleep, squeezing in the hunt for Glendower. The jobs felt like so much wasted time: in five years, no one would care if he'd worked at a trailer factory. They'd only care if he'd graduated from Aglionby with perfect grades, or if he'd found Glendower, or if he was still alive. And Ronan didn't have to worry about any of that.

Two years earlier, Adam had made his decision to

come to Aglionby, and, in his head, it was sort of because of Ronan. His mother had sent him to the grocery store with her bank card – all that had been on the conveyer belt was a tube of toothpaste and four cans of microwave ravioli – and the cashier had just told him there were insufficient funds in her bank account to cover the purchase. Though it was not his failing, there was something peculiarly humiliating and intimate about the moment, hunched at the head of a shopping line, turning out his pockets to pretend he might have the cash to cover instead. While he fumbled there, a shaved-headed boy at the next register moved swiftly through, swiping a credit card and collecting his things in only a few seconds.

Even the way the other boy had moved, Adam recalled, had struck him: confident and careless, shoulders rolled back, chin tilted, an emperor's son. As the cashier swiped Adam's card again, both of them pretending the machine might have misread the magnetic stripe, Adam watched the other boy go out to the kerb to where a shiny black car waited. When the boy opened the door, Adam saw the other two boys inside wore raven-breasted jumpers and ties. They were despicably carefree as they divvied up the drinks.

He'd had to leave the cans and the toothpaste on the conveyer belt, eyes hot with shamed tears that wouldn't fall.

He'd never wanted to be someone else so badly.

In his head, that boy was Ronan, but in retrospect, Adam thought it couldn't have been. He wouldn't have been old enough to have his driver's licence yet. It was just some other Aglionby student with a working credit card and exquisite car. And also, that day wasn't the only reason he'd decided to fight to come to Aglionby. But it was the catalyst. The imagined memory of Ronan, careless and shallow but with pride fully intact, and Adam, cowed and humiliated while a line of old ladies waited behind him.

He still wasn't that other boy at the register. But he was closer.

Adam looked at his battered old watch to see how late Gansey was. He told Ronan, "Give me your phone."

With a raised eyebrow, Ronan retrieved the phone from the roof of the BMW.

Adam punched in the psychic's number. It rang just twice and then a breathy voice said, "Adam?"

Startled at the sound of his name, Adam replied, "Blue?"

"No," the voice said. "Persephone." Then, to someone in the background, "Ten dollars, Orla. That was the bet. No, the caller ID doesn't say anything at all. See?" Then, back to Adam, "Sorry about that. I'm terrible when there's competition involved. You're the Coca-Cola T-shirt one, right?"

It took Adam a moment to realize that she meant the top he'd worn to the reading. "Oh, um. Yeah."

"How wonderful. I'll go get Blue."

There was a brief, uncomfortable moment while voices murmured in the background of the telephone. Adam swatted at gnats; the car park needed to be mowed again. The tarmac was hard to see in some places.

"I didn't think you'd call," Blue said.

Adam must not have truly expected to get Blue on the

phone, because the surprise he felt when he heard her voice made his stomach feel hollowed out. Ronan was smirking in a way that made him want to punch his arm.

"I said I would."

"Thanks for the flowers. They were pretty." Then she hissed:

"*Orla, get out of here!*"

"It seems busy there."

"It's always busy here. There are three hundred and forty-two people who live here, and they all want to be in this room. What are you doing today?" She asked it very naturally, like it was the most logical thing in the world for them to have a conversation on the phone, like they were already friends.

It made it easier for Adam to say, "Exploring. Do you want to come with?"

Ronan's eyes widened. No matter what she said now, the phone call had been worth it for the genuine shock on Ronan's face.

"What sort of exploring?"

Shielding his eyes, Adam lifted his eyes to the sky. He thought he could hear Gansey coming. "Mountains. How do you feel about helicopters?"

There was a long pause. "How do you mean? Ethically?"

"As a mode of transportation."

"Faster than camels, but less sustainable. Is there going to be a helicopter in your future today?"

"Yeah. Gansey wants to look for the ley line and they're usually easier to spot from the air."

"And of course he just . . . got a helicopter."

"He's Gansey."

There was another long pause. It was a thinking pause, Adam thought, so he didn't interrupt it. Finally, Blue said, "OK, I'll come. Is this a. . . What is this?"

Adam replied truthfully, "I have no idea."

TWENTY-ONE

It was remarkably easy to disobey Maura.

Maura Sargent had very little experience disciplining children, and Blue had very little experience being disciplined, so there was nothing to stop Blue from going with Adam when he met her in front of the house. She didn't even feel guilty, yet, because she had no practice in that, either. Really, the most remarkable thing about the entire situation was how *hopeful* she felt, against all odds. She was going against her mother's wishes, meeting with a boy, meeting with a *raven* boy. She should've been dreading it.

But it was very difficult to imagine Adam as a raven boy as he greeted her, his hands neatly in his pockets, scented with the dusty odour of mown grass. His bruise was older and therefore more dreadful looking.

"You look nice," he said, walking with her down the pavement.

She was uncertain if he was being serious. She wore heavy boots she'd found at the Goodwill (she'd attacked them with embroidery thread and a very sturdy needle) and a dress she'd made a few months earlier, constructed from several different layers of green fabric. Some of them striped. Some of them crochet. Some of them transparent. It made Adam look quite conservative, like she was abducting him. They did not, Blue mused with a bit of unease, look anything like a couple.

"Thanks," she replied. Then, fast, before she could lose her nerve, "Why did you want my number?"

Adam kept walking, but he didn't look away. He seemed shy until he didn't. "Why wouldn't I?"

"Don't take this the wrong way," Blue replied. Her cheeks felt a little warm, but she was well into this conversation and she couldn't back down now. "Because I know you're going to think I feel bad about it, and I don't."

"All right."

"Because I'm not pretty. Not in the way that Aglionby boys seem to like."

"I go to Aglionby," Adam said.

Adam did not seem to go to Aglionby like other boys went to Aglionby.

"I think you're pretty," he said.

When he said it, she heard his Henrietta accent for the first time that day: a *long* vowel and *pretty* like it rhymed with *biddy*. In a nearby tree, a cardinal went *wheek. wheek. wheek.* Adam's trainers scuffed on the pavement. Blue considered what he had said and then she considered it some more.

"*Pshaw*," she said finally. She felt like when she'd first read his card with the flowers. Weirdly undone. It was like his words had spun tight some sort of thread between them, and she felt like she ought to somehow ease the tension. "But thanks. I think you're pretty, too."

He laughed his surprised laugh.

"I have another question," Blue said. "Do you remember the last thing my mother said to Gansey?"

His rueful face made it clear that he did.

"Right." Blue took a deep breath. "She said she wouldn't help. But I didn't."

After he'd called, she'd hastily scrawled an unspecific map to the unnamed church where she'd sat with Neeve on St Mark's Eve. It was just a few scratched parallel lines to indicate the main road, some spidery named cross streets, and finally, a square labelled only THE CHURCH.

She handed Adam this map, unimpressive on a wrinkled piece of notebook paper. Then, from her bag, she handed him Gansey's journal.

Adam stopped walking. Blue, a metre ahead of him, waited as he frowned at the things in his hands. He held the journal very carefully, like it was important to him, or perhaps like it was important to someone who was important to him. Desperately she wanted him to both trust her and respect her, and she could tell from his face that she didn't have much time to accomplish either.

"Gansey left that at Nino's," she said quickly. "The book. I know I should've given it back at the reading, but my mom . . . well, you saw her. She doesn't normally – she isn't normally like that. I didn't know what to think. Here's the thing. I want to be in on this thing, that you guys are doing. Like, if there really is something supernatural going on, I want to see it. That's all."

Adam merely asked, "Why?"

With him, there was never any option but the truth, said as simply as possible. She didn't think he would stand for anything else. "I'm the only person in my family who's not psychic. You heard my mom; I just make things easier for people who *are* psychic. If magic exists, I just want to see it. Just once."

"You're as bad as Gansey," Adam said, but he didn't sound as if he thought that was very bad at all. "He doesn't need anything but to know it's real."

He tilted the notebook paper this way and that. Blue was instantly relieved; she hadn't realized how still he'd been until he'd begun to move again, and now it was like tension had been bled out of the air.

"That's the way to the corpse ro – the ley line," she explained, pointing at her scratchy map. "The church is on the ley line."

"You're sure?"

Blue gave him a deeply withering look. "Look, either you're going to believe me or not. *You're* the one who asked me along. 'Exploring'!"

Adam's face melted into a grin, an expression so unlike his usual one that his features needed to completely shift to accommodate it. "So you don't do anything quiet, do you?"

The way he said it, she could tell that he was impressed with her in the way that men were usually impressed with Orla. Blue very much liked that, especially since she hadn't had to do anything other than be herself to earn it. "Nothing worth doing."

"Well," he said, "I think you'll find I do pretty much everything quiet. If you can be all right with that, I guess we'll be fine."

It turned out that she had walked or biked past Gansey's apartment every single day of the year, on the way to school and to Nino's. As they walked towards the massive warehouse, she spotted the fiendishly orange glint of the Camaro in the overgrown car park and, only a hundred metres away, a glistening navy blue helicopter.

She hadn't really believed the part about the helicopter. Not in a way that prepared her for seeing an actual, life-sized helicopter, sitting there in the car park, looking normal, like someone would park an SUV.

Blue stopped in her tracks and breathed, "Whew."

"I know," Adam said.

And here, again, was Gansey, and again Blue had a strange shock of reconciling the image of him as a spirit and the reality of him beside a helicopter.

"*Finally!*" he shouted, jogging out towards them. He was still wearing those idiotic Top-Siders she'd noticed at the reading, this time paired with cargo shorts and a yellow polo shirt that made it look as if he were prepared for any sort of emergency, so long as the emergency involved him falling on to a yacht. In his hand he held a container of organic apple juice.

He pointed his no-pesticides juice at Blue. "Are you coming with?"

Just as at the reading, Blue felt cheap and small and stupid just by being in his presence. Clipping her Henrietta vowels as best as she could, she answered, "Coming along in the helicopter you just happen to have at your beck and call, you mean?"

Gansey slung a burnished leather backpack over his burnished cotton shoulders. His smile was gracious and inclusive, as if her mother hadn't recently refused to assist him in any way, as if she hadn't just been borderline rude. "You say that like it's a bad thing."

Behind him, the helicopter began to roar to life. Adam

stretched out the journal to Gansey, who looked startled. Just a tiny bit of his composure slid, enough for Blue to see once more that it was part of his President Mobile Phone mask.

"Where was it?" yelled Gansey.

And he had to yell. Now that it was running, the blades of the helicopter didn't so much roar as scream. Air beat against Blue's ears, more feeling than sound.

Adam pointed at Blue.

"Thanks," Gansey shouted back. It was a default answer, she saw; he fell back on to his powerful politeness when he was taken by surprise. Also, he was still watching Adam, taking his cues from him as to how he should react to her. Adam nodded, once, briefly, and the mask slipped just a little more. Blue wondered if the President Mobile Phone demeanour ever vanished completely when he was around his friends. Maybe the Gansey she'd seen in the churchyard was what lay beneath.

That was a sobering thought.

The air rumbled around them. Blue felt like her dress would fly away. She asked, "Is this thing safe?"

"Safe as life," Gansey replied. "Adam, we're behind schedule! Blue, if you're coming, tighten your liberty bodice and come on." As he ducked to approach the helicopter, his shirt, too, flapped against his back.

Blue was suddenly a little nervous. It wasn't that she was scared, exactly. It was just that she hadn't psychologically prepared herself for leaving the ground with a bunch of raven boys when she'd woken up this morning. The helicopter, for all its size and noise, seemed like a pretty insubstantial thing to trust her life to, and the boys felt like strangers. Now, it felt like she was truly disobeying Maura.

"I've never flown," she confessed to Adam, a shout to be heard over the whine of the helicopter.

"Ever?" Adam shouted back.

She shook her head. He put his mouth right against her ear so that she could hear him. He smelled like summer and cheap shampoo. She felt a tickle go all the way from her belly button to her feet.

"I've flown once," he replied. His breath was hot on her skin. Blue was paralysed; all she could think was *This is how close a kiss is.* It felt every bit as dangerous as she'd imagined. He added, "I hated it."

A moment passed, both of them motionless. She needed to tell him that he couldn't kiss her – just in case he was her true love – but how could she? How could she tell a boy that before she even knew if he wanted to kiss her at all?

She felt him take her hand. His palm was sweaty. He really did hate flying.

At the door to the helicopter, Gansey looked back over his shoulder at them, his smile complicated when he saw them holding hands.

"I hate this," Adam shouted at Gansey. His cheeks were red.

"I know," Gansey yelled back.

Inside the helicopter, there was room for three passengers on a bench seat in the back, and one in a utilitarian seat beside the pilot. The interior would have resembled the back seat of a really big car if the seat belts hadn't had five-point fasteners that looked like they belonged in an X-wing fighter. Blue didn't like to think why passengers had to be strapped down so securely; possibly they were expecting people to be bounced against the walls.

Ronan, the raven boy who was more raven boy than the others, was already installed in a window seat. He didn't smile when he looked up. Adam, punching Ronan's arm, took the middle seat, while Blue took the remaining window seat. As she toyed with the seat belt straps, Gansey leaned into the cabin to knock knuckles with Adam.

A few minutes later, when Gansey climbed into the front seat beside the pilot, she saw that he was grinning, effusive and earnest, incredibly excited to be going wherever they were going. It was nothing like his previous, polished demeanour. It was some private joy that she managed to be in on by virtue of being in the helicopter and, just like that, Blue was excited, too.

Adam leaned towards her as if he was about to say something, but ultimately, he just shook his head, smiling, like Gansey was a joke that was too complicated to explain.

In the front, Gansey turned to the pilot, who surprised Blue a little – a young woman with an impressively straight nose, her brown hair swept into a beautiful knot, headphones clamping down any loose strands. She seemed to find Blue and Adam's proximity far more interesting than Gansey had.

The pilot shouted at Gansey, "Aren't you going to introduce us, Dick?"

Gansey made a face.

"Blue," he said, "I'd like you to meet my sister, Helen."

TWENTY-TWO

There wasn't much Gansey didn't like about flying. He liked airports, with their masses of people all *doing* things, and he liked planes, with their thick-paned windows and fold-out trays. The way that a jet charged down a runway reminded him of how the Camaro pressed him back in the driver's seat when he hit the gas. The whine of a helicopter sounded like productivity. He liked the little knobs and toggles and gauges of cockpits, and he liked the technological backwardness of the simple clasp seat belts. Gansey derived a large part of his pleasure from meeting goals, and a large part of that large part was pleased by meeting goals efficiently. There was nothing more efficient than aiming for your destination as the crow flew.

And of course, from three hundred metres, Henrietta took Gansey's breath away.

Below them, the surface of the world was deeply green, and cutting through the green was a narrow, shining river, a mirror to the sky. He could follow it with his eyes all the way to the mountains.

Now that they were in the air, Gansey was feeling a little anxious. With Blue here, he was beginning to feel as if possibly he'd overdone it with the helicopter.

He wondered if it would make Blue feel better or worse to know that it was Helen's helicopter, that he hadn't paid anything today for the use of it. Probably worse. Remembering his vow to at least do no harm with his words, he kept his mouth shut.

"There she is," Helen's voice reported directly into Gansey's ears; in the helicopter, they all wore headsets to allow them to converse through the ceaseless noise of the blades and the engine. "Gansey's girlfriend."

Ronan's snort barely made it through his headset, but Gansey had heard it often enough to know it was there.

Blue said, "She must be pretty big to see her from up here."

"Henrietta," Helen replied. She peered to the left of the helo as she banked. "They're getting married. They haven't set a date yet."

"If you're going to embarrass me, I'll throw you out and fly myself," Gansey said from the seat beside her. This was not a true threat. Not only would he not push Helen out at this altitude, he wasn't legal to fly without her. Also, truth be told, he wasn't very good at flying a helicopter, despite several lessons. He seemed to lack the important ability to orient himself vertically as well as horizontally, which led to disagreements involving trees. He comforted himself with the knowledge that, at least, he could parallel park very well.

"Did you get Mom a birthday present?" Helen asked.

"Yes," Gansey replied. "Myself."

Helen said, "The gift that keeps on giving."

He said, "I don't think that minor children are required to get gifts for their parents. I'm a dependent.

That's the definition of dependent, is it not?"

"You, a dependent!" his sister said, and laughed. Helen had a laugh like a cartoon character: *Ha ha ha ha!* It was an intimidating laugh that tended to make men suspect that they were possibly the brunt of it. "You haven't been a dependent since you were four. You went straight from kindergarten to old man with a studio apartment."

Gansey made a dismissive hand gesture. His sister was known for hyperbole. "What did *you* get her?"

"It's a surprise," Helen replied loftily, tapping some sort of toggle switch with a pink-nailed finger. The pink was the only fanciful thing about her. Helen was beautiful in the way a super-computer was beautiful: sleek with elegant but utilitarian styling, full of top-notch technological know-how, far too expensive for most people to possess.

"That means it's glassware."

Gansey's mother collected rare painted plates with the same obsessive fervor that Gansey collected facts about Glendower. He had a hard time seeing the allure of a plate robbed of its original purpose, but his mother's collection had been featured in magazines and was insured for more than his father, so clearly she was not alone in her passion.

Helen was stony. "I don't want to hear it. You didn't get her anything."

"I didn't say anything about it!"

"You called it glassware."

He asked, "What should I have said?"

"They're not all glass. This one I've found her is not glass."

"Then she won't like it."

Helen's face shifted from stony to very stony. She

glowered at her GPS. Gansey didn't like to think of how much time she'd invested in her non-glass plate. He didn't like to see either of the women in his family disappointed; it ruined perfectly good meals.

Helen was still silent, so Gansey began to think about Blue. Something about her was discomfiting him, though he couldn't put his finger on it. Taking a mint leaf from his pocket, Gansey put it into his mouth and watched the familiar Henrietta roads snake below them. From the air, the curves looked less perilous than they felt in the Camaro. What *was* it about Blue? Adam was not suspicious of her, and he was suspicious of everyone. But then again, he was clearly infatuated. That, too, was unfamiliar ground for Gansey.

"Adam," he said. There was no answer, and Gansey looked over his shoulder. Adam's headphones were looped around his neck and he was leaned over beside Blue, pointing something out on the ground below. As she'd shifted, Blue's dress had got hitched up and Gansey could see a long, slender triangle of her thigh. Adam's hand was braced a few centimetres away on the seat, knuckles pale with his hatred of flying. There was nothing particularly intimate about the way they sat, but something about the scene made Gansey feel strange, like he'd heard an unpleasant statement and later forgotten everything about the words but the way they had made him feel.

"Adam!" Gansey shouted.

His friend's head jerked up, face startled. He hurried to pull his headset back on. His voice came through the headphones. "Are you done talking about your mom's plates?"

"Very. Where should we go this time? I was thinking maybe back to the church where I recorded the voice."

Adam handed Gansey a wrinkled piece of paper.

Gansey flattened the paper and found a crude map. "What's this?"

"Blue."

Gansey looked at her intently, trying to decide if she had anything to gain by misdirecting them. She didn't flinch from his gaze. Turning back around, he spread the paper flat on the controls in front of him. "Make that happen, Helen."

Helen banked to follow the new direction. The church Blue directed them towards was probably forty minutes' drive from Henrietta, but as the bird flew, it was only fifteen. Without a quiet noise from Blue, Gansey would've missed it. It was a ruin, hollowed and overgrown. A narrow line of an old, old stone wall was visible around it, as well as an impression on the ground where an additional wall must have originally been. "That's it?"

"That's all there is left."

Something inside Gansey went very still and quiet.

He said, "What did you say?"

"It's a ruin, but—"

"No," he said. "Say precisely what you said before. Please."

Blue cast a glance towards Adam, who shrugged. "I don't *remember* what I said. Was it . . . that's all there is?"

That's all.

Is that all?

That was what had been nagging him all this time. He *knew* he recognized her voice. He knew that Henrietta accent, he knew that cadence.

It was Blue's voice on the recorder.

Gansey.

Is that all?

That's all there is.

"I'm not made out of fuel," Helen snapped, as if she'd already said it once and Gansey had missed it. Maybe he had. "Tell me where to go from here."

What does this mean? Once more, he began to feel the press of responsibility, awe, something bigger than him. At once he was anticipatory and afraid.

"What's the lay of the line, Blue?" Adam asked.

Blue, who had her thumb and forefinger pressed against the glass as if she was measuring something, answered, "There. Towards the mountains. Fly. . . Do you see those two oak trees? The church is one point, and another point is right between them. If we make a straight line between those two, that's the path."

If it had been Blue he'd been talking to on St Mark's Eve, what did that *mean*?

"Are you certain?" This was Helen, in her brisk supercomputer voice. "I only have an hour and a half of fuel."

Blue sounded a little indignant. "I wouldn't have *said* it if I wasn't sure."

Helen smiled faintly and pushed the helicopter in the direction Blue had indicated.

"Blue."

It was Ronan's voice, for the first time, and everyone, even Helen, twisted their heads towards him. His head was cocked in a way that Gansey recognized as dangerous. Something in his eyes was sharp as he stared at Blue. He asked, "Do you know Gansey?"

Gansey remembered Ronan leaning against the Pig,

playing the recording over and over again.

Blue looked defensive under their stares. She said reluctantly, "Only his name."

With his fingers linked loosely together, elbows on his knees, Ronan leaned forward across Adam to be closer to Blue. He could be unbelievably threatening.

"And how is it," he asked, "you came to know Gansey's name?"

To her credit, Blue didn't back down. Her ears were pink, but she said, "First of all, get out of my face."

"What if I don't?"

"Ronan," said Gansey.

Ronan sat back.

"I would like to know, though," Gansey said. His heart felt like it weighed nothing at all.

Looking down, Blue bunched a few of the layers of her improbable dress in her hands. Finally, she said, "I guess that's fair." She pointed at Ronan. She looked angry. "But *that* is not the way to get me to answer anything. Next time he gets in my face, I let you find this thing on your own. I'll – look. I'll tell you how I knew your name if you explain to me what that shape is that you have in your journal."

"Tell me why we're negotiating with terrorists?" Ronan asked.

"Since when am I a terrorist?" demanded Blue. "Seems to me I came bringing something you guys wanted and you're being dicks."

"Not all of us," Adam said.

"I am not being a dick," Gansey said. He was uncomfortable with the idea that she might not like him. "Now, what is this thing you want to know?"

Blue reached her hand out. "Hold on, I'll show you what I mean."

Gansey let her take the journal again. Leafing through the pages, she turned it to him so that she could see the one in question. The page detailed an artefact he'd found in Pennsylvania. He'd also doodled on it in several places.

"I believe that is a man chasing a car," Gansey said.

"Not that. This." She pointed to one of the other doodles.

"They're ley lines." He stretched out a hand for the journal. For a strange, hyperaware moment, he realized how closely she watched him as he took it. He didn't think it missed her notice how his left hand curved familiarly around the leather binding, how the thumb and finger on his right hand knew just how much pressure to apply to coax the pages to spread where he wanted them to. The journal and Gansey were clearly long-acquainted, and he wanted her to know.

This is me. The real me.

He didn't want to analyse the source of this impulse too hard. He focused on flipping through the journal instead. It took him no time at all to find the desired page – a map of the United States, marked all over with curving lines.

He traced a finger over one line that stretched through New York City and Washington, D.C. Another intersecting line that stretched from Boston to St Louis.

A third that cut horizontally across the first two, stretching through Virginia and Kentucky and on westward. There was, as always, something satisfying about tracing the lines, something that called to mind scavenger hunts and childhood drawings.

"These are the three main lines," Gansey said. "The ones that seem to matter."

"Seem to matter how?"

"How much of this did you read?"

"Um. Some. A lot. Most."

He continued, "The ones that seem to matter as far as finding Glendower. That line across Virginia is the one that connects us to the UK. The United Kingdom."

She rolled her eyes dramatically enough that he caught the gesture without turning his head. "I know what the UK is, thanks. The public school system isn't that bad."

He'd managed to offend again, with no effort at all. He concurred, "Surely not. Those other two lines have a lot of reports of unusual sightings on them. Of . . . paranormal stuff. Poltergeists and Mothmen and black dogs."

But his hesitation was unnecessary; Blue didn't scoff.

"My mother drew that shape," she said. "The ley lines. So did Nee – one of the other women here. They didn't know what it was, though, only that it would be significant. That's why I wanted to know."

"Now you," Ronan said to Blue.

"I – saw Gansey's spirit," she said. "I've never seen one before. I don't see things like that, but this time, I did. I asked you your name, and you told me. 'Gansey. That's all there is.' Honestly, it's part of the reason why I wanted to come along today."

This answer satisfied Gansey fairly well – she was, after all, the daughter of a psychic, and it matched the account his recorder gave – though it struck him as a partial answer. Ronan demanded, "Saw him where?"

"While I was sitting outside with one of my half aunts."

This seemed to satisfy Ronan as well, because he asked, "What's the other half of her?"

"God, Ronan," Adam said. "Enough."

There was a moment of tense silence, occupied only by the continuous droning whine of the helicopter. They were waiting, Gansey knew, for his verdict. Did he believe her answer, did he think they should follow her directions, did he trust her?

Her voice was on the recorder. He felt like he didn't have a choice. What he was thinking, but didn't want to say with Helen listening in, was, *You're right, Ronan, it's starting, something's starting.* He was also thinking, *Tell me what you think of her, Adam. Tell me why you trust her. Don't make me decide for once. I don't know if I'm right.* But what he said was, "I'm going to need everyone to be straight with each other from now on. No more games. This isn't just for Blue, either. All of us."

Ronan said, "I'm always straight."

Adam replied, "Oh, man, that's the biggest lie you've ever told."

Blue said, "OK."

Gansey suspected that none of them were being completely honest with their replies, but at least he'd told them what he wanted. Sometimes all he could hope for was getting it on the record.

The headsets fell silent as Adam, Blue and Gansey

all stared intently out of the window. Below them was green and more green, everything toy-like and quaint from this height, a play-set of velvet fields and broccoli trees.

"What are we looking for?" Helen asked.

Gansey said, "The usual."

"What's 'the usual'?" Blue asked.

The usual more often than not turned out to be acres of nothing, but Gansey said, "Sometimes, the ley lines are marked in ways that are visible from the air. Like in the UK, some of the lines are marked with horses carved into hillsides."

He'd been in a small fixed-wing plane with Malory the first time that he'd seen the Uffington Horse, a hundred-metre horse scraped into the side of an English chalk hill. Like everything associated with the ley lines, the horse was not quite . . . ordinary. The horse was stretched and stylized, an elegant, eerie silhouette that was more suggestion of a horse than actual horse.

"Tell her about Nazca," murmured Adam.

"Oh, right," Gansey said. Even though Blue had read much of the journal, there was a lot that wasn't in it, and unlike Ronan and Adam and Noah, she hadn't lived this life for the past year. It was suddenly difficult not to be excited by the idea of explaining it all to her. The story always sounded more plausible when he laid all of the facts out at once.

He continued, "In Peru, there are hundreds of lines cut into the ground in the shapes of things like birds and monkeys and men and imaginary creatures. Thousands of years old, but they only make sense from the air. From an aeroplane. They're too big to see from the ground. When you're standing next to them, they just look like scraped footpaths."

"You've seen them in person," Blue said.

When Gansey had seen the Nazca Lines for himself, massive and strange and symmetrical, he'd known that he wouldn't be able to give up until he found Glendower. The scale of the lines was what had struck him first – hundreds upon hundreds of feet of curious drawings in the middle of the desert. He'd been stunned by the precision. The drawings were mathematical in their perfection, faultless in their symmetry. And the last thing to hit him, right in his gut, was the emotional impact, a mysterious, raw ache that wouldn't go away. Gansey felt like he couldn't survive not knowing if the lines *meant* something.

That was the only part of his hunt for Glendower that he could never seem to explain to people.

"Gansey," Adam said. "What's that, there?"

The helicopter slowed as all four passengers craned their necks. By now, they were deep into the mountains, and the ground had risen to meet them. All around them were rippling flanks of mysterious green forests, a rolling dark sea from above. Among the slopes and gullies, however, was a slanting, green-carpeted field marked by a pale fracture of lines.

"Does it make a shape?" he asked. "Helen, *stop*. Stop!"

"Do you think this is a bicycle?" demanded Helen, but the helicopter's forward progress stopped.

"Look," Adam said. "There's a wing, there. And there, a beak. A bird?"

"No," Ronan said, voice cold and even. "Not just a bird. It's a raven."

Slowly the form became clear to Gansey, emerging from the overgrown grass: a bird, yes, neck twisted backwards and wings pressed as if in a book. Tail feathers splayed and claws simplified.

Ronan was right. Even stylized, the dome of the head, the generous curve of the beak and the ruffle of feathers on its neck made the bird unmistakably a raven.

His skin prickled.

"Put the helicopter down," Gansey said immediately.

Helen replied, "I can't land on private property."

He cast an entreating gaze at his sister. He needed to write down the GPS coordinates. He needed to take a photo for his records. He needed to sketch the shape of it in his journal. More than anything, he needed to touch the lines of the bird and make it real in his head. "Helen, two seconds."

Her return look was knowing; it was the sort of condescending look that might have caused arguments when he was younger and more easily riled. "If the landowner discovers me there and decides to press charges, I could lose my licence."

"Two seconds. You saw. There's no one around here for miles and miles, no houses."

Helen's gaze was very level. "I'm supposed to be at Mom and Dad's in two hours."

"Two seconds."

Finally, she rolled her eyes and sat back in her seat. Shaking her head, she turned back towards the controls.

"Thank you, Helen," Adam said.

"Two seconds," she repeated grimly. "If you aren't done by then, I'm taking off without you."

The helicopter landed five metres away from the strange raven's heart.

TWENTY-THREE

As soon as the helicopter had touched down, Gansey leapt from the cabin and strode into the thigh-high grass as if he owned the place, Ronan by his side. Through the open door of the helo, Blue heard him say Noah's name to the phone before repeating the GPS coordinates for the field. He was energized and powerful, a king in his castle.

Blue, on the other hand, was a little slower. For a multitude of reasons, her legs felt a little gelled after flying. She wasn't sure if not telling Gansey the entire truth about St Mark's Eve was the right decision, and she was worried about Ronan trying to speak to her again.

It smelled wonderful in the middle of this field, though — all grass and trees and, somewhere, water, and lots of it. Blue thought she might live here quite happily. Beside her, Adam shielded his eyes. He looked at home here, his hair the same colourless brown as the tips of old grass, and he looked more handsome than Blue remembered. She thought about how Adam had taken her hand earlier and considered how much she'd like for him to do it again.

With some surprise, Adam said, "Those lines are pretty invisible from here." He was right, of course. Though

Blue had just seen the raven as they touched down beside it, whatever geographical feature had made the shape was now completely hidden. "I still hate flying. Sorry about Ronan."

"The flying part wasn't bad," Blue said. Actually, aside from Ronan, she had kind of liked it – the sense of floating in a very noisy bubble where all directions were possible. "I thought it would be worse. You sort of have to give up control, don't you, and then it's OK. Now, Ronan. . ."

"He's a pit bull," Adam said.

"I know some really nice pit bulls." One of the dogs Blue walked each week was a cow-printed pit bull with as nice a smile as you could hope for in a canine.

"He's the kind of pit that makes the evening news. Gansey's trying to retrain him."

"How noble."

"It makes him feel better about being Gansey."

Blue didn't doubt it. "Sometimes he's very condescending."

Adam looked at the ground. "He doesn't mean to be. It's all that blue blood in his veins."

He was about to say something else when a shout interrupted him.

"*ARE YOU LISTENING, GLENDOWER? I AM COMING TO FIND YOU!*" Gansey's voice, ebullient and ringing, echoed off the tree-covered slopes around the field. Adam and Blue found him standing in the middle of a clear, pale path, his arms stretched out and his head tilted back as he shouted into the air. Adam's mouth made the soundless shape of a laugh.

Gansey grinned at them both. He was hard to resist in

this form: glowing with rows and rows of white teeth, a college brochure in the making.

"Oyster shells," he said, leaning to pick up one of the pale objects that made up the path. The fragment was pure white, the edges blunt and worn. "That's what makes up the raven. Like they use for roads down in the tidewater area. Oyster shells on bare rock. What do you think of *that*?"

"I think that's a lot of oyster shells to bring from the coast," Adam replied. "I also think Glendower would've come from the coast, too."

Gansey pointed at Adam by way of a reply.

Blue put her hands on her hips. "So you think they put Glendower's body on a boat in Wales, sailed over to Virginia, then brought him up to the mountains. Why?"

"Energy," Gansey replied. Rummaging in his bag, he removed a small black box that looked a lot like a very small car battery.

Blue asked, "What's that? It looks expensive."

He twiddled with switches on the side as he explained, "An electromagnetic-frequency reader. It monitors energy levels. Some people use them for ghost hunting. It's supposed to have a high reading when you're near a spirit. But it's also supposed to read high when you're near an energy source. Like a ley line."

She scowled at the gadget. A box to register magic seemed to insult both the box holder and magic. "And of course you have an electromagnorific button thing. Everyone has one of them."

Gansey held the reader above his head as if he were calling aliens. "You find it not normal?"

She could tell that he very much wanted her to say that he wasn't normal, so she replied, "Oh, I'm sure it's quite normal in *some* circles."

He looked a little hurt, but most of his attention was on the reader, which showed two faint red lights. He remarked, "I'd like to be in those circles. So, like I said, energy. One of the other names for the ley line is corpse—"

"Corpse road," Blue interrupted. "I know."

He looked pleased and magnanimous, as if she were a prize pupil. "So school me. You probably know better than I."

As before, his accent was the broad, glorious old Virginia accent, and Blue's words felt clumsy beside him.

"I just know that the dead travel in straight lines," she said. "That they used to carry corpses in straight lines to churches to bury them. Along what you call the ley line. It was supposed to be really bad to take them any other route than the way they'd choose to travel as a spirit."

"Right," he said. "So it stands to reason there's something about the line that fortifies or protects a corpse. The soul. The . . . *animus*. The quiddity of it."

"Gansey, seriously," Adam interrupted, to Blue's relief. "Nobody knows what quiddity is."

"The *whatness*, Adam. Whatever it is that makes a person what they are. If they removed Glendower from the corpse road, I think the magic that keeps him asleep would be disrupted."

She said, "Basically, you mean he would die for good if he was removed from the line."

"Yes," Gansey said. The blinking lights on his machine had begun to flash more heavily, leading them over the raven's beak and towards the tree line where Ronan already stood. Blue lifted her arms up so the heads of the grass wouldn't hit the backs of her hands; it was up to her waist in some places.

She asked, "And why not just leave him in Wales? Isn't that where they want him to wake up and be a hero?"

"It was an uprising, and he was a traitor to the English crown," Gansey said. The easy way that he began the story, at once striding through grass and eyeing the EMF reader, let Blue know that he had told it many times before. "Glendower fought the English for years, and it was ugly, all struggle between noble families with mixed allegiances. The Welsh resistance failed. Glendower disappeared. If the English had known where he was, dead or alive, there's no way they'd treat his body the way the Welsh wanted it treated. Haven't you heard of being hung, drawn and quartered?"

Blue asked, "Is it as painful as conversations with Ronan?"

Gansey cast a glance over to Ronan, who was a small, indistinct form by the trees. Adam audibly swallowed a laugh.

"Depends on if Ronan is sober," Gansey answered.

Adam asked, "What is he doing, anyway?"

"Peeing."

"Trust Lynch to deface a place like this five minutes after getting here."

"Deface? Marking his territory."

"He must own more of Virginia than your father, then."

"I don't think he's ever used an indoor toilet, now that I consider it."

This all seemed very manly and Aglionby to Blue, this calling of one another by last names and bantering about outdoor urinary habits. It also seemed like it could go on for a long time, so she interrupted, changing the subject back to Glendower. "They'd really go to all this trouble to hide his body?"

Gansey said, "Well, Ned Kelly."

He delivered the nonsensical statement so matter-of-factly that Blue felt abruptly stupid, as if maybe the public school system really *was* lacking.

Then Adam said, with a glance towards Blue, "Nobody knows who Ned Kelly is, either, Gansey."

"Really?" Gansey asked, so innocently startled by this that it was clear that Adam had been right before – he hadn't meant to be condescending. "He was an Australian outlaw. When the British caught him, they did awful things with his body. I think the chief of police used his head as a paperweight for a while. Just think what Glendower's enemies would do to him! If the Welsh wanted a shot at Glendower being resurrected, they would've wanted his body unmolested."

"Why the mountains, then?" Blue insisted. "Why isn't he right on the shore?"

This seemed to remind Gansey of something, because instead of replying to her, he turned to Adam. "I called Malory about that ritual, to see if he'd tried it. He said he didn't think it could be performed just anywhere on the ley line. He guessed it had to be done on the 'heart' of it, where the most energy is. I'm thinking that some place like that is also where they'd want Glendower."

Adam turned to Blue. "What about *your* energy?"

The question took her by surprise. "What?"

"You said that you made things louder for other

psychics," Adam said. "Is that about energy?"

Blue was absurdly pleased that he remembered, and also absurdly pleased that he'd replied to her instead of Gansey, who was now swatting gnats out of his eyes and waiting for her response.

"Yes," she said. "I guess I make things that need energy stronger. I'm like a walking battery."

"You're the table everyone wants at Starbucks," Gansey mused as he began to walk again.

Blue blinked. "What?"

Over his shoulder, Gansey said, "Next to the wall plug." He pressed the EMF reader into the side of a tree and observed both objects with great interest.

Adam shook his head at Blue. To Gansey, he said, "I'm *saying* that she could maybe turn a regular part of the ley line into a doable place for the ritual. Wait, are we going in the woods? What about Helen?"

"It hasn't been two seconds," Gansey said, although it clearly had been. "That's an interesting idea about the energy. Though – can your battery get drained? By things other than conversations about prostitution?"

She didn't dignify this comment with an immediate response. Instead, she thought about how her mother had said there was nothing to fear from the dead and how Neeve had seemed disbelieving. The church watch had obviously taken *something* from her; maybe there were worse consequences that she had yet to discover.

"Well, this is interesting," Gansey remarked. He straddled a tiny stream at the very edge of the trees. It was really just water that had bubbled up from an underground source, soaking the grass. Gansey's attention was focused entirely on the EMF reader he held directly above the water. The meter was pegged.

"Helen," Adam said warningly. Ronan had rejoined them and both boys looked in the direction of the helicopter.

"I said *this is interesting*," Gansey repeated.

"And I said *Helen*."

"Just a couple of metres."

"She'll be angry."

Gansey's expression was baleful and Blue could see immediately that Adam wouldn't hold out against it.

"I did *tell* you," Adam said.

The stream trickled sluggishly out of the woods from between two diamond-barked dogwoods. With Gansey in the lead, they all followed the water into the trees. Immediately, the temperature dropped several degrees. Blue hadn't realized how much insect noise there was in the field until it was replaced by occasional birdsong under the trees. This was a beautiful, old wood, all massive oak and ash trees finding footing among great slabs of cracked stone. Ferns sprang from rocks and verdant moss grew up the sides of the tree trunks. The air itself was scented with green and growing and water. The light was golden through the leaves. Everything was alive, alive.

She breathed. "This is lovely."

It was for Adam, not Gansey, but she saw Gansey glance over his shoulder at her. Beside him, Ronan was curiously muted, something about his posture defensive.

"What are we even looking for?" Adam asked.

Gansey was a bloodhound, the EMF reader leading him along the widening stream. The moving water had become too wide to straddle, and now it ran in a bed of pebbles and sharp fragments of rock and, strangely enough, a few of the oyster shells. "What we're always looking for."

Adam warned, "Helen is going to hate you."

"She'll text me if she gets too mad," Gansey said. To demonstrate, he slid his phone out of his pocket. "Oh — there's no signal."

Given their location in the mountains, the lack of signal was unsurprising, but Gansey stopped short. While the four of them made an uneven circle, he thumbed through the screens on his phone. In his other hand, the EMF reader glowed solid red. His voice sounded a little strange when he asked, "Is anyone else wearing a watch?"

Weekends were not generally days of precise timing for Blue, so she was not, and Ronan had only his few knotted leather strands around his arm. Adam lifted his wrist. He wore a cheap-looking watch with a grubby band.

"I am," he said, adding ruefully, "but it doesn't seem to be working."

Without speaking, Gansey turned the face of his phone to them. It was set to the clock function and it took Blue a moment to realize that none of the hands were moving. For a long moment the four of them just looked at the three still hands on the phone's clock face. Blue's heart marked off every second the clock didn't.

"Is it—" Adam started, and then stopped. He tried again, "Is it because the power is being affected from the energy of the line?"

Ronan's voice was cutting. "Affecting your watch? Your windup watch?"

"It's true," Gansey answered. "My phone's still on. So's the reader. It's only that the time has . . . I wonder if. . ."

But there were no answers and they all knew it.

"I want to go on," Gansey said. "Just a little further."

He waited to see if they would stop him. No one said anything, but as Gansey set off again, clambering over the top of a slab of stone, Ronan beside him, Adam glanced at Blue. His expression asked, *Are you OK?*

She *was* OK, but in the way she'd been OK before the helicopter. It was not that she was scared of flashing lights on the EMF reader or Adam's watch refusing to work, but she hadn't got out of bed in the morning expecting to encounter a place where possibly time didn't work.

Blue stretched her hand out.

Adam took it without hesitation, like he'd been waiting for her to offer it. He said in a low voice, just for her, "My heart is beating like crazy right now."

Strangely enough, it was not his fingers twined in hers that affected Blue the strongest, it was where his warm wrist pressed against hers above their hands.

I need to tell him he can't kiss me, she thought.

But not yet. Right now, she wanted to feel his skin pressed against hers, both of their pulses rapid and uncertain.

Hand in hand, they climbed after Gansey. The trees grew even larger, some of them grown together into trunks like castles, turreted and huge. The canopy soared high overhead, rustling and reverent. Everything was green, green, green. Somewhere ahead, water splashed.

For one brief moment, Blue thought she heard music.

"Noah?"

Gansey's voice sounded forlorn. He'd stopped by a mighty beech tree and now he searched around himself. Catching up to him, Blue realized he'd stopped by the shore of a mountain pool that fed the stream they'd been following. The pool was only a few centimetres deep and perfectly clear. The water was so transparent that it begged to be touched.

"I thought I heard—" Gansey broke off. His eyes dropped to where Adam held Blue's hand. Again, his face was somehow puzzled by the fact of their hand-holding. Adam's grip tightened, although she didn't think he meant for it to.

This was a wordless discussion, too, though she didn't think either of the boys knew what they were trying to say.

Gansey turned to the pool of water. In his hand, the EMF reader had gone dark. Crouching, he hovered his free hand over the water. His fingers were spread wide, millimetres from the surface. Beneath his hand, the water shifted and darkened, and Blue realized that there were a thousand tiny fish just underneath. They flashed silver and then black as they moved, clinging to the faint shadow he cast.

Adam asked, "How are there fish here?"

The stream they'd followed into the woods was far too shallow for fish, and above them, the pool seemed to be fed by rainfall from higher up the mountain. Fish didn't come from the sky.

Gansey replied, "I don't know."

The fish tumbled and coursed over one another, ceaselessly moving, tiny enigmas. Again, Blue thought she heard music, but when she looked at Adam, she thought perhaps it had just been the sound of his breathing.

Gansey looked up to them and she saw in his face that he loved this place. His bald expression held something new: not the raw delight of finding the ley line or the sly pleasure of teasing Blue. She recognized the strange happiness that came from loving something without knowing why you did, that strange happiness that was sometimes so big that it felt like sadness. It was the way she felt when she looked at the stars.

Just like that, he was a little bit closer to the Gansey that Blue had seen in the churchyard and she found she couldn't bear to look at him.

Instead, she pulled her hand free from Adam to go to the beech tree Gansey stood beside. Carefully, she stepped over the exposed knots of the beech's roots and then she laid her palm on its smooth, grey bark. Like the tree behind her house, this beech's bark was as cold as winter and oddly comforting.

"Adam." This was Ronan's voice, and she heard Adam's footsteps moving cautiously and slowly around the edge of the pool towards it. The sound of snapping branches became softer as he moved further away.

"I don't think these fish are real," Gansey said softly.

It was such a ridiculous thing to say that Blue turned to look at him again. He was tipping his hand back and forth as he watched the water.

"I think they're here because I thought they ought to be here," Gansey said.

Blue replied sarcastically, "OK, God."

He twisted his hand again; she saw the fish's forms flash in the water once more. Hesitant, he went on: "At the reading, what was it that the one woman said? With the hair? She said it was about – perception – no, intention."

"Persephone, Intention is for cards," Blue said "That's for a reading, for letting someone into your head, to see patterns in the future and the past. Not for *fish*. How could intention work on a fish? Life isn't negotiable."

He asked, "What colour were the fish when we arrived?"

They'd been black and silver, or at least they had looked it in the reflection. Gansey, she was certain, was reaching for signs of inexplicable magic, but she wasn't going to be swayed so easily. Blue and brown could look black or silver, depending on the light. Nonetheless, she joined him, crouching in the moist dirt beside the pool. The fish were all dark and indistinct in the shadow of his hand.

"I was watching them and wondering how they'd got here and then I remembered that there was a kind of trout that often live in smaller creeks," Gansey said. "Wild brook trout, I think they're called. I thought, that would make a little more sense. Maybe they were introduced by man, somehow, in this pool, or a pool further up the stream. That's what I was thinking. Brook trout are silver on top and red on the bottom."

"*OK*," she said.

Gansey's outstretched hand was very still. "Tell me there were no red fish in this pool when we arrived."

When she didn't answer, he looked at her. She shook her head. There'd definitely been no red.

He pulled his hand back quickly.

The tiny school of fish darted and leapt for cover, but not before Blue saw that every one of them was silver and red.

Not a little red, but bright red, sunset red, red as a dream. Like they had never been any other colour.

"I don't understand," Blue said. Something in her ached, though, like she did understand, but couldn't put words to it, wrap her thoughts around it. She felt like she was a part of a dream this place was having, or it was a part of a dream of hers.

"I don't, either."

They both turned their head at the same time then, at the sound of a voice from their left.

"Was that Adam?" Blue asked. It seemed strange that she had to ask, but nothing felt very definite.

Again they heard Adam's voice, more clearly this time. He and Ronan stood on the other side of the pool. Just behind him was an oak tree. A man-sized rotten cavity gaped blackly in its trunk. In the pool at his feet was a reflection of both Adam and the tree, the mirror image colder and more distant than reality.

Adam rubbed his arms fiercely, as if chilled. Ronan stood beside him, looking over his shoulder at something Blue couldn't see.

"Come here," Adam said. "And stand in there. And tell me if I'm losing my mind." His accent was pronounced, which Blue was beginning to learn meant that he was too bothered to hide it.

Blue peered at the cavity. Like all holes in trees, it looked moist and uneven and black, the fungus in the bark still working away at enlarging the crater. The edges of the entrance were jagged and thin, making the tree's continued survival seem miraculous.

"Are you OK?" Gansey asked.

"Close your eyes," Adam told him. His arms were crossed, his hands gripping his biceps. The way he was breathing reminded Blue of what it felt like to wake after a nightmare, heart pounding, breath snagging, legs aching from a chase you never really ran. "After you stand in there, I mean."

"Did you go in there?" Gansey asked Ronan, who shook his head.

"He's the one who pointed it out," Adam said.

Ronan said, flat as a board, "I'm not going in there." When he said it, it sounded like principle instead of cowardice, like his refusal to take a card at the reading.

"I don't mind," Blue said. "I'll go."

It was hard for her to imagine being intimidated when surrounded by a tree, no matter how strange the forest around it might be. Stepping into the cavity, she turned so that she faced the outside world. The air inside the cavity smelled damp and close. It was warm, too, and although Blue knew it must be because of the rotting process, it made the tree seem as warmblooded as her.

In front of her, Adam's arms were still gripped around himself. *What does he think will happen in here?*

She closed her eyes. Almost at once, she could smell rain – not the scent of rain coming, but the living, shifting odour of a storm currently waging, the wide-open scent of a breeze moving through water. Then she became aware that something was touching her face.

When she opened her eyes, she was both in her body and watching it, nowhere near the cavity of the tree. The Blue that was before her stood close to a boy in an Aglionby jumper. There was a slight stoop to his posture, and his shoulders were spattered darkly with rain. It was his fingers that Blue felt on her face. He touched her cheeks with the backs of his fingers.

Tears coursed down the other Blue's face. Through some strange magic, Blue could feel them on her face as well. She could feel, too, the sick, rising misery she'd felt in the churchyard, the grief that felt bigger than her. The other Blue's tears seemed endless. One drop slid after another, each following an identical path down her cheeks.

The boy in the Aglionby jumper leaned his forehead against Blue's. She felt the pressure of his skin against hers and suddenly she could smell mint.

It'll be OK, Gansey told the other Blue. She could tell that he was afraid. *It'll be OK.*

Impossibly, Blue realized that this other Blue was crying because she loved Gansey. And that the reason Gansey touched her like that, his fingers so careful with her, was because he knew that her kiss could kill him. She could feel how badly the other Blue wanted to kiss him, even as she dreaded it. Though she couldn't understand why, her real, present day memories in the tree cavity were clouded with other false memories of their lips nearly touching, a life this other Blue had already lived.

OK. I'm ready – Gansey's voice caught, just a little. *Blue, kiss me.*

Shaken, Blue opened her eyes for real, and now she saw the darkness of the cavity around her and smelled the dark, rotten scent of the tree again. Her guts were twisted with the ghostly grief and desire she'd felt in the vision. She was sick and embarrassed, and when she stepped out of the tree, she couldn't look at Gansey.

"Well?" Gansey asked.

She said, "It's . . . something."

When she didn't elucidate further, he took her place in the tree.

It had seemed so very real. Was this the future? Was this an alternate future? Was this just a waking dream? She couldn't imagine falling in love with Gansey, of all people, but in that vision, it had seemed not just plausible, but indisputable.

As Gansey turned inside the cavity, Adam took her arm and dragged her closer. He wasn't gentle, but Blue didn't think he meant to be rough. She did startle, though, when he wiped her face with the heel of his other hand; she had been crying real tears.

"I want you to know," Adam whispered furiously, "I would never do that. It wasn't real. I'd *never* do that to him."

His fingers were tight on her arm, and she felt him shaking. Blue blinked at Adam, wiping her cheeks dry. It took her a moment to realize that he must have seen something entirely different than she had.

But if she asked him what he had seen, she'd have to tell him what she saw.

Ronan was staring at them, raw, as if he knew what had happened in the tree, even without attempting it himself.

A metre away in the cavity, Gansey's head was bowed. He looked like a statue in a church, his hands clasped in front of him. There was something very ancient about him just then, with the tree arched over him and his eyelids rendered colourless in the shadows. He was himself, but he was something else, too – that something that Blue had first seen in him at the boys' reading, that sense of *other*ness, of *something more*, seemed to radiate from that still portrait of Gansey enshrined in the dark tree.

Adam's face was turned away, and now, *now*, Blue knew what his expression was: shame. Whatever he had seen in his vision in the hollowed tree, he was certain Gansey was seeing it, too, and he couldn't bear it.

Gansey's eyes flicked open.

"What did you see?" Blue asked.

He cocked his head. It was a slow, dreamlike gesture.

Gansey said, "I saw Glendower."

TWENTY-FOUR

As Adam had warned, it had not taken two seconds to explore the raven cut into the ground, follow the creek into the woods, watch the fish change colours, discover a hallucinatory tree and return to Helen.

According to Gansey's watch, it had taken seven minutes.

Helen had been furious. When Gansey told her that seven minutes was a miracle, and really, they should've been gone forty, it had caused such an argument that Ronan, Adam and Blue had removed their headphones to allow the siblings to duke it out. Without the headphones, of course, the three of them in the rear seat were robbed of the power of speech. It should have created an awkward silence, but instead, it was easier without words.

"It's impossible," Blue said, the moment the helicopter had left the car park quiet enough to speak. "Time couldn't have stopped while we were in the woods."

"Not impossible," Gansey replied, crossing the car park to the building. He ripped open the door to Monmouth's first floor and shouted up into the dim stairwell, "Noah, are you home?"

"It's true," Adam said. "According to ley-line theory, time can be a fluid thing right on the line."

It was one of the more commonly reported effects of ley lines, especially in Scotland. In Scottish folklore, there was a long-held myth that travellers could be "pixy-led", or led astray by territorial fairies. Hikers would set out along a straight trail only to find themselves inexplicably lost, standing in a location they had no recollection of walking to, far away from their starting point, their watch showing minutes before or hours after they'd left. Like they'd tripped on a wrinkle in space/time.

The ley line's energy playing tricks.

"What about that thing in the tree?" Blue asked. "Was that a hallucination? A dream?"

Glendower. It was Glendower. Glendower. Glendower.

Gansey couldn't stop seeing it. He felt excited, or scared, or both.

"I don't know," he said. He pulled out his keys and swatted Ronan's hand away when he snatched for them. It would be a cold, cold day in a Virginia summer when Ronan was allowed to drive his car. He'd seen what Ronan did to his own car and the idea of what he'd do with a few dozen more horsepower at his command was unthinkable. "But I intend to find out. Come on, let's go."

"Go? Where?" Blue asked.

"Prison," Gansey said agreeably. The other two boys were already jostling her towards the Pig. He felt high as a kite, euphoric. "The dentist. Some place awful."

"I have to be back by. . ." But she trailed off. "I don't know when. Sometime reasonable?"

"What's reasonable?" Adam asked, and Ronan laughed.

"We'll get you back before you turn into a pumpkin." Gansey was about to add *Blue* to the end of this statement, but it felt strange to call her that. "Is Blue a nickname?"

Beside the Camaro, Blue's eyebrows got suddenly pointy.

Hurriedly, Gansey added, "Not that it's not a cool name. Just that it's . . . unusual."

"Weird-ass." This was from Ronan, but he said it as he chewed absently on one of the leather straps on his wrist, so the effect was minimized.

Blue replied, "Unfortunately, it's nothing normal. Not like *Gansey*."

He smiled tolerantly at her. Rubbing his smooth chin with its recently assassinated chin hairs, he studied her. She barely came up to Ronan's shoulder, but she was every bit as *big* as he, every bit as present. Gansey had a sense of incredible *rightness*, then, with everyone assembled by the Pig. Like Blue, not the ley line, was the missing piece that he'd been needing all these years, like the search for Glendower wasn't truly under way until she was part of it. She was right like Ronan had been right, like Adam had been right, like Noah had been right. When each of them had joined him, he'd felt a rush of relief, and in the helicopter, he'd felt exactly the same way when he'd realized it was her voice on the recorder.

Of course, she could still walk away.

She won't, he thought. *She has to feel it, too.*

He said, "I've always liked the name Jane."

Blue's eyes widened. "Ja – what? Oh! No, no. You can't just go around naming people other things because you don't like their real name."

"I like *Blue* just fine," Gansey said. He didn't believe she was really offended; her face didn't look like it had at Nino's when they'd first met, and her ears were turning pink. He thought, possibly, he was getting a little better at not offending her, although he couldn't seem to stop teasing her. "Some of my favourite shirts are blue. However, I also like *Jane*."

"I'm not answering to that."

"I didn't ask you to." Opening the door of the Camaro, he pushed the driver seat forward. Adam obediently climbed in the back.

Blue pointed at Gansey. "I'm not answering to that."

But she got in. Ronan retrieved his MP3 player from the BMW before getting into the passenger seat, and even though the Pig's aftermarket CD player wasn't really working, Ronan kicked the dash until a loudly obnoxious electronic track came on. Gansey tugged open the driver's side door. Really, he should be making Ronan do his homework before Aglionby kicked him out. But instead, he shouted for Noah one last time and then climbed into the car.

"Your sense of what constitutes cool music is frightful," he told Ronan.

From the back seat, Blue shouted, "Does it always smell like petrol?"

"Only when it's running!" Gansey called back.

"Is this thing *safe*?"

"Safe as life."

Adam shouted, "Where are we going?"

"Gelato. Also, Blue's going to tell us how she knew where the ley line was," Gansey said. "We're going to strategize and decide what the next move is and we're going to pick Blue's brain about energy. Adam, you're going to tell me everything you remember about time and ley lines, and Ronan, I want you to tell me again what you'd found out about dreamtime and song lines. Before we go back there again, I want to find out everything we can about making sure it's safe."

But that wasn't what happened. What happened was they drove to Harry's and parked the Camaro next to an Audi and a Lexus and Gansey ordered flavours of gelato until the table wouldn't hold any more bowls and Ronan convinced the staff to turn the overhead speakers up and Blue laughed for the first time at something Gansey said and they were loud and triumphant and kings of Henrietta, because they'd found the ley line and because it was starting, it was starting.

TWENTY-FIVE

Gansey, energized, set the boys out on Glendower-related tasks for the next three days, and to Adam's surprise, Blue managed to come along for each of them. Though she never said as much, it was clear she was keeping them a secret, because she never contacted the boys by phone or met up with them near 300 Fox Way. Despite their lack of formal planning and psychic ability, they all had schedules largely dictated by school, so they managed to meet up to explore with remarkable precision.

Exploring, however, did not include going back to the strange wood. Instead, they spent time at the courthouse, finding out who owned the land underneath the raven. Looking up microfiche in the Henrietta library, trying to determine if the strange wood had a name. Discussing the history of Glendower. Marking the ley line on the map, measuring how wide it seemed to be. Tramping around in fields, turning over rocks, making circles of stones and measuring the energy that came from them.

They also ate a lot of cheap food from convenience stores; this was Blue's fault. After that first triumphant gelato party, Blue insisted on paying for all of her food herself, which limited where they could eat. She despised when any of the boys tried to buy food for her, but she seemed to hate it the most when Gansey offered.

At one store, Gansey had started to pay for Blue's crisps and she'd snatched them away.

"I don't want you to buy me food!" Blue said. "If you pay for it, then it's like I'm . . . be – be—"

"Beholden to me?" Gansey suggested pleasantly.

"Don't put words in my mouth."

"It was *your* word."

"You *assumed* it was my word. You can't just go around assuming."

"But that is what you meant, isn't it?"

She scowled. "I'm done with this conversation."

Then Blue had bought her own crisps, though it was clear the price was dear to her and nothing to Gansey. Adam was proud of her.

After the first day, too, Noah came with them, and this also pleased Adam, because Noah and Blue got along well. Noah was a good bellwether for people. He was so shy and awkward and invisible that he could be easily ignored or made fun of. Blue was not only kind to him, but actually seemed to get along with him. Strangely enough, this relieved Adam, who felt like Blue's presence among them was largely his doing. He now so rarely made decisions without Gansey or Ronan or Noah that he doubted his judgement when he acted alone.

The days slid easily by with the five of them doing everything but returning to the strange pool and the dreaming tree. Gansey kept saying, *We need more information.*

Adam told Blue, "I think he's afraid of it."

He knew *he* was. The ever-pervasive vision he'd had in the tree kept creeping into his thoughts. Gansey dead, dying, because of him. Blue looking at Adam, shocked. Ronan, crouched beside Gansey, his face miserable, snarling, *Are you happy now, Adam? Is this what you wanted?*

Was it a dream? Was it a prophecy?

Gansey told Adam, "I don't know what it is."

Historically, this phrase had been a very good way of losing Adam's respect. The only way to counteract admitting to not knowing something was to immediately follow it with the words *but I'll find out*. Adam didn't give people much time to find out: only as much time as he'd give himself. But Gansey never let him down. They'd find out what it was. Only – Adam wasn't sure, this time, that he wanted to know.

By the end of the second week, the boys had settled into a routine of waiting for Blue at the end of the school day, then setting off into whatever mission Gansey had assigned them. It was an overcast spring day that felt more like autumn, cold and damp and steel grey.

While they waited, Ronan decided to finally take up the task of teaching Adam how to drive a stick shift. For several minutes, it seemed to be going well, as the BMW had an easy clutch, Ronan was brief and to the point with his instruction, and Adam was a quick study with no ego to get in the way.

From a safe vantage point beside the building, Gansey and Noah huddled and watched as Adam began to make ever quicker circles around the car park. Every so often their hoots were audible through the open windows of the BMW.

Then – it had to happen eventually – Adam stalled the

car. It was a pretty magnificent beast, as far as stalls went, with lots of noise and death spasms on the part of the car. From the passenger seat, Ronan began to swear at Adam. It was a long, involved swear, using every forbidden word possible, often in compound-word form. As Adam stared at his lap, penitent, he mused that there was something musical about Ronan when he swore, a careful and loving precision to the way he fit the words together, a black-painted poetry. It was far less hateful sounding than when he *didn't* swear.

Ronan finished with, "For the love of. . . Parrish, take some care, this is not your mother's 1971 Honda Civic."

Adam lifted his head and said, "They didn't start making the Civic until '73."

There was a flash of fangs from the passenger seat, but before Ronan truly had time to strike, they both heard Gansey call warmly, "Jane! I thought you'd never show up. Ronan is tutoring Adam in the ways of manual transmissions."

Blue, her hair pulled every which way by the wind, stuck her head in the driver's side window. The scent of wild flowers accompanied her presence. As Adam catalogued the scent in the mental file of things that made Blue attractive, she said brightly, "Looks like it's going well. Is that what that smell is?"

Without replying, Ronan climbed out of the car and slammed the door.

Noah appeared beside Blue. He looked joyful and adoring, like a Labrador retriever. Noah had decided almost immediately that he would do anything for Blue, a fact that would've needled Adam if it had been anyone other than Noah.

Blue permitted Noah to pet the crazy tufts of her hair, something Adam would have also liked to do, but felt would mean something far different coming from him.

"OK, let's go," Gansey said. He was being theatrical about it, flipping open his journal, checking his watch, waiting for someone to ask him where they were going.

Through the car window, Adam asked, "Where today?"

Gansey swept up a backpack from the ground. "The wood."

Blue and Adam looked at each other, startled.

"Time," Gansey said grandly, striding past them towards the Camaro, "is wasting."

Blue jumped back as Adam scrambled from the driver's seat of the BMW. She hissed to him, "Did you know this?"

"I didn't know anything."

"We have to be back in three hours," Ronan said. "I just fed Chainsaw but she'll need it again."

"This," Gansey replied, "is precisely why I didn't want to have a baby with you."

They bundled into the car with the comfort of routine, climbing into the Camaro though all logic suggested they take the BMW instead. Ronan and Gansey scuffled briefly over his keys (Gansey won, as he won everything). Adam, Blue and Noah climbed into the tiny back seat, in that order. Noah shrank up the side of the car, trying desperately not to touch Blue. Adam didn't take quite so much care. For the first ten minutes on the first day, Adam had been polite, but it quickly become clear that Blue didn't mind when his leg touched hers.

Adam was all right with that.

Everything was the same as before, but for some

reason, Adam's heart was thumping. New spring leaves, jerked from the trees by the suddenly cold wind, scurried across the lot. He saw goosebumps through the loopy crocheted cardigan Blue wore. She reached to take a handful of both his shirt and Noah's, and tugged them both to her like blankets.

"You're always cold, though, Noah," she said.

"I know," he replied, bleak.

Adam wasn't certain what came first with Blue — her treating the boys as friends, or them all becoming friends. It seemed to Adam that this circular way to build relationships required a healthy amount of self-confidence to undertake. And it was a strange sort of magic that it felt like she'd always been hunting for Glendower with them.

With his shoulder pressed against Blue's crocheted one, Adam leaned forward between the two front seats and asked, "Gansey, don't we have any heat?"

"If it starts."

The engine was turning over, over, over, over. Adam felt cold enough for his teeth to chatter, though there was no way that the temperature was that low. He was cold on the *inside*. He ordered, "Gas. Give it more gas."

"That is with gas."

Ronan punched Gansey's right leg down, his palm on Gansey's knee. The engine wailed high and caught. Gansey drily thanked Ronan for his assistance.

"Your heart," Blue said in Adam's ear. "I can feel it in your arm. Are you nervous?"

"It's just," he replied, "I'm not sure where we're going."

★

Because they were travelling by Camaro, not by helicopter, it took longer to get to the coordinates Gansey had marked in his journal. When they arrived, parking the car at an empty holiday cabin and walking the rest of the way, they found the woods had a far different character under a cloudy sky. The raven was stark and dead among the grass, bony white shells in the foliage. The trees at the forest's edge seemed taller than before, giants even among the towering mountain trees. Everything was in shadow on the sunless day, but the stretch of scrubby grass at the edge of the forest seemed darker still.

Adam's heart was still a flighty thing. He had to confess to himself that until now he probably had never really believed Gansey's supernatural explanation for the ley line, not in a way that he'd really internalized. Now, it was real. Magic existed and Adam didn't know how much that changed the world.

For a long moment, they all silently stared into the woods as if facing an adversary. Gansey rubbed a finger over his lip. Blue clutched her arms around herself, jaw clenched with the cold. Even Ronan seemed disquieted. Only Noah looked as he always did, his arms loose, shoulders hunched.

"I feel watched," Blue said finally.

Gansey replied, "High EMF readings can do that. Haunting cases have often come down to old, exposed wiring. High readings can make you feel watched. Unnerved. Nauseous, suspicious. It plays with the hardwiring of your brain."

Noah tipped his head far back to look at the slowly moving tops of the trees. It was the opposite of Adam's instinct, which was to search between the trunks of the trees for movement.

"But," Adam added, "it can go the other way, too. High readings can give spirits the power they need to manifest, right? So you *are* more likely to be watched or haunted even as you're feeling watched or haunted."

Gansey said, "And of course water can reverse that, too. Makes EMF and energy into positive feelings."

"Hence," Ronan chipped in, not to be outdone, "all the healing springs crap out there."

Blue rubbed her arms. "Well, the water's in there, not out here. Are we going in?"

The trees sighed. Gansey narrowed his eyes.

"Are we invited?" Adam asked.

"I think," Noah replied, "you invite yourself."

He was the first to step in. Ronan muttered angrily, probably because Noah – *Noah* – had more courage than any of them. He plunged in after him.

"Wait." Gansey looked at his watch. "It's 4:13. We need to remember that later." He followed Noah and Ronan in.

Adam's heart pounded. Blue stretched out her hand, and he took it. *Don't crush her fingers*, he thought.

And they went in.

Under the canopy, it was even dimmer than in the field. The shadows beneath fallen trees were flat black, and the trunks were painted in chocolate, charcoal, onyx.

"Noah," whispered Gansey. "Noah, where did you go?"

Noah's voice came from behind them. "I didn't go anywhere."

Adam spun, still clutching Blue's hand, but there was nothing there but branches quivering in the faint breeze.

"What did you see?" Gansey asked. When Adam turned back, Noah was standing just ahead of Gansey.

Plays with the hardwiring of your brain.

"Nothing."

Ronan, a hunched black shape a few metres off, asked, "Where are we going?"

Anywhere but that tree, Adam thought. *I don't want to see that again.*

Gansey poked in the dirt for signs of the stream they'd followed before. "Back the same way, I guess. Proper experiment recreates the conditions, doesn't it? The creek's shallower this time, though. Harder to see. It wasn't far, was it?"

They had only been walking along the shallow streambed for a few minutes, however, when it became apparent that the landscape was unfamiliar. The trees were tall, thin and spindly, all slanted as if from some great wind. Great crags of rock shoved up from the poor soil. There was no sign of the streambed, the pool, the dreaming tree.

"We've been misdirected," Gansey said.

His tone was at once blunt and accusatory, as if the wood itself had done it.

"Also," Blue pointed out, dropping Adam's hand, "did you notice the trees?"

It took Adam a moment to realize what she meant. A few of the leaves that clung to the branches were still pale yellow, but now it was the yellow of autumn, not spring. Most of the leaves that surrounded them were the dusky red-green of shifting autumn. The leaf litter at their feet was brown and orange, leaves killed by the early frost of a winter that shouldn't be near.

Adam was torn by wonder and anxiety.

"Gansey," he said, "what time do you have?"

Gansey twisted his wrist. "It's 5:27 p.m. Second hand's still running."

In a little over an hour, they'd walked through two seasons. Adam caught Blue's eye. She just shook her head. What else was there to do?

"Gansey!" Noah called. "There's writing over here!"

On the other side of a rock outcropping, Noah stood by a great block of chin-height stone. Its face was sheared and cracked, striated with lines like Gansey's ley sketches. Noah pointed at a few dozen words painted low on the rock. Whatever ink the author had used, it was worn and uneven: black in some places, deep plum in others.

"What language is that?" Blue asked.

Adam and Ronan answered as one: "Latin."

Ronan crouched swiftly by the rock.

"What does it say?" Gansey asked.

Ronan's eyes darted back and forth as he scanned the text. Unexpectedly, he smirked. "It's a joke. This first part. The Latin is pretty crappy."

"A joke?" Gansey echoed. "About what?"

"You wouldn't find it funny."

The Latin was difficult, and Adam gave up trying to read it. Something about the letters, however, disturbed him. He couldn't put his finger on it. The very shape of them. . .

Warily, he asked, "Why is there a joke written on a random stone?"

The mirth had run out of Ronan's face. He touched the words, traced the letters. His chest rose and fell, rose and fell.

"Ronan?" asked Gansey.

"There's a joke," Ronan answered finally, not looking away from the words, "in case I didn't recognize my own handwriting."

This, Adam realized, was what had distressed him about the words. Now that it had been pointed out, it was obvious that the handwriting was Ronan's. It was just so out of context, painted on this rock with an arcane pigment, smudged and worn by the weather.

"I don't understand," Ronan said. He kept tracing and retracing the letters. He was badly shaken.

Gansey rallied. He couldn't bear to see any of his number rattled. Voice firm, like he was certain, like he was lecturing on world history, he said, "We saw before how the ley line played with time. We can see it right now on my watch. It's flexible. You haven't been here before, Ronan, but it doesn't mean you didn't come here later. Minutes later. Days, years, leave yourself a message, write a joke so you'd believe it was you. Knowing there was a chance time might fold you here to find it."

Well done, Gansey, Adam thought. Gansey had crafted his explanation to steady Ronan, but Adam, too, felt more reasonable. They were explorers, scientists, anthropologists of historical magic. This was what they wanted.

Blue asked, "Then what does it say after the joke?"

"*Arbores loqui latine,*" Ronan replied. "The trees speak Latin."

It was meaningless, a riddle perhaps, but nonetheless, Adam felt the hairs of his neck crawl. They all glanced at the trees that surrounded them; they were fenced by one thousand different shades of green fastened to a million wind-blown claws.

"And the last line?" Gansey asked. "That last word doesn't look like Latin."

"*Nomine appellant*," Ronan read. "Call it by name." He paused. "Cabeswater."

TWENTY-SIX

"Cabeswater," Gansey repeated.

There was something about the word itself that was magical. *Cabeswater.* Something old and enigmatic, a word that didn't seem to belong in the New World. Gansey read the Latin on the rock again – the translation seemed obvious, once Ronan had done the heavy lifting – and then, like the others, he looked around at the surrounding trees.

What is this thing you've done? he asked himself. *Where have you brought them?*

"I vote we find water," Blue said. "To make the energy do whatever Ronan said it would do that was better. And then . . . I think we should say something in Latin."

"It sounds like a plan," Gansey agreed, wondering at the strangeness of this place, that such a nonsensical suggestion should seem so practical. "Should we go back the way we came, or go further in?"

Noah said, "Further."

Since Noah rarely expressed an opinion, his word reigned. Setting off again, they doubled back and forth across their own trail in search of water. And as they walked, the leaves fell around them, red and then brown and then grey, until the trees were naked. Frost appeared in the shadows.

"Winter," Adam said.

It was impossible, of course, but again, so was everything that had come before it. It was, Gansey thought, like when he'd driven through the Lake District with Malory. After a while, there had been too much incredible beauty for him to process, and it had become invisible.

It was impossible that it was winter. But it was no more impossible than anything else that had happened.

They had come to a stand of naked willow trees on a gentle slope, and below them was the twist of a slow-moving, shallow creek. Malory had once told Gansey that where there were willows, there was water. Willows propagated, he said, by dropping seeds in moving water that then carried them downstream, allowing them to root on some distant shore.

"And," Blue added, "there's water."

Gansey turned to the others. Their breath came in clouds, and they all looked badly underdressed. Even the colour of their skin looked wrong: too sun-flushed for this colourless winter air. Tourists from another season. He became aware that he was shivering, but he didn't know if it was from the newly wintry cold or from anticipation.

"OK," he said to Blue. "What did you want to say in Latin?"

Blue turned to Ronan. "Can you just say hello? That's polite."

Ronan looked pained; polite was not his style. But he said, "*Salve.*" To Blue, he said, "That actually means *be well*."

"Super job," she replied. "Ask if they'll speak with us."

Now Ronan looked even more pained, because this made him look ridiculous, and that was even less his style, but he tilted his head back to the treetops and said, "*Loquere tu nobis?*"

They all stood quietly. A hiss seemed to be rising, as if a faint winter breeze rustled the leaves in the trees. But there were no leaves left on the branches to rustle.

"Nothing," Ronan replied. "What did you expect?"

"Quiet," ordered Gansey. Because now the hissing was definitely more than a rustle. Now it had resolved into what sounded distinctly like whispered, dry voices. "Do you hear that?"

Everyone but Noah shook their heads.

"I do," said Noah, to Gansey's relief.

Gansey said, "Ask them to say it again."

Ronan did.

The hissing rustle came again, and now, it seemed obvious that it was a voice, obvious that it had never been leaves. Plainly, Gansey heard a crackly statement in Latin. He wished, suddenly, that he'd studied harder in class as he repeated the words phonetically to Ronan.

"They say they've been speaking to you already, but you haven't been listening," Ronan said. He rubbed the back of his shaved head. "Gansey, are you messing with me? Do you really hear something?"

"Do you think Gansey's Latin is that good?" Adam replied tersely. "It was *your* handwriting on the rock, Ronan, that said they spoke Latin. Shut up."

The trees hissed again, and Gansey repeated them to Ronan. Noah corrected one of the verbs Gansey had misheard.

Ronan's eyes darted to Blue. "They said they're happy to see the psychic's daughter."

"Me!" Blue cried.

The trees hissed a reply and Gansey repeated the words.

"I don't know what that means," Ronan said. "They're also happy to once more see — I don't know what that word is. *Greywaren?* If it's Latin, I don't know it."

Ronan, whispered the trees. *Ronan Lynch.*

"It's you," Gansey said with wonder, his skin creeping. "Ronan Lynch. They said your name. It's *you* they're happy to see again."

Ronan's expression was guarded, his feelings hidden.

"*Again.*" Blue pressed her hands to her cold-red cheeks, her eyes wide, her face holding all the awe and excitement that Gansey felt. "Amazing. The trees? Amazing."

Adam asked, "Why can only you and Noah hear them?"

In stumbling Latin — even in class, he rarely spoke it, and it was strange to try to translate his thoughts from words he could see written in his head to spoken ones — Gansey said, "*Hic gaud-emus. Gratias tibi . . . loquere — loqui pro nobis.*" He looked at Ronan. "How do I ask why you can't hear them?"

"God, Gansey. If you paid attention in—" Closing his eyes, Ronan thought for a moment. "*Cur non te audimus?*"

Gansey didn't need Ronan to translate the trees' hushed answer; the Latin was simple enough.

He said aloud, "The road isn't awake."

"The . . . ley line?" Blue suggested. A little wistfully, she added, "But that doesn't explain why only you and Noah can hear it."

The trees murmured, *Si expergefacere via, erimus in debitum.*

"If you wake the line, they'll be in your debt," Ronan said.

For a moment, they were all quiet, then, looking at one another. It was a lot to take in. Because it wasn't merely that the trees were speaking to them. It was that the trees themselves were sentient beings, capable of watching their movements. Was it only the trees in this strange wood, or did every tree observe their movements? Had they always been trying to speak to them? There was no way of knowing, either, if the trees were good or bad, if they loved or hated humans, if they had principles or compassion. They were like aliens, Gansey thought. Aliens that we have treated very badly for a very long time. *If I were a tree, I would have no reason to love a human.*

It was happening. All of these years, he had been looking for this.

Gansey said, "Ask them if they know where Glendower is."

Adam looked startled. Without pausing, Ronan translated.

It took a moment for the hissing voices to reply, and again, Gansey didn't need a translation.

"No," Gansey said. Something inside him had tightened and tightened and tightened until he'd asked the question. He'd thought hearing the answer would release it, but it didn't. Everyone else was looking at him; he wasn't sure why. Maybe something in his face was wrong. It felt wrong. He looked away from them all and said, "It's very cold. *Valde frigida.* What's the way out? Please? *Amabo te, ubi exitum?*"

The trees whispered and hissed, and Gansey realized he might have been mistaken; it might have been only one voice, all along. He wasn't entirely sure he'd ever heard it aloud, either, now that he thought about it. It was possible that it had been said directly in his head this entire time. It was a disconcerting thought and it distracted his listening. Noah had to help him recall everything that had been said, and Ronan had to think for a very long moment before he was able to translate.

"Sorry," Ronan said. He was concentrating too hard to remember to look cool or surly. "It's difficult. It's – they said that we need to go back through the year. Against . . . the road. The line. They said if we go back along the creek and turn left at the big . . . sycamore? *Platanus?* I think sycamore. Then we'll find something they think we want to find. Then we'll be able to walk out of the woods and find our way back to our . . . to our day. I don't know. I missed parts, but I think – I'm sorry."

"It's OK," Gansey said. "You're doing really well." In a low voice, he asked Adam, "Do you think we should do it? It occurs to me they might not be trusted."

Adam's furrowed brow meant that this had occurred to him as well, but he replied, "Do we have another choice?"

"I think we should trust them," Blue said. "They knew me and Ronan. Somehow. And the rock didn't say not to. Right?"

She had a point. Ronan's handwriting, with its great care to prove its origin to them, had given them the key to speak to the trees, not a warning.

"Back we go," Gansey said. "Careful not to slip." Then, louder, he said, "*Gratias. Reveniemus.*"

"What did you say?" Blue asked.

Adam replied for him. "Thanks. And that we'd be back."

It wasn't difficult to adhere to the directions Ronan had translated. The creek was wide here, the water cold and slow between white-frosted banks. Following it took them steadily downhill, and gradually, the air around them began to warm. Sparse red leaves spotted the branches, and by the time Blue pointed out a massive sycamore, the peeling white and grey trunk too wide for her to put her arms around, they were in the sticky grips of summer. The leaves were full and green, moving and rubbing against one another in a constant murmured rustle. If there was a voice now, Gansey wasn't certain he'd hear it.

"We missed summer before," Adam pointed out. "When we came the other way. We went straight to autumn."

"Magical mosquitos," Ronan said, smacking his arm. "What a great place this is."

Following the voice's directions, they turned left at the massive sycamore. Gansey wondered what it was that the trees thought they would want to find. He thought there was only one thing he was looking for.

Then the trees opened up into a summery clearing, and it became obvious what the voice had meant.

In the clearing, entirely out of place, was an abandoned car. A red Mustang. Newer model. At first, it appeared to be covered with mud, but a closer inspection revealed that it was, in fact, coated with layers and layers of pollen and leaf litter. Leaves had caught in drifts in the cracks of the hood and under the spoiler, gathered over the windscreen wipers and bunched around the tyres. A sapling grew out from under the car, wrapping around the front fender. The scene was reminiscent of old shipwrecks, ancient boats turned into coral reefs by the wiles of time.

Behind the car stretched a badly overgrown track that seemed to lead out of the woods; this must have been the way out the trees meant.

"Bling," Ronan remarked, kicking one of the tyres. The Mustang had massive, expensive wheels, and now that Gansey looked more closely at the car, he saw that it was covered with aftermarket details: big rims, new spoiler, dark window tint, gaping exhaust. *New money*, his father would've said, *burns in the pocket*.

"Look," Adam said. He rubbed a finger over the dust of the back window. Next to a Blink-182 sticker was an Aglionby decal.

"Figures," Blue said.

Ronan tried the driver's side door; it came open. He laughed, once, sharp. "There's a mummified hamburger in here."

They all crowded around to see the interior, but apart from the dry, half-eaten hamburger on the passenger seat, still sitting on its wrapper, there was not much to see.

This car, too, was a riddle, like Blue's voice on the recorder. Gansey felt as if it was directed specifically at him.

"Open the boot," he ordered.

The boot had a jacket in it, and beneath that, an odd collection of sticks and springs. Frowning, Gansey withdrew the contraption, holding it by the largest rod. The pieces swung into place, several sticks hanging and twisting beneath the main one, and he understood all at once.

"It's a dowsing rod."

He turned to Adam, wanting verification.

"Coincidence," Adam said. Of course meaning that it wasn't.

Gansey had the peculiar sensation he had first felt in the car park outside Nino's, when Adam had warned him that he thought someone else was looking for the ley line. Then he realized that Blue and Noah were no longer in sight. "Where's Blue and Noah?"

At her name, Blue reappeared, stepping over a log and back into the clearing. She said, "Noah's throwing up."

"Why is he doing that?" Gansey asked. "Is he sick?"

"I'll ask him," she replied. "As soon as he's finished *puking*."

Gansey winced.

"I think you'll find that Gansey prefers the word *vomiting*. Or *evacuating*," Ronan said brightly.

"I think *retching* is the most specific word, in this case," Blue corrected pointedly.

"Retching!" said Ronan without concern; this, finally, was something he knew something about. "Where is he? Noah!" He pushed away from the Mustang and started back the way that Blue had come.

Blue noticed the dowsing rod in Gansey's hands. "Was *that* in the car? A dowsing rod!"

He shouldn't have been surprised she knew what it was; even if she wasn't psychic, her mother was, and this was technically a tool of the trade. "The boot."

"But that means that someone else was looking for the ley line!"

On the other side of the Mustang, Adam drew his fingers through the pollen on the side of the car. He looked disquieted. "And they decided it was more important than their car."

Gansey glanced up at the trees around them, then back

at the expensive car. In the distance, he heard the low voices of Ronan and Noah. "I think we'd better go. I think we need more information."

TWENTY-SEVEN

As Blue got ready to go out the following Sunday morning, she was officially conflicted. Sundays were dog-walking days. Actually, Sundays and Thursdays were dog-walking days, but Blue had begged off the previous two weeks to spend time with the boys, so it felt like it had been a long time since she'd seen her dogs-by-proxy. The problem was that she was running distinctly low on money, and moreover, guilt at disobeying Maura was finally beginning to weigh on her. It had got so that she couldn't look her mother in the eye over dinner, but it was impossible, now, to imagine giving up the boys. She had to find a way to reconcile the two.

But first, she had to walk the dogs.

On the way out to Willow Ridge, the phone in the kitchen rang and Blue, a glass of cloudy apple juice in one hand and the laces of a high-top trainer in the other, grabbed it.

"Hello?"

"I'd like to speak to Blue, please, if she's in."

It was Gansey's unmistakable, polite voice, the one he used to turn straw into gold. Clearly, he had known what he risked calling here, and clearly, he had been prepared to speak to someone other than Blue about it. Despite her growing suspicion that her secrecy couldn't last, she wasn't sure how she felt about the fact that he could've blown her cover.

"Blue is getting ready to go walk other people's dogs," she said, setting down the juice and tugging on the trainer, phone shoved between her ear and shoulder. "And it's a good thing you got her and not someone else."

"I was prepared for that eventuality," Gansey said. It was strange to hear him over the phone; his voice didn't quite sound like his face looked. "Still, I'm glad I caught you. How are you doing? Well, I trust?"

He doesn't mean to be condescending, Blue told herself. She told herself several times. "You trust right."

"Brilliant. Look. Adam's working today and Ronan's at church with his brothers, but I'd like to go out and just . . . look around." He added, quickly, "Not to the woods. I was thinking maybe to that church on your map. Do you want to. . ."

He faltered. *Gansey* was faltering? It took Blue a moment of his silence to realize that he was asking if she wanted to go with him. It took her another moment to realize that she'd never been anywhere with him without the other boys.

"I have to walk dogs."

"Oh," Gansey replied, sounding deflated. "Well, OK."

"But it'll only take an hour."

"Oh," he repeated, about fourteen shades brighter. "Shall I pick you up, then?"

Blue glanced furtively over her shoulder towards the living room. "Oh no – I'll, uh, meet you in the car park."

"Brilliant," he said again. "Top shelf. I think this'll be interesting. See you in an hour."

Top shelf? Gansey without Adam – Blue wasn't certain how this would work. Despite Adam's tentative interest in her, the boys seemed to act as a unit, a single, multiheaded entity. To see any of them without the presence of the others felt a little ... dangerous.

But there wasn't an option of not going with Gansey. She wanted to explore as much as he did.

No sooner had Blue hung up than she heard her name being called.

"Bloo-OOOO-oooooo, my child, my child, come in here!"

This was Maura's voice, and the sing-song rhythm to it was highly ironic. With a sinking sensation, Blue followed it into the living room, where she found Maura, Calla and Persephone drinking what Blue suspected were screwdrivers. When she walked into the room, the women all looked up at her with indolent smiles. A pack of lionesses.

Blue raised her eyebrows at the cocktails. The morning light through the windows turned the drinks a brilliant, translucent yellow. "It's only ten o'clock."

Calla reached out, enclosing Blue's wrist with her fingers, and dragged her on to the mint green love seat. Her glass was already mostly empty. "It's a Sunday. What else would we do?"

"*I* have to go walk dogs," Blue said.

From her blue-striped chair across the room, Maura sipped her screwdriver and made a wild face. "Oh, Per*seph*one. You make them with *far* too much vodka."

"My hand always slips," Persephone said sadly from a wicker bench in front of the window.

When Blue started to rise, Maura said, a thinly veiled

iron behind her tone, "Sit with us a moment, Blue. Talk to us about yesterday. And the day before. And the day before. And – oh, let's just talk about these past few weeks."

Blue realized then that Maura was furious. She had seen her furious only a few times before, and having it directed at her made her skin go instantly clammy.

"Well, I was. . ." She trailed off. A lie seemed pointless.

"I'm not your dungeon master," interrupted Maura. "I'm not going to bolt you in your room or send you to a convent, for crying out loud. So you can just stop all the sneaking around stuff right now."

"I wasn't—"

"You were. I have been your mother since you've been born and I promise you, you were. So I take it you and Gansey get along, then?" Maura's expression was annoyingly knowing.

"*Mom.*"

"Orla told me about his muscle car," Maura continued. Her voice was still angry and artificially bright. The fact that Blue was well aware that she'd earned it made the sting of it even worse. "You aren't planning on kissing him, are you?"

"Mom, that will *never* happen," Blue assured her. "You *did* meet him, didn't you?"

"I wasn't sure if driving an old, loud Camaro was the male equivalent of shredding your T-shirts and gluing cardboard trees to your bedroom walls."

"Trust me," Blue said. "Gansey and I are nothing like each other. And they aren't cardboard. They're repurposed canvas."

"The environment breathes a sigh of relief." Maura attempted another sip of her drink; wrinkling her nose, she shot a glare at Persephone. Persephone looked martyred. After a pause, Maura noted, in a slightly softer voice, "I'm not entirely happy that you're getting in a car without air bags."

"*Our* car doesn't have air bags," Blue pointed out.

Maura picked a long strand of Persephone's hair from the rim of her glass. "Yes, but you always take your bike."

Blue stood up. She suspected that the green fuzz of the sofa was now adhered to the back of her leggings. "Can I go now? Am I in trouble?"

"You are in trouble. I told you to stay away from him and you didn't," Maura said. "I just haven't decided what to do about it yet. My feelings are hurt. I've consulted with several people who tell me that I'm within my rights to feel hurt. Do teenagers still get grounded? Did that only happen in the eighties?"

"I'll be very angry if you ground me," Blue said, still wobbly from her mother's unfamiliar displeasure. "I'll probably rebel and climb out of my window with a bedsheet rope."

Her mother rubbed a hand over her face. Her anger had completely burned itself out. "You're well into it, aren't you? That didn't take long."

"If you don't tell me not to see them, I don't have to disobey you," Blue suggested.

"This is what you get, Maura, for using your DNA to make a baby," Calla said.

Maura sighed. "Blue, I know you're not an idiot. It's just, sometimes smart people do dumb things."

Calla growled, "Don't be one of them."

"Persephone?" asked Maura.

In her small voice, Persephone said, "I have nothing to add." After a moment of consideration, she added, however, "If you are going to punch someone, don't put your thumb inside your fist. It would be a shame to break it."

"OK," Blue said hurriedly. "I'm out."

"You could at least say sorry," Maura said. "Pretend like I have some power over you."

Blue wasn't sure how to reply to this. Maura had all sorts of control of Blue, but it wasn't usually the sort that came with ultimatums or curfew. So she just said, "I'm sorry. I should've told you I was going to do what you didn't want me to do."

Maura said, "That was not as satisfying as I imagined it would be."

Calla caught Blue's wrist again, and for a moment Blue was worried that Calla would sense the level of strangeness surrounding Gansey's quest. But she merely swallowed the last of her drink before purring, "What with all this running around, don't forget our movie night on Friday, Blue."

"Our – movie – night—" Blue repeated.

Calla's eyebrows hardened. "You promised."

For a shapeless moment, Blue tried to remember when she had ever talked about a movie night with Calla, and then she realized what this was really about: the conversation from days and days ago. About tossing Neeve's room.

"I forgot that was this week," Blue replied.

Maura swirled her drink, which still looked mostly full. She always preferred watching other people drink to doing it herself. "Which movie?"

"*Even Dwarfs Started Small*," Calla replied immediately. "In the original German: *Auch Zwerge haben klein angefangen*."

Maura winced, though Blue couldn't tell if it was at the movie or at Calla's accent. She said, "Just as well. Neeve and I are out that evening."

Calla raised an eyebrow and Persephone picked at a string on her lace stockings.

"What are you doing?" Blue asked. *Looking for my father? Scrying in pools?*

Maura stopped swirling her drink. "Not hanging out with Gansey."

At least Blue could still be certain that her mother would never lie to her.

She just wouldn't say anything at all.

TWENTY-EIGHT

"Why the church?" Blue asked from the passenger seat of the Camaro. She'd never ridden in the front before, and in the passenger seat, the sensation of the car being a few thousand parts flying in uneasy formation was even more pronounced.

Gansey, installed comfortably behind the wheel with expensive sunglasses and Top-Siders, took his time answering. "I don't know. Because it's on the line, but it's not as . . . whatever Cabeswater is. I have to think more about Cabeswater before we go back."

"Because it's like we're going into someone's house." Blue tried not to look at Gansey's boat shoes; she felt better about him as a person if she pretended he wasn't wearing them.

"Exactly! That's exactly what it feels like." He pointed at her like he pointed at Adam when Adam made a comment he approved of. Then he put his hand back on the gear stick to stop its rattling.

Blue found it a thrilling idea, actually, that the trees were thinking creatures, that they could speak. That they *knew* her.

"Turn here!" Blue ordered, as Gansey nearly passed the ruined church. With a broad smile, he hauled on the wheel and dropped down a few gears. With only a few protesting rubber noises, they made it into the overgrown drive. As they did, the glovebox fell open and shot its contents on to Blue's lap.

"Why do you even *have* this car?" she asked. Gansey shut off the engine, but her legs still felt like they vibrated in time with it.

"Because it is a classic," he replied primly. "Because it's unique."

"But it's a piece of crap. Don't they make unique classics that don't—" Blue demonstrated her point by unsuccessfully shoving the door to the glovebox shut a few times. Now, as she reinserted the box's contents and slammed the door shut, it once again ejected its contents on to her legs.

"Oh, they do," Gansey said, and she thought she detected a bit of an edge to his voice. Not anger, really, but irony. He put a mint leaf in his mouth and climbed out of the car.

Blue replaced the car's registration and an ancient strip of beef jerky in the glovebox, and then she inspected the other object that had fallen into her lap. It was an EpiPen – a syringe meant to restart someone's heart in the case of a severe allergic reaction. Unlike the beef jerky, its expiration date was current.

"Whose is this?" she asked.

Gansey was already out of the car, holding the EMF reader and stretching as if he'd been in the car for hours instead of thirty minutes. She noticed that he had impressive arm muscles, probably related to the Aglionby rowing team sticker she'd noticed on the glovebox. Glancing over his shoulder at her, he replied, dismissive, "Mine. You've got to jimmy that latch to the right, then it'll shut."

She did as he recommended and, sure enough, the

glovebox latched, the EpiPen safely replaced inside.

On the other side of the car, Gansey tipped his head back to look at the storm clouds: living things, moving towers. In the very deep distance, they were nearly the same colour as the blue edge of the mountains. The road they'd come in on was a dappled blue-green river twisting back towards town. The indirect light of the sun was peculiar: nearly yellow, thick with humidity. Apart from the birds, there was no sound but the slow, faraway growl of thunder.

"I hope the weather holds," he remarked.

He strode over to the ruined church. This, Blue had discovered, was how Gansey got places – *striding*. Walking was for ordinary people.

Standing beside him, Blue found the church eerier in the daylight, as she always did. Growing inside the ruined walls among collapsed bits of roof, knee-high grass and trees as tall as her strove towards the sunlight. There was no evidence there had ever been any pews, or any congregation. There was something bleak and meaningless about it: death with no afterlife.

She remembered standing here with Neeve, all those weeks ago. She wondered if Neeve really was looking for her father, and if she was, what she intended to do with him if she found him. She thought about the spirits walking into the church and she wondered if Gansey—

Gansey said, "I feel like I've been here before."

Blue didn't know how to answer. She'd already told him one half-truth about St Mark's Eve and she wasn't sure it was right to tell him the other half. Moreover, she wasn't sure it felt *true*. Standing next to him in his very alive state, she couldn't imagine that he would be dead in less than a year. He was wearing a teal polo shirt, and it seemed impossible that someone in a teal polo shirt could perish of anything other than heart disease at age eighty-six, possibly at a polo match.

Blue asked, "What's your magic-o-meter doing right now?"

Gansey turned it towards her. His knuckles were pale, bone pressed through skin. Red lights flashed across the surface of the meter.

He said, "It's pegged. Same as in the wood."

Blue surveyed their surroundings. In all likelihood, all of this was private property, even the ground the church was on, but the area behind the church looked more remote. "If we go that way, it seems less like we'll be shot for trespassing. We can't be low profile because of your shirt."

"Aquamarine is a wonderful colour and I won't be made to feel bad for wearing it," Gansey said. But his voice was a bit thin and he glanced back at the church again. Just then he looked younger than she'd ever seen him, his eyes narrowed, hair messed up, features unstudied. Young and, strangely enough, afraid.

Blue thought: *I can't tell him. I can never tell him. I have to just try to stop it from happening.*

Then Gansey, suddenly charming again, flipped a hand in the direction of her purple tunic dress. "Lead the way, Eggplant."

She found a stick to poke at the ground for snakes before they set off through the grass. The wind smelled like rain, and the ground rumbled with thunder, but the weather held. The machine in Gansey's hands blinked red constantly, only flickering to orange when they stepped too far away from the invisible line.

"Thanks for coming, Jane," Gansey said.

Blue shot him a dirty look. "You're welcome, *Dick*."

He looked pained. "Please don't."

This genuine expression robbed all of the glee of using his real name. She kept walking.

"You're the only one who doesn't seem fazed by this," he said after a moment. "It's not that I'm accustomed to it, but I've run across some unusual things before and I guess I just . . . but Ronan and Adam and Noah all seem . . . nonplussed."

Blue pretended she knew what *nonplussed* meant. "I live with this, though. I mean, my mother is a psychic. All her friends are psychics. This is – well, it's not like it's *normal*. But it's how I always thought it would feel to be them. You know, to see things that other people don't."

"I spent years trying to get it to do this," Gansey admitted. There was something about the timbre of his voice that surprised Blue. It wasn't until he spoke again she realized he was using the tone she'd heard him use with Adam. "I've spent eighteen months trying to find the Henrietta line."

"Was it what you expected?"

"I don't know what I expected. I'd read all about the effects of the line but I never thought it would be so pronounced. So . . . I never expected the trees. I never expected it to happen so fast, either. I'm used to getting one clue every month, and then beating that dead horse until another one comes along. Not this." He paused, his smile wide and benevolent. "This is all down to you.

Putting us on the line, finally. I could kiss you."

Though he was obviously joking, Blue skittered to the side.

"What was that for?"

She asked, "Do you believe in psychics?"

"Well, I *went* to one, didn't I?"

"That doesn't mean anything. Lots of people go to psychics just for a laugh."

"I went because I believe. Well, I believe in ones that are good at what they do. I just think there's quite a lot of hooey you have to wade through to get to them. Why?"

Blue viciously stabbed the ground with her snake stick. "Because my mom's told me, ever since I was born, that if I kiss my true love, he'll die."

Gansey laughed.

"Don't laugh, you—" Blue was going to say *bastard* but it felt too strong and she lost the nerve.

"Well, it's just a very precautionary-sounding sort of thing, isn't it? Don't date or you'll go blind. Kiss your true love and he bites it."

"It's not just her!" Blue protested. "Every psychic or medium I've ever met tells me the same thing. Besides, my mom's not like that. She wouldn't just play around with something like that. It's not *pretend.*"

"Sorry," Gansey said, realizing she was genuinely annoyed with him. "I was being a dick again. Do you know how he's supposed to die, this unlucky guy?"

Blue shrugged.

"Ah. Devil's in the details, I guess. So you just kiss nobody, in a precautionary way?" He watched her nod. "That seems grim, Jane. I won't lie."

She shrugged again. "I don't usually tell people. I don't know why I told you. Don't tell Adam."

Gansey's eyebrows spiked up towards his hairline. "It's like that, is it?"

Her face went instantly hot. "No. I mean. . . No. *No.* It's just, because it's not – because I don't know – I would rather play it safe."

Blue fantasized that time had begun again with them getting out of the car and her instead striking up a conversation about the weather or which classes he was taking. It didn't seem like her face would ever stop burning.

Gansey's voice, when he replied, was a little rough. "Well, if you killed Adam, I'd be quite upset."

"I'll do my best not to."

For a moment, the silence was uneven and uncomfortable, and then he said, his voice more ordinary, "Thanks for telling me. I mean, trusting me with something like that."

Relieved, Blue replied, "Well, you told me about how you felt about Ronan and Adam and the nonplussing thing. Only, I still want to know. . . Why are you looking? For Glendower?"

He smiled ruefully, and for a moment, Blue was afraid that he was about to switch over to flippant, glossy Gansey, but in the end, he just said, "It's a difficult story to summarize."

"You're in a pre–Ivy League high school. Try."

"All right. Where to start? Maybe – you saw my EpiPen. It's for bee stings. I'm allergic. Badly."

Blue stopped in her tracks, alarmed. Hornets nested on the ground, and this was prime territory for them: quiet areas close to trees. "Gansey! This is *the countryside*. Where bees live!"

He made a dismissive gesture, as if eager to be off this particular subject. "Keep poking things with your stick and it'll be OK."

"My *stick*! All week we've been walking in the woods! That seems awfully—"

"Cavalier?" Gansey suggested. "The truth is that there's not even really a point having an EpiPen. The last they told me was that it would only work if I got stung once, and even then, they don't know. I was four the first time I had to go to a hospital for a sting, and the reactions only got worse after that. It is what it is. It's this or live in a bubble."

Blue thought about the Death card, and how her mother hadn't actually interpreted it for Gansey. It was possible, she thought, that the card hadn't been about Gansey's foretold tragedy at all, but rather about his life – how he walked side by side with death everyday.

With her stick, Blue thwacked the ground ahead of them. "OK, go on."

Gansey sucked in his lips and then released them. "Well, seven years ago, I was at a dinner party with my parents. I can't remember what it was for. I think one of my dad's friends had got the party nomination."

"For . . . *Congress*?"

The ground beneath their feet or the air around them vibrated with thunder.

"Yeah. I don't remember. You know how you sometimes don't remember everything right? Ronan says that memories are like dreams. You never remember how you got to the front of the classroom with no clothes on. Anyway, the party was dull – I was nine or ten. It was all little black dresses and red ties and any sort of food you wanted, as long as it was shrimp. A few of us kids started to play hide-and-seek. I remember thinking I was too old to play hide-and-seek, but there was nothing else to do."

Blue and he entered a narrow copse of trees, sparse enough that grass grew between them instead of brambles. This Gansey, this story-telling Gansey, was a different person altogether from any of the other versions of him she'd encountered. She couldn't *not* listen.

"It was hot as Hades. It was spring, but it had suddenly decided it was summer. Virginia spring. You know how that is. Heavy, somehow. There was no shade in the back garden, but there was this great forest that bounded it. Dark and green and blue. Like diving into a lake. In I went, and it was fantastic. Only five minutes and I couldn't see the house."

Blue stopped poking the ground. "Did you get lost?"

Gansey shook his head a little.

"I stepped on a nest." His eyes were narrowed in that way people do when they're trying hard to appear casual, but it was obvious this story was anything but casual to him. "Hornets, like you said. They nest on the ground. I don't have to tell you. But I didn't know back then. The first thing I felt was a little prickle on my sock. I thought I'd stepped on a thorn – there were a ton of them, those green, whip-shaped ones – but then I felt another. They were just such small hurts, you know?"

Blue felt a little sick.

He continued, "But then I felt one on my hand, and by the time I jumped away, I saw them. All over my arms."

Somehow, he'd managed to take her there, to put her in that moment of discovery. Blue's heart felt dragged down, snared with venom.

"What did you do?" she asked.

"I knew I was dead. I knew I was dead before I started to feel everything start to go wrong in my body. Because I'd been to the hospital for just one sting and this was, like, a hundred. They were in my hair. They were in my *ears*, Blue."

She asked, "Were you scared?"

He didn't have to answer. She saw it in the hollow of his eyes.

"What happened?"

"I died," he said. "I felt my heart stop. The hornets didn't care. They were still stinging me, even though I was dead."

Gansey stopped. He said, "This is the difficult part."

"Those are my favourite," Blue replied. The trees were quiet around them; the only sound was the growl of thunder. After a pause, she added, a little ashamed, "Sorry. I didn't mean to be . . . but my whole life is the 'difficult part'. Nobody believes in what my family does. I'm not going to laugh."

He exhaled slowly. "I heard a voice. It was a whisper. I won't forget what it said. It said: '*You will live because of Glendower. Someone else on the ley line is dying when they should not, and so you will live when you should not.*'"

Blue was very quiet. The air pressed on them.

"I told Helen. She said it was a hallucination." Gansey brushed a hanging vine from his face. The brush was getting thicker here, the trees closer. They probably needed to turn back. His voice was peculiar. Formal and certain. "It was not a hallucination."

This was the Gansey who had written the journal. The truth of it, the magic of it, possessed her.

She asked, "And that's enough to make you spend your life looking for Glendower?"

Gansey replied, "Once Arthur knew the grail existed, how could he not look for it?"

Thunder growled beneath them again, the hungry snarl of an invisible beast.

Blue said, "That's not really an answer."

He didn't look at her. He replied, voice terrible, "I *need* to, Blue."

Every light on the EMF reader went out.

Equal parts relieved to be back on safe ground and disappointed not to pry deeper into the real Gansey, Blue touched the machine. "Did we step off the line?"

They retreated several metres, but the machine didn't turn back on.

"Is the battery dead?" she suggested.

"I don't know how to check." Gansey switched it off and then on again.

Blue stretched out her hand for the reader. The moment she took it from him, the lights burst red. Solid red, no blinking. She turned from side to side. Orange to her left. Red to her right.

They met each other's eyes.

"Take it back," Blue said.

But as soon as Gansey touched the EMF reader, the lights went dead again. When the thunder came this time, seductive and simmering, she felt like it started something inside her trembling that didn't stop after the sound had died.

"I keep thinking there must be a logical explanation," Gansey said. "But there hasn't been all week."

Blue thought there probably was a logical explanation, and she thought it was this: Blue made things louder. Only she had no idea what she was amplifying at the moment.

The air shuddered again as thunder grumbled. There was no sign of the sun now. All that was left was the heavy green air around them.

He asked, "Where is it steering us?"

Letting the solid red light lead them, Blue stepped hesitantly through the trees. They had only made it a few metres when the machine went dead again. No amount of switching hands or manipulation would encourage it to flicker again.

They stood with the machine between them, heads bowed close, looking silently at the dark face of it.

Blue asked, "What now?"

Gansey stared down between their feet, directly below the machine. "Step back. There's—"

"Oh my gosh," Blue said, jerking away from Gansey. Then, again: "Oh my—"

But she couldn't finish the sentence, because she had just stepped off something that looked an awful lot like a human arm bone. Gansey was the first to crouch, brushing away the leaves from the bone. Sure enough, beneath the first arm bone was a second. A filthy watch encircled the wrist bone. Everything looked fake, a skeleton in the woods.

This can't be happening.

"Oh no," Blue breathed. "Don't touch it. Fingerprints."

But the corpse was long beyond fingerprints. The bones were clean as a museum piece, the flesh long since rotted off, and there were only threads remaining of whatever the person had worn. Picking carefully at leaves, Gansey uncovered the entire skeleton. It lay crumpled, one leg crooked up, arms sprawled to either side of its skull, a freeze-frame of tragedy. Time had spared strange elements and taken others: the watch was there, but the hand was not. The shirt was gone, but a tie remained, rippled over the hills and valleys of the collapsed rib bones. The shoes were dirty but unchanged from exposure. The socks, too, were preserved inside the leather shoes, ankle-height bags of foot bones.

The skull's cheek was smashed in. She wondered if that was how the person had died.

"Gansey," Blue said, voice flat. "This was a kid. This was a kid from Aglionby."

She pointed at his ribcage. Crooked between two bare ribs was an Aglionby patch, the synthetic fibres of the embroidery impervious to the weather.

They stared at each other over the body. Lightning lit the sides of their faces. Blue was very aware of the skull beneath Gansey's skin, his cheekbones so close to the surface, high and square like those on the Death card.

"We should report it," she said.

"Wait," he replied. It only took him a moment to find the wallet beneath the hip bone. It was good leather, spattered and bleached, but mostly unmolested. Gansey flipped it open, eyeing the multicoloured edges of credit cards that lined one side. He spotted the top edge of a driver's licence and thumbed it out.

Blue heard Gansey's breath catch in naked shock.

The face on the driver's licence was Noah's.

TWENTY–NINE

At eight p.m., Gansey called Adam at the trailer factory.

"I'm coming to get you," he said, and hung up.

He didn't say it was important, but this was the first time he'd ever asked for Adam to leave work, so it had to be. Outside, the Camaro idled in the car park, the uneven tripping of the engine echoing across the darkness. Adam got in.

"I'll explain when we get there," said Gansey.

He put the car into gear, stomping the accelerator hard enough that the back tyres squeaked on the tarmac as they left. From Gansey's expression, Adam thought that something had happened to Ronan. Maybe, finally, *Ronan* had happened to Ronan. But it wasn't the hospital that they drove to. The Camaro tore straight into the car park outside Monmouth Manufacturing. Together, they climbed the dark, creaking stairs to the first floor. Under Gansey's hands, the door fell open, crashing against the wall.

"Noah!" he shouted.

The room stretched out, limitless in the dark. Against the windows, the miniature Henrietta was a false skyline. Gansey's alarm clock beeped continuously, sounding a warning for a time that had long since passed.

Adam's fingers searched unsuccessfully for the light switch.

Gansey shouted again, "We need to talk. Noah!"

The door to Ronan's room opened, releasing a square of light. Ronan was silhouetted in the doorway, one hand curled against his chest, the raven foundling hunched down between his fingers. He pulled a pair of silkily expensive headphones from his ears and looped them around his neck. "Man, you're back late. Parrish? I thought you were working."

So Ronan knew no more than Adam did. Adam felt a cold bit of relief over this, which he quickly extinguished.

"I *was*." Adam finally found the light switch. The room was transformed into a twilight planet, the corners alive with sharp-mouthed shadows.

"Where's Noah?" demanded Gansey. He jerked the alarm clock's power cord out of the wall to silence it.

Ronan took in Gansey's state and raised an eyebrow. "He's out."

"*No*," Gansey said, emphatic, "he is not. *Noah!*"

He backed into the centre of the room, turning to look at the corners, the rafters, searching places no one would ever find a roommate. Adam hesitated by the door. He couldn't figure out how this could be over Noah: Noah, who could go unnoticed for hours, whose room was pristine, whose voice was never raised.

Gansey stopped searching and turned to Adam.

"Adam," he demanded, "what is Noah's last name?"

Before Gansey had asked, Adam felt as if he must have known. But now the answer slid away from his mouth and then from his thoughts entirely, leaving his lips parted. It was like losing his way to class, losing his way home, forgetting the phone number for Monmouth Manufacturing.

"I don't know," Adam admitted.

Gansey pointed at Adam's chest like he was shooting a gun or making a point. "It's Czerny, by the way. Zerny. Chair-knee. However it's pronounced. Noah Czerny." Throwing his head back, he shouted to the air, "I know you're here, Noah."

"Dude," Ronan remarked. "You're flipped."

"Open his door," Gansey ordered. "Tell me what's in there."

With a graceful shrug, Ronan slid out of his doorway and turned the knob on Noah's door. It fell open, revealing the corner of an always-made bed.

"It looks like a nunnery as usual," Ronan said. "All the personality of a mental facility. What am I looking for? Drugs? Girls? Guns?"

"Tell me," Gansey said, "which classes you share with Noah."

Ronan snorted. "None."

"Me neither," Gansey replied. He looked at Adam, who shook his head slightly. "Nor Adam. How is that possible?" He didn't wait for an answer, though. "When does he eat? Have you *ever* seen him eat?"

"I don't really care," Ronan said. He stroked Chainsaw's head with a single finger and she tilted her beak up in response. It was a strange moment in a strange evening, and if it had happened the day before, it would've struck Adam that he rarely saw such thoughtless kindness from Ronan.

Gansey shot questions at both of them. "Does he pay rent? When did he move in? Have you ever questioned it?"

Ronan shook his head. "Dude, you have really left the reservation. What is your problem?"

"I spent the afternoon with the police," Gansey said. "I went out with Blue to the church—"

Now jealousy stabbed Adam, deep and unexpected, a wound that kept stinging, no less painful for him not being certain what, precisely, had inflicted it.

Gansey continued, "Don't look at me like that, both of you. The point is this. We found a body. Rotted to bones. Do you know whose it was?"

Ronan's gaze held Gansey's, solid.

Adam felt like he had dreamt the answer to this question.

Behind them, the door to the apartment suddenly slammed shut. They whirled to face it, but there was no one there, only the fluttering of map corners on the wall to show that it had moved.

The boys stared at the subtle movement of the paper, listened to the echo of the slam.

There was no breeze. Adam's skin crawled.

"Mine," Noah said.

As one, they spun back around.

Noah stood in the doorway to his room.

His skin was pale as parchment and his eyes were shadowed and unspecific, as they always were after dark. There was the ubiquitous smudge on his face, only now, it looked like dirt, or blood, or possibly like a hollow, his bones crushed beneath his skin.

Ronan's posture was wound tight. "Your room was empty. I just looked in it."

"I told you," Noah said. "I told everyone."

Adam had to close his eyes for a long moment.

Gansey, if anything, looked finally back under control. What Gansey needed out of life was facts, things he could write in his journal, things he could state twice and underline, no matter how improbable those facts were. Adam realized that all along Gansey had not really known what he was going to find when he'd brought Adam back here. How could he have? How could anyone truly believe—

"He's dead," Gansey said. His arms were tight over his chest. "You're really dead, aren't you?"

Noah's voice was plaintive. "I *told* you."

They stared at him, just a metre away from Ronan. Really, he was so much less *real* than Ronan, Adam thought – it should have been obvious. It was ludicrous that they hadn't noticed. Ridiculous that they had not thought about his last name, about where he came from, about the classes he did or did not go to. His clammy hands, his pristine room, his unchanging smudgy face. He had been dead as long as they'd known him.

Reality was a bridge breaking beneath Adam.

"Shit, man," Ronan said, finally. A little desperate. "All those nights you gave me grief about keeping you awake and you don't even need to sleep."

Adam asked, barely audible, "How did you die?"

Noah turned his face away.

"No," Gansey said, purpose crystallized in the word. "That's not the question, is it? The question is: who *killed* you?"

Now Noah wore the retreating expression that came when something made him uncomfortable. His chin turned, his eyes hooded and alien. Adam was suddenly profoundly aware that Noah was a dead thing and he was not.

"If you can tell me," Gansey said, "I can find a way to put the police on the trail."

Noah's chin ducked further, his expression somehow black, his eye sockets hollowed and skull-like. Were they looking at a boy? Or something that looked like a boy?

Adam wanted to say, *Don't push him, Gansey*.

In Ronan's hands, Chainsaw began to scream. Bright, frantic caws that split the air. It was as if there was nothing in the world but the sound of her frenzied cries. It seemed impossible that such a small body could make such a huge sound.

Noah lifted his head, his eyes wide open and ordinary. He looked frightened.

Ronan folded a hand over Chainsaw's head until she quietened.

Noah said, "I don't want to talk about it."

His shoulders were drawn up around his ears, and he looked, now, like the Noah that they had always known. The Noah they had never questioned as being one of them.

One of the *living*.

"OK," said Gansey. Then, again: "OK. What would you like to do?"

"I'd like. . ." Noah began, trailing off as he always did, shrinking back into his room. Was this what Noah did when he was alive, Adam wondered, or was this a function of being dead, of trying to hold an ordinary conversation?

Ronan and Adam both glanced to Gansey at once. It seemed like there was nothing to be done or said. Even Ronan seemed subdued, his normal barbs hidden. Until they were sure what the new rules were, he, too, seemed reluctant to find out how otherworldly Noah could be when provoked.

Looking away from the others, Gansey asked, "Noah?"

The space in Noah's doorway was empty.

At the threshold of Noah's room, Ronan pushed the door all the way open. The room inside was stark and untouched, the bed so clearly unslept in.

The world hummed around Adam, suddenly charged with possibilities, not all of them pleasant. He felt like he was sleepwalking. Nothing was the truth until he could put his hands on it.

Ronan began to swear, long and filthy and continuous, without stopping for breath.

Gansey's thumb worried over his bottom lip. He asked Adam, "What's going on?"

Adam replied, "We're being haunted."

THIRTY

Blue was more distressed than she thought she would've been by the fact that Noah was dead. From talking to the police, it was clear that he'd *never* been alive, at least not since she'd met him, but still, she felt a curious grief over it. For starters, Noah's presence in Monmouth changed distinctly after they discovered his body. They never seemed to get the entire Noah any more: Gansey would hear Noah's voice in the car park, or Blue would see his shadow fall across the pavement as she headed over to Monmouth, or Ronan would find scratches on his skin.

He had always been a ghost, but now he was acting it.

"Maybe," Adam had suggested, "it's because his body's been removed from the ley line."

Blue just kept thinking of the skull with its face smashed in, of Noah retching at the sight of the Mustang. Not throwing up. Just going through the actions of it, because he was *dead*.

She wanted to find whoever did it and she wanted him to fester in a cell for the rest of his life.

Blue was so engrossed in Noah's plight that she nearly forgot that she and Calla were supposed to search Neeve's room on Friday. Calla must have recognized that she was distracted, because she'd left a cheekily obvious note on the fridge for Blue to find before school: BLUE – DON'T FORGET MOVIE NIGHT TONIGHT. Swiping the sticky note from the door, Blue stuffed it into her backpack.

"Blue," Neeve said.

Blue jumped as far into the air as a human being could manage, spinning at the same time. Neeve sat at the kitchen table, a mug of tea in front of her, a book in her hand. She wore a cream shirt the precise colour of the curtains behind her.

"I didn't see you there!" Blue gasped. The sticky note in her backpack felt like a burning confession.

Neeve smiled mildly and placed her book face down. "I haven't seen much of you this week."

"I've . . . been . . . out . . . with . . . friends." Between each word, Blue told herself to stop sounding suspicious.

"I've heard about Gansey," Neeve said. "I advised Maura that it wasn't wise to try to keep you apart. You're clearly meant to cross paths."

"Oh. Uh. Thanks for that."

"You seem distressed," Neeve said. With one of her lovely hands, she patted the seat of the chair beside her. "Would you like me to look at anything for you? Do a reading?"

"Oh, thanks for that, but I can't – I have to make it to school," Blue said quickly. Part of her wondered if Neeve asked these things out of kindness, or if she asked them out of reverse psychology, because she knew what Calla and Blue were planning. Either way, Blue didn't want any part of the scrying Neeve did. Bundling her things towards the doorway, she did a kind of casual half wave over her shoulder.

She had made it only a few steps when Neeve said to her back, "You're looking for a god. Didn't you suspect that there was also a devil?"

Blue froze in the doorway. She turned her head, but didn't quite face Neeve.

"Oh, I haven't been poking around," Neeve said. "What you're doing is big enough for me to see while I'm looking at other things."

Now Blue faced her. Neeve's mild expression hadn't changed; her hands were cupped around the mug.

"Numbers are easy for me," Neeve said. "They came first, really. I could always pull them out of thin air. Important dates. Telephone numbers. They're the easiest. But death's the next easiest. I can tell when someone's touched it."

Blue clutched her backpack straps. Her mother and her friends were strange, yes, but they *knew* they were strange. They knew when they were saying something weird. Neeve didn't seem to have that filter.

She replied finally, "He'd been dead a long time."

Neeve shrugged. "There'll be more before it's done."

Lost for words, Blue just slowly shook her head.

"I'm just warning you," Neeve said. "Watch for the devil. When there's a god, there's always a legion of devils."

THIRTY-ONE

For the first time ever, Adam wasn't happy to have a day off from Aglionby. With Friday a scheduled teacher workday, Gansey had reluctantly gone to his parents' for his mother's belated birthday, Ronan was drinking and boorish in his room, and Adam was left studying at Gansey's desk at Monmouth Manufacturing in his absence. The public school had classes as normal, but he could always hope that Blue would come over when she was done.

The apartment felt oppressive without anyone else in the main room. Part of Adam wanted to lure Ronan out of his room for company, but most of him realized that Ronan was, in his unappealing and unspoken way, grieving for Noah. So Adam remained at Gansey's desk, scratching at some Latin homework, aware that the light that came in the windows didn't seem to light the floorboards as well as it ordinarily did. The shadows shifted and clung. Adam smelled the mint plant on Gansey's desk, but he also smelled Noah – that combination of his deodorant and soap and sweat.

"Noah," Adam said to the empty apartment. "Are you here? Or are you out haunting Gansey?"

There was no response.

He looked down at his paper. The Latin verbs looked

nonsensical, a made-up language. "Can we fix it, Noah? Whatever's made you like this, instead of like you were before?"

Adam jumped at a crash directly beside the desk. It took him a moment to realize that Gansey's mint plant had been swept to the floor. A single triangle of the clay pot had fractured, and lay beside a dusting of soil.

"That's not going to help," Adam said calmly, but he was shaken. He wasn't sure, however, what *would* help. After they'd discovered Noah's bones, Gansey had called the police to find out more, but they hadn't learned much – only that Noah had been missing for seven years. As always, Adam had urged reticence, and this time, Gansey had listened, withholding their discovery of the Mustang from the police. The car would lead them to Cabeswater, and that was too complicated, too public.

When a knock came at the door, Adam didn't answer right away, thinking it was Noah again. But then the knock came once more, and this time, Declan's voice: "*Gansey!*"

With a sigh, Adam climbed to his feet, replacing the mint plant before going to open the door. Declan stood on the threshold in neither his Aglionby uniform nor his internship suit, and he seemed like a different person in his jeans, even if they were impeccably dark and expensive. He looked younger than Adam normally thought of him.

"Declan. Hi."

"Where's Gansey?" Declan demanded.

"Not here."

"Oh, come on."

Adam didn't like to be accused of lying. He usually had better ways of getting what he wanted. "He went home for his mother's birthday."

"Where's my brother?"

"Not here."

"Now you are lying."

Adam shrugged. "Yeah. I am."

Declan started past him, but Adam held out his arm, blocking the door. "Now's really not a good time. And Gansey said it wasn't a good idea for you two to talk without him around. I think he's right."

Declan didn't step back. His chest pressed into Adam's arm. Adam knew only this: there was no way that Declan could speak to Ronan right now. Not if Ronan had been drinking, not if Declan was already angry. Without Gansey here, there was sure to be a fight. That was the only thing that was important.

"You're not going to fight me, are you?" Adam asked, as if he wasn't nervous. "I thought that was Ronan's thing, not yours."

It worked better than Adam could have imagined; Declan immediately fell back a step. Reaching into his back pocket, Declan withdrew a folded envelope. Adam recognized the Aglionby crest on the return address.

"He's getting kicked out," Declan said, stuffing the envelope towards Adam. "Gansey *promised* me he would turn his grades around. Well, that hasn't happened. I trusted Gansey, and he let me down. When he gets back, let him know he's got my brother kicked out."

This was more than Adam could stand.

"Oh no," he said. He hoped Ronan was listening. "Ronan did that all by himself. I don't know when you both are going to see that only Ronan can keep himself in Aglionby.

Some day, he has to pick for himself. Until then, you're both wasting your time."

But no matter how true, there was no argument that Adam Parrish could present in his Henrietta accent that would move someone like Declan.

Adam refolded the envelope. Gansey was going to be sick over this. For a brief, brief moment, Adam considered not sharing the letter until it was too late, but then he knew he didn't have it in him. "I'll make sure this gets to him."

"He's moving out," Declan said. "Remind Gansey of that. No Aglionby, no Monmouth."

Then you've killed him, Adam thought, because he couldn't imagine Ronan living under a roof with his brother. He couldn't imagine Ronan living under a roof without Gansey, period. But all he said was, "I'll tell him."

Declan retreated down the stairs, and a moment later, Adam heard his car pull out of the car park.

Adam opened the envelope and slowly read the letter inside. With a sigh, he returned to the desk and picked up the phone that sat beside the now-broken mint pot. He dialled from memory.

"Gansey?"

Several hours away, Gansey was just losing interest in his mother's birthday. Adam's call had spoiled any buoyancy left in his mood, and it hadn't taken long after that for Helen and Gansey's mother to become engaged in a full-on politely disappointed conversation that they both pretended wasn't over Helen's non-glass glassware. During a particularly tense non-exchange, Gansey put his hands in his pockets and walked out to his father's garage.

Ordinarily, home – a sprawling, Cotswold-stone mansion outside of Washington, D.C. – had a sort of nostalgic comfort to it, but today, Gansey had no patience for it. All he could think about was Noah's skeleton and Ronan's terrible grades and the trees speaking Latin.

And Glendower.

Glendower, lying in his fine armour, barely illuminated in the darkness of his tomb. In Gansey's vision in the tree, he had seemed so real. Gansey had touched the dusted surface of the armour, run his fingers over the spearhead that lay beside him, blown dust off the cup curled in Glendower's armoured right hand. He'd moved to the helmet and hovered his hands over it. This was the moment he'd been waiting for, the uncovering, the waking.

And that was when the vision had ended.

Gansey had always felt as if there were two of him: the Gansey who was in control, able to handle any situation, able to talk to anyone, and then, the other, more fragile Gansey, strung out and unsure, embarrassingly earnest, driven by naive longing. That second Gansey loomed inside him now, more than ever, and he didn't like it.

He punched the key code (Helen's birthday) into the pad by the garage door. The garage, as large as the house, was all stone and wood and arched ceilings, a stable housing several thousand horses tucked away under hoods.

Like Dick Gansey III, Dick Gansey II also adored old cars, but unlike Dick Gansey III, all of the elder Gansey's cars had been returned to elegant perfection by teams of restoration experts who were familiar with terms like *rotisserie* and *Barrett-Jackson*. Most had been imported from Europe and many had right-hand drive or came with owner's manuals in foreign languages. And most important, his father's cars were all famous in some way: they'd been owned by a celebrity or been part of a movie shoot or had once been involved in a collision with a historical figure.

Gansey settled on a Peugeot the colour of vanilla ice cream that had probably been owned by Lindbergh or Hitler or Marilyn Monroe. Leaning back in the seat, his feet resting on the pedals, Gansey thumbed through the cards in his wallet and eventually dialled the school guidance counsellor, Mr Pinter. While the phone rang, he conjured up that in-control version of himself that he knew lurked inside.

"Mr Pinter? I'm sorry to call you after hours," Gansey said. He ran his pile of business and credit cards over the steering wheel. The interior of the entire car reminded him a lot of his mother's kitchen mixer. The gearshift looked like it might make a serviceable meringue when it wasn't moving the car from first to second. "This is Richard Gansey."

"Mr Gansey," Pinter said. He took a very long time to say the syllables, during which Gansey imagined him struggling to put a face to the name. Pinter was a tidy, motivated man that Gansey called "very traditional" and Ronan deemed "a cautionary tale".

"I'm calling on behalf of Ronan Lynch."

"Ah."

Pinter didn't need any time to put a face to that name. "Well, I can't really discuss the specifics of Mr Lynch's imminent expulsion—"

"With all due respect, Mr Pinter," Gansey interrupted, fully aware that he was not allotting any due respect to him by so doing, "I'm not sure you're aware of our specific situation."

He scratched the back of his head with a credit card while

he explained Ronan's fragile emotional state, the agonizing trials of sleepwalking, the affirming joys of Monmouth Manufacturing and the strides they'd made since Ronan came to live with him. Gansey concluded with a thesis statement of just how successful he was certain Ronan Lynch would be, once he found a way to patch the haemorrhaging, Niall-Lynch-shaped hole in his heart.

"I'm not entirely convinced that Mr Lynch's future success is the kind that Aglionby nurtures," Pinter said.

"Mr Pinter," Gansey protested, although he was inclined to agree with him on this point. He spun the knob on the window crank. "Aglionby has an incredibly varied and complex student body. It's one of the reasons why my parents selected it for me."

Really, it had been four hours of Google and a persuasive phone call with his father, but Pinter didn't need to know that.

"Mr Gansey, I appreciate your concern for your frie—"

"Brother," Gansey interrupted. "Really, I've come to see him as a brother. And to my parents, he's a son. In every sense of the word. Emotionally, practically, *fiscally*."

Pinter didn't say anything.

"Last time he visited, my father thought the Aglionby library looked a little sparse in the nautical history department," Gansey said. He stuck the credit card in the air vents to see how far it would go before meeting resistance. He had to grab the card before it disappeared in the bowels of the car. "He remarked that it looked like an, oh, thirty-thousand-dollar-sized gap in the funding."

Pinter's voice was a little deeper as he said, "I don't think you understand why Mr Lynch's time at Aglionby is being threatened. He utterly flaunts school regulations and seems to have nothing but contempt for his academics. We have given him leeway considering his extremely difficult personal circumstances, but he seems to forget that attending Aglionby Academy is a privilege, not a chore. His expulsion is meant to be effective Monday."

Gansey leaned forward and rested his head against the steering wheel. *Ronan, Ronan, why. . .*

He said, "I know he's screwing up. I know he should've been kicked out a long time ago. Just give me to the end of the school year. I can get him through his finals."

"He hasn't been to any *classes*, Mr Gansey."

"I can get him through his finals."

For a long moment there was silence. Gansey heard a television playing in the background.

Finally, Pinter said, "He has to make Bs in all of his finals. And toe the line until then or he's out of Aglionby immediately. He doesn't have any more chances."

Sitting up, Gansey let out his breath. "Thank you, sir."

"Also, don't forget about your father's interest in our nautical history section. I'll be watching for it."

And Ronan thought he had nothing to learn from Pinter. Gansey smiled grimly at the dashboard, though he was as far away from amused as he'd ever been. "The boats have always been a big part of our life. Thanks for picking up the phone after hours."

"Enjoy your weekend, Mr Gansey," Pinter replied.

Gansey clicked END and tossed the phone on to the dashboard. Closing his eyes, he breathed a swear word. Gansey had dragged Ronan through his midterms. Surely he could do it again. He had to do it again.

The Peugeot rocked as someone got into the passenger seat. For a breathless moment, Gansey thought, *Noah?*

But then, his father said, "Are you being seduced by this French beauty? This makes your mullet car seem pretty coarse, doesn't it?"

Gansey opened his eyes. Beside him, his father ran a palm over the dash of the car and then inspected it for dust. He squinted at Gansey as if he could determine the state of his son's health and mental facilities merely by looking at him.

"It's nice," Gansey said. "Not really me, though."

"I'm surprised your jalopy got you here," his father said. "Why don't you take the Suburban back?"

"The Camaro's OK."

"Smells like petrol."

Now Gansey could imagine his father pecking around the Camaro where it was parked in front of the garage, his hands behind his back as he sniffed for fluid leakage and observed nicks in the paint.

"It's fine, Dad. It's *exemplary.*"

"I doubt that," his father said, but amiably. Richard Gansey II was rarely anything but. *A lovely man, your father,* people told Gansey. *Always smiling. Nothing flaps him. Such a character.* This last bit was because he collected strange old things and looked in holes in walls and had a journal of things that had happened on the fourteenth of April every year since history began. "Do you have any idea why your sister purchased that hideous bronze plate for three thousand dollars? Is she angry at your mother? Is she trying to play a practical joke?"

"She thought Mom would like it."

"It's not *glass.*"

Gansey shrugged. "I tried to warn her."

For a moment they sat there. His father asked, "Do you want to start it up?"

Gansey didn't care, but he found the key in the ignition and turned it. The engine turned over immediately, springing to obedient life, nothing like the Camaro.

"Bay four, open," his father said, and the garage door in front of them began to power open. When he saw Gansey's glance, he explained, "I had voice controls installed. The only difficulty is that if you shout very loudly outside, the door closest to you will open. Obviously, that is detrimental to security. I'm working on that. We did have an attempted break-in a few weeks ago. They only made it as far as the front gate. Installed a weight-based system out there."

The garage door opened on the Camaro, parked directly in front of them, blocking their exit. The Pig was low and defiant and rough around the edges in comparison to the demure, self-contained, always smiling Peugeot. Gansey felt a sudden and irrepressible love for his car. Buying it was the best decision of his life.

"I never get used to that thing," Gansey's father said, eyeing the Pig without malice.

Once, Gansey had overhead his father saying, *Why in the world did he even* want *that car?* and his mother replying, *Oh, I know why.* One day he would find an opportunity to bring up that conversation with her, because he wanted to know why she thought he had bought it. Analysing what motivated him to put up with the Camaro made Gansey feel unsettled, but he knew it had something to do with how sitting in this perfectly restored Peugeot made him feel. A car was a wrapper for its contents, he thought, and if he looked on the inside like any of the cars in this garage looked on the outside, he couldn't live with himself. On the outside, he knew he looked a lot like his father. On the inside, he sort of wished he looked more like the Camaro. Which was to say, more like Adam.

His father asked, "How are you doing in school?"

"Great."

"What's your favourite class?"

"World History."

"Good teacher?"

"Perfectly adequate."

"How's your scholarship friend doing? Finding the classes harder than public school?"

Gansey turned the driver's side mirror so that it reflected the ceiling. "Adam's doing well."

"He must be pretty smart."

"He's a genius," Gansey said, with certainty.

"And the Irish one?"

Gansey couldn't bring himself to make up a convincing lie for Ronan, not so soon after the call with Pinter. Just then, it felt very weighty to be Gansey the younger. He replied, "Ronan is Ronan. It's hard for him without his father."

Gansey Sr, didn't ask about Noah and Gansey realized he couldn't remember him ever doing so. In fact, he couldn't remember ever mentioning Noah to his family at all. He wondered if the police would call his parents about him finding the body. If they hadn't already, it seemed unlikely that they would. They'd given Gansey and Blue cards with the number of a counsellor on it, but Gansey thought they both probably needed help of a different variety.

"How's the ley-line hunt going?"

Gansey considered how much to say. "I've actually made some breakthroughs that I hadn't expected. Henrietta is looking promising."

"So things aren't going badly? Your sister said you seemed a little melancholy."

"*Melancholy?* Helen's an idiot."

His father clucked his tongue. "Dick, you don't mean that. Word choice?"

Gansey turned off the engine and exchanged a look with his father. "She bought Mom a bronze plate for her birthday."

Gansey Sr, made a little *hm* noise, which meant that Gansey Jr, had a point.

"Just so long as you're happy and keeping busy," his father said.

"Oh," Gansey said, retrieving his phone from the dash. Already his mind was churning over how to crunch three months of study into Ronan's brain, how to return Noah to his former self, how to convince Adam to leave his parents' house even though Henrietta no longer seemed like such a dead end, what cunning thing he could say to Blue when he saw her next. "I'm keeping busy."

THIRTY-TWO

When Blue knocked on the door of Monmouth Manufacturing after school, Ronan answered the door.

"You guys weren't waiting outside," Blue said, feeling a little self-conscious. After all this time, she'd never been inside and she felt a little like a trespasser merely by standing in the decrepit stairwell. "I thought maybe you weren't here."

"Gansey's partying with his mother," Ronan said. He smelled like beer. "And Noah's fucking dead. But Parrish is here."

"Ronan, let her in," Adam said. He appeared at Ronan's shoulder. "Hey, Blue. You've never been up before, have you?"

"Yeah. Should I not—"

"No, come—"

There was a bit of a fumble and then Blue was inside and the door was shut behind her and both of the boys were watching her reaction carefully.

Blue gazed around the first floor. It looked like the home of a mad inventor or an obsessed scholar or a very messy explorer; after meeting Gansey, she was beginning to suspect that he was all of these things. She said, "What's the downstairs look like?"

"Dust," Adam replied. He used his foot to discreetly move a pair of dirty jeans, boxers still tucked inside them, out of Blue's direct line of sight. "And concrete. And more dust. And dirt."

"Also," said Ronan, moving off towards a pair of doors at the other end of the floor, "dust."

For a moment, Ronan and Adam craned their necks, looking around the spread-out space as if they, too, were seeing it for the first time. The vast room, painted red with afternoon sun through the dozens of windowpanes, was beautiful and cluttered. It reminded Blue of the feeling she had when she had first seen Gansey's journal.

For the first time in days, she thought about the vision of his fingers resting on her face.

Blue, kiss me.

For one half of a breath, Blue closed her eyes to reset her thoughts.

"I have to feed Chainsaw," Ronan said, a sentence that made absolutely no sense to Blue. He disappeared into the tiny office and shut the door behind himself. An inhuman squawking noise emitted from within, which Adam didn't comment on.

"We're not doing anything today, obviously," Adam said. "Do you want to hang out?"

Blue looked around for a sofa. It would be easier to hang out with a sofa. There was an unmade bed in the middle of the room, a very expensive-looking leather armchair (the sort with glossy brass bolts holding the leather in place) situated in front of one of the floor-to-ceiling windows, and a desk chair with papers scattered across it. No sofa.

"Has Noah—?"

Adam shook his head.

Blue sighed. Maybe, she thought, Adam was right about Noah's body. Maybe moving it off the ley line had stolen his energy.

"Is he here?" she asked.

"It feels like it. I don't know."

To the empty air, she said, "You can use my energy, Noah. If that's what you need."

Adam's expression was enigmatic. "That's brave of you."

She didn't think so; if it was something that she needed to be brave about, she was certain her mother wouldn't have her along to the church watch. "I like to be useful. So, do you live here, too?"

Adam shook his head, his eyes on the spread of Henrietta outside the windows. "Gansey would like me to. He likes all of his things in one place." His voice was a little bitter, and after a pause, he added, "I shouldn't say things like that. He doesn't mean it badly. And we're – it's just, this place is Gansey's. Everything in it is Gansey's. I need to be an equal, and I can't be, living here."

"Where *do* you live?"

Adam's mouth was very set. "A place made for leaving."

"That's not really an answer."

"It's not really a place."

"And it would be terrible to live here?" She leaned her head back to gaze at the ceiling far above. The entire place smelled dusty, but in the good, old way of a library or a museum.

"Yes," Adam replied. "When I get out on my own, it will be to some place I made myself."

"And that's why you go to Aglionby."

He levelled that gaze on her. "And that's why I go to Aglionby."

"Even though you're not rich."

He hesitated.

"Adam, I don't care," Blue said. Parsed on the most basic level, it wasn't really the most gutsy sentence ever said, but it felt gutsy to Blue when she said it. "I know other people do, but I don't."

He made a little face and then inclined his head in the slightest of nods. "Even though I'm not rich."

"True confession—" Blue said. "I'm not rich, either."

Adam laughed out loud at that, and she discovered that she was starting to really like this laugh that burst out of him and seemed to surprise him every time. She was a little scared of the knowledge that she was starting to like it.

He said, "Oh. Hey. Come over here. You'll like this."

The floor creaking under him, he led the way past the desk to the windows on the far side. Blue felt a sense of dizzying height here; these massive old factory windows began only a few centimetres above the old wide floorboards, and the ground floor was much taller than the ground floor of her house. Crouching, Adam began pawing through a row of cardboard file boxes that were shoved against the windows.

Eventually he dragged one of the boxes away from the window and gestured for Blue to sit beside him. She did. Adam readjusted his posture so that he was more settled; his knee bone pressed against Blue's. He was not looking at her, but there was something about his posture that betrayed his awareness of her. She swallowed.

"These are things that Gansey's found," Adam said. "Things not cool enough for museums, or things they couldn't prove were old, or things he didn't want to give away."

"In this box?" Blue asked.

"In all the boxes. This is the Virginia box." He tipped it enough that the contents spilled between them, along with a prodigious quantity of dirt.

"Virginia box, huh? What are the other boxes?"

There was something of a little boy in his smile. "Wales and Peru and Australia and Montana and other strange places."

Blue took a forked stick from the pile. "Is this another dowsing rod?" Though she had never used one, she knew some psychics used them as a tool to focus their intuition and to lead them in the direction of lost items, or dead bodies, or hidden bodies of water. A low-tech version of Gansey's fancy EMF reader.

"I guess. Might just be a stick." Adam showed her an old Roman coin. She used it to scrape some ages-old dust off a tiny sculpted stone dog. The dog was missing a back leg; the jagged wound revealed stone lighter than the rest of the grubby surface.

"He looks a little hungry," Blue commented. The stylized dog sculpture reminded her of the raven carved into the side of the hill – head bent back, body elongated.

Adam picked up a stone with a hole in it and looked at her through it. The shape of it perfectly covered the last remnants of his bruise.

Blue selected a matching stone and looked at him through its matching hole. One side of his face was red with the afternoon light. "Why are these in the box?"

"Water bored these holes," Adam said. "Seawater. But he

found them in the mountains. I think he said they matched some of the stones he found in the UK."

He was still looking at her through the hole, the stone making a strange eyeglass. She watched his throat move, and then, he reached out and touched her face.

"You sure are pretty," he said.

"It's the stone," she replied immediately. Her skin felt warm; his fingertip touched just the very edge of her mouth. "It's very flattering."

Adam gently pulled the stone out of her hand and set it on the floorboards between them. Through his fingers he threaded one of the flyaway hairs by her cheek. "My mother used to say, 'Don't throw compliments away, so long as they're free'." His face was very earnest. "That one wasn't meant to cost you anything, Blue."

Blue plucked at the hem on her dress, but she didn't look away from him. "I don't know what to say when you say things like that."

"You can tell me if you want me to keep saying them."

She was torn by the desire to encourage him and the fear of where it would lead. "I like when you say things like that."

Adam asked, "But what?"

"I didn't say *but*."

"You meant to. I heard it."

She looked at his face, fragile and strange under the bruise. It was easy to read him as shy or uncertain, she thought, but he really wasn't either. *Noah* was. But Adam was just quiet. He wasn't lost for words; he was observing.

But knowing those things about him didn't help her answer the question: should she tell him about the danger of a kiss? It had been so much easier to tell Gansey, when it felt like it didn't really matter. The last thing she wanted to do was to scare Adam off by tossing around phrases like *true love* right after she'd met him. But if she *didn't* say anything, there was a chance that he might steal a kiss and then they'd both be in trouble.

"I like it when you say those things, *but* – I'm afraid you'll kiss me," Blue admitted. Already this seemed like an untenable path to set off on. When he didn't immediately say anything, she hurried on, "We've just met. And I . . . I'm . . . I'm *very young.*"

Halfway through, she lost her nerve to explain the prediction, but she wasn't sure what part of her felt this was a better confession to blurt out. *I'm very young.* She winced.

"That seems. . ." Adam sought words. "Very sensible."

The precise adjective Neeve had found for Blue that very first week. So she truly was sensible. This was distressing. She felt like she'd done so much work to appear as eccentric as possible, and still, when it came down to it, she was *sensible.*

Both Adam and Blue looked up at the sound of footsteps crossing the floor towards them. It was Ronan, holding something under his arm. He cautiously lowered himself until he sat cross-legged beside Adam and then sighed heavily, as if he had been part of the conversation to this point and it tired him. Blue was equal parts relieved and disappointed at his presence effectively ending any more talk about kissing.

"Do you want to hold her?" Ronan asked.

That was when Blue discovered that the thing that Ronan was holding was alive. For a brief moment, Blue was actually incapable of doing anything but contemplating the irony that one of the raven boys actually possessed a raven.

By then, it was clear that Ronan had decided the answer was no.

"What are you doing?" Blue asked as he withdrew his hand. "I want to."

She wasn't exactly sure that she did – the raven was not quite done-looking – but it was a matter of principle. She realized, again, that she was trying to impress Ronan only because he was impossible to impress, but she comforted herself that at least all she was doing in pursuit of his approval was holding a baby bird. Ronan carefully bundled the raven into her cupped palms. The little bird felt like she weighed nothing at all, and her skin and feathers felt humid where they'd been in contact with Ronan's hands. The raven tipped her huge head back and goggled at Blue and then Adam, beak cracked.

"What's her name?" Blue asked. Holding her was frightening and lovely; she was such a small, tenuous little life, her pulse tapping rapidly against Blue's skin.

Adam answered witheringly, "Chainsaw."

The raven opened her beak wide, goggling even more than before.

"She wants you again," Blue said, because it was clear that she did. Ronan accepted the bird and stroked the feathers on the back of her head.

"You look like a supervillain with your familiar," Adam said

Ronan's smile cut his face, but he looked kinder than Blue had ever seen him, like the raven in his hand was his heart, finally laid bare.

They all heard a door open on the other side of the room. Adam and Blue looked at each other. Ronan ducked his head, just a little, as if he was waiting for a blow.

No one said anything as Noah settled down in the gap left between Ronan and Blue. He looked as Blue remembered him, his shoulders hunched forward and his hands restlessly moving from place to place. The ever-present smudge on his face was clearly where his cheek had been smashed in. The longer she stared at him, the more certain she became that she was at once seeing his dead body and his live one. That smudge was her brain's way of reconciling those facts.

Adam was the first to say something.

"Noah," he said. He lifted his fist.

After a pause, Noah bumped knuckles with him. Then he rubbed the back of his neck.

"I'm feeling better," he said, as if he'd been ill instead of dead. The things from the box were still spread out all over the floor between them; he began to sort through them. He picked up something that looked like a carved bit of bone; it must've had a larger pattern on it once, but now all that was left was something that looked like the edge of an acanthus leaf and possibly some raised scrolling. Noah held it against his throat like an amulet. His eyes were averted from either of the other two boys, but his knee touched Blue's.

"I want you to know," Noah said, pressing the carved bone against his Adam's apple, hard, as if it would squeeze the words from him, "I was . . . *more* . . . when I was alive."

Adam chewed his lip, looking for a response. Blue thought she knew what he meant, though. Noah's resemblance to the crookedly smiling photo on the driver's licence Gansey had discovered was akin to a photocopy's resemblance to an original painting. She couldn't imagine the Noah she knew driving that tricked-out Mustang.

"You're enough now," Blue said. "I missed you."

With a wan smile, Noah reached over and petted Blue's hair, just like he used to. She could barely feel his fingers.

Ronan said, "Hey, man. All those times you wouldn't give me notes because you said I should go to my classes. You *never* went to classes."

"But you *did*, didn't you, Noah?" Blue interrupted, thinking of the Aglionby badge they'd found with his body. "You were an Aglionby student."

"Are," Noah said.

"*Were*," Ronan said. "You don't go to classes."

"Neither do you," Noah replied.

"And he's about to be a *were*, too," Adam broke in.

"*OK!*" Blue shouted, her hands in the air. She was starting to feel a deep sensation of cold, as Noah pulled energy from her. The last thing she wanted to do was to get completely drained, like she had at the churchyard. "The police said you'd been missing seven years. Does that seem right?"

Noah blinked at her, vague and alarmed. "I don't . . . I can't. . ."

Blue held her hand out.

"Take it," she said. "When I'm at readings with my mom, and she needs to get focused, she holds my hand. Maybe it will help."

Hesitant, Noah reached out. When he laid his palm against hers, she was shocked by how chilled it was. It was not merely cold, but somehow empty as well, skin without a pulse.

Noah, please don't die for real.

He let out a heaving sigh. "God," he said.

And his voice sounded different from before. Now it

sounded closer to the Noah she knew, the Noah who had passed as one of them. Blue knew she wasn't the only one to notice it, because Adam and Ronan exchanged sharp glances.

She watched his chest rise and fall, his breaths becoming more even. She hadn't really noticed, before, if he'd been breathing at all.

Noah shut his eyes. He still held the carved bone loosely in his other hand, rested palm up on his Top-Siders. "I can remember my grades, the date on them – seven years ago."

Seven years. The police had been right. They were talking with a boy who had been dead for seven years.

"The same year Gansey was stung by hornets," Adam said softly. Then he said, "'*You will live because of Glendower. Someone else on the ley line is dying when they should not, and so you will live when you should not.*'"

"Coincidence," Ronan said, because it wasn't.

Noah's eyes were still closed. "It was supposed to do something to the ley line. I don't remember what he said it was supposed to do."

"Wake it up," Adam suggested.

Noah nodded, his eyelids still pressed closed. Blue's entire arm felt chilled and numb. "Yeah, that. I didn't care. It was always his deal, and I was just going along with him because it was something to do. I didn't know he was going to. . ."

"This is the ritual Gansey was talking about," Adam said to Ronan. "Someone *did* try it. With a sacrifice as the symbolic way to touch the ley line. You were the sacrifice, weren't you, Noah? Someone killed you for this."

"My face," Noah said softly, and he turned his head away, pressing his ruined cheek into his shoulder. "I can't remember when I stopped being alive."

Blue shuddered. The late afternoon light bathing the boys and the floor was spring, but it felt like winter in her bones.

"But it didn't work," Ronan said.

"I almost woke up Cabeswater," Noah whispered. "We were close enough to do that. It wasn't for nothing. But I'm glad he never found that. He doesn't know. He doesn't know where it is."

Blue shivered unconsciously, a product of both Noah's cold hand in hers and the horror of the story. She wondered if this was what it felt like for her mother and her aunts and her mother's friends when they were doing a séance or a reading.

Do they hold hands with dead people?

She had thought *dead* was something more permanent, or at least something more obviously not alive. But Noah seemed unable to be either.

Ronan said, "OK, it's time to stop fucking around. Who did it, Noah?"

In Blue's grip, Noah's hand trembled.

"Seriously, man. Spill it. I'm not asking you for notes. I'm asking who smashed your head in."

When Ronan said it, there was something angry and honourable about it, but it was an anger that included Noah, too, that somehow made him culpable.

There was humiliation in his voice when Noah answered, "We were friends."

Adam said, rather more ferocious than he'd been a moment before, "A friend wouldn't kill you."

"You don't understand," Noah whispered. Blue was afraid that he would disappear. This, she understood, had been a secret, carried inside him for seven years, and he still didn't want to confess it. "He was upset. He'd lost everything. If he'd been thinking straight, I don't think he would've . . . he didn't mean to . . . we were friends like — are you afraid of Gansey?"

The boys didn't answer; they didn't have to. Whatever Gansey was to them, it was bulletproof. Again, though, Blue saw the shame flit across Adam's expression. Whatever had transpired between the two of them in his vision, it was still worrying at him.

"Come on, Noah. A name." This was Ronan, head cocked, keen as his raven. "Who killed you?"

Lifting his head, Noah opened his eyes. He took his hand out of Blue's and put it in his lap. The air was freezing around all of them. The raven was hunched far down into Ronan's lap, and he held one hand over the top of her, protectively.

Noah said, "But you already know."

THIRTY-THREE

It was dark by the time Gansey left his parents' house. He was full of the restless, dissatisfied energy that always seemed to move into his heart after he visited home these days. It had something to do with the knowledge that his parents' house wasn't truly home any more – if it had ever been – and something to do with the realization that they hadn't changed; he had.

Gansey rolled down the window and stuck his hand out as he drove. The radio had stopped working again and so the only music was the engine; the Camaro was louder after dark.

The conversation with Pinter gnawed at Gansey. Bribery. So that's what it had come to. He thought this feeling inside him was shame. No matter how hard he tried, he kept becoming a Gansey.

But how else was he supposed to keep Ronan in Aglionby and at Monmouth? He went over the talking points for his future conversation with Ronan, and all of them sounded like things Ronan wouldn't listen to. Was it so hard for him to go to class? How *hard* could it be to make it through just another year of school?

He still had a half hour to go until he got to Henrietta. At a tiny town that consisted only of an artificially bright petrol station, Gansey got caught at a traffic light that turned red for invisible cross traffic.

All Ronan had to do was go to class, do the reading, get the grade. And then he was free and he had his money from Declan and he could do whatever the hell he wanted.

Gansey checked his phone. No signal. He wanted to talk to Adam.

The breeze through the open window scented the interior of the car with leaves and water, growing things and secret things. More than anything, Gansey wanted to spend more time in Cabeswater, but class would take up much of the coming week – there could be no cutting for either of them after the talk with Pinter – and after school, he had to drag Ronan through his homework. The world was opening up in front of Gansey and Noah needed him and Glendower seemed like a possibility again, and instead of going out there and seizing the chance, Gansey had to babysit. *Damn* Ronan.

The light turned green. Gansey punched the accelerator so hard that the tyres squealed and smoked. The Pig exploded off the line. *Damn* Ronan. Gansey punched his way through the gears, fast, fast, fast. The engine drowned out the pound of his heart. *Damn* Ronan. The needle climbed on the speedometer, touched the red warning area.

Gansey hit the speed limit. The car had plenty more. The engine did well in this cool air and it was fast and uncomplicated and he wanted badly to see what would happen in the rest of the gears.

He checked himself, heaving a ragged sigh.

If he'd been Ronan, he would've kept going. The

thing about Ronan was that he had no limits, no fears, no boundaries. If Gansey had been Ronan, he would've crushed the accelerator to the floor until the road or a cop or a tree stopped him. He would cut class tomorrow to go see the forest. He'd tell Ronan it was his problem that he was getting expelled, if he would have cared about him at all.

Gansey didn't know how to be that person.

Beneath him, the Camaro abruptly shuddered. Gansey let off the accelerator and stared at all of the badly lit gauges, but nothing stood out to him. A moment later, the car shuddered again and Gansey knew he was done for.

He just had time to find a fairly flat place to pull off when the engine went dead, just as it had on St Mark's Day. As he coasted off the abandoned road, he tried the key, but there was nothing.

Gansey allowed himself the meagre pleasure of a breathed-out swear word, the very worst he had knowledge of, and then he climbed out of the car and opened the hood. Adam had taught him the basics: changing spark plugs, draining oil. If there had been a belt hanging loose or a newly jagged hose end jutting from the bowels of the car, he might have been able to fix it. As it was, the engine was an enigma.

He removed his phone from his back pocket and discovered that he had merely a sliver of reception. Enough to taunt him, but not enough to place a call. Gansey walked around the car a few times, his phone held above his head like Lady Liberty. Nothing.

Somewhat bitterly, Gansey recalled his father's suggestion that he take the Suburban back.

He wasn't certain how much distance he'd covered since the petrol station at the light, but it felt like he must be closer to the edge of Henrietta. If he started to walk towards town, he might get reception before he found a petrol station. Maybe he should just stay put. Sometimes, when the Pig stopped, it would start working again after the engine had cooled down a little.

But he was too restless to sit.

He had barely finished locking the car, however, when headlights pulled in behind the Camaro, blinding him. Turning his face away, Gansey heard a car door slam and footsteps crunch in the loose fill by the highway.

For a blink, the figure in front of him was unfamiliar, a homunculus instead of a man. Then Gansey recognized him.

He said, "Mr Whelk?"

Barrington Whelk wore a dark-coloured jacket and running shoes, and there was something strange and intense about the oversized features of his face. It was as if he needed to ask a question but couldn't find the words.

He didn't ask "car trouble?" or "Mr Gansey?" or any of the things Gansey thought he might say.

Instead, he licked his lips and said, "I want that book of yours. And you'd better give me your phone, too."

Gansey thought he must have misheard. He asked, "Excuse me?"

Whelk produced a small, impossibly real-looking handgun from the pocket of his dark jacket. "That book you bring to class. And your phone. Hurry up."

It was somehow difficult to process the fact of the gun. It was hard to go from the idea that Barrington Whelk was creepy in a way that was entertaining to joke about with

Ronan and Adam to the idea that Barrington Whelk had a gun and was pointing it at Gansey.

"Well." Gansey blinked. "OK."

There didn't seem to be anything else to say. He preferred his life to nearly all of his possessions, with the possible exception of the Camaro, and Whelk hadn't asked for that. Gansey handed his phone to Whelk.

"My journal's in the car," he explained.

"Get it." Whelk pointed the pistol at Gansey's face.

Gansey unlocked the Camaro.

The last time he had seen Whelk, he'd been turning in a quiz about fourth declension Latin nouns.

"Don't think about trying to take off in that," Whelk said.

It hadn't occurred to Gansey that if the Camaro had been operating properly, fleeing would've been an option.

"I also want to know where you've been going this week," Whelk said.

"Pardon?" Gansey asked politely. He had been rummaging in the back seat for the journal, and the crinkling papers had drowned Whelk's voice out.

"Don't push me," Whelk snapped. "The police called the school. I can't believe it. After seven years. Now there's going to be a million questions. It's only going to take them *two seconds* to answer a lot of those questions with my name. This is all on you. Seven years and I thought I was – I'm screwed. You've screwed me."

As Gansey emerged from the Camaro, his journal in his hands, he realized what Whelk was saying: Noah. This man in front of him had killed Noah.

Gansey was beginning to feel something somewhere in

his gut. It still didn't feel like fear. It was something strung out like a rope bridge, barely supporting weight. It was the suspicion that nothing else in Gansey's life had ever been real except for this moment.

"Mr Whelk—"

"Tell me where you've you been."

"Up the mountains near Nethers," Gansey said, his voice remote. It was the truth, and in any case, it didn't matter if he lied or not; he'd entered the GPS coordinates into the journal he was about to hand over.

"What did you find? Did you find Glendower?"

Gansey flinched, and the flinch surprised him. Somehow he'd convinced himself this was about something else, something more logical, and the sound of Glendower's name shocked him. "No," Gansey replied. "We found a carving in the ground." Whelk held his hand out for the journal. Gansey swallowed.

He asked, "Whelk – sir – are you sure this is the only way?"

There was a soft, unmistakable *click*. It was a sound that had been made recognizable by hours of action-adventure movies and video games. Though Gansey had never heard it in person before, he knew exactly what sound a pistol made when the safety was taken off.

Whelk placed the barrel of the gun on Gansey's forehead.

"No," Whelk said. "This is the other way."

Gansey had that same detached feeling that he'd had in Monmouth Manufacturing, looking at the wasp. At once he saw the reality: a gun pressed against the skin above his eyebrows, so cold as to feel sharp – and also the possibility: Whelk's finger pulling back, a bullet burrowing into his skull, death instead of finding a way to get back to Henrietta.

The journal weighted his hands. He didn't need it. He knew everything in it.

But it was *him*. He was giving everything that he'd worked for away.

I will get a new one.

"If you'd just asked," Gansey said, "I would've told you everything in there. I would've been happy to. It wasn't a secret."

The handgun trembled against Gansey's forehead. Whelk said, "I can't believe that you're saying anything when I have a gun to your head. I can't believe you would bother to say that."

"That's how," replied Gansey, "you know it's the truth." He let Whelk take the journal from him.

"You disgust me," Whelk said, holding the book to his chest. "You think you're invincible. Guess what. So did I."

When he said that, Gansey knew Whelk was going to kill him. That there was no way that someone could have that much hatred and bitterness in his voice while holding a gun and not pull the trigger.

Whelk's face tensed.

For a moment, there was no time: just the space between when one breath escaped and another rushed in.

Seven months before, Ronan had taught Gansey how to throw a hook.

Hit with your body, not just your fist.

Look where you're punching.

Elbow at ninety degrees.

Don't think about how much it will hurt.

Gansey. I told you: don't think about how much it will hurt.

He swung.

Gansey forgot nearly everything Ronan had told him, but he remembered to look, and it was only that, and luck, that knocked the gun into the gravel by the road.

Whelk bellowed a wordless shout.

They both dived for the gun. Gansey, stumbling on to one knee, kicked blindly in the direction of it. He heard his foot connect with something. Whelk's arm first, then something more solid. The gun skittered in the direction of the car's rear wheels, and Gansey scrabbled around the far side of the Camaro. The light from Whelk's headlights didn't reach to this side. His only thought was to find cover, to be still in the darkness.

There was silence on the other side of the car. Struggling to keep his gasping breaths in check, Gansey laid his cheek against the warm metal of the Pig. His thumb throbbed where he'd hit the gun.

Don't breathe.

By the road, Whelk swore again and again and again. The gravel crunched as he crouched by the car. He couldn't find the gun. He swore again.

In the far-off distance, an engine hummed. Another car, possibly, coming this way. A rescuer or, at least, a witness.

For a moment, Whelk was completely silent, and then, abruptly, he broke into a run, his footsteps softening as he made it back to his own car.

Ducking his head, Gansey peered under the body of the Pig, which was ticking as it cooled down. He saw the slender silhouette of the gun between the rear tyres, illuminated from behind by Whelk's headlights.

He wasn't sure if Whelk was retreating or going for a

torch. Gansey backed further into the darkness. Then he waited there, his heart crashing in his ears, grass scraping at his cheek.

Whelk's car charged on to the highway, roaring towards Henrietta.

The other car passed by right after. Oblivious.

Gansey lay in the grass of the ditch for a long time, listening to the humming of insects in the trees around him and the breathing sounds the Pig made as the engine settled. His thumb was really starting to hurt where he'd hit the gun. Really, he'd got off light. But still. It hurt.

And his journal. He felt raw: the chronicle of his fiercest desires stripped from him by force.

After Whelk's car failed to return, Gansey climbed to his feet and went around to the other side of the Camaro. He got down on to his knees and crawled as far under the car as he could manage, hooking the edge of the gun with his good thumb. Gingerly, he put the safety back on. He could hear Blue's voice when they found Noah's body: *fingerprints!*

Gansey, moving as in a dream, opened the car door and dropped the gun on the passenger seat. It felt like another night, another car, another person had left his parents' house.

He closed his eyes and turned the key.

The Pig coughed and coughed, but then the engine caught.

He opened his eyes. Nothing about the night looked the same as before.

He turned on his headlights, and then drove back on to the road. Pressing the accelerator, he tested the engine. It held, no stutters.

Slamming down the accelerator, he raced towards Henrietta. Whelk had killed Noah and he knew his cover was blown. Wherever he was heading next, he had nothing left to lose.

THIRTY-FOUR

Blue had never been a big fan of the attic, even before Neeve moved in. Numerous slanting roof lines provided dozens of opportunities to hit your head on a sloping ceiling. Unfinished wood floorboards and areas patched with prickly plywood were unfriendly to bare feet. Summer turned the attic into an inferno. Moreover, there generally was nothing up there but dust and wasps. Maura was a die-hard not-collector and so anything unused was forced upon neighbours or Goodwill. There was really no reason to visit the attic.

Until now.

As it grew late, Blue had left Ronan, Adam and Noah behind to discuss if it was possible to implicate their Latin teacher in Noah's death, if the police had not already established a link. Adam had called only five minutes after she'd got home to tell her that Noah had vanished the instant she'd left.

So it was true. She really *was* the table at Starbucks everyone wanted.

"I think we have an hour," Calla said as Blue opened the attic door. "They should be back around eleven. Let me go first. In case. . ."

Blue raised an eyebrow. "What is it you're thinking she has up here?"

"I don't know."

"Ferrets?"

"Don't be ridiculous."

"Wizards?"

Calla eased by Blue and began to climb the stairs. The single light bulb that illuminated the attic didn't reach far down the stairs. "That's more likely. Oh, it *smells*."

"That's the ferrets."

From her vantage point further up the stairs, Calla shot Blue a look that Blue suspected was more dangerous than anything they'd find in the attic. Calla was right, however. The air that moved slowly around them was rather malodorous; Blue couldn't place the scent, though it hinted at familiar things, like rotting onions and feet.

"Smells like sulphur," Blue said. "Or a dead body."

Thinking of the horrid voice coming from Neeve's mouth before, she wouldn't be surprised by either.

"Smells like asafetida," Calla corrected grimly.

"What's that?"

"Either something that is delicious in curry, or something that is very useful in witchcraft."

Blue tried to breathe through her mouth. It was hard to imagine something that smelled so convincingly of a dead person's feet being delicious in anything. "Which do you think it is?"

Calla had reached the top of the stairs.

"Not curry," she said.

Now that Blue stood at the top of the stairs, she could see that Neeve had transformed the attic into something quite different from what she remembered. A mattress covered with throw rugs lay directly on the floor. Around the room, unlit candles of different heights, dark bowls, and glasses of water were gathered in groups. Bright painters' tape made patterns on the floor between some of the objects. Beside Blue's feet, a half-burned plant stalk rested on a plate dusted with ashes. In one of the narrow dormers, two full-length, footed mirrors faced each other, reflecting mirrored images back and forth at each other *in perpetuum*.

Also, it was cold. The attic should not have been cold after the day's heat.

"Don't touch anything," Calla told Blue. Which Blue found ironic, considering why they'd come.

Blue didn't touch anything, but she did walk further into the room, peering at a small statue of a woman with eyes in her belly. The entire room was giving her a crawling feeling. "She must be making a lot of curry."

Behind them, the stairs creaked, and both Calla and Blue leapt.

"May I come up?" Persephone asked. It was an irrelevant question, as she was already "up". Wearing a lace frock Blue had made her, she stood at the top of the stairs. Her hair was tied up tightly, which signalled that she was not afraid to get her hands dirty.

"*Persephone*," Calla thundered. She'd got over her shock and was now merely angry at being shocked. "You should make some noise when you enter rooms."

"I did let the stair squeak," Persephone pointed out. "Maura said she'll be back at midnight, so be done by then."

"She knows?" This was both Blue and Calla in unison.

Persephone crouched to look at a black leather mask with a long pointed beak. "You didn't think she believed you about the dwarf movie, did you?"

Calla and Blue exchanged a look. Blue mused over what this meant: that Maura wanted to know more about Neeve as much as they did.

Blue asked, "Before we start, are you going to explain why Neeve *said* she was here in Henrietta?"

Calla moved around the room, rubbing her hands together as if she were either warming herself or planning what to pick up first. "That's quite simple. Your mother had her out here to find your father."

"Well," Persephone corrected, "that is not quite true. Maura told me Neeve approached her first. Neeve said she might be able to find him."

"Out of the blue?" Calla asked.

"I'd prefer if you didn't use that expression," Blue said.

"Out of nowhere?" Calla repeated. She picked up a candle. "That seems strange."

Blue crossed her arms. "I'm still missing a lot of details here."

Calla switched the candle from her left hand to her right. "Basically, your father showed up eighteen years ago, swept Maura off her feet, made her an absolutely useless friend for a year, got her pregnant and then vanished after you were born. He was cagey and cute, so I assumed he was trailer-park trash with a police record."

"*Calla!*" Persephone admonished.

"It doesn't bother me," Blue replied. How could she be bothered by a stranger's past? "I just want to know the facts."

Persephone shook her head. "Do you have to be so sensible?"

Blue shrugged. She asked Calla, "What's that candle telling you?"

Holding the candle out from her body, Calla squinted. "Just that it was used for a scrying spell. Locating objects, which is what I'd expect."

As Calla rummaged through more things, Blue thought about what she'd just learned about her father and found she still maintained her unreasonable fondness for him. She was also pleased that he'd been cute. She said, "I heard Mom telling Neeve that the search was meant to be like looking him up online."

"That sounds true," Calla said. "It was just curiosity. It's not as if she's been pining for him."

"Oh," Persephone murmured, "I don't know about that."

This made Blue's ears prick with interest. "Wait, you think my mother is still in love with — does he have a name?"

"Puppy," replied Calla, and Persephone giggled, clearly recalling memories of Maura insensible with love.

"I refuse to believe Mom ever called some man *puppy*," Blue said.

"Oh, but she did. Also *lover*." Calla picked up an empty bowl. There was a crust in the bottom, as if it had once held a liquid with some body to it. Like pudding. Or blood. "And *butternut*."

"You are *making that up*." Blue was ashamed for her mother.

Persephone, a little red from trying not to laugh, shook her head. Large hanks of hair had escaped from her knot, making her look as if she had escaped a tornado. "I'm afraid not."

"Why would you even *call* someone—"

Turning to Blue with extremely jagged eyebrows, Calla said, "Use your imagination", and Persephone exploded into helpless laughter.

Blue crossed her arms. "Oh, really." Her seriousness only served to dissolve any self-control the two women had left. Laughing uncontrollably, they began to trade other pet names Maura had apparently coined eighteen years earlier.

"Ladies," Blue said sternly. "We only have forty-five minutes. Calla, touch that." She pointed to the mirrors. Of all the odd things in the room, she found them the creepiest, and that seemed as good a reason as any to try them.

Swallowing a laugh, Calla stepped over to the mirrors. There was something unnerving about the utter impracticality of two reflecting surfaces pointed only at each other.

"Don't stand between them," Persephone warned.

"I'm not an idiot," Calla retorted.

Blue asked, "Why not stand between them?"

"Who knows what she's doing with them. I don't want my soul put in a bottle in some other dimension or something." Calla gripped the edge of the closest mirror, careful to stand out of the view of the other. Frowning, she pawed a hand towards Blue. Blue obligingly stepped forward and allowed Calla to press her fingers over her shoulder.

A moment passed, quiet but for the insects outside the window.

"Our little Neeve is quite ambitious," Calla growled finally, tightening her fingers on both Blue and the mirror's edge. "Apparently her level of fame is not enough for her. Television programmes are for nobodies."

"Don't be sarcastic, Calla," Persephone said. "Tell us what you see."

"I see her wearing that black mask over there, standing in between these mirrors. I must be seeing her back wherever she came from, because she has four mirrors. Two other larger ones behind each of these. I can see her in each of the four mirrors, and she's wearing the mask in all of them, but she looks different in each one. She's thinner in one of them. She's wearing black in one. Her skin looks wrong in a different one. I'm not sure what they are... They might be possibilities." Calla stopped. Blue felt a little chill at the idea of four different Neeves. "Bring me the mask. No, not you, Blue, stay here. Persephone—?"

Persephone gingerly retrieved the mask. Again, there was a pause as Calla read the object, her knuckles pressed white.

"She was disappointed when she bought this," Calla said. "She'd got a bad review, I think, of one of her books? Or to one of her shows? No. She'd seen numbers for one or the other, and they were disappointing. I definitely see the numbers, and that's what she's imagining when she buys this. She was comparing herself to Leila Polotsky."

"Who's that?" Blue asked.

"A psychic more famous than Neeve," Calla said.

"I didn't know that was possible," Blue replied. A television show and four books seemed more famous than any psychic could hope for in a disbelieving world.

"Oh, it's very possible," Calla asked. "Ask Persephone."

"I don't know about that," Persephone said. Blue wasn't

sure if she was talking about being famous or about asking her.

Calla blew onward. "Anyway, our woman Neeve wishes she could travel the world and get some respect. And this mask helps her visualize that."

"What's this have to do with her being here?" Blue asked.

"I don't know yet. I need a better object." Calla released the mirror and returned the mask to its hook on the wall.

They poked about the room. Blue found a switch made of three sticks tied together with a red ribbon, and a red mask to match the black one. Near the window, she found the source of the hideous smell: a little cloth bag with something sewed into it.

She gave the bag to Calla, who held it for just a moment before saying dismissively, "That's the asafetida. It's just a protection charm. She got spooked by a dream and made it."

Crouching, Persephone hovered her hands over one of the bowls. The way she held her palms out, fingers barely moving, reminded Blue of Gansey holding his hand out over the shallow pool of water in Cabeswater. Persephone said, "There is quite a lot of uncertainty in all of this, isn't there? That's what I feel. Perhaps it's quite as simple as this: she did come to help Maura but is getting a little carried away by Henrietta."

"Because of the corpse road?" asked Blue. "I caught her scrying in the middle of the night and she told me the corpse road made it easy to be psychic here."

Calla sneered before turning to rummage in the things beside the bed.

"Easier and harder," Persephone said. "It's got a lot of

energy, so it's like having you in the room all the time. But it's like your boys. It's quite loud."

My boys! Blue thought, first in a huff, then flattered, then in a huff again.

Persephone asked, "Calla, what are you finding out?"

Calla's back was to them as she replied, "Eleven months ago, a man called Neeve on the phone to ask her if he could bring her to Henrietta, Virginia, for an all-expenses-paid trip. While she was there, she was supposed to use any means at her disposal to pinpoint a ley line and a 'place of power' that he knew was close by but couldn't find. She told him she wasn't interested but decided upon further thought that she might investigate this possibility on her own. She guessed Maura might let her stay in town if she came offering to help locate her old boyfriend."

Persephone and Blue wore matching astonished expressions.

"That's amazing!" Blue said.

Calla turned around. She was holding a small notebook, which she waved at them. "*That* is Neeve's day planner."

"Oh, technology." Persephone sighed. "I thought I heard a car. I'll be right back."

While Persephone padded down the stairs as silently as she'd climbed them, Blue sidled over to Calla, hooking her chin on Calla's shoulder so she could catch a glimpse for herself. "Where does it say all that?"

Calla flipped back through pages of Neeve's handwriting and showed her the pages of mundane notes on appointment times, publishing deadlines and lunch dates. Then she flipped back to the notes for the call with the Henrietta man. It was all as Calla had said, with one notable exception. Neeve had also jotted down the man's name and phone number.

Every muscle in Blue's body went slack.

Because the name of the man who'd called Neeve all those months ago was a rather peculiar one that Blue, by now, knew quite well: Barrington Whelk.

Behind them, the single stair creaked again. Persephone said something that was a bit like *ahem*.

"That was still a little sinister," Calla said, turning.

Persephone's hands were clasped before her. "I have two pieces of bad news." She turned to Blue. "First of all, your raven boys are here, and one of them seems to have broken his thumb on a gun."

Behind Persephone, there was another creak as a second person climbed the stairs. Blue and Calla both twitched a little as Neeve appeared beside Persephone, her gaze eternal and unwavering.

"Secondly," Persephone added, "Neeve and Maura came home early."

THIRTY-FIVE

The kitchen was quite full. It had never been a large kitchen to start with, and by the time three boys, four women, and one Blue were in it, felt like it hadn't been made with enough floor. Adam was polite, helping Persephone make tea for everyone in the room, though he had to keep asking, *Where are the mugs? And now where are the spoons? What about the sugar?* Ronan more than made up for Adam's calm, though — he took up enough room for three people with his restless pacing. Orla came down for the gossip but stared so admiringly at Ronan that Calla yelled at her to leave and give everyone more space.

Neeve and Gansey sat at the breakfast table. Adam and Ronan looked just as they had when Blue had seen them last, but Gansey's eyes were different. She spent a minute too long trying to figure out what was different — it was a combination, she decided, between them being a little brighter and the skin around them a little tighter.

His arm stretched out across the table in front of him. His thumb was splinted.

"Could someone cut this hospital bracelet off?" he asked. There was something gallant and hectic about the deliberately offhand way he asked it. "I feel like an invalid. Please."

Handing him a pair of scissors, Persephone remarked, "Blue, I did *tell* you about putting your thumb outside of your fist if you were going to hit someone."

"You didn't tell me to tell *him*," Blue retorted.

"OK," Maura said from the doorway, rubbing her forehead with her fingers. "There are a few things going on here, obviously. Someone just tried to kill *you*." This was to Gansey. "*You two* are telling me that your friend was killed by the man who just tried to kill him." This was to Ronan and Adam. "*You three* are telling me that Neeve had a phone call with the man who killed your friend and just now tried to kill Gansey." This was to Blue, Persephone and Calla. "And *you're* telling me that you've had nothing to do with him since that phone call."

This last one was to Neeve. Though Maura had spoken to each of them, they all kept looking at Neeve.

"And you let them go through my things," Neeve replied.

Blue expected her mother to look chastened, but instead Maura seemed to grow taller. "And with good reason, obviously. I can't believe you didn't tell me the truth. If you wanted to play around on the corpse road, why didn't you just ask? How do you know I would have said no? Instead, you pretended like you were actually committed to—"

She paused and looked at Blue.

Blue finished, "To finding Butternut."

"Oh, God," Maura said. "Calla, this is your fault, isn't it?"

"No," Blue said. She had to try very hard to pretend that the boys weren't all looking at her in order to say this. "I think I can be mad here, too. Why didn't you just tell me that you didn't really know my father and you had me without getting married? Why is that a big secret?"

"I never said I didn't really know him," Maura replied, voice hollow. She had an expression on her face that Blue didn't like; it was a little too emotional.

Blue looked at Persephone instead. "How do you know I wouldn't have just been happy with the truth? I don't *care* if my father was a deadbeat named Butternut. It doesn't change anything right now."

"His name wasn't really Butternut, was it?" Gansey asked Adam in a low voice.

Neeve's voice, mild as always, cut through the kitchen. "I think this has all been oversimplified. I *was* spending time looking for Blue's father. It's just not *all* I was looking at."

Calla snapped, "Then why all the secretive behaviour?"

Neeve looked very pointedly at Gansey's splinted thumb. "It is the sort of discovery that lends itself to danger. Surely you all feel the pull of secrecy as well, or you would have shared everything you knew with Blue."

"Blue is not psychic," Maura said crisply. "Most of what we didn't pass along were things that would only be meaningful while doing a reading or scrying into the corpse road."

"You also didn't tell me," Gansey said. He was looking at his thumb, his eyebrows pulled together. Suddenly, Blue realized what looked different about him: he was wearing a pair of wire-framed glasses. They were the thin, subdued sort of glasses that you usually didn't notice until they were pointed out. They made him look at once older and more serious, or maybe that was just his expression in general at the moment. Though she would never, ever tell him, she preferred this Gansey to the wind-tossed, effortlessly handsome one. He went on, "At the reading, when I asked about the ley line, you withheld that information from me."

Now Maura looked a little chastised. "How was I supposed to know what you would do with it? So, where is this man now? Barrington? Is that *really* his name?"

"Barrington Whelk," Adam and Ronan replied in unison. They exchanged a wry look.

"At the hospital, the police told me they're looking for him. Henrietta police *and* state police," Gansey said. "But they said he wasn't at his house and that it looked like he'd packed."

"I believe he's what you call *on the lam*," Ronan said.

"Do you think he still has interest in you?" Maura asked.

Gansey shook his head. "I don't know if he ever cared about *me*. I don't think he had a plan. He wanted the journal. He wants Glendower."

"But he doesn't know where Glendower is?"

"*No one* does," Gansey replied. "I have a colleague" – Ronan sniggered when Gansey used the word *colleague*, but Gansey pressed on – "in the UK who told me about the ritual that Whelk used Noah for. It's possible he'll try it again in a different place. Like Cabeswater."

"I think we should wake it up," Neeve said.

Again, everyone stared at her. She seemed unperturbed, a sea of calm, hands folded in front of her.

"Excuse me?" Calla demanded. "I'm pretty sure I heard it involved a dead body."

Neeve cocked her head. "Not necessarily. A sacrifice isn't always death."

Gansey looked dubious. "Even assuming that is true, Cabeswater is a bit of a strange place. What would the rest of the ley line be like if we woke it up?"

"I'm not sure. I can tell you right now that it will be woken, though," Neeve said. "I don't even need my scrying bowl to see that." She turned on Persephone. "Do you disagree?"

Persephone held her mug in front of her face, hiding her mouth. "No, that's what I see as well. Someone *will* wake it in the next few days."

"And I do not think you want it to be Mr Whelk," Neeve went on. "Whoever wakes up the corpse road will be favoured by the corpse road. Both the one who sacrifices and the one who is sacrificed."

"Favoured like Noah is favoured?" Blue interrupted. "He doesn't seem very lucky."

"From what I've heard here, he was living a physical life in an apartment with these boys," Neeve remarked. "That seems far preferable to a traditional spirit's existence. I would count that as favourable."

Gansey ran a pensive finger over his lower lip. He said, "I'm not certain about this. Noah's favour is also tied to the ley line, isn't it? When his body was moved, he lost a lot of his presence. If one of us did the ritual, would we be tied to the ley line the same way, even if the sacrifice didn't involve death? There's too much we don't know. It's more practical to *stop* Whelk from performing the ritual again. We could just give the location of Cabeswater to the police."

"*NO.*"

Both Neeve and Maura said it at once. Neeve, however, won for overall impressiveness by pairing her outburst with leaping from her chair.

"I thought you went to Cabeswater," she said.

"We did."

"Didn't you feel that place? Do you want it destroyed? How many people do you want tramping through it? Does it seem like a place that can exist full of tourists? It's . . . *holy*."

"What I'd like," Gansey said, "is to neither send the police to Cabeswater nor wake the ley line. I would like to find out more about Cabeswater, and then I'd like to find Glendower."

"What about Whelk?" Maura asked.

"I don't know," he admitted. "I just don't want to bother with him at all."

Several exasperated faces turned on Gansey. Maura said, "Well, he's not going to just go away because you don't want to deal with him."

"I didn't say it was possible," Gansey replied, not looking up from his splint. "I just said that it was what I would like."

It was a naive answer, and he knew it.

Gansey continued, "I'm going back to Cabeswater. He took my journal, but I'm not letting him take Glendower, too. I'm not going to stop looking just because he's looking, too. And I'm going to fix Noah. Somehow."

Blue looked at her mother, who was just watching, her arms crossed. And she said, "I'll help you."

THIRTY-SIX

"The buck stops here," Ronan said, pulling up the hand brake. "Home shit home."

In the dark, the Parrish family's double-wide was a dreary grey box, two windows illuminated. A silhouette at the kitchen window drew aside the curtains to look at the BMW. He and Adam were alone in the car; Gansey had driven the Camaro from the hospital to Fox Way, so he drove it back to Monmouth as well. It was a comfortable enough arrangement; Adam and Ronan weren't in a fight at the moment, and both of them were too startled by the day's events to start a new one.

Adam reached in the back for his messenger bag, the one gift he'd ever permitted Gansey to give him, and only because he didn't need it. "Thanks for the ride."

Another silhouette, distinctly Adam's father, had joined the first at the window. Adam's stomach curdled. He tightened his fingers around the strap of his bag, but he didn't get out.

"Man, you don't have to get out here," Ronan said.

Adam didn't comment on that; it wasn't helpful. Instead he asked, "Don't you have homework to do?"

But Ronan, as the inventor of sly remarks, was impervious

to them. His smile was ruthless in the glow from the dash. "Yes, Parrish. I believe I do."

Still Adam didn't get out. He didn't like the agitation of his father's silhouette. But, it was unwise to loiter in the car — especially *this* car, an undeniably Aglionby car — flaunting his friendships.

"Do you think they'll arrest Whelk before class tomorrow?" Ronan asked. "Because if they do, I'm not doing the reading."

"If he shows up for class," Adam replied, "I think that the reading will be the least of his concerns."

There was quiet, and then Ronan said, "I better go feed the bird."

But he looked down at the gearshift instead, eyes unfocused. He said, "I keep thinking about what would've happened if Whelk had shot Gansey today."

Adam hadn't let himself dwell on that possibility. Every time his thoughts came close to touching on the near miss, it opened up something dark and sharp edged inside him. It was hard to remember what life at Aglionby had been like before Gansey. The distant memories seemed difficult, lonely, more populated with late nights where Adam sat on the steps of the double-wide, blinking tears out of his eyes and wondering why he bothered. He'd been younger then, only a little more than a year ago. "But he didn't."

"Yeah," said Ronan.

"Lucky you taught him that hook."

"I never taught him to break his thumb."

"That's Gansey for you. Only learns enough to be superficially competent."

"Loser," Ronan agreed, and he was himself again.

Adam nodded, steeling himself. "See you tomorrow. Thanks again."

Ronan looked away from the house, out across the black field. His hand worked on the steering wheel; something was frustrating him, but with Ronan, there was no telling if it was still Whelk or something else entirely. "No problem, man. See you tomorrow."

With a sigh, Adam climbed out. He knocked on the top of the BMW, and Ronan pulled slowly away. Above him, the stars were brutal and clear.

As Adam stepped up the three steps to the house, the front door opened, light flashing down across his legs and feet. His father left the door hanging open as he stood in it, staring down his son.

"Hi, Dad," Adam said.

"Don't 'hi, dad' me," his father replied. He was already revved up. He smelled like cigarettes, although he didn't smoke. "Come home at midnight. Trying to hide from your lies?"

Warily, Adam asked, "What?"

"Your mother was in your room today and she found something. Can you guess what it would be?"

Adam's knees were slowly liquefying. He did his best to keep most of his Aglionby life hidden from his father, and he could think of several things about himself and his life that wouldn't please Robert Parrish. The fact that he didn't know precisely what had been found was agonizing. He couldn't meet his father's eyes.

Robert Parrish grabbed Adam's collar, forcing his chin up. "Look at me when I'm talking to you. A pay stub. From the factory."

Oh.

Think fast, Adam. What does he need to hear?

"I don't understand why you're angry," Adam said. He tried to keep his voice as level as possible, but now that he knew it was about the money, he didn't know how to get out of it.

His father drew Adam's face a bare centimetre from his, so that Adam could feel the words as well as hear them. "You lied to your mother about how much you made."

"I didn't lie."

This was a mistake and Adam knew it as soon as the words were out of his mouth.

"*Do not look in my face and lie to me!*" his father shouted.

Even though he knew it was coming, Adam's arm was too slow to protect his face.

When his father's hand hit his cheek, it was more sound than feeling: a pop like a distant hammer hitting a nail. Adam scrambled for balance, but his foot missed the edge of the stair and his father let him fall.

When the side of Adam's head hit the railing, it was a catastrophe of light. He was aware in a single, exploded moment of how many colours combined to make white.

Pain hissed inside his skull.

He was on the ground by the stairs without any recollection of the second between hitting the railing and the ground. His face was caked with dust; it was in his mouth. Adam had to put together the mechanics of breathing, of opening his eyes, of breathing again.

"Oh, come on," his father said, tired. "Get up. Really."

Adam slowly pushed himself to his hands and knees. Rocking back, he crouched, knees braced on the ground,

347

while his ears rang, rang, rang. He waited for them to clear. There was nothing but an ascending whine.

Halfway down the drive, he saw the brake lights on Ronan's BMW.

Just go, Ronan.

"You're not playing that game!" Robert Parrish snapped. "I'm not going to stop talking about this just because you threw yourself on the ground. I know when you're faking, Adam. I'm not a fool. I can't believe you'd make this kind of money and throw it away on that damn school! All of those times you've heard us talking about the power bill, the phone?"

His father was far from done. Adam could see it in the way he pushed off his feet with every step down the stairs, from the coil in his body. Adam drew his elbows into his body, ducking his head, willing his ears to clear. What he needed to do was put himself in his father's head, to imagine what he had to say to defuse this situation.

But he couldn't think. His thoughts crashed explosively across the dirt in front of him, in time with the rhythm of his heart. His left ear screamed at him. It was so hot that it felt wet.

"You lied," growled his father. "You told us that school was giving you money to go. You didn't tell me you were making" – he stopped long enough to withdraw a battered piece of paper from his shirt pocket. It shook in his hand – "eighteen thousand, four hundred and twenty-three dollars a year!"

Adam gasped an answer.

"What's that?" His father came in close. Grabbing Adam's collar, he pulled his son up, as easy as he'd lift a dog. Adam stood, but only just. The ground was sliding away from him and he stumbled. He had to struggle to find the words again; something was fractured inside him.

"Partial," Adam gasped. "Partial scholarship."

His father bellowed something else at him, but it was into his left ear and there was nothing but a roar on that side.

"*Do not ignore me*," his father growled. And then, inexplicably, he turned his head from Adam, and he shouted, "What do *you* want?"

"To do this," Ronan Lynch snarled, smashing his fist into the side of Robert Parrish's face. Beyond him, the BMW sat, the driver's side door hanging open, headlights illuminating clouds of dust in the darkness.

Ronan, said Adam. Or maybe he only thought it. Without his father holding him up, he staggered.

Grabbing Ronan's shirt, Adam's father propelled him back towards the double-wide. But it only took Ronan a moment to get his feet under him. His knee found Parrish's gut. Doubled over, Adam's father snatched a hand towards Ronan. His fingers passed harmlessly over Ronan's shaved head. It set him back just half a second. Parrish crashed his skull into Ronan's face.

Out of his right ear, Adam heard his mother screaming at them to stop. She was holding the phone, waving the phone at Ronan like that would make him stop. There was only one person who could stop Ronan, though, and Adam's mother didn't have that number.

"Ronan," said Adam, and this time he was certain he said it out loud. His voice sounded strange to him, stuffed with cotton. He took a step and the ground slid out from under him entirely. *Get up, Adam.* He was on his hands and knees.

The sky looked the same as the ground. He felt fundamentally broken. He couldn't stand. He could only watch his friend and his father grappling a metre away. He was eyes without a body.

The fight was dirty. At one point Ronan went down and Robert Parrish kicked, hard, at his face. Ronan's forearms came up, all instinct, to protect himself. Parrish lunged in to rip them free. Ronan's hand lashed out like a snake, dragging Parrish to the ground with him.

Adam caught bits and pieces: his father and Ronan rolling, dragging, punching. Red and blue flashing strobes bounced off the sides of the double-wide, lighting the fields for a second at a time. The cops.

His mother was still yelling.

It was all just noise. What Adam needed was to be able to stand, to walk, to think, and then he could stop Ronan before something awful happened.

"Son?" An officer knelt beside him. He smelled like juniper. Adam thought he might choke on it. "Are you OK?"

With the officer's hand helping him, Adam stumbled to his feet. Across the dirt, another officer dragged Ronan off Robert Parrish.

"I'm OK," Adam said.

The cop released his arm and then, as quickly, caught it again. "Boy, you're not OK. Have you been drinking?"

Ronan must have caught this question because, from across the lot, he shouted an answer. It involved a lot of profanity and the phrase *beats the shit*.

Adam's vision shifted and cleared, shifted and cleared. He could make out Ronan, dimly. Appalled, he asked, "Is he being cuffed?"

This can't happen. He can't go to jail because of me.

"Have you been drinking?" the cop repeated.

"No," Adam replied. He was still not steady on his feet; the ground slanted and pitched with every move of his head. He knew he looked drunk. He needed to get himself together. Only this afternoon he'd touched Blue's face. It had felt like anything was possible, like the world soared out in front of him. He tried to channel that sensation, but it felt apocryphal. "I can't—"

"Can't what?"

Can't hear out of my left ear, Adam thought.

His mother stood on the porch, watching him and the cop, her eyes narrowed. Adam knew what she was thinking, because they'd had the conversation so many times before: *Don't say anything, Adam. Tell him you fell down. It really was a little your fault, wasn't it? We'll deal with it as a family.*

If Adam turned his father in, everything crashed down around him. If Adam turned him in, his mother would never forgive him. If Adam turned him in, he could never come home again.

Across the lot, one of the officers put his hand on the back of Ronan's head, guiding him down into the police car.

Even without the hearing in his left ear, Adam heard Ronan's voice clearly. "I said I've *got* it, man. Do you think I've never been in one of these before?"

Adam couldn't move in with Gansey. He had done so much to make sure that when he moved out, it would be on his own terms. Not Robert Parrish's. Not Richard Gansey's.

On Adam Parrish's terms, or not at all.

Adam touched his left ear. The skin was hot and painful, and without his hearing to tell him when his finger was close to his ear cavity, his touch felt imaginary. The whine in the ear had subsided and now there was . . . nothing. There was nothing at all.

Gansey said, *You won't leave because of your pride?*

"Ronan was defending me." Adam's mouth was dry as the dirt around them. The officer's expression focused on him as he went on. "From my father. All this . . . is from him. My face and my. . ."

His mother was staring at him.

He closed his eyes. He couldn't look at her and say it. Even with his eyes closed, he felt like he was falling, like the horizon pitched, like his head tilted. Adam had the sick feeling that his father had managed to knock something crucial askew.

And then he said what he couldn't say before. He asked, "Can I . . . can I press charges?"

THIRTY-SEVEN

Whelk missed the good food that came with being rich.

When he'd been home from Aglionby, neither of his parents had ever cooked, but they'd hired a chef to come in every other evening to make dinner. Carrie, the chef's name had been, an effusive but intimidating woman who adored chopping things up with knives. God, he missed her guacamole.

Currently, he sat on the kerb of a now-closed service station, eating a dry burger he'd bought from a fast-food joint several kilometres away; the first fast-food burger he'd had in seven years. Uncertain of just how hard the cops might be looking for his car, he'd parked out of the reach of the streetlight and returned to the kerb to eat.

As he chewed, a plan was falling into shape, and the plan involved sleeping in the back seat of his vehicle and making another plan in the morning. It was not confidence inspiring and his spirits were low. He should've just abducted Gansey, now that he considered it, but abduction took so much more planning than theft, and he hadn't left the house prepared to put someone in his boot. He hadn't left the house prepared to do anything, actually. He'd merely seized the opportunity when Gansey's car had broken down. If he'd considered the matter at all, he would've abducted Gansey for the ritual later, after he'd got to the heart of the ley line.

Except that Gansey would never have been a good target; the manhunt for his killer would be monumental. Really, the Parrish kid would have been a better bet. No one would miss a kid born in a trailer. He always turned his homework in on time, though.

Whelk grimly took another bite of the dusty burger. It did nothing to lift his mood.

Beside him, the pay phone began to ring. Until then, Whelk hadn't even been aware that the phone was there; he thought mobile phones had driven pay phones out of business years before. He eyed the only other car parked in the service station to see if anyone was awaiting a call. The other vehicle was empty, however, and the sagging right tyre indicated that it had been parked in the service station for longer than a few minutes.

He waited anxiously as the phone rang twelve times, but no one appeared to answer it. He was relieved when it stopped, but not enough to remain where he was. He wrapped up the other half of his burger and stood up.

The phone began to ring again.

It rang all the while that he walked to the rubbish bin on the other side of the service station's door (COME IN, WE ARE OPEN! lied the flip-around sign on the door), and it rang all the while he returned to the kerb to retrieve one of the fries that he'd missed, and it rang the entire time that he walked back to where he'd parked his car.

Whelk was not prone to philanthropy, but it occurred to him that whoever was on the other side of that pay phone was really trying to get a hold of someone. He returned to the pay phone, which was still ringing – such an old-fashioned ring, really, now that he thought of it, phones just didn't sound like this any more – and he removed the phone from its cradle.

"Hello?"

"Mr Whelk," Neeve said mildly. "I hope you are having a good evening."

Whelk clung to the phone. "How did you know where to contact me?"

"Numbers are a very simple thing for me, Mr Whelk, and you aren't difficult to find. Also I have some of your hair." Neeve's voice was mild and eerie. No live person, Whelk thought, should sound so much like a computerized voicemail menu.

"Why are you calling me?"

"I'm glad that you asked," Neeve remarked. "I am calling regarding the idea that you proposed the last time we spoke."

"The last time we spoke, you said you weren't interested in helping me," Whelk replied. He was still thinking about the fact that this woman had collected one of his hairs. The image of her moving slowly and mildly through his dark abandoned apartment was not a pleasant one. He turned his back to the service station and looked out into the night. Possibly she was out there, somewhere; perhaps she had followed him and that was how she knew where to call him. But he knew that was not true. The only reason he'd contacted her in the first place was because he knew she was the real thing. Whatever that "thing" might be.

"Yes, about helping you," Neeve said. "I've changed my mind."

THIRTY-EIGHT

"Hey, Parrish," Gansey said.

The Camaro was parked in the shade of the walkway just outside the glass hospital doors. As Gansey had waited for Adam to emerge, he'd watched them open and close for invisible patients. Now he sat behind the wheel as Adam lowered himself into the passenger seat. Adam was strangely unmarked; usually after encounters with his father, there were bruises or scratches, but this time, the only thing Gansey could see was a slight reddening of his ear.

"They told me you didn't have insurance," Gansey said. They'd also told him Adam would probably never hear out of his left ear again. This was the hardest thing to internalize, that something permanent but invisible had happened. He waited for Adam to say he'd find a way to pay for it. But Adam just turned his hospital bracelet around and around on his wrist.

Gansey added carefully, "I took care of it."

This was where Adam always said something. Where he got angry. Where he snapped, *No, I won't take your damn money, Gansey. You can't buy me.* But he just turned that paper bracelet around and around and around.

"You win," Adam said finally. He rubbed a hand through

his uneven hair. He sounded tired. "Take me to get my stuff."

Gansey had been about to start the Camaro, but he took his hand away from the ignition. "I didn't win anything. Do you think this is how I wanted it?"

"Yes," Adam replied. He didn't look at him. "Yes, I do."

Hurt and anger warred furiously inside Gansey. "Don't be shitty."

Adam picked and picked at the uneven end where the paper bracelet sealed. "I'm telling you that you can say 'I told you so'. Say 'if you left earlier, this wouldn't have happened'."

"Did I say that before? You don't have to act like it's the end of the world."

"It is the end of the world."

An ambulance pulled in between them and the hospital doors; the lights weren't on, but the paramedics leapt out of the cab and hurried to the back to attend to some silent emergency. Something behind Gansey's breastbone felt red-hot. "Moving out of your dad's place is the end of the world?"

"You know what I wanted," Adam said. "You know this wasn't it."

"You act like it's my fault."

"Tell me you're unhappy about how this is going down."

He wouldn't lie; he wanted Adam out of that house. But there had never been a part of him that wanted him hurt to accomplish that. There had never been a part of him that wanted Adam to have to run instead of march triumphantly out. There had never been a part of him that wanted Adam to look at him like he was looking at him now. So it was the truth when he replied, "I'm unhappy about how this is going down."

"Whatever," Adam shot back. "You've wanted me to move out for ever."

Gansey despised raising his voice (in his head, his mother said, *People shout when they don't have the vocabulary to whisper*), but he heard it happening despite himself and so, with effort, he kept his voice even. "Not like this. At least you have a place to go. 'End of the world'. . . What is your *problem*, Adam? I mean, is there something about my place that's too repugnant for you to imagine living there? Why is it that everything kind I do is pity to you? Everything is charity. Well, here it is: I'm *sick* of tiptoeing around your principles."

"God, I'm sick of your condescension, Gansey," Adam said. "Don't try to make me feel stupid. Who whips out *repugnant*? Don't pretend you're not trying to make me feel stupid."

"This is the way I talk. I'm sorry your father never taught you the meaning of *repugnant*. He was too busy smashing your head against the wall of your trailer while you apologized for being alive."

Both of them stopped breathing.

Gansey knew he'd gone too far. It was too far, too late, too much.

Adam shoved open the door.

"Fuck you, Gansey. Fuck you," he said, voice low and furious.

Gansey closed his eyes.

Adam slammed the door, and then he slammed it again when the latch didn't catch. Gansey didn't open his eyes. He didn't want to see what Adam was doing. He didn't want to see if people were watching some kid fight with a boy in a bright orange Camaro and an Aglionby jumper. Just then he hated his raven-breasted uniform and his loud car and every three- and four-syllable word his parents had used in casual conversation at the dinner table and he hated Adam's hideous father and Adam's permissive mother and most of all, most of all, he hated the sound of Adam's last words, playing over and over.

He couldn't stand it, all of this inside him.

In the end, he was nobody to Adam, he was nobody to Ronan. Adam spit his words back at him and Ronan squandered however many second chances he gave him. Gansey was just a guy with a lot of stuff and a hole inside him that chewed away more of his heart every year.

They were always walking away from him. But he never seemed able to walk away from them.

Gansey opened his eyes. The ambulance was still there, but Adam was gone.

It took Gansey a few moments to locate him. He was already several hundred metres away, walking across the car park towards the road, his shadow a small, blue thing beside him.

Gansey leaned across the car to roll down the passenger window, and then he started the Pig. By the time he circled around the loading area to get to the car park, Adam had made it out to the manicured four-lane divided highway that ran by the hospital. There was some traffic, but Gansey pulled up along where Adam walked, making the cars in the right lane pass him, some honking.

"Where are you going?" he shouted out. "Where do you have to go?"

Of course Adam knew he was there – the Camaro was louder than anything – but he just kept walking.

"Adam," Gansey repeated. "Just tell me not back there." Nothing.

"It doesn't have to be Monmouth," Gansey tried a third time. "But let me take you wherever you're going."

Please just get in the car.

Adam stopped. Climbing in jerkily, he pulled the door shut. He didn't do it hard enough, so he had to try two more times. They were silent as Gansey pulled back into traffic. Words pressed against his mouth, begged to be said, but he kept silent.

Adam didn't look at him when he said, finally, "It doesn't matter how you say it. It's what you wanted, in the end. All your things in one place, all under your roof. Everything you own right where you can see. . ."

But then he stopped. He dropped his head into his hands. His thumbs worked through the hair above his ears, over and over, the knuckles white. When he sucked in his breath, it was the ragged sound that came from trying not to cry.

Gansey thought of one hundred things that he could say to Adam about how it would be all right, how it was for the best, how Adam Parrish had been his own man before he'd met Gansey and there was no way he'd stop being his own man just by changing the roof over his head, how some days Gansey wished that he could be him, because Adam was so very real and true in a way that Gansey couldn't ever seem to be. But Gansey's words had somehow become unwitting weapons, and he didn't trust himself to not accidentally discharge them again.

So they drove in silence to get Adam's things and when they left the trailer park for the last time, his mother watching from behind the kitchen window, Adam didn't look back.

THIRTY-NINE

When Blue first arrived at Monmouth Manufacturing that afternoon, she thought it was empty. Without either car in the car park, the entire street had a disconsolate, abandoned feeling. She tried to imagine being Gansey, seeing the warehouse for the first time, deciding it would be a great place to live, but she couldn't picture it. No more than she could imagine looking at the Pig and deciding it was a great car to drive, or Ronan and thinking he was a good friend to have. But somehow, it worked, because she loved the apartment, and Ronan was starting to grow on her, and the car. . .

Well, the car she could still live without.

Blue knocked on the door to the stairwell. "Noah! Are you here?"

"I'm here."

She was unsurprised when his voice came from behind her instead of from the other side of the door. When she turned, she seemed to see his legs first, and then, slowly, the rest of him. She still wasn't sure he was actually all there, or if he had been there all along – it was hard to make a decision about existence and Noah these days.

She allowed him to pet her hair with his icy fingers.

"Not so spiky as usual," he said sadly.

"I didn't get much sleep. I need sleep for quality spikes. I'm glad to see you."

Noah crossed his arms, then uncrossed them, then put his hands in his pockets, then removed them. "I only ever feel normal when you're around. I mean, normal like I was before they found my body. That still wasn't like what I was when I was. . ."

"I don't believe that you were really that different when you were alive," Blue told him. But it was true that she still couldn't reconcile this Noah with that abandoned red Mustang.

"I think," Noah said cautiously, remembering, "that I was worse then."

This line of discussion seemed in danger of making him vanish, so Blue asked quickly, "Where are the others?"

"Gansey and Adam are getting Adam's stuff so he can move in," Noah said. "Ronan went to the library."

"Move in! I thought he said . . . wait – Ronan went *where*?"

With lots of pauses and sighs and staring off into the trees, Noah described the previous night's events to her, ending with, "If Ronan had got arrested for punching Adam's dad, he would've been out of Aglionby no matter what happened. No way they'd let an assault charge ride. But Adam pressed charges so Ronan would get off the hook. 'Course that means Adam has to move out because his dad hates him now."

"But that's awful," Blue said. "Noah, that's *awful*. I didn't know about Adam's dad."

"That's the way he wanted it."

A place for leaving. She remembered how Adam had referred to his home. And now, of course, she remembered his awful bruises and a dozen comments between the boys that had seemed inexplicable at the time, all veiled references to his home life. Her first thought was a strangely unpleasant one – that she hadn't been a good enough friend for Adam to share this with her. But it was fleeting and replaced almost immediately with the horrific realization that Adam had no family. Who would she be without hers?

She asked, "OK, wait, so why is Ronan at the library?"

"Cramming," Noah said. "For an exam on Monday."

It was the nicest thing Blue had ever heard of Ronan doing.

The phone rang then, clearly audible through the floor above them.

"You should pick that up!" Noah said abruptly. "Hurry!"

Blue had lived too long with the women at 300 Fox Way to question Noah's intuition. Jogging quickly to keep up with him, she followed him into the stairwell and then up the stairs to the doorway. It was locked. Noah made a series of incomprehensible gestures, more agitated than she'd seen him.

He burst out, "I could do it if—"

If he had more energy, Blue thought. She touched his shoulder at once. Immediately fortified by her energy, Noah leaned against the latch, wiggling the lock open and throwing the door free. She hurled herself at the phone.

"Hello?" she gasped into the receiver. The phone on the desk was an old-fashioned black rotary number, completely in keeping with Gansey's love of the bizarre and barely functional. Knowing him, it was possible he had a landline merely to justify having this particular phone on his desk.

"Oh, hello, dear," said an unfamiliar voice at the other end of the line. Already she could hear a significant accent. "Is Richard Gansey there?"

"No," replied Blue. "But I can take a message."

This, she felt, had been her role in life so far.

Noah prodded her with a cold finger. "Tell him who you are."

"I'm working with Gansey," Blue added. "On the ley line."

"Oh!" said the voice. "Well. How lovely to meet you. What did you say your name was? I'm Roger Malory."

He was doing something extremely complicated with his *r*'s that made him difficult to understand.

"Blue. My name's Blue Sargent."

"Blair?"

"Blue."

"Blaize?"

Blue sighed. "Jane."

"Oh, Jane! I thought that you were saying *Blue* for some reason. It's nice to meet you, Jane. I'm afraid I have bad news for Gansey. Would you let him know that I attempted that ritual with a colleague – that chap from Surrey I mentioned before, endearing man, really, with terrible breath, though – and it just didn't go very well. My colleague, he will be all right, the doctors just say it will be a few weeks before the skin heals. The grafts are working splendidly, they say."

"Wait," Blue said. She grabbed the closest piece of paper from Gansey's desk; it looked like a bit of calculus or something. He'd already doodled a cat attacking a man on it, so she figured it was safe to use. "I'm writing this all down. This is the ritual to wake the ley line, right? What exactly went wrong?"

"That is very hard to say, Jane. Suffice to say the ley lines are even more powerful than Gansey and I had anticipated. They may be magic, they may be science, but they are undoubtedly energy. My colleague stepped quite easily out of his skin. I was certain I'd lost him; I didn't think a man could bleed that much without perishing. Oh, when you tell Gansey all this, don't tell him that. The boy has quite a thing about death and I don't like to upset him."

Blue hadn't noticed Gansey having a "thing" about death, but she agreed not to tell him.

"But you've still not said what you *tried*," Blue pointed out.

"Oh, haven't I?"

"Nope. Which means we might do it by accident, if we don't know."

Malory chuckled. It was a sound a lot like sucking just the whipped cream off hot chocolate. "Indeed you're right. It was quite logical, really, and it was based on one of Gansey's ideas from long ago, to tell you the truth. We set up a new stone circle using stones we found to have excellent energy readings – that's dowsing terms, of course, Jane, I don't know how well you know all these things but it's nice to see a girl involved with all this; ley lines tend to be a man's game and it's nice to hear a lady like yourself—"

"Yes," Blue agreed. "It's great. I'm enjoying myself. So, you set up a stone circle?"

"Oh yes, right. We set seven stones in a circle on what we hoped was the centre of the ley line and we twiddled them about in position until we had a quite high energy reading in the middle. Sort of like positioning a prism, I think, to focus the light."

"And that's when your partner's skin came off?"

"Round about then. He was taking a reading in the middle and he – I'm sad to say I cannot remember exactly what he said, as I was so overcome by what came after – but he made some sort of light remark or joke or what-have-you – you know how young people are, Gansey himself can be quite one for the levity—"

Blue wasn't certain that Gansey *was* quite one for the levity, but she made a mental note to look out for it in the future.

"—and he said something about losing his skin or shedding his skin or something like that. And apparently these things are quite literal. I'm not certain how his *words* triggered any sort of reaction and I don't think we've woken this line, at least not properly, but there it is. Disappointing, really."

"Apart from your partner living to tell the tale," Blue said.

Malory said, "Well, *I'm* the one who's having to tell it."

She thought this was a joke. In any case, she laughed and didn't feel bad about it. Then she thanked Malory, exchanged niceties with him, and hung up.

"Noah?" she asked the room, because Noah had disappeared. There was no reply, but outside, she heard car doors slamming and voices.

Blue replayed the phrase in her head: *My colleague stepped quite easily out of his skin.* Blue *didn't* have a "thing" with death and even she thought it painted a rather horrible and vivid image in her mind.

A moment later, she heard the door clap shut on the ground floor and feet stomping up the stairs.

Gansey was first into the room, and he clearly hadn't expected to find anyone there, because his features hadn't been arranged at all to disguise his misery. When he saw Blue, he immediately managed to pull a cordial smile from somewhere.

And it was so very convincing. She had seen his face just a second before, but even having seen his expression, it was hard to remind herself that the smile was false. Why a boy with a life as untroubled as Gansey's would have needed to learn how to build such a swift and convincing false front of happiness was beyond her.

"Jane," he said, and she thought she heard a little of his unhappiness in his bright voice, even if his face no longer betrayed it. "Sorry you had to let yourself in."

Noah's voice and nothing more manifested at Blue's ear, a cold, cold whisper: *They fought.*

Adam and Ronan came in then. Ronan was bent double with a duffel bag and backpack on his back, and Adam carried a dented Froot Loops box with a Transformer poking out of the top.

"Nice Transformer," Blue said. "Is that the police car one?"

Adam looked at Blue, unsmiling, as if he didn't really see her. Then, a moment too late, he replied, "Yes."

Ronan, still weighed down with the luggage, headed across the floor towards Noah's room, saying "Ha. Ha. Ha" in time with his footsteps. It was the kind of laughing that came from being the only person laughing.

"This guy called," Blue said. She held up the piece of paper where she'd jotted his name. The place she'd written it made it look like the doodled cat was calling it out.

"Malory," Gansey said with less than his usual enthusiasm. As Adam carried the box after Ronan, he watched his back with narrowed eyes. It wasn't until Noah's door closed behind them that Gansey tore his eyes away and looked at Blue. The apartment felt empty without the others, like they'd gone into another world instead of another room.

Gansey asked, "What did he want?"

"He tried the ritual on the ley line and he said it went wrong and his other person – his, uh, colleague? – got hurt."

"Hurt how?"

"Just hurt. Badly hurt. By energy," Blue said.

With force, Gansey kicked off his shoes. One flew over his miniature Henrietta and the other made it all the way to the side of his desk. It slammed off the old wood and slid to the ground. Under his breath, Gansey said, "*Yee haw.*"

Blue said, "You seem upset."

"Do I?" he asked.

"What did you and Adam fight about?"

Gansey cast a glance at Noah's closed door. "How did you know?" he asked wearily. He threw himself on his unmade bed.

"Please," Blue said, because even if Noah hadn't told her, she would've known.

He muttered something into his bedsheets and waved a hand at the air. Blue crouched by the bed and leaned on her arms at the head of it.

"What now? With a lot less pillow in your mouth this time?"

Gansey didn't turn his head, so his voice remained muffled. "My words are unerring tools of destruction, and I've come unequipped with the ability to disarm them. Can you believe I'm only alive because Noah died? What a fine sacrifice that was, what a fine contribution to the world I am." He made another little twirling hand gesture without removing his face from his pillow. It was probably meant to make it look as if he was merely joking. He went on, "Oh, I know I'm being self-pitying. Ignore me. So Malory thinks it is a bad idea to wake the ley line? Of course he does. I enjoy dead ends hugely."

"You *are* being self-pitying." But Blue sort of liked it. She'd never seen anything like the real Gansey for so long at one time. It was too bad he had to be miserable to make it happen.

"I'm nearly done. You don't have much more of this to bear."

"I like you better this way."

For some reason, admitting this made her face go hot right away; she was very glad that he still had his face pressed into his pillow and the other boys were still in Noah's room.

"Crushed and broken," Gansey said. "Just the way women like 'em. Did he say this guy was badly hurt?"

"Yes."

"Well, then, that's off." He rolled over on to his back so that he was looking at Blue upside down where she leaned on his bed. "It's not worth the risk."

"I thought you said you *needed* to find Glendower."

"I do," Gansey said. "They don't."

"So you'll do it yourself?"

"No, I'll find another way. I would love to have the ley line's power pointing giant arrows to where he is, but I'll just keep plodding along the old way. What sort of hurt was this guy?"

Blue made a noncommittal noise, remembering Malory's exhortation to spare him the details.

"Blue. What sort?" His gaze was unflinching, as if staring were easier when their faces were upside down to each other.

"He said something about losing his skin and then, apparently, his skin came off. Malory didn't want me to tell you that."

Gansey's mouth pursed. "He still remembers when I . . . never mind. His skin came right off? That's grim."

"What's grim?" asked Adam, coming across the floor.

Ronan, taking in Blue's posture and Gansey below, observed, "If you spat, Blue, it would land right in his eye."

Gansey moved to the opposite side of the bed with surprising swiftness, glancing at Adam and away again as quickly. "Blue said Malory tried to wake the line and the man with him got seriously hurt. So we're not doing it. Not right now."

Adam said, "I don't care about the risk."

Ronan picked his teeth. "Me neither."

"You have nothing to lose," Gansey said, pointing at Adam. He looked at Ronan. "And you don't care if you live or die. That makes you both bad judges."

"You have nothing to gain," Blue pointed out. "That makes you an equally bad judge. But I think I agree. I mean, look at what happened to your British friend."

"Thank you, Jane, for being the voice of reason," Gansey said. "Do not look at me like that, Ronan. Since when did we decide waking up the ley line is the only way to find Glendower?"

"We don't have time to find another way," Adam insisted. "If Whelk wakes it up, he'll get an advantage. Plus, he speaks Latin. What if the trees know? If he finds Glendower, he gets the favour, and he gets away with killing Noah. Game over, bad guy takes all."

All trace of vulnerability had vanished from Gansey's countenance as he swung his legs over the side of the bed. "It's a bad idea, Adam. Find me a way to do it without hurting someone and I'm for it. Until then – we wait."

"We don't have *time*," Adam said. "Persephone said someone will wake the ley line in just a few days."

Gansey stood up. "Adam, what's happening now is that someone on the other side of the world has no skin because he fooled around with the ley line. We've *seen* Cabeswater. This isn't a game. It's very real and very powerful and *we're not screwing with it.*"

He held Adam's gaze for a long, long moment. There was something unfamiliar in Adam's expression, something that made Blue think that she didn't really know him at all.

In her mind, Blue imagined him handing the single tarot card to her mother, and as she remembered how Maura had interpreted the two of swords, she thought, sadly, *My mother is very good at what she does.*

"Sometimes," Adam said, "I don't know how you live with yourself."

FORTY

Barrington Whelk was not pleased with Neeve. For starters, since getting in the car, she had done nothing but eat hummus and crackers, and the combination of the garlic odour and cracker chewing was incredibly aggravating. The thought that she was filling his driver's seat with crumbs was one of the more troubling ones he'd had in a week of extremely troubling thoughts. Also, the very first thing she had done after they exchanged hellos was to use her Taser on him. This was followed by the ignominy of being tied up in the back of his own car.

It is not enough that I should have to put up with a shitty car, Whelk thought. *Now I'm going to die in it.*

She hadn't told him she intended to kill him, but Whelk had spent the last forty minutes unable to easily see much but the floor behind the passenger seat. Lying there was a wide, flat clay bowl containing a collection of candles, scissors and knives. The knives were sizable and sinister, but not a guarantee of imminent murder. The rubber gloves that Neeve wore now, and the extra set inside the bowl, were.

Likewise, Whelk couldn't be certain they were headed towards the ley line, but from the amount of time Neeve had spent perusing the journal before setting off down the road, he suspected it was a good guess. Whelk was not much for postulation – but he thought his fate was probably meant to be the same as Czerny's, seven years earlier.

A ritual death, then. A sacrifice, with his blood seeping down through the earth until it reached the sleeping ley line below. Rubbing his tied wrists against each other, he turned his head towards Neeve, who held the wheel with one hand as she ate crackers and hummus with the other. To add insult to injury, she was listening to some kind of trance nature sounds CD on his car's radio. Perhaps preparing herself for the ritual.

His death on the ley line would, Whelk thought, have a sort of circularity to it.

But Whelk didn't care for circularity. He cared for his lost car, his lost respect. He cared for the ability to sleep at night. He cared for languages dead long enough that they wouldn't change on him. He cared for the guacamole his parents' long-gone chef used to make.

Also, Neeve hadn't tied him tightly enough.

FORTY–ONE

After leaving Monmouth Manufacturing, Blue returned home and retreated to the far side of the beech in the back garden to try to do homework. But she found herself spending less time solving for x and more time solving for *Noah* or *Gansey* or *Adam*. She'd given up and leaned back by the time Adam appeared. He stepped into the dim green shadow of the tree from the house side.

"Persephone said you were out here." He just hung there at the edge of the shadow.

Blue thought about saying *I'm so sorry about your dad*, but instead she just stretched out a hand towards him. Adam gave an unsteady sigh of the sort that she could see from two metres away. Wordlessly, he sat beside her and then laid his head on her lap, his face in his arms.

Startled, Blue didn't immediately react, other than to glance over her shoulder to make certain that the tree hid them from the house. She felt a little like she'd been approached by a wild animal, and she was at once flattered by its trust and worried that she'd scare it away. After a moment, she carefully stroked a few fine, dusty strands of his hair while she looked at the back of his neck. It made her chest hum to touch him and smell the dust-and-oil scent of him.

"Your hair is the colour of dirt," she said.

"It knows where it came from."

"That's funny," Blue noted, "because then mine should be that colour, too."

His shoulders moved in response. After a moment, he said, "Sometimes I'm afraid he'll never really understand me."

She ran a finger along the back of his ear. It felt dangerous and thrilling, but not as dangerous and thrilling as it would have been to touch him while he was looking at her.

"I'm only going to say this once and then I'm going to be done with it," she said. "But I think you're awfully brave."

He was quiet for a long, long moment. A car whirred through the neighbourhood. The wind moved through the beech leaves, turning them upside down in a way that meant rain later.

Without lifting his head, Adam said, "I'd like to kiss you now, Blue, young or not."

Blue's fingers stopped moving.

"I don't want to hurt you," she said.

He pulled himself free of her, sitting just a few centimetres away. His expression was bleak, nothing like when he'd wanted to kiss her before. "I'm already all hurt up."

Blue didn't think this was really about kissing her, and that made her cheeks burn. It wasn't supposed to be a kiss at all, but if it had, it definitely shouldn't be like this. She said, "There's still worse than what you've got."

Something about this made him swallow and turn his face away. His hands were limp in his lap. *If I'd been anybody else in the world,* she thought, *this would've been my first kiss.* She wondered what it would've been like to kiss this hungry, desolate boy.

Adam's eyes moved, following the shifting light through the leaves above. He didn't look at her when he said, "I don't remember how your mother said I was supposed to solve my problem. At the reading. The choice I couldn't make."

Blue sighed. *This* was what all this was really about, and she had known it all along, even if he hadn't. " 'Make a third option', she said. Next time you should bring a notebook."

"I don't remember her saying the part about the notebook."

"That's because it was me saying that part, right now. Next time you get your cards read, take notes. That way you can compare it to what actually happens and you'll know if the psychic is a good one."

Now he looked at her, but she wasn't sure if he was really *looking* at her. "I'll do that."

"I'll save you the trouble this time, though," Blue added, tilting her head back as he climbed to his feet. Her fingers and skin longed for the boy she'd held hands with days before, but he didn't seem to be the boy standing before her. "My mother's a good one."

Shoving his hands in his pockets, he rubbed his cheek on his shoulder. "So you think I should listen to her?"

"No, you should listen to me."

Adam's hastily constructed smile was thin enough to break. "And what do you say?"

Blue was suddenly afraid for him. "Keep being brave."

There was blood everywhere.

Are you happy now, Adam? Ronan snarled. He knelt beside Gansey, who convulsed in the dirt. Blue stared at Adam, and the horror in her face was the worst thing. It was his fault.

Ronan's face was wild with loss. *Is this what you wanted?*

At first, when Adam opened his eyes from the gory dream, his limbs tingling from the adrenaline of it, he wasn't sure where he was. He felt like he levitated; the space around him was all wrong, too little light, too much space overhead, no sound of his breath coming back at him from the walls.

Then he remembered where he was, in Noah's room with its close walls and soaring ceilings. A new wave of misery washed over him and he could identify its source very precisely: homesickness. For uncountable minutes, Adam lay there awake, reasoning with himself. Logically, Adam knew that he had nothing to miss, that he effectively had Stockholm syndrome, identifying with his captors, considering it a kindness when his father *didn't* hit him. Objectively, he knew that he was abused. He knew the damage went deeper than any bruise he'd ever worn to school. He could endlessly dissect his reactions, doubt his emotions, wonder if he, too, would grow up to hit his own kid.

But lying in the black of the night, all he could think was, *My mother will never speak to me again. I'm homeless.*

The specter of Glendower and the ley line hung in Adam's mind. They seemed closer than ever before, but the possibility of a successful outcome also felt more tenuous than ever before. Whelk was out there and he'd been searching for this for even longer than Gansey. Surely, left to his own devices, he'd find what he wanted sooner than they would.

We need to wake up the ley line.

Adam's head was a jumble of thoughts: the last time

his father had hit him, the Pig pulling up beside him with Gansey inside, Ronan's doppelganger at the cash register on that day when he decided he must go to Aglionby, Ronan's fist slamming into his father's face. He was full of so many wants, too many to prioritize, and so they all felt desperate. To not have to work so many hours, to get into a good college, to look right in a tie, to not still be hungry after eating the thin sandwich he'd brought to work, to drive the shiny Audi that Gansey had stopped to look at with him once after school, to go home, to have hit his father himself, to own an apartment with granite worktops and a television bigger than Gansey's desk, to belong somewhere, to go home, to go home, to go home.

If they woke the ley line, if they found Glendower, he could still have those things. Most of them.

But again, he saw Gansey's wounded form, and he saw, too, Gansey's wounded face from earlier today, when they'd fought. There just wasn't a way that Adam would put Gansey in peril.

But there also wasn't any way that he was going to let Whelk slide in and take what they'd worked so hard for. *Wait!* Gansey could always afford to wait. Adam couldn't.

He was decided, then. Creeping quietly around the room, Adam put things in his bag. It was hard to predict what he would need. Adam slid the gun from beneath the bed and looked at it for a long moment, a black, sinister shape on the floorboards. Earlier, Gansey had seen him unpacking it.

"What's *that*?" he'd demanded, horrified.

"You know what it is," Adam had replied. It was Adam's father's gun, and though he wasn't sure his father would ever use it on his mother, he wasn't taking the chance.

Gansey's anxiety over the gun had been palpable. It was possible, Adam thought, that it was because of Whelk sticking one in his face. "I don't want it in here."

"I can't sell it," Adam had said. "I already thought of that. But I can't, legally. It's registered in his name."

"Surely there's a way to get rid of it. Bury it."

"And have some kid find it?"

"I don't want it in here."

"I'll find a way to get rid of it," Adam had promised. "But I can't leave it there. Not now."

Adam didn't want to bring it along with him tonight, not really.

But he didn't know what he'd need to sacrifice.

He checked the safety and put it in the bag. Climbing to his feet, he turned towards the door and just managed to stifle a sound. Noah stood directly in front of him, hollow eyes on level with Adam's eyes, smashed cheek on level with Adam's ruined ear, breathless mouth centimetres from Adam's sucked-in breath.

Without Blue there to make him stronger, without Gansey there to make him human, without Ronan there to make him belong, Noah was a frightening thing.

"Don't throw it away," Noah whispered.

"I'm trying not to," Adam replied, picking up his messenger bag. The gun in it made it feel unnaturally weighted. *I checked the safety, didn't I? I did. I know I did.*

When he straightened, Noah was already gone. Adam walked through the black, freezing air where he had just been and opened the door. Gansey was crumpled on his bed, earbuds in, eyes closed. Even with the hearing gone in his left ear, Adam could hear the tinny sound of the music, whatever

Gansey had played in order to keep himself company, to lure himself to sleep.

I'm not betraying him, Adam thought. *We're still doing this together. Only, when I come back, we'll be equals.*

His friend didn't stir as he let himself out of the door. As he left, the only sound he heard was the whisper of the night wind through the trees of Henrietta.

FORTY-TWO

Gansey woke in the night to find the moon full on his face.

Then, when he opened his eyes again, waking properly, he realized there was no moon – the few lights of Henrietta reflected a dull purple off the low cloud cover and the windows were spattered with raindrops.

There was no moon, but something like a light had woken him. He thought he heard Noah's voice, distantly. The hairs on his arms slowly prickled.

"I can't understand you," he whispered. "I'm sorry. Can you say it louder, Noah?"

The hair on the back of his neck rose as well. A cloud of his breath hung in the suddenly cold air in front of his mouth.

Noah's voice said: "Adam."

Gansey scrambled out of bed, but it was too late. Adam was not in Noah's old room. His things were scattered about. He'd packed, he'd gone. But no – his clothing stayed behind. He hadn't meant to leave for good.

"Ronan, get up," Gansey said, shoving open Ronan's door. Without waiting for a response, he moved to the stairwell and pushed out on to the landing to look out of the broken window that overlooked the car park. Outside, the rain misted down, a fine spray that just made halos around the distant house lights.

Somehow, he already knew what he'd find, but still, the reality was a jolt: the Camaro was missing. It would've been easier for Adam to hot-wire than Ronan's BMW. The roar of the engine starting was probably what had woken Gansey in the first place, the moonlight merely a memory of the last time he'd been woken.

"Man, Gansey, what?" Ronan asked. He stood in the doorway to the stairwell, scrubbing his hand over the back of his head.

Gansey didn't want to say it. If he said it out loud, it was real, it had really happened, Adam had really done it. It wouldn't have hurt if it was Ronan; this was the sort of thing he'd expect from Ronan. But it was Adam. *Adam.*

I did tell him, right? I did say that we were to wait. It's not that he didn't understand me.

Gansey tried several different ways to think of the situation, but there wasn't any way he could paint it that made it hurt less. Something kept fracturing inside him.

"What's going on?" The tone of Ronan's voice had changed.

There was nothing left but to say it.

"Adam's gone to wake the ley line."

FORTY-THREE

Just a kilometre away at 300 Fox Way, Blue looked up as a tap came on her cracked bedroom door.

"Are you sleeping?" Maura asked.

"Yes," Blue replied.

Maura let herself in. "Your light was on," she observed, and with a sigh, she sat on the end of Blue's bed, looking as soft as a poem in the dim light. For several long minutes, she didn't say anything at all, merely picked through Blue's reading selections piled on the card table shoved against the end of the mattress. There was nothing unfamiliar about this quiet between them; for as long as Blue could remember, her mother had come into her room in the evening and together they'd read books on separate ends of the bed. Her old twin mattress had seemed roomier when Blue was small, but now that Blue was human-sized, it was impossible to sit without knees touching or elbows rubbing.

After a few moments of fretting through Blue's books, Maura rested her hands in her lap and looked around at Blue's tiny room. It was lit to a dim green by the lamp on the nightstand. On the wall opposite the bed, Blue had pasted canvas trees decorated with collaged and found-paper leaves, and she'd glued dried flowers over the entirety of her wardrobe door. Most of them still looked pretty good, but some of them were a little long in the tooth. Her ceiling fan was hung with coloured feathers and lace. Blue had lived here the entire sixteen years of her life, and it looked like it.

"I think I'd better say sorry," Maura said finally.

Blue, who had been reading and re-reading an American Lit assignment without much success, laid her book down. "For what?"

"For not being straightforward, I guess. Do you know, it's really hard to be a parent. I blame it on Santa Claus. You spend so long making sure your kid doesn't know he's fake that you can't tell when you're supposed to stop."

"Mom, I found you and Calla wrapping my presents when I was, like, six."

"It was a metaphor, Blue."

Blue tapped her literature book. "A metaphor's supposed to clarify by providing an example. That didn't clarify."

"Do you know what I mean or not?"

"What you mean is that you're sorry you didn't tell me about Butternut."

Maura glowered at the door as if Calla stood behind it. "I wish you wouldn't call him that."

"If you'd been the one to tell me about him, then I wouldn't be using what Calla told me."

"Fair enough."

"So what *was* his name?"

Her mother lay back on the bed. She was crossways on it, so she had to draw her knees up to brace her feet on the edge of the mattress, and Blue had to withdraw her own legs to keep them from being crushed.

"Artemus."

"No wonder you preferred Butternut," Blue said. But before her mother had time to say anything, she said, "Wait – isn't Artemus a Roman name? Latin?"

"Yeah. And I don't think it's a bad name. I didn't raise you to be judgemental."

"Sure you did," Blue said. She was wondering if it was a coincidence that there was so much Latin in her life at the moment. Gansey was beginning to rub off on her, because coincidences no longer seemed so coincidental.

"Probably," Maura agreed after a moment. "So, look. This is what I know. I think your father has something to do with Cabeswater or the ley line. Way back before you were born, Calla and Persephone and I were messing around with things we probably shouldn't have been messing around with—"

"Drugs?"

"Rituals. Are *you* messing around with drugs?"

"No. But maybe rituals."

"Drugs might be better."

"I'm not interested in them. Their effects are proven – where's the fun in that? Tell me more."

Maura tapped a rhythm on her stomach as she stared up. Blue had copied a poem on to the ceiling just above her, and it was possible she was trying to read it. "Well, he appeared after this ritual. I think he was trapped in Cabeswater and we released him."

"You didn't *ask*?"

"We didn't . . . have that sort of relationship."

"I don't want to know what sort it was, actually, if it didn't involve talking."

"We *did* talk. He was a really decent person," Maura said. "He was very kind. People bothered him. He thought we should be more concerned with the world around us and how our actions would affect things years down the road. I liked that part of him. It wasn't preachy, just who he was."

"Why are you telling me this?" Blue asked, because she was a little distressed to see the unsteady press of Maura's lips against each other.

"You said you wanted to know about him. I was telling you about him, because you're a lot like him. He would've liked to see your room with all the shit you've put on the walls."

"Gee, thanks," Blue said. "So why did he leave?"

Right after she asked the question, she realized it may have been too blunt.

"He didn't leave," Maura said. "He disappeared. Right when you were born."

"That's called leaving."

"I don't think he did it on purpose. Well, I did, at first. But now I've been thinking about it and learning more about Henrietta and I think . . . you're a very strange child. I've never met anybody who makes psychics hear things better. I'm not exactly sure we didn't accidentally do another ritual when you were born. I mean, a ritual where you being born was the final bit. It might have got him stuck back in there."

Blue said, "You think this is my fault!"

"Don't be ridiculous," Maura said, sitting up. Her hair was all frazzled from lying on it. "You were only a baby – how could anything be your fault? I just thought maybe that was what happened. That was why I called Neeve about looking for him. I wanted you to understand why I called her."

"Do you even really know her?"

Maura shook her head. "*Pft*. We didn't grow up together, but we've got together a few times over the years, just a day or two here or there. We've never been friends, much less real sisters. But her reputation . . . I never thought it would get weird like it has."

Footsteps moved softly in the hallway and then Persephone stood in the doorway. Maura sighed and looked down at her lap, as if she'd been expecting this.

"I don't mean to interrupt. But in either three or seven minutes," Persephone said, "Blue's raven boys are going to pull down the street and sit in front of the house while they try to find a way to convince her to sneak out with them."

Her mother rubbed the skin between her eyebrows. "I know."

Blue's heart raced. "That seems awfully specific."

Persephone and her mother exchanged a quick glance.

"That's another thing I wasn't quite truthful about," Maura said. "Sometimes Persephone, Calla and I are very good with specifics."

"Only sometimes," Persephone echoed. Then, a little sadly, "More and more often, it seems."

"Things are changing," Maura said.

Another silhouette appeared at the doorway. Calla said, "Also, Neeve still hasn't come back. And she scuttled the car. It won't start."

Outside the window, they all heard the sound of a car pulling up in front of the house. Blue looked at her mother entreatingly.

Instead of replying, her mother looked at Calla and Persephone. "Tell me we're wrong."

Persephone said in her soft way, "You know I can't tell you that, Maura."

Maura stood up. "You go with them. We'll take care of Neeve. I hope you know how big this thing is, Blue."

Blue said, "I have an inkling."

FORTY–FOUR

There are trees and then there are trees at night. Trees after dark become colourless and sizeless and moving things. When Adam got to Cabeswater, it felt like a living being. The wind through the leaves was like the bellows of an exhaled breath and the hiss of the rain on the canopy like a sucked-in sigh. The air smelled like wet soil.

Adam cast a torch beam into the edge of the trees. The light barely penetrated the woods, swallowed by the fitful spring rain that was beginning to soak his hair.

I wish I could've done this in the daytime, Adam thought.

He didn't have a phobia of the dark. A phobia meant that the fear was irrational, and Adam suspected there was plenty to be afraid of in Cabeswater after the sun had gone down. *At least,* he reasoned, *if Whelk is here and using a torch, I'll see him.*

It was a cold comfort, but Adam had come too far to turn back. He cast another glance around himself – one always felt observed here – and then he stepped over the invisible gurgle of the tiny creek, into the woods.

And it was bright.

Jerking his chin down, eyes squeezed shut, he shielded his face with his own torch. His eyelids burned red with the difference from black to light. Slowly, he opened them again. All around him, the forest glowed with afternoon light. Dusty gold shafts pierced the canopy and made dapples of the insubstantial brook to his left. In the slanting light, the leaves were made yellow, brown, pink. The furred lichen on the trees was a murky orange.

The skin of his hand in front of him had become rose and tan. The air moved slowly around his body, somehow tangible, gold flaked, every dust mote a lantern.

There was no sign of night, and there was no sign of anyone else in the trees.

Overhead, a bird called, the first that he remembered hearing in the wood. It was a long, clarion song, just four or five notes. It was like a sound the hunting horns made in the autumn. *Away, away, away.* It both awed him and saddened him, Cabeswater's brand of bittersweet beauty.

This place should not exist, Adam thought, and at once, he hastily thought the opposite. Cabeswater had become bright just as Adam had wished that it wouldn't be dark, just as it had changed the colour of the fish in the pool as soon as Gansey had thought it would be better if they were red. Cabeswater was as literal as Ronan was. He didn't know if he could *think* it into nonexistence and he didn't want to find out.

He needed to guard his thoughts.

Switching off the torch, Adam dropped it into his bag and moved along the tiny creek they'd first followed. The rain had swelled it, so the creek was easier to follow towards its source, wending a way through newly flattened grasses down the mountain.

Ahead, Adam saw slowly moving reflections on the tree trunks, the strong, slanting afternoon light mirroring off the mysterious pool they'd found the first day. He was nearly there.

He stumbled. His foot had turned on something unforgiving and unexpected.

What is this?

At his feet was an empty, wide-mouthed bowl. It was a glistening, ugly purple, strange and man-made in this place.

Puzzled, Adam's eyes slid from the dry bowl at his feet to another bowl about three metres away, equally conspicuous among the pink and yellow leaves on the ground. The second bowl was identical to the one at his feet, only it was full to the brim with a dark liquid.

Adam was again struck by how out of place this clearly man-made thing was in the middle of these trees. Then he was puzzled again when he realized that the surface of the bowl was undisturbed and perfect; no leaves or silt or twigs or insects marred the black liquid. Which meant the bowl had been filled only recently.

Which meant—

The adrenaline hit his system a second before he heard a voice.

Tied in the back of the car, it had been hard for Whelk to know when he should make his play for freedom. The fact was, Neeve clearly had a plan, which was far more than Whelk could say of himself. And it seemed extremely unlikely that she'd try to kill him until she'd set up the finer details of the ritual. So Whelk allowed himself to be driven in his own car, now reeking of garlic and full of crumbs, to the edge of the woods. Neeve was not brave enough to take his car off-road – a fact for which he was very grateful – so she parked it in a little gravel turn-around and made them both walk the rest of the way. It was not yet dark, but still, Whelk stumbled over hummocks of field grass on the way.

"Sorry," Neeve said. "I did look on Google Maps for a closer place to park."

Whelk, who was annoyed by absolutely everything about Neeve, from her soft, fluffy hands to her crinkled broom skirt to her curled hair, replied, without much civility, "Why are you bothering to apologize? Aren't you planning on killing me?"

Neeve winced. "I wish you wouldn't say it like that. You're meant to be a sacrifice. Being a sacrifice is quite a fine thing, with a lovely tradition behind it. Besides, you deserve it. It's fair."

Whelk said, "If you kill me, does that mean that someone else ought to kill you in fairness? Down the road?"

He tripped over another clump of grass, and this time, Neeve did not apologize or answer his questions. Instead, she fixed a gaze of interminable length on him. It was not so much keenly penetrating as exhaustively extensive. "For a brief time, Barrington, I'll admit that I was feeling slight regret over choosing you. You seemed very pleasant until I Tasered you."

It's a hard thing to hold a civil conversation after recalling that one party has used a Taser on the other, so both of them finished the walk in silence. It was a strange feeling for Whelk to be back inside the woods where he'd last seen Czerny alive. He'd thought that woods were woods and he wouldn't be affected by returning, especially at a different time of the day. But something about the atmosphere immediately took him back to that moment, the skateboard in his hand, the sad question gasped in Czerny's dying sounds.

The whispers hissed and popped in his head, like a fire just getting under way, but Whelk ignored them.

He missed his life. He missed everything about it: the carelessness, the extravagant Christmases at home, the accelerator beneath his foot, free time that felt like a blessing instead of an empty curse. He missed skipping classes and taking classes and spray-painting the Henrietta sign on I-64 after getting astonishingly drunk on his birthday.

He missed Czerny.

He had not let himself think it once in the past seven years. He had tried instead to convince himself of Czerny's uselessness. Tried to remind himself of the practicality of the death instead.

But instead, he remembered the sound Czerny made the first time he hit him.

Neeve didn't have to tell Whelk to sit quietly while she arranged the ritual. Instead, as she laid out the five points of a pentagram with an unlit candle, a lit candle, an empty bowl, a full bowl, and three small bones arranged in a triangle, he sat with his knees pulled up to his chin and his hands still tied behind him and wished he could find it in himself to cry. Something to relieve this terrible weight inside him.

Neeve caught a glimpse of him and imagined that he was upset over his approaching death. "Oh," she said mildly, "don't be like that. It will not hurt very much." She reconsidered what she had said, and then corrected, "At least for very long."

"How are you going to kill me? How does this ritual work?"

Neeve frowned at him. "That is not an easy question.

That is like asking a painter why he chooses the colours he does. Sometimes it is not a *process*, but a *feeling*."

"Fine, then," Whelk said. "What are you *feeling*?"

Neeve pressed a perfectly shaped mauve fingernail to her lip as she surveyed her work. "I have made a pentagram. It is a strong shape for any sort of spell and I work well with it. Others find it challenging or too constricting, but it satisfies me. I have my lit candle to give energy and my unlit candle to invite it. I have my scrying bowl to see the other world and I have my empty bowl for the other world to fill. I have crossed the leg bones of three ravens I killed to show the corpse road the nature of the spell I mean to do. And then I think I will bleed you out in the centre of the pentagram while invoking the line to wake."

She stared hard at Whelk at this, and then added, "I may tweak it as I go along. These things need to be flexible. People rarely show interest in the mechanics of my work, Barrington."

"I'm very interested," he said. "Sometimes the process is the most interesting part."

When she turned her back to get her knives, he slipped his hands from the binding. Then he selected a fallen branch and crashed it down on her head with as much force as he could muster. He didn't think it would be enough to kill her, because it was still green and flexible, but it certainly brought her to her knees.

Neeve moaned and shook her head slowly, so Whelk gave her another blow for good measure. He tied her up with the bindings he'd removed from himself – he did them up rather tightly, having learned from her errors – and dragged her semi-unconscious form into the middle of the pentagram.

Then he looked up and saw Adam Parrish.

It was the first time Blue had felt as if it were truly dangerous for her to be in Cabeswater – dangerous because she made things louder. More powerful. By the time they got to the woods, the night already felt charged. The rain had given way to an intermittent drizzle. The combination of the charged feeling and the rain had made Blue look quite anxiously at Gansey when he got out of the car, but his shoulders were barely damp and he wasn't wearing his Aglionby uniform. He had definitely been wearing the raven jumper when she saw him at the church watch, and his shoulders had definitely been wetter. Surely she hadn't managed to change his future enough to make tonight the night he died, had she? Surely she had been meant all along to meet him, since she was supposed to kill him or fall in love with him. And surely Persephone wouldn't have let them go if she'd sensed that tonight was the night Gansey died.

Making a path with their torch beams, they found the Pig parked near where they'd found Noah's Mustang. Several trampled paths led from the car to the woods, as if Adam had been unable to decide where he wanted to enter.

At the sight of the Camaro, Gansey's face, which had already been grim, became positively stony. None of them spoke as they broached the boundary of the trees.

At the edge of the woods, the feeling of charge, of *possibility*, immediately became more pronounced. Shoulder to shoulder, they entered the trees and between one blink and the next, they found themselves surrounded by a dreamy afternoon light.

Even having braced herself for magic, Blue was breathless with it.

"What is Adam thinking?" Gansey muttered, but not to anyone in particular. "How can you mess with. . ." He lost interest in answering his own question.

Before them was Noah's Mustang, in the unearthly golden light looking even more surreal than the first time they'd found it. Shafts of sun punched opaquely through the canopy, making stripes over the pollen-coated roof.

Standing by the front of the car, Blue caught the boys' attention. They joined her, staring at the windscreen. Since they had last been in the clearing, someone had written a word on the dusty glass. In round, handwritten letters, it said: MURDERED.

"Noah?" Blue asked the empty air – though it didn't feel so empty. "Noah, are you here with us? Did you write this?"

Gansey said, "Oh."

It was a very flat little sound and instead of asking him to clarify, Blue and Ronan followed his gaze to the driver's side window. An invisible finger was in the process of tracing another letter on the glass. Though Blue had felt that Noah must've been the one to write the first word on the glass, in her head she had pictured him having a body while he did it. Far more difficult was watching letters appear spontaneously. It made her think of the Noah with the dark hollows for eyes, the smashed-in cheek, the barely human form. Even in the warm afternoon woods, she felt cold.

It's Noah, she thought. *Drawing energy from me. That's what I feel.*

On the glass, the word took shape.

MURDERED

It began another word. There was not enough space left between the *D* and the new word, and so the second word partially obliterated the first.

MURDERED

And again, again, again, across each other:

MURDERED

MURDERED

MURDERED

The writing continued until the driver's side glass was clear, entirely swept clean by an invisible finger, until there were so many words that none of them could be read. Until it was only a window into an empty car with the memory of a burger on the passenger seat.

"Noah," Gansey said, "I'm so sorry."

Blue wiped away a tear. "Me, too."

Stepping forward, leaning over the hood of the car, Ronan pressed his finger to the windscreen, and while they watched, he wrote:

REMEMBERED

Calla's voice spoke in Blue's head, so clearly that she wondered if everyone else could hear it: *A secret killed your father and you know what it was.*

Without any comment, Ronan put his hands into his pockets and strode deeper into the woods.

Noah's voice hissed in Blue's ear, cold and urgent, but she couldn't understand what he was trying to say. She asked him to repeat it, but there was silence. She waited in vain for another few seconds, but still – nothing. Adam was right: Noah was getting less and less.

Now that Ronan had had a few moments' head start, Gansey seemed anxious to get going. Blue understood entirely. It seemed important to keep them all within sight of one another. Cabeswater felt like a place for things to get lost at the moment.

"Excelsior," Gansey said bleakly.

Blue asked, "What does that even mean?"

Gansey looked over his shoulder at her. He was, once more, just a little bit closer to the boy she'd seen in the churchyard.

FORTY-FIVE

"For the love of God," said Whelk when he saw Adam standing beside the bowl he had just kicked. Whelk held a very large and efficient-looking knife. He was scruffy and unshaven and looked like an Aglionby boy after a bad weekend. "*Why?*"

His voice held genuine aggravation.

Adam had not seen his Latin teacher since he'd discovered he'd killed Noah, and he was surprised by the rush of emotion the sight of Whelk caused. Especially when he realized that this was once again a ritual, with yet another sacrifice in the middle of it. In this context, it took him a moment to place Neeve's face — that night at 300 Fox Way. Neeve gazed at him from the centre of the circle made from points on a pentagram. She didn't look quite as *afraid* as he thought someone tied in the middle of a diabolic symbol might be expected to look.

Adam had several things he thought about saying, but when he opened his mouth, it was none of those things.

"Why Noah?" he asked. "Why not someone horrible?"

Whelk closed his eyes for a bare second. "I'm not having this conversation. Why are you *here*?"

It was obvious that he wasn't sure what to do with the

fact of Adam – which was fair, because Adam had no idea
what to do with the fact of Whelk. The only thing he had
to do was keep him from waking the ley line. Everything
else (disabling Whelk, saving Neeve, avenging Noah) was
negotiable. He remembered, all at once, that he had his
father's gun in his bag. It was possible that he could point
that at Whelk and convince him to do something, but what?
In the movies, it looked simple: whoever had the gun won.
But in reality, he couldn't point the gun at Whelk *and* tie
him up at the same time, even if he had something to tie him
with. Whelk could overpower him. Maybe Adam could use
Neeve's binding to. . .

Adam withdrew the gun. It felt heavy and malevolent in
his hand. "I'm here to stop this from happening again. Untie
her."

Whelk said again, "For the love of God."

He took two steps to Neeve and put his knife
against the side of her face. Her mouth tightened, just
a very little. He said, "Just put down the gun so that I
don't slice her face off. Actually, throw it over here. And
make sure you put the safety on before you throw
it or you might end up just shooting her anyway."

Adam had a sneaking suspicion that, if he'd been Gansey,
he would've been able to talk his way out of this. He would
straighten his shoulders and look impressive and Whelk
would've done whatever he wanted. But he was not Gansey,
so all he could think to say was, "I didn't come here for
anyone to die. I'm going to throw the gun out of my reach,
but I'm not going to throw it into your reach."

"Then I cut her face off."

Neeve's face was quite placid. "You'll ruin the ritual if

you do. Weren't you listening? I thought you were interested in the process."

Adam had the curious, discomfiting sensation of seeing something unusual when he looked at her eyes. It was like he saw a brief flash of Maura and Persephone and Calla in them.

Whelk said, "Fine. Throw the gun over there. Don't come any closer, though." To Neeve, he said, "What do you mean it won't work? Are you bluffing?"

"You may throw the gun," Neeve told Adam. "I won't mind."

Adam tossed the gun into the brush. He felt terrible as he did, but he felt better when he wasn't holding it.

Neeve said, "And, Barrington, the reason why it will not work is because the ritual needs a sacrifice."

"You were planning on killing me," Whelk said. "You expect me to believe that it doesn't work the other way around?"

"Yes," Neeve replied. She didn't look away from Adam. Again, he thought he saw a flash of something when he was looking at her face: a black mask, two mirrors, Persephone's face. "It must be a personal sacrifice. Killing me wouldn't accomplish that. I'm nothing to you."

"But I'm nothing to you," Whelk said.

"But killing is," she replied. "I've never killed anyone. I give up my innocence if I kill you. That is an incredible sacrifice."

When Adam spoke, he was surprised by how clearly the contempt came through. "And you've already killed someone, so you don't have that to give up."

Whelk began to swear, very softly, as if no one else were

there. Leaves the colour and shape of pennies drifted down around them. Neeve was still staring at Adam. The sensation of seeing some place else in her eyes was now undeniable. It was a black, mirrored lake, it was a voice deep as the earth, it was two obsidian eyes, it was another world.

"Mr Whelk!"

Gansey!

Gansey's voice had come from just behind the hollowed-out vision tree, and then the rest of him followed as he strode into view. Behind him were Ronan and Blue. Adam's heart was a bird and a stone; his relief was palpable, but so was his shame.

"Mr Whelk," Gansey said. Even in his glasses and with his musty bedhead, he was in full Richard Gansey III splendour – shiny and powerful. He didn't look at Adam. "The police are on their way. I really recommend you step away from that woman to avoid making this any worse."

Whelk looked as if he was going to reply, but then he didn't. Instead, everyone looked at the knife in his hand and the ground just below it.

Neeve was gone.

At once, they all looked around the pentagram, at the hollowed-out tree, at the pool – but it was ridiculous. Neeve could not have slithered away without anyone seeing, not in ten seconds' time. She had not moved. She had *disappeared*.

For a moment, nothing happened. Everyone was frozen in a diorama of uncertainty.

Whelk plunged from the pentagram. It took Adam only a bare second to realize that he was lunging in the direction of the gun.

Ronan hurled himself towards Whelk at the same moment

that Whelk rose with the gun. Whelk smashed the side of it into Ronan's jaw. Ronan's head snapped back.

Whelk pointed the pistol at Gansey.

Blue shouted, "*Stop!*"

There was no time.

Adam threw himself into the middle of the pentagram.

Curiously, there was no sound here, not in any reasonable way. The end of Blue's cry was muffled, as if it had been shoved under water. The air was still around him. It was as if time itself had become a sluggish thing, barely existing. The only true sensation he felt was that of electricity – the barely perceptible tingling of a lightning storm.

Neeve had said that it wasn't about the killing, that it was about the sacrifice. It was obvious that stymied Whelk completely.

But Adam knew what sacrifice meant, more than he thought Whelk or Neeve had ever had to know. He knew that it wasn't about killing someone or drawing a shape made of bird bones.

When it came down to it, Adam had been making sacrifices for a very long time, and he knew what the hardest one was.

On his terms, or not at all.

He wasn't afraid.

Being Adam Parrish was a complicated thing, a wonder of muscles and organs, synapses and nerves. He was a miracle of moving parts, a study in survival. The most important thing to Adam Parrish, though, had always been free will, the ability to be his own master.

This was the important thing.

It had always been the most important thing.

This was what it was to be Adam.

Kneeling in the middle of the pentagram, digging his fingers into the soft, mossy turf, Adam said, "I sacrifice myself."

Gansey's cry was agonized. "Adam, no! *No.*"

On his terms, or not at all.

I will be your hands, Adam thought. *I will be your eyes.*

There was a sound like a breaker being thrown. A crackle.

Beneath them, the ground began to roll.

FORTY-SIX

Blue was thrown into Ronan, who was already crouched, rising from where Whelk had hit him. In front of her, the great stone slabs among the trees rippled as if they were water, and the pool tipped and splashed from its banks. There was a great sound all around them like a train bearing down, and all Blue could think was, *Nothing really bad has ever really happened to me.*

The trees heaved towards one another as if they would pull free from the soil. Leaves and branches rained down, thick and furious.

"It's an earthquake!" Gansey shouted to them. He had one arm thrown up over his head and the other hooked around a tree. Debris coated his hair.

"Look what you've done, you crazy bastard!" Ronan shouted to Adam, whose gaze was sharp and wary as he stood in the pentagram.

Will it stop? Blue wondered.

An earthquake was such a shocking thing, such a *wrong* thing, that it didn't seem impossible to believe that the world had been inherently broken and that it would never be right again.

As the ground shifted and groaned around them, Whelk

staggered to his feet, the gun in hand. It was a blacker and uglier thing than it had seemed before, from a world where death was unfair and instant.

Whelk was able to keep his footing. The bucking of the rocks was beginning to slow, though everything still tilted like a fun house.

"What would *you* know what to do with power?" he snapped at Adam. "What a waste. What a fucking waste."

Whelk pointed the gun at Adam, and, without any ceremony, he pulled the trigger.

Around them, the world went still. The leaves quivered and the water lapped slowly at the pool's banks, but otherwise, the ground was quiet.

Blue screamed.

Every set of eyes was on Adam, who remained standing in the middle of the pentagram. His expression was perplexed. He cast his gaze over his chest, his arms. There was not a mark on him.

Whelk had not missed, but Adam had also not been shot, and the two were somehow the same thing.

There was a crushing sadness to Gansey's face as he looked at Adam. That was the first clue Blue got that something was inherently different, irretrievably altered. If not about the world, then about Cabeswater. And if not about Cabeswater, then about Adam.

"Why?" Gansey asked Adam. "Was I so awful?"

Adam said, "It was never about you."

"But, Adam," Blue cried, "what have you *done*?"

"What needed to be done," Adam replied.

From his place a metre away, Whelk made a strangled noise. When his bullet had failed to wound Adam, he'd dropped the gun by his side, defeated as a child in a game of pretend.

"I think you should give that back to me," Adam told Whelk. He was shaking, a little. "I don't think Cabeswater wants you to have it. I think if you don't give it to me, it might take it."

Suddenly, the trees began to hiss as if a breeze was coming through them, though no wind touched Blue's skin. Adam's and Ronan's faces wore matching shocked expressions, and a moment later, Blue realized that it was not hissing: it was voices. The trees were speaking, and now she could hear them, too.

"Take cover!" Ronan shouted.

There was another sound like rustling, only this resolved itself very quickly into a more concrete noise. It was the sound of something massive moving through the trees, snapping branches and trampling underbrush.

Blue yelled, "Something's coming!"

She clutched at both Ronan and Gansey, snagging their sleeves. Only a few metres behind them was the craggy mouth of the hollowed-out vision tree, and it was there that she pulled them. For a moment, before the tree's magic enveloped them, they had time to see what was bearing down on them — a tremendous rippling herd of white-horned beasts, coats glinting like ice-crusted snow, snorts and cries choking the air. They were shoulder to shoulder, hectic and heedless. When they tossed their heads back, Blue saw that they were somehow like that raven carved into the hillside, like that dog sculpture she'd held, strange and sinuous. The thunder of them, of their pressed bodies, rumbled the ground like another earthquake. The herd, snorting, began to part around the pentagram-marked circle.

Beside her, Ronan breathed a soft swear word, and Gansey, pressed up against the warm wall of the tree, turned his face away as if he could not bear to see them.

The tree pulled them into a vision.

In this vision, the night smeared jewelled reflections across wet, steaming tarmac, stoplights turning from green to red. The Camaro sat at a kerb, Blue in the driver's seat. Everything was soaked in the smell of petrol. She caught a glimpse of a collared shirt in the passenger seat; this was Gansey. He leaned across the gearshift towards her, pressing fingers to the place her collarbone was exposed. His breath was hot on her neck.

Gansey, she warned, but she felt unstable and dangerous.

I just want to pretend, Gansey said, the words misting on her skin. *I want to pretend that I could.*

The Blue in the vision closed her eyes.

Maybe it wouldn't hurt if I kiss you, he said. *Maybe it's only if you kiss me—*

In the tree, Blue was jostled from behind, jolting her from the vision. She just had time to see Gansey – the real Gansey – with widened eyes as he pushed past her and out of the tree.

FORTY-SEVEN

Gansey only allowed himself a confused moment of a vision – his fingers, somehow, touching Blue's face – and then he threw himself out of the tree, jostling the real Blue out of his way. He needed to see what had happened to Adam, though in his heart he felt a dreadful premonition, like he already knew what he would see.

Sure enough, Adam still stood in the circle, unharmed, his arms adrift by his sides. The gun hung in one of his hands. Just a metre away, outside of the circle, Whelk lay broken. His body was covered with leaf litter, as if he'd lain there for years, not minutes. There was not as much blood as one would expect in a trampling, but there was something broken in his appearance nonetheless. A sort of rumpled look to his form.

Adam was just staring at him. His uneven hair was mussed in the back, and it was the only hint that Adam had moved at all since Gansey had last seen him.

"Adam," Gansey gasped. "How did you get the gun?"

"The trees," Adam said. That chilling remoteness was in his voice, the sound that meant that the boy Gansey knew was pressed somewhere far down inside him.

"The trees? God! Did you shoot him!"

"Of course not," Adam said. He put the gun on the ground, carefully. "I only used it to keep him from coming in here."

Horror was rising up inside Gansey. "You let him get trampled?"

"He killed Noah," Adam said. "It's what he deserved."

"No." Gansey pressed his hands over his face. There was a body here, a *body*, and it used to be alive. They didn't even have the authority to choose an alcoholic beverage. They couldn't be deciding who deserved to live or die.

"You really wanted me to let a murderer in here?" demanded Adam.

Gansey couldn't begin to explain the size of this awfulness. He only knew that it burst inside him, again and again, fresh every time he considered it.

"He was just alive," he said helplessly. "He just taught us four irregular verbs last week. And you killed him."

"Stop saying that. I didn't *save* him. Stop telling me what I should believe is wrong or right!" Adam shouted, but his face looked as miserable as Gansey felt. "Now the ley line is awake and we can find Glendower on it and everything will be as it should be."

"We have to call the police. We have to—"

"We don't have to do anything. We leave Whelk to be worn away, just like he left Noah."

Gansey turned away, sickened. "What about justice?"

"That *is* justice, Gansey. That's the real thing. This place is all about being real. About being fair."

This all felt inherently wrong to Gansey. It was like the truth, but turned sideways. He kept looking at it, and looking at it, and it still had a young man dead who looked an awful lot like Noah's crippled skeleton. And then there was Adam, his appearance unchanged, but still – there was something in his eyes. In the line of his mouth.

Gansey felt loss looming.

Blue and Ronan had emerged from the tree, and Blue's hand covered her mouth at the sight of Whelk. Ronan had an ugly bruise rising on his temple.

Gansey simply said, "He died."

"I think we should get out of here," Blue said. "Earthquakes and animals and – I don't know how much of an effect I'm having, but things are. . ."

"Yes," Gansey said. "We need to go. We can decide what to do about Whelk outside."

Wait.

They all heard the voice this time. In English. None of them moved, unconsciously doing precisely what the voice had asked.

Boy. Scimus quid quaeritis.

(Boy. We know what you're looking for.)

Though the trees could have meant any of the boys, Gansey felt as if the words were directly particularly at him. Out loud, he said, "What am I looking for?"

In response, there was a babble of Latin, words tumbling over one another. Gansey crossed his arms over his chest, hands fisted. They all looked at Ronan for a translation.

"They said there've always been rumours of a king buried somewhere along this spirit road," Ronan said. His eyes held Gansey's. "They think he may be yours."

FORTY-EIGHT

It was a fine, sunny day at the very beginning of June when they buried Noah's bones. It had taken several weeks for the police department to finish their work with evidence, and so it was the end of the school year before the funeral took place. A lot had taken place in between Whelk's death and Noah's funeral. Gansey had recovered his journal from police evidence and quit the rowing team. Ronan successfully scraped through his finals to Aglionby's satisfaction and unsuccessfully repaired the apartment door lock. Adam, with probable help from Ronan, moved from Monmouth Manufacturing to a room belonging to St Agnes Church, a subtle distance that affected both boys in different ways. Blue triumphantly welcomed the end of the school year and the beginning of more freedom to explore the ley line. Power failures plagued the town of Henrietta a total of nine times and the phone system failed almost half as many times. Maura, Persephone and Calla went through the attic and dismantled Neeve's things. They'd told Blue that they still weren't precisely sure what they'd done when they rearranged her mirrors that night.

"We'd meant to disable her," Persephone acknowledged.

"But we seem to have disappeared her instead. It's possible she will reappear at some point."

And slowly their lives found an equilibrium, though it didn't seem they'd ever return to normal. The ley line was awake and Noah was all but gone. Magic was real, Glendower was real and something was starting.

"Jane, not to be blunt, but this is a funeral," Gansey said to Blue as she made her way across the field towards them. He and Ronan looked like groomsmen in their impeccable black suits.

Blue, lacking any black wardrobe options, had hastily stitched a few metres of cheap black lace over a green T-shirt she'd converted into a dress a few months earlier. She hissed furiously, "This was all the better I could do!"

"Like Noah cares," Ronan said.

"Did you bring something else for later?" Gansey asked.

"I'm not an idiot. Where's Adam?"

Gansey said, "He's at work. He's coming later."

Noah's bones were being buried in the Czerny family plot in a remote valley graveyard. His newly dug grave lay near the edge of the long, sloping graveyard on the side of a rocky hill. A tarp covered the fresh heap of dirt from grieving eyes. Noah's family stood right next to the hole. The man and the two girls wept, but the woman stared off into the trees, dry-eyed. Blue didn't have to be a psychic, though, to see how sad the woman was. Sad and proud.

Noah's voice, cool and barely there, whispered in her ear. "Please say something to them."

Blue didn't reply, but she turned her head in the direction of his voice. She could nearly feel him, standing just behind

415

her shoulder, breath on her neck, hand pressed anxiously to her arm.

"You know I can't," she replied in a low voice.

"You *have* to."

"I would look like a crazy person. What good would it do? What could I possibly say?"

Noah's voice was faint but desperate. His distress hummed through her. "*Please.*"

Blue closed her eyes.

"Tell her I'm sorry I drank her birthday schnapps," Noah whispered.

God, Noah!

"What are you doing?" Gansey reached out and caught her arm as she started towards the grave.

"Humiliating myself!" She tugged free. As Blue approached Noah's family, she rehearsed ways to make herself sound less insane, but she didn't like any of them. She'd been with her mother often enough to suspect how this would go. *Noah, only for you. . .* She eyed the sad, proud woman. Up close, her make-up was impeccable, her hair carefully rolled at the ends. Everything was knotted and painted and sprayed under control. All of that sadness was shoved so deep inside her that her eyes weren't even red. Blue wasn't fooled.

"Mrs Czerny?"

Both of Noah's parents' heads turned to her. Blue selfconsciously ran a hand down one of the pieces of lace. "I'm Blue Sargent. I, uh, wanted to say that I'm sorry for your loss. Also, my mother's a psychic. I have a" — already their expressions were transforming unpleasantly — "message from your son."

Immediately, Mrs Czerny's face darkened. She merely shook her head and said, quite calmly, "No, you don't."

"Please don't do this," said Mr Czerny. It was taking all he had to be civil, which was better than she'd expected. Blue felt bad for having interrupted their private moment. "Please just go."

Tell her, whispered Noah.

Blue took a breath. "Mrs Czerny, he's sorry for drinking your birthday schnapps."

For a moment there was silence. Mr Czerny and Noah's sisters looked from Blue to Noah's mother. Noah's father opened his mouth and then Mrs Czerny started to cry.

None of them noticed when Blue walked away from the grave.

Later, they dug him up. At the mouth of the access road, Ronan lounged beside his BMW with its hood ajar, acting as both roadblock and look out. Adam operated the backhoe Gansey had rented for the occasion. And Gansey transferred Noah's bones to a duffel bag while Blue shone the torch over them to be certain they were all there. Adam reburied the empty casket, leaving a fresh grave identical to the one they'd begun with.

When they ran back to the BMW, giddy and breathless with their crime, Ronan told Gansey, "This will all come out and bite you in the ass, you know, when you're running for Congress."

"Shut up and drive, Lynch."

They reburied his bones at the old ruined church, which was Blue's idea.

"No one will bother them here," she said. "And we know it's on the ley line. And it's holy ground."

"Well," said Ronan, "I hope he likes it. I've pulled a muscle."

Gansey scoffed, "Doing what? You were standing watch."

"Opening my hood."

After they'd finished covering the last of the bones, they stood quietly inside the ruined walls. Blue stared at Gansey, in particular, his hands in his pockets, his head tilted down towards where they had just interred Noah. It felt like no time and all the time in the world since she'd seen his spirit walk this very path.

Gansey. That's all there is.

She wouldn't, she vowed, be the one to kill him.

"Can we go home? This place is so creepy."

Euphoric, they all spun. Noah, rumpled and familiar, was framed in the arched doorway of the church, more solid than Blue remembered ever seeing him. Solid in form, anyway. He peered around the crumbled walls with a timorous expression.

"Noah!" Gansey cried gladly.

Blue hurled her arms around his neck. He looked alarmed, and then pleased, and then he petted the tufts of her hair.

"Czerny," Ronan said, trying out the word.

"No," Noah protested, around Blue's arm. "I'm serious. This place creeps me the hell out. Can we go?"

Gansey's face broke into a relieved, easy grin. "Yes, we can go home."

"I'm still not eating pizza," Noah said, backing out of the church with Blue.

Ronan, still in the ruins, looked over his shoulder at them. In the dim light of the torches, the tattooed hook that edged out above his collar looked like either a claw or a finger or part of a fleur-de-lis. It was nearly as sharp as his smile.

"I guess now would be a good time to tell you," he said. "I took Chainsaw out of my dreams."

ACKNOWLEDGEMENTS

At this point, I feel like I'm always thanking the usual suspects, but they must be thanked nonetheless. Everyone at Scholastic, and particularly: my editor, David Levithan, for his patience during this novel's prolonged gestation. Dick and Ellie for their continued belief in me. Rachel C., Tracy, and Stacy for their boundless enthusiasm, no matter how bizarre an idea I toss their direction. Becky, for booze I didn't drink but Gansey did. Cacao.

A special shout-out to my Scholastic UK people, Alyx, Alex, Hannah and Catherine, for working very hard to get me on ley lines.

Thanks to my agent, Laura Rennert, who lets me run with scissors, and to my tireless critique partners, Tessa "Dead in a Ditch" Gratton and Brenna "This is Interesting" Yovanoff.

I'm also grateful to everyone else who read for me: Jackson Pearce, who is so very shiny; Carrie, who really does make good guacamole; Kate, first and last reader; Dad, for dangerous handguns; and Mom, for cycloliths. Thanks to Natalie, as well, who did not read but did give me really awful music that helped an incredible amount.

And, as always, I am grateful to my husband, Ed, who always makes the magic seem obvious.

GET CARRIED AWAY BY THIS BREATHTAKING ADVENTURE.
IT WILL MAKE YOUR HEART RACE.

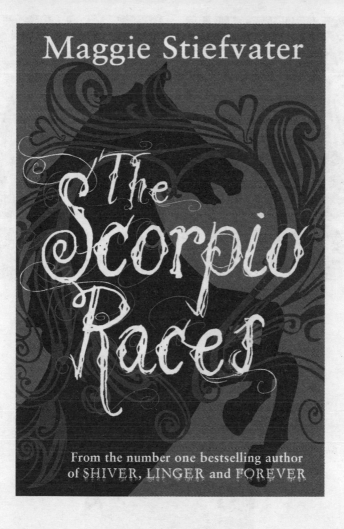

Maggie Stiefvater

The Scorpio Races

From the number one bestselling author
of SHIVER, LINGER and FOREVER

L♥ve Maggie

LOOK OUT FOR THIS NUMBER 1 BESTSELLING LOVE STORY.
COMPELLING. ROMANTIC. ABSOLUTELY ADDICTIVE.

AND DON'T MISS THESE STUNNING
DARK ROMANCES THAT WILL TAKE YOU
INTO THE WORLD OF FAERIE.

Love Maggie